Margaret

4/22

NORTH-WEST BY SOUTH

D1396200

Also by Nancy Cato and available from
New English Library

ALL THE RIVERS RUN

NORTH-WEST
BY SOUTH
Nancy Cato

NEW ENGLISH LIBRARY/TIMES MIRROR

First published in Great Britain by
William Heinemann Ltd in 1965

This edition published by
New English Library Limited in 1980

Copyright © 1965 by Nancy Cato

Thanks are due to Mr Hal Porter for permission to quote
from his poem, 'Hobart Town 1837'.

All rights reserved. No part of this publication may be
reproduced or transmitted in any form or by any means,
without permission of the publishers.

First NEL paperback edition December 1980

Conditions of sale: This book is sold subject
to the condition that it shall not, by way
of trade or otherwise, be lent, re-sold,
hired out, or otherwise circulated without
the publisher's prior consent in any
form of binding or cover other than that
in which it is published and without a
similar condition including this condition
being imposed on the subsequent purchaser.

NEL Books are published by
New English Library Limited,
Barnard's Inn, Holborn,
London EC1N 2JR.
Printed and bound in Great Britain by
©ollins, Glasgow

45004932 9

Acknowledgements

In collecting material for this book, I wish to acknowledge the assistance of the Mitchell Library, Sydney; the National Library, Canberra; the Melbourne Public Library and Archives; and the South Australian Public Library and Archives Department, for making available manuscript material, early newspapers, and facilities for using microfilm.

Particular thanks are due to the State Public Library of Tasmania and the Research Department of the Tasmanian Archives, Hobart, and to the Royal Society, Hobart. Also to Miss Linley Thomas, librarian of the Royal Geographical Society of South Australia's York Gate Library, for access to their remarkable collection of early Australiana; to Mr H. A. Lindsay for reading the MS for errors; and to Mr N. J. B. Plomley of the History Department of Sydney University, for private research material.

Much help was given by Professor Kathleen Fitzpatrick's *Sir John Franklin in Tasmania*, and Mr Justice Barry's *Alexander Maconachie of Norfolk Island*.

N.C.

Return, and sing for extra logs, Sir John;
Refill the Monteith with a burning brew;
The final decade left ticks freezing on
And Northwest icebergs inch upon your view.
Watchman Death – eternal clown –
Crows the hour through Hobart Town.

Hal Porter

BOOK ONE

Arrival

I am ready to sigh for simplicity and peace, and obscurity in some distant land, a land like Australia, where to breathe the very air is happiness, and existence ... is in itself enjoyment.

– Lady Franklin, Journal

Chapter One

*And the Spirit of God moved upon the face of the waters.
. . .* The words of the Bible came up often to his mind when
he stood alone on deck, far out of sight of land. Here at sea,
circumscribed by the vast uncomplicated ring of the horizon,
John Franklin felt nearest to his Maker.

*They that go down to the sea in ships, and do business in
great waters: these see the works of the Lord, and His
wonders in the deep.*

He had seen leviathan and walrus and octopus, the Great
Barrier Reef of coral, icebergs as big as islands. Looking
now to southward over the long rollers of the Southern
Ocean, he could see in imagination the Antarctic wastes
where Cook had found freezing waters clogged with grinding floes, farther south beyond the Antarctic Circle.

His own journeys to those strange unwelcoming seas
which lie towards the 70th parallel had all been in the north
– and he had not finished with Arctic exploration yet. Ever
since he was twelve years old and first beheld the sea, he had
known that here was his spiritual home. Since he was fourteen he had known he wanted to be an explorer.

But never again would he take on a land expedition to
the shores of the Polar Sea.

The dreadful slogging march, day after day, of exhausted
bodies; Richardson and Hepburn with their skeleton-like
frames, the great sunken eyes in their bony skulls; and the
strange, hollow sound of their voices. And they'd reached
the Fort on the return journey to find no provisions waiting
for them, after they'd lived for weeks on nothing but lichen
scraped from rocks! The two Canadian *voyageurs* dying
slowly before their eyes, and the rest of them almost too
weak to drag the bodies outside and scrape a handful of

snow over them ...

Michel, who'd had to be shot like a wild beast after he killed young Hood – Michel who had come back fat and sleek after going off with Belanger (who was never seen again), in his eyes the glitter of lust for man-meat as he stared at the weakest of the party.

The meals that had kept the last four of them alive were almost as ghastly: boiled shoes, a fried leather gun-case, putrid deerskins and charred, powdered bones. When Hepburn shot a single partridge they'd fallen on it like animals. His first hunger appeased, he had looked at his companions' faces, smeared with blood and feathers, and thought how thin is the shell of civilization.

Little wonder he enjoyed his food nowadays, was a bit overweight. Only those who had been actually starving knew what it meant. ...

He withdrew his far-sighted gaze from the distance and the past, and gave an approving glance at the set of the sails. The Captain knew his business. It was pleasant to be a passenger for a change, with the other passengers paying him every deference; but the *Fairlie* was cluttered with women and children, even babies.

They'd had to bury several at sea. He thought of one young mother swooning to the hot deck that day in the tropics, when the tiny bundle slipped from under the large bright flag. A cursed calm, and the sharks swam round all day.

That was one complication you didn't get in the Navy, or on voyages of exploration. Women and children! He found it much easier to get on with men. He'd felt it almost an act of treachery when any of his friends got married. Richardson, marrying a niece young enough to be his daughter! Of course he himself had married again, for that matter; but it was for intellectual sympathy and a mother for his little Eleanor. He admired a good brain before a pretty face. This time he'd been lucky enough to find both in the same person.

Jane was below now, indefatigably writing up her journal.

She had a real horror of wasting time. A great eye for detail, a boundless appetite for the new and strange, and a capacity for ignoring danger and discomfort which in a man would have made a great explorer.

Well, she'd married an explorer as the next best thing. Now, at fifty, he felt ready as ever to tackle a new expedition. But there was nothing doing in the Arctic, and the war with France was over so that there was nothing doing in the Navy either; and since the *Investigator* voyage with Matthew Flinders they had cleared up the last details of the coast of New Holland.

Lately he had kicked his heels in London, living in his wife's house with a rich father-in-law. He hated inactivity almost as much as Jane did. His great ambition was to discover the North-west Passage from the Atlantic to the Pacific, the dream of Englishmen since the days of Frobisher. .. So what was he doing here, at the opposite end of the earth?

Well, he owned he would like to see again the great South Land he had visited as a midshipman: a land over which, in his memory, lay ever the golden haze of youth. And he had been the very first to plant the Union Jack on its southern shores.

Jane, of course, was wild to see New Holland – or Australia, as she preferred to call it. She had been full of enthusiasm as soon as his appointment was mooted. Certainly it was a great honour to be appointed by the King: Captain Sir John Franklin, RN, KCB, KCH, Lieutenant-Governor of Van Diemen's Land.

It showed at least that his naval service was appreciated, just as his knighthood had set the seal of approval on his explorations by land and sea. And one thing he liked, Sir John told himself, was to be appreciated.

With the help of Almighty God, he would discharge his new and unfamiliar duties with the same distinction. They could rely on him, at least, to do his duty.

31 Dec. 1836. If only the voyage could last forever, still to be *going* there, but never to arrive! I hate the end of a journey. How could Captain Parry have felt if he had actually reached the Pole? What then would have remained to him?

Yet I am longing to see Australia: Van Diemen's Land I have thought of as a kind of Paradise on earth, a spiritual agapemone. Why then does this strange foreboding move in me when I think that in perhaps a week we shall be there? I must then take up the duties of a Governor's Lady; and sometimes I feel that I shall stifle in the confines of an official life, living as it were in a glass jar with all my actions scrutinized and commented upon: like the poor corked-up Chameleons they brought on board at Cape Town who lifted up their mouths to the mouth of the bottle before they died of suffocation....

The small hand paused, poised above the notebook, then dipped the point of the quill once more. Idly it began making tall, sloping Js. 'Jane Griffin' it wrote, then 'Jane, Lady Franklin'.... Musing on the fatality of the letter N: Griffin, Franklin, it might have been Butini – or Colquhoun, the little Scottish minister who had taken a lock of her hair to India. And that queer Benson. And Eleanor Porden might have lived to be Lady Franklin instead. Poor, talented, ill-fated Eleanor! *Dead, dead, go to thy deathbed.* And in her place sleeps Jane.

At the back of her active mind a note was made: Eleanor – Latin verbs. On the voyage young Eleanor had been allowed to fall into lazy habits, as her governess seemed permanently seasick, and Jane had had to take her in hand herself. It remained to be seen how Miss Williamson would turn out, but she was ladylike and had excellent references.

The trouble with Eleanor was mental laziness. She spent too much time lying about the deck with the young Maconachies, and gossiping with the eldest girl; or begging to have the piano brought up from the hold so they could dance to it while Sophy played. Sophy Cracroft was an admirable young lady, and she played to perfection. Sir John said she took after her mother, his favourite sister. But Eleanor was lacking in perseverance. She hadn't Sir John's tenacious character, though she was ridiculously like him in appearance. And even her father –

Jane sighed and rubbed her forehead, where she felt a headache beginning. It was she who had to be the strong one these days, to carry them all. It was this idle shipboard life that led to trouble. Once he had arrived and begun his new duties he would be too occupied, please God, to yield to self-indulgence! His sense of duty, his feeling that he must give of his best, would strengthen him and his health would improve in consequence.

Her pen dipped again and made an angular capital A. Beneath she wrote:

> *On revient toujours, toujours,*
> *À ses premiers amours ...*

Adolphe Butini ... Heavens, how long ago! And it didn't sound right at all. Jane went with John, an honest English name, even if her forebears had been Huguenots and French. Jane and John, John and Jane, till death do us part. Dear, solid, lovable, honest John! Only she knew the timid child who dwelt deep within his bluff exterior, the great baby she had so often soothed on her childless breast.

She tore the page from her journal, screwed it into a ball and tossed it out of the cabin porthole, to float away like a tiny iceberg in the wake. Like the past it slipped behind, like Uncle Guillemard and the carefree days at Tredrea; Switzerland and the Butinis; Russia and Egypt, Greece and Malta.

Ever since South Africa they had been in the Antipodes, with strange constellations overhead, and the Magellanic Clouds like two misty islands in the great glittering ocean of the midnight sky. One day ... One day the name of Franklin would be numbered with Magellan's and Cook's among the great explorers. She would like to come back in a hundred years' time and see the map of the world. As Magellan and Cook belonged to the Pacific, Franklin belonged to the Arctic Ocean, and it was he who would discover the North-west Passage, she felt perfectly sure. He was already a Polar hero when she married him. Her ambition would make him greater still.

A sudden draught lifted the papers on the table, and a tremor of cold shook her fine shoulders.

The diary lay open from which she was writing up her journal: 'A man overboard ... a large shark and an octopus caught ... a near collision at night. ...'

At Cape Town she had climbed Table Mountain with Archdeacon Hutchins, in spite of Sir John's remonstrances: she could never resist a mountain, and he was too heavy and short of breath to accompany her. She smiled at a mental picture of the future head of the Church in Van Diemen's Land scudding lightly down the slope, an umbrella open in one hand and a bunch of white chrysanthemums (gathered on the summit) in the other. He had still managed to look dignified.

Then there were the lectures given by Captain Maconachie in the evenings; some rather putting the ladies to the blush, and shocking the Archdeacon so much that he retired to his cabin.

The Captain was an old friend of Sir John's from the Navy. It would be delightful to have him with them in the new colony, but she saw that he might well become an embarrassment with his outspoken ways and tactless Scottish dogmatism. And the little Maconachies! He let them run wild, believing in 'the freedom o' the indiveedual to develop withoot restraint', and he let them read *anything*. If Eleanor –

There came a tap on her cabin door, and in came the man himself: first his long head with its vigorous curls and deep-set fanatical eyes, then his whole tall energetic figure.

14

'Well, Captain Maconachie.' Jane put down her pen and regarded him with a gleam of amusement in the depths of her blue eyes. She rested her small, firm chin on one small, firm hand. 'Have you decided yet on the subject of your next lecture? The Archdeacon's been complaining that the last one was more suitable to a medical convention than to a mixed audience. And the ladies –'

'Och! The Archdeacon is nothing but an old woman himself. But, the fact o' it is, Mrs Maconachie has been scolding me aboot it. She said – she said such frankness was unca'd for. And though I dinna agree – I dinna agree, mind ye! – I've promised to stick to something more acceptable. For the future. Aye! And him with his back-to-front collar and closed-in mind needna be afraid of phrenology. The lecture will be suitable even for young gels.'

'Phrenology Captain Maconachie! That's an interesting subject now. I went to a phrenologist in London once. He told me I had a large bump of hopefulness.'

'That's why I'm here, ma'am, to ask if ye'll co-operate by letting me feel your head and expound upon it at the lecture. I want to get a lady and a gentleman. And next to Mrs Maconachie ye've the most interesting head on board – and I mean the contents as well as the contour.'

Jane blushed slightly. 'Thank you, Captain Maconachie, I'm honoured; but I cannot agree. It's against my nature to put myself up for a show, even if Sir John would allow it. I have a real horror of eyes looking at me, indeed I cannot bear it. I thought you were aware of this weakness of mine.'

Alexander Maconachie turned down his mobile lips disbelievingly. After all the lady was going to take up the position of First Lady in the land – she could hardly hope to escape the public eye there. To him the limelight was meat and drink; he was incapable of being silent or unobtrusive in any gathering.

'Ah well,' he said, 'perhaps I can persuade Mrs Maconachie to take part. Her head's a good one and I ken it well. But she's aye busy with the bairns at just that time o' night.

15

The stewardess is no' to be trusted, and the nanny is awa' having her own meal.'

'I'll send Stewart along to help. She's very dependable. Marie will be here to help get Eleanor to bed, but she wouldn't do with your little ones as she only speaks French.'

'Och, the bairns understand French – Mrs Maconachie and I have had to start convairsing in Spanish,' he said with a twinkle in his eye. 'But thank you, Lady Franklin. That will aid my wife conseederably.'

Lying on the sunwarm deck with her fair head on a striped cushion, close to the lee rail where the sea frothed past only feet below, Eleanor was talking with Mary Anne Maconachie, known as Minnie.

'Your mamma's a great traveller, isn't she?' Minnie was asking. 'Mamma was telling us the other day that she had been to Russia, and down the Nile in a boat, and climbed Mount Olympus and all.'

'Ye-es. But she's not a real explorer like my papa. And she isn't really my mamma. My mamma is dead. She was a very clever writer, she could write poetry and everything, and Papa loved her best.'

'How do you know?' Minnie had her father's long nose and enquiring mind.

'I just know,' said Eleanor vaguely. But of course it was obvious. He hadn't given the new Mamma even one little baby, and they had been married for years. She fingered her mother's pearl and garnet brooch, entwined with a lock of her hair, which she always wore. 'He thought I needed another mamma to look after me, but she was always travelling. And she gives me dull books to read – botany and natural history and stuff. She thinks ladies ought to be interested in science.'

'So does my Papa. He says he doesn't mind what we read, so long as it's scientifically correct. He won't let us read the Bible or fairy stories.'

'*Not* read the *Bible*!' Eleanor looked shocked.

'He doesn't want our minds confused with all those stories about Noah and Jonah in the Book of Genesis –'

'Jonah isn't in Genesis.'

'– because he says they are only fairy stories, and sensible people don't need fairy stories.'

'I don't know. I always liked stories about mermaids,' said Eleanor, gazing down into the white-marbled blue-black water.

'Yes, but you don't believe in them!'

'No-o.'

Mary Anne's sharp elbow found her ribs. 'Look, there's your cousin Sophy with Mr Elliott. Sara says she is a monstrous flirt.'

Eleanor looked, and looked away. She couldn't understand all this gaping and giggling over young men. She never wanted to marry, and loved only her dear kind Papa. He was the most important person on board; absolutely everyone tried to get next to him when he walked on the deck. And when they arrived at Hobart Town, he would be Governor of the whole Colony, and she would be almost like a princess. She longed for the new land, even if it meant regular school lessons again.

Mrs William Henty was taking the air on deck with her husband. She leaned rather heavily on his arm, for she was still weak from the shock of grief. Little Babet, her only son, lay below the laughing white-capped surface of this ocean she would always hate – down in the dark unimaginable depths in the little weighted wooden coffin the carpenter had made for him.

He had seemed to pick up a little while they stayed at Cape Town, but back there, two weeks out from the Cape, the end had come. Her little son, not two years old, who never ventured far from her skirts, had been launched into that vast waste of water, alone. His grave was just a point of latitude and longitude upon the map.

There had been no dancing on deck that night and the

next day, being Sunday, all the passengers had attended Divine Service, and pressed her hand in silent sympathy when it was over. Lady Franklin, with her gentle and kind manner, had seemed genuinely distressed. They had both put everyone at ease on board from the beginning: in spite of their retinue of aides and servants, they kept up no state but behaved with simple amiability.

They were a congenial crowd altogether, the passengers – but oh, she longed for land, for peace and quiet, for her sister-in-law's welcoming arms! William said they were nearly there.

'La-and ho-o-o!'

The cry came from the look-out in the foretop; he pointed away to the north-east. Before long the misty outline of South-west Cape was looming on the port bow, and passengers ran to line the lee rail, laughing with excitement.

Young Mrs Henty, a smile upon her wan face, Eleanor Franklin, her prim ringlets blown across her eyes, and the little Maconachies stood together, staring and pointing. Beyond that blue smudge lay their new home, and the unknown future.

Jane, called from her cabin by Sir John, felt a strange sinking at her heart as she looked at him. He had put on weight on the voyage, and he smelt of snuff. 'Come, my love,' he said importantly as his short legs stepped over the coaming. She knew he was excited by the sparkle in his eyes, but his face wore its habitual look of calm benevolence. So, in the *Trent*'s long-boat, he had looked at the attacking sea-bears and the heaving ice floes; so he had looked, no doubt, at his own boiled shoes served up against starvation on that long journey to the shores of the Polar Sea.

Phrenology! He had a noble, intellectual brow, as her sister had remarked when they first met him, and a sensitive mouth above a chin like a knob of moulded iron. Yet he was a man of action rather than intellect, and often it was she who had to make up his mind for him; but once made up it was immovable as a rock.

They went on deck and stood beside Captain and Mrs Maconachie, who deferentially made way for Lady Franklin at the rail.

Alexander Maconachie's piercing eyes seemed to look beyond the wraith of land to the prison buildings and penal settlements of which he had read. He was intensely interested in the whole subject of transportation as a means of dealing with crime.

Of the four of them, only one was not glad to see land and know that the voyage was nearly over; but for all it was as well that they could not see what the future held for them in the Southern Hemisphere.

Chapter Two

Hobart Town,
6 Jan. 1837.

My Dear Father,

This morning Sir John made his public landing, while
we ladies walked quietly through the garden to the
Government House.

The weather is almost as cold as the name of the month
would imply at home, though here the middle of summer.
The place looks beautiful. ... Sir George Frankland, the
Surveyor-General, a gentleman of singular wit and
humour and most amiable manners, brought me on board
a bouquet of beautiful native flowers, a most characteristic
and acceptable gift from my new country. . . .

Jane looked from her escritoire to her dressing-table, where
the mirror gave back in double profusion the spires of pink
heath, the starry white clematis, and a tiny flower blue as
the Hobart Town sky above the great brown organ-pipes of
Mount Wellington. The summit of this mountain, which
rose almost from the water's edge, looked so close in the
clear sparkling atmosphere that she had already resolved
to climb it before the year was out. (She collected mountains
as in her youth she had collected beaux.)

She went to the open window and breathed deeply. It was
almost like being at sea – and she still had the illusion of
the floor moving slightly under her feet – there was a
glimpse of wind-ruffled blue water from nearly every
window. The air had a freshness not all of salt, but com-
pounded of sea and eucalyptus scrub and dry grass : an
essence, subtle and invigorating, distilled by the sun in the
sky's blue cup.

She remembered, in all the journals she had read of

voyages to Australia and sojourns within its shores, how the writers dwelt on the effect of the atmosphere on their spirits. There was, they said, an actual physical enjoyment in breathing, and the simple fact of existence was felt to be a blessing.

Already in this pure and exhilarating air she felt herself sensibly inhaling life and vigour both of mind and body. God grant it might have the same effect on Sir John! Perhaps in this genial climate, cool and bracing as it was today without being clammy, brilliantly sunny without being too hot, he would not feel the need of the stimulants which were so bad for him.

She was worried about his cough, which kept him awake at night, and by his high colour and sudden fits of irritability. Spirits, especially the rum and hot water he liked to take at bedtime, the doctors said only increased his plethoric tendency.

It was no use her remonstrating, of course. It was the one subject of all that he was most touchy about: any suggestion that he was not as young as he was, or that his health and faculties were not all they should be, and he fired up at once.

She leant far out over the window-sill and plucked a thin, straight leaf from one of the gum trees growing close to the house, higher than these upstairs windows. Holding the leaf up to the light, she could see the glistening globules of essential oil, the transparent cells. It was the simplest of leaves, just one straight vein dividing the two flat lobes, and shaped like a faintly-curving dagger. Its surface had the waxy sheen of polished leather. Its scent, and the spiky-leaved flowers behind her, reminded her of Greece, of Athens and the dry thymey slopes below the Acropolis.

Here she was in a distant land, a whole strange island waiting to be explored. . . . She longed to set off at once, to climb the mountains, sail the coasts, explore the rivers, gaze upon the hidden inland lakes. It was like a big present just waiting to be untied.

21

Miss Williamson knocked at the door and put her head in. 'Come in!' called Jane. 'Come here and smell this atmosphere. There! Is it not exhilarating, like champagne?'

'Champagne always gives me a sick headache, my lady. I think it is too sour for my stomach.' Miss Williamson often spoke as if her head were blocked with a cold, the consonants coming out dead and distorted.

'Oh, tut! But *smell* the *air*! It's just as I expected: glorious. I know I shall be better in health, my headaches will go at last, I shall be a new woman in a new land.'

'Lady Franklin, Eleanor wants to know if we may go for a walk outside the grounds. Sir John is willing to accompany us if you say she may.'

'Of course you may! I'd like to come too, but I must finish my letters and then I must write an advertisement for a French chef, if such a thing is to be found in Van Diemen's Land. The housekeeper seems capable, and at least she is not a convict. Eckh! It's unpleasant to think that one's laundress is a convicted felon, and the kitchen-maid might be a murderess for all we know.'

'I hardly think that is likely,' said Miss Williamson with a faint smile. 'I shall go and tell Eleanor to put her bonnet on, then.'

Jane sat down again at her desk. It was a pity Miss Williamson was so unprepossessing, with those large teeth and that heavy pallid face and glasses – but at least they would be less likely to lose her through marriage. She began making a list of furniture they would need. There was not even a set of dining-room chairs. She would like to get some with inlaid brass backs, like those they had at home; but it would take too long to get them sent out....

Half an hour later Miss Williamson and Eleanor came in, all aglow.

'Mamma, we went outside the gates, and we were just walking along Macquarie Street when someone said, "There's the Guv'nor!" and they all began to cheer like anything. Such a crowd collected that Papa said we had better come back. Isn't it exciting?'

'And a man called out, "There's the chap what ate his shoes,"' added Miss Williamson with a laugh that showed all of her large teeth.

'Well, my love, they don't seem to be dissatisfied with their new Lieutenant-Governor. Quite the contrary, in fact.' Sir John was smiling broadly above the high collar of his uniform. He strutted a little, pleased with himself and his outing.

'It says more, perhaps, for how much they disliked their *retiring* Governor,' said Jane judiciously.

'By Jove, it does too! I hadn't thought of that. Poor old Arthur rubbed 'em all the wrong way, you know. He was most unpopular – most unpopular all round, except for the few officials he'd appointed. Stephen was telling me, the Attorney-General. Man with his head screwed on the right way.'

'May I go and play with Kitty and Mary Anne, Mamma?' Eleanor, having taken off her bonnet, darted away almost before Jane had given her consent, and without hearing Miss Williamson's beginning remonstrance about putting the bonnet in her own room first.

'That child has become rather giddy lately,' said Jane.

'Oh, she's a well-disposed child: she'll settle down. There's no harm in Eleanor,' said John comfortably. 'Quite the contrary! She's a good child on the whole.'

'Miss Williamson,' said Jane briskly, 'I want you to make sure that she gets up by six every morning. She can prepare her lessons for the day, and then go for a walk in the garden before breakfast.' And when Miss Williamson had gone, 'I feel sure that early rising is best for Eleanor,' said Jane, who usually had her breakfast in bed. 'She has a tendency towards laziness which needs to be overcome vigorously; and then lying in bed in the mornings, at her particular age, is likely to encourage thoughts she would be better without. Don't you agree, my love?'

'Eh? Oh! Yes, yes, I'm sure you're right. I like a breath

23

of fresh air myself at that time of day. Nothing like a turn round the deck before breakfast to give you an appetite.'

'Yes; but do remember, my love, that you *aren't* at *sea* any longer.'

Chapter Three

' "At first sight this region of giant plutonic fragments would seem impracticable to the step of the delicate female foot. . . . But the courage and activity of the ladies were beyond all praise. . . . Without bruise or scratch they reached the flagstaff on the highest peak." Oh dear!' Jane laughed, and put down her copy of the *Hobart Town Courier* on the bed. She sipped her morning tea. 'Sir John, they are being pompous about my climbing Mount Wellington now,' she called. 'I declare, it was nothing to Hymettus; at one stage I thought I'd never get down from there at all.'

'You have extraordinary energy, my love.' Sir John came in from his adjoining room, barrel-shaped in his dressing-gown. He smiled at her complacently. 'Herbs from Mount Hymettus, olives from the Mount of Olives, sea-water from the Dead Sea, burnt peas from Pompeii! And what was there on top of this mountain to be worth collecting?'

'Oh, a few pieces of volcanic rock; and some fossiliferous limestone from the Sassafras valley at the bottom. But there is a most glorious view. I sat on the cairn and Mr Frankland pointed out the capes and bays on the map, and there it was all spread out like a giant coloured atlas below. Everything reduced as in a painting: at breakfast I counted five large ships between the legs of a roast fowl.'

'I think you just climbed the thing because of the challenge. You could never resist a mountain. It's your hidden wish to dominate. As soon as you see something larger than yourself you have to subjugate it – as you subjugated me.'

'You were certainly *larger*, my dear, as well as higher – in the public esteem, I mean.' She looked affectionately at his broad, solid figure in the plush dressing-gown, at his broad, kind, cleanshaven face above it. 'What do you weigh now, Sir J., is it fifteen stone?'

'All of that, I fear. My new uniforms are a shade tight already. And yet you can still wear that crimson silk you had made up in Malta.'

'That old thing! I most certainly cannot; it's quite out of fashion. Nobody is wearing –'

'I meant, you can still get into it. You never change, you're uncommonly young and slim for your age. And not even a grey hair! Your poor fat old husband will be thought to have robbed the nursery.

'Oh, fiddlesticks.' She moved the paper impatiently. She did not like this self-deprecatory tone; she felt an irritable proprietorship in all who belonged to her, and could not bear that they should not be well-thought-of. It had given her real pain when the impudent colonial press, in the midst of friendly notices of Sir John's arrival, had described him as 'of short stature, and rather corpulent; he is very active for his age, which looks to be about sixty.' And he was barely fifty yet!

I could have had a grown-up son by now, she mused ... that is, if I'd married early.

'O my dear!' she sighed. The sparkle of mischief that was never far from the surface had gone out of her soft blue eyes. 'If only I could have given you a son, as *she* gave you a daughter.'

'My dearest Jane, you must give over brooding on that old woe. For myself, as you know, I care not in the least so long as I have you. It was childbirth that fatally weakened poor Eleanor's health, and I wouldn't want your life risked for all the sons in Christendom. Besides – confess it! – you've enjoyed your freedom. Think if you'd had a brood of six like Mrs Maconachie, or nine like Mrs Bedford, how your adventures would have been cut short. And that girlish figure – where would it be?'

'It's true. *Tu as raison*.' She began to smile again. 'I have had a wonderfully interesting life for a woman. But I wish I'd been a man and could have gone to the Arctic with you.'

26

'*I* don't wish you'd been a man – perish the thought.'

He sat on the side of the big bed and kissed her bare shoulder. She patted his balding head, pulled her peignoir a little higher and went back to the paper. Men were tiresome creatures at times, and didn't seem to get any less so with age. She knew her wifely duty, but it did not extend to the daytime. She poured herself another cup of tea from the silver tea-pot.

'It's just as well I'm not a jealous sort of chap,' he said, playing with one of her brown ringlets, 'or I should have put a stop to your travelling about the world without me. I know the havoc you caused among the hearts of my brother-officers in the Navy. You and Mary must've had more beaux than any other two young ladies in London. And even now you've got Montagu eating out of your hand.'

'O fie! You like to think everyone admires me, you're proud as Punch about it.'

'But it's true.'

'He's on our list for the Tuesday Drawing-Room, with his wife; and that devastating old bore Mr Justice Pedder, who insists on telling me long dull anecdotes of the Court, and Mr Alfred Stephen – though *he* is amusing and clever.'

'And what about Montagu – what d'you think about him?'

'He's handsome and gentlemanly, of course, an accomplished flatterer; rather oily I sometimes think. Mary Maconachie says as smooth as a snake, and just as trustworthy.'

'Oh, come! He seems an open, friendly, helpful sort of fellow to me.'

'My dearest, *everyone* seems an open, friendly sort of fellow to you – at first. It's because your own nature is open and candid. No wonder the unscrupulous take advantage of you.'

'What nonsense!' He took a turn about the room, rather annoyed. He knew his mind was not as acute and agile as his wife's. He usually trusted her judgement. But Montagu, his Colonial Secretary! He had to be a trustworthy man.

27

He knew the ropes, he had run the Colony for years under Arthur, and he was essential to its smooth running still.

Imagine a ship with a first officer you couldn't trust; why, she'd come to grief in no time. He thought nostalgically of the *Rainbow* he'd commanded for so long: she'd been known as 'The Celestial Rainbow' in the Service because of the harmony that prevailed on board.

Here in Hobart Town the intrigue and backbiting, waspish tempers and continual quarrels made him feel ill. He'd rather face the inhuman cold of the Polar Sea any day.

As though Jane were following his thought, as she sometimes did, she said with a sigh, 'Oh dear! Who would have thought to find that people in the Antipodes are more conscious of social levels than in the capitals of the world! They are so touchy about precedence, I've offended two or three wives already.... Sir J., *must* we give a reception every Tuesday?'

'Colonel Arthur always did; and I feel it is our duty. It is expected of us.'

'Say no more!' She pulled a mock-solemn face.

'Duty' was a word which ranked with 'God' in Sir John's vocabulary; duty had kept him from joining her in Egypt, from letting her join him in Greece. Sea-going wives were not popular with the naval authorities. But here they were, in a sense, on duty together. She meant to make a success of it; and she would help him to the best of her abilities, wherever he would let her, even to drafting dispatches and official letters.

'But can't you warn him, open his eyes to this slimy serpent before it's too late?'

At breakfast in their own room over the library, Mary Maconachie questioned her stern-faced captain. She knew Alexander's nobility of mind, and respected his judgement; and she could see as well as her husband that Montagu was running things to please the Arthur faction. A collision with the free Colonists was bound to come.

'It's no good, my dear. I've aye tried to get Sir John to see Montagu's insincerity, but it's quite useless. He willna give up his comfortable belief in the mon's goodness of heart until Mr M. stabs him in the back. To argue aboot it – weel, it's like trying to force a piece of barley sugar from the mouth of a bairn. The sweetie melts away in the process; and nothing remains but the deesagreeable impression left on both sides of the contest.'

'I'm afraid for you – for us.'

'Aye, they'll never forgi'e me for seeing through them, o' course.'

'At least you're a man, thank God, and not a sheep,' she said, looking at him with burning dark eyes as he stood, stripped to the waist, brushing his vigorous thatch before the dressing-table.

'Aye, and have proved it six times over,' he said, with a laughing glance in the mirror.

'And quite enough, too,' she said tartly. 'If you quarrel with Sir John over the Arthurites and we are turned out of Government House without a roof over our heads –'

'It'll no' come to that, Mary. Have faith in your Alexander.'

'I do have faith!' It was true; he was the only god she believed in. But she had no very high opinion of the Lieutenant-Governor. While everyone obeyed him, or seemed to, all would be well; but once question his authority and he would react like a stern naval commander on his quarter-deck: 'I'll have no mutiny aboard this vessel!' And then the heads would begin to roll.

She couldn't help liking Lady Franklin, with her kindly unassuming ways, her lively wit and sense of hmour. How bored she must be with her stolid lord and master! Yet they seemed to get on well, in fact Sir John's devotion was obvious, and she was devoted heart and mind to furthering his career. He always liked to make a show of consulting her before coming to a decision. And that, no doubt, was why Montagu had set out to make himself charming to

Lady F. – the power behind the throne!

Yet Mr Montagu was perhaps in for an unpleasant surprise. Sir John had the obstinacy of a mule, and after asking for an opinion was just as likely to take the opposite course from sheer contrariness. And nothing would shake him once his mind was made up.

She took her boiled egg from the tray and sliced viciously at its bald dome, as if it had been the smooth round skull of Sir John himself.

Chapter Four

'What a delightful young man! But such a sad face,' said Jane.

'But did you see it light up when we got on to the subject of botany? What a pity he lives in Launceston – he would certainly be an asset to Hobart Town society.'

'He has been highly recommended to us by Sir William Hooker.' Lady Franklin was paying an afternoon visit to Mrs Maconachie in her suite of upstairs rooms. In the great house they met for certain only at dinner, so had formed the habit of dropping in on each other for a chat over the previous day's doings. They were discussing the arrival of Mr Ronald Campbell Gunn, police magistrate in the north, who was on a visit to the capital.

'He came to look us over, I do believe,' said Jane. 'He had heard that we were favourable to natural history, and the poor man has evidently been pining for some congenial company. Wasn't he disgusted with Colonel Arthur? "All that immense Government garden and Domain growing nothing but cabbages for the Governor's horses!" I believe I shall engage him to lay out a garden of native plants – to advise me how to go about it, at all events.'

'That's an interesting project! You must seek out some suitable land, some unspoiled brushland. Everyone here is busy making the place look like a bit of Old England, with pansies and geraniums and daffodils. Yet there are some beautiful native flowers.'

'I know it. And they are not scentless, as people keep asserting. Think of the scent of wattle blossom.' She looked over her friend's shoulder at the work she was doing. It was an elaborate piece of floral tapestry-work in wool. 'Mary Maconachie, you'll ruin your eyes with that thing, I declare! It's a pretty design, but the stitches are so small you will be needing eyeglasses.'

Mary Maconachie looked up with unwonted shyness. 'Do you know who this is for? It's for you – for a footstool.'

'But how very kind! What a dear you are. I *wondered* at your sitting so long over fancy-work, when your interest is more in real plants than embroidered ones. I could never abide needlework as a girl. But I do appreciate it; I admire it all the more in others.'

Mr Gunn was delighted with Lady Franklin's idea for a botanic garden devoted to native plants. Nobody but himself, and a few enthusiasts like Robert Lawrence and Dr Milligan, had ever shown any interest in them. He said he would write off at once to Sir William Hooker to send out a good man as a gardener.

A sober man was more important, Lady Franklin suggested, and he agreed. 'So many out here take to drink,' she added. For a moment it seemed that a darker shadow slipped over the painfully knit brows of Ronald Gunn. When animated his face was bright enough, though in repose there was a hint of tragedy about his lips. He interested her intensely.

' 'Tis easy enough to ken the cause of most of the drunkenness in the colony,' said Captain Maconachie in his brisk brook-no-argument manner. ' 'Tis due precisely to its being a penal settlement; and the meesery induced by the system is aye reflected through society at every level.'

'But surely the assigned servants –'

'They are in the worrst case of all: nothing but slaves of capreecious masters. Och, when I think o' it, I don't wonder there should be some drunkenness; I wonder that there's any sober!'

'Really, Captain, I can't go along with you there,' said Gunn, rather stiff. 'It's not so in the north, I assure you.'

'Mr Gunn, where you are is not so far from Flinders Island, the Aboriginal settlement,' said Lady Franklin brightly. 'I wonder would you like to go along with us when

32

Sir John and I visit the island? You might get some new specimens of plants for Sir William Hooker.'

'I should like that above anything! You are too kind, Lady Franklin. There's a wonderful growth of *Xanthorrhea*, the grass tree, which I've long wanted to see.'

When next he wrote to Sir William Hooker about a consignment of plants for Kew Gardens, he recorded the delight of meeting congenial minds.

> Sir John and Lady Franklin are sincerely desirous of forwarding the cause of Natural History in this colony. A Society has been formed and Lady F. is about purchasing a Piece of ground out of her private income for a Collection of our Indigenous Plants.... This is true love of Science. It will come exclusively out of her own pocket, and on her departure she intends handing it over for the Good of the Colony. She is a most amiable and estimable Lady – and has certainly secured my best Feelings.

Eleanor Franklin, with Minnie and Kitty Maconachie, all of them wearing bonnets to protect their complexions from the morning sun, were planting seeds in their own plot in the Government House garden.

Eleanor had been up at six to prepare her lessons, then had walked in the grounds with her dear Papa for half an hour before breakfast. When Mamma had one of her headaches she didn't come down for breakfast but it was a merry meal, and the only one at which children and grown-ups met.

Eleanor scowled at the seeds in her hand. In a minute Miss Williamson would send for her, and she'd have to start reading about the Athenians in Sicily, or the androgynous plants, or work at Latin translation.

She hated Caesar's expeditions into Gaul.

Writing lessons were boring, too. She didn't mind writing up her diary, setting the letters down anyhow, the sentences climbing up and down hill. But Papa and Mamma wanted her to write in copperplate.

While they were doing their Progress in Launceston, Miss W. had refused to send the loving letter she had written, because it was blotted and the hand not neat enough. She still thought it easier to read than Papa's spiky scrawl.

She did it over again, and received a stern note in reply. 'You know this is all part of the same haste and inconsiderateness I have had to reprove you for at other times,' he wrote. 'And "Yours affectionately", my dear child, is not enough to your parents. It should be something like "Your affectionate and dutiful daughter", or "child".'

He advised her to take Sophy's letters as a model, as her hand was clear and well-formed and she made no spelling mistakes. This added to Eleanor's sense of injury. It was not fair, Sophy was so much older, to make comparisons with her. And Sophy was a flirt, and Mamma treated her like her own daughter, laughing with her over private jokes which Eleanor was supposed to be 'too young' to understand.

Sometimes she hated Sophy Cracroft.

Her other cousin Mary Franklin was much nicer, not so clever but a sweet girl and always very kind. She and Sophy went down for balls and dinner-parties and drawing-room receptions while Eleanor had to stay upstairs and peep over the bannisters, hearing tantalizing laughter and music from below. Mary always found time to run upstairs and bring her some tidbit from the supper tables.

At the first ball the chef, Charles Napoleon, who Mamma thought would be so good because she admired everything French, had covered the platters of cold chicken with a bright pink sauce so that it looked like coloured blancmange, and nobody ate it.

Eleanor and the Maconachie children had a wonderful feast of chicken afterwards, for the sauce was quite tasty in spite of its sickly appearance.

Now the dining-room was dark with the wooden shutters put up to enclose the verandas for the New Year Ball, and she had permission to stay up till midnight if she could keep awake. She was very fond of dancing, and thought nostalgically of the quadrilles and country dances on the *Fairlie*'s deck, with sudden lurches of the ship adding to the merriment.

Even Miss Williamson was going to the ball tomorrow night. She had been fussing all yesterday with her costume – as if anyone would look at *her*! Whereas everyone would have wanted to dance with the Governor's daughter.

Eleanor crumbled some earth over the last of the seeds, pulled off her gardening-gloves, and got up to follow Minnie and Kitty to the gate of the garden enclosure. Kitty dropped back and waited for her. Eleanor said:

'Mary Anne, I think you should let me walk ahead.'

'Why, pray? I'm older than you.'

'Yes, but *I* am Miss Franklin, remember.'

'You certainly don't let anyone forget it!' Mary Anne Maconachie tossed her head and walked first through the gate.

Eleanor hurried after her. 'I was only joking, Minnie,' she said placatingly. Her broad face wore a bland, innocent expression, but her eyes were sharp.

Eleanor was curled up on the box-couch in Lady Franklin's boudoir, watching Marie put the finishing touches to her Mamma's evening toilette.

She loved this couch, which was covered in a pretty design of pink roses climbing over a black lattice on a cream ground. It was her favourite perch on these occasions, when she was admitted almost like a grown-up to the secret rites of the dressing-table.

Mamma certainly looked lovely when she was dressed up. Tonight her gown was of shimmering India silk, shot with blue and green, with a deep border at the hem of embroidered silver grapes and vine leaves. Her train was trimmed with blond and silver cord, and blue and silver grapes were caught in her piled-up dark hair.

35

'*Ah, que Madame est belle!*' murmured Marie. '*Mais un peu pâle ce soir.*' She gazed critically at her mistress's reflection. '*Une peu du rouge? Un soupçon –*'

'*Pas de rouge.*' Marie always had to be dissuaded from making her look like Jezebel; as if there were not enough gossip about her Paris gowns! She would soon have a high enough colour with the business of greeting guests and trying to remember who was not on speaking terms with whom.

She looked forward to the evening with the familiar shrinking nervousness which had made her violently sick when she was presented at Court.

Only one thing made the thought of the ball agreeable to her. Mr Alfred Stephen would be there – no longer Attorney-General, but still disposed to be friendly to the Governor. He had resigned to concentrate on his own practice. His wife had died after her ninth confinement last year, poor woman. Jane had been to visit the seven remaining children at his large and beautifully appointed home in Macquarie Street. It was amazing to see the state kept up in these Colonial homes: the massive, well-proportioned rooms, the expensive furniture all brought out from Home.

Mr Stephen had a keen intellect and an unexpected sense of fun, so that there had been an instant *rapport* between them. He made up delightful extempore verses about pompous Hobartonians, and his shrewd sparkling glance under his fly-away eyebrows, across the crowded heads at a Levée, could lift her from the depths of boredom.

Also he was an undoubted gentleman, as was Mr Montagu; so many of the men she was expected to receive were not. He was a handsome man, not tall but well-proportioned, with fine, strong features and dignified side-whiskers. She had seen a lively twinkle of appreciation, together with some astonishment, light up his eyes when they rested on her for the first time.

Rather recently widowed he might be, and father of a large family, but he was not blind to a merry glance and slim shoulders.

Jane gazed with modified approval at her own reflection, her small figure given dignity by curls and head-dress. She smiled indulgently in the mirror at Eleanor, watching with intensity and evident admiration, her large chin resting on her clasped hands as she leaned over the end of the couch.

Jane thanked her maid and rose from the dressing-table chair of quilted satin.

'You look beautiful, Mamma,' said Eleanor, almost sincere. She was thinking how she would like to dress up herself and go down and dance with her Papa, who loved her best. 'That's a gorgeous gown, really and truly it is! Mamma, in six months I'll be fourteen, and then *I'll* be able to go to balls and parties, shall I not?'

'We'll see when the time comes, my child. Meanwhile you should be thinking more of your studies, and not such giddy things as balls. Keep still, pet, while I tie your ribbons. I declare, your hair looks as if you had been dragged through a bramble bush.'

(Balls and parties, fiddlesticks! We must get these ideas out of her foolish little head, I'm afraid she's not as serious-minded as I'd like to see her. She must not be allowed to grow up too soon, or she'll be wanting to marry a colonist, or even worse, an emancipist! From what I've seen of Hobarton young ladies, they'd rather marry with an ex-convict than not marry at all.)

'But there aren't any bramble bushes in Van Diemen's Land!' cried Eleanor, pert and laughing. 'You should say – er, er – you should say a fern tree!'

'That's enough, miss. You may carry my fan to the top of the stairs; but no dropping bread-pellets on Mr Gregson's head this time, or straight to bed you go.'

'It was Lachie Maconachie who –'

'Hush! No tales out of school. And no silly-billies, mind.'

'And I may stay up until midnight? Mary has promised to bring me some supper.'

'Very well. Since it's Saturday tomorrow. There, child! Be careful; you'll disarrange my coiffure.'

In the great drawing-room, the hall and ante-room,

candles twinkled in crystal chandeliers and silver candelabra; in the Octagon Room the band was tuning up.

It was a scratch band, for Colonel Elliott had refused the regimental band's services on the ground that his wife had not been invited to Government House. But Mrs Elliott's character and reputation were not above reproach, and Jane was not going to be blackmailed into receiving her.

She threw the gleaming peacock-silk train over her gloved arm and descended the stairs. Her back was straight, her brow serene. Only a close observer could have detected the faint tremor of the feather fan, the slightly quickened rise and fall of her bosom, which betrayed the intense nervousness she had never been able to conquer.

Chapter Five

Walking at dusk over the rough, hilly track from the cluster of huts near the coast which made up the Aboriginal settlement, Ronald Campbell Gunn could scarcely believe his good fortune. He must, surely, be dreaming.

Yet the solid figure of Sir John Franklin striding along beside him, puffing slightly from exertion, was certainly real. So was the slight form of his Lady, sturdily and energetically crossing fallen trees and prickly shrubs, and ignoring the rents made in full skirts, the dust and grass-seeds clinging to them. It was delightful to see Sir John's solicitude that she should not fall, and her cheerful good-humour when a broken twig spiked her ankle. He was charmed by their complete naturalness, and their making this expedition on foot in the name of science, to see the growth of *Xanthorrhea arborea*, the Tasmanian grass tree.

Who could have imagined Colonel Arthur doing such a thing! For natural history, or anything unconnected with money or the penal system, he'd shown a contemptuous indifference.

Gunn found the Franklins wonderfully sympathetic. Since poor Robert Lawrence's death there was no one within a hundred miles with a knowledge of botany; his one contact with a scientific mind the correspondence with Hooker on the other side of the world.

'Oh, Mr Gunn! Pray look! Look at them.'

Lady Franklin, plunging eagerly on ahead, had paused on top of a slight rise, and turned a smiling animated face towards him.

Beyond lay the grasstree plain, covered as far as they could see with the weird, stunted shapes of *Xanthorrhea*. It might have been a mob of wild black men with shaggy heads and uplifted spears, struck suddenly into stillness. In the grey evening light they had a look of arrested motion.

Gunn had read descriptions of them in flower, when the dark peduncles were covered with pale creamy florets from top to bottom, and decorated with foraging butterflies and honey-eating birds; but now there was something infinitely grim and forbidding in their aspect, suited to the wind-whipped barren island where a dwindling race was exiled.

On the way, once out of earshot of the superintendent, Mr Robinson – an odd little man given to pompous poly-syllables frequently mispronounced – they had discussed the evident pining away of the people under his care.

Only ten children on the whole settlement, and the total number reduced to ninety-eight from nearly two hundred sent there in Governor Arthur's time! Robinson had put them through their paces like so many performing animals. They answered the questions of the Catechist, Mr Clarke, in a mechanical fashion: 'Where is God?' – 'God is in heppen'; 'What is your soul?' – 'My sould is immortal.'

The women had showed their laborious needlework, the men their gardens; but Gunn had seen the hopeless, lost darkness in their eyes.

No, said the superintendent unctuously, they did not have corroborees any longer, as he (Mr Robinson) found they disturbed his rest. No, they did not go out hunting, as they had plenty of Government rations; no, he did not encourage 'walkabouts' as the idea was to civilize the natives and make home-loving Christians out of them....

It was unthinkable, said Lady Franklin as they walked along, that a whole race of human beings should be allowed to become extinct. Sir John wanted to do something practi-cal to help them, but what? They were safe on the island from unscrupulous white men, sealers and sawyers and old lags who would corrupt them with drink and other temp-tations.

They were an interesting race, Gunn opined, and far from being low in the scale of human beings as many seemed to think. Yet the early settlers had shot them like kangaroos.

They had never needed to stir themselves much. There were no competitors for the food which abounded in the bush and on the shore – they didn't even bother to fish, except that the women dived to get shellfish from the rocks – and they had not needed to be inventive, to build houses or grow crops. A simple breakwind, a firestick, and his hunting weapons were all a man needed to set up house.

They had probably lived an undisturbed and idyllic life on this beautiful island for thousands of years before they were seen and described by Péron and Labillardière. Until the panicky massacre by the whites at Risdon Cove, they appeared to have been a gentle and inoffensive race; but once roused they had fought bitterly for thirty years to keep their homeland.

Now, as the three Europeans turned their backs on those plants so aboriginal and primitive in form, the darkness spread round them, seeming to flow up from the ground and out from the undergrowth. Ahead there appeared a row of bobbing red lights: melodious voices calling, guttural laughter, loud coo-ees. It was now quite dark.

As the lights approached they could make out the figures of the Ringtail Possum and Bong, last of the Lenah Valley tribes; Wooneteah Cootmena, whose name meant 'thunder and lightning'; Parley and his wife, Wanganippi, now re-named Hannibal and Queen Evelene; Augustus and Lalla Rookh, whose pretty native name had been Truganini; but Mr Robinson had thought their old names undignified and preferred something more classical.

The natives were carrying torches made of smouldering bark. Shed from living trees, it lay everywhere in curved dry strips on the ground. As soon as one burned down they picked up another and lit it from the old one, and the wind of their progress made it glow brightly. The torches made a reddish light in which white teeth and dark eyes glistened strangely.

The effect was most picturesque; Lady Franklin was charmed. But after greeting them Sir John walked along

41

silently, brooding over the insoluble problem of these unfortunate creatures. He could not forget the reproachful voice of one of the old men who had spoken to him out of the hearing of Robinson.

'Ah, Mitta Guberna, you take-it him own country, white man : take-it him lubra, him own kangaroo-ground; me no like-it dis way. More better you kill-it right out.'

Well, the old ones had a right to be bitter, he supposed. They remembered the implacable war between white and black, and there had been terrible atrocities on both sides. But surely the younger ones could adjust themselves, grow up to be useful Christian citizens?

Mr Robinson seemed to think so. The superintendent of the Queen's Orphan School at Newtown seemed to think so – at least he had several mixed-blood children there who were very bright at their studies.

They were cheerful and animated enough tonight, but it was hard to tell how much this was the result of the unusual excitement of visitors.

'They are a happy and contented community, are they not?' said Mr Robinson as he welcomed them back to the establishment. 'Mr Clarke will tell you that they are phenomenally fond of Bible-reading, and the women take a simple pride in the housewifely arts in their cottages.

'In the morning the men will give a text-reading; the girls will sing hymns; and the women will recite from the Psalms of David.'

Jane turned her back on him. She had felt an instantaneous and inexplicable dislike for the little man, with his rosy cheeks and his sanctimonious manner. Sir John seemed impressed by his show of Christianity, and besides he always admired physical bravery.

There was no doubt Mr Robinson had shown courage in going into the wildest parts of the bush, alone and unarmed, to bring back the formerly hostile natives as his friends. He was known in Van Diemen's Land as the Conciliator. Did some of them now regret the trust they had placed in him, she wondered? There was a certain cold-shouldering of Truganini – ah, Lalla Rookh, of course – by the older ones, as though they still resented having listened to her persuasion to 'come quietly' to the earthly heaven Mr Robinson promised them. For Robinson had won her round first; and it was she, Jane suspected, who had been his best shield against hostile spears.

As the little Government vessel *Breeze* flew over the waves like the fresh wind she was named after, Lady Franklin paced the deck with Mr Gunn while Sir John took an after-dinner nap in his cabin.

'Sir John seems contented with Robinson's supervision of the natives. Tell me truly what you think, Mr Gunn. Are they doomed?' Her face was hidden by her bonnet as she spoke, but her voice deepened on the last word and she looked up with such a tragic expression that he was surprised. There was something a little fey about her today. Did she have some definite premonition of their end?

'Perhaps; unless something can be done to arrest their decline. But – Lady Franklin, do you know the native cherry?'

'No, I don't think I do. Why?'

'Well, it's a small tree which flourishes in the shade of big gums. When the axe destroys the forest, the cherry tree begins to sicken, and gradually dies out. That's how it seems to be with the natives. Their natural habitat has been disturbed, and they are slowly fading away. Also, of course, they've been transplanted.'

'Then you think they *are* doomed? Pray God you may be wrong.'

'You know, while those Bible-reading performances were going on this morning, one old gin pulled at my sleeve, and said very softly, "Well, mitter, blackfellow soon all gone." *She* knew.'

Jane bit her lip and walked faster, as if to leave behind her unhappy thoughts. He said, striding after her, 'It's a strange place, this Van Diemen's Land, is it not? Yes, I know you like "Tasmania" better, and it's much more euphonious, but I used to think sometimes – in these last few years – that the other was more appropriate. The Demons' Land! The place of evil spirits.'

'Demons, Mr Gunn!'

'You may think me fanciful, but Lady Franklin, you have never camped alone in the depths of the bush. Sometimes in a dark and silent gully, surrounded by those enormous trees, I have felt – presences – as if the "debbil-debbils" of the Aborigines were all around me. Or perhaps the spirits of the unhappy murdered tribes.'

'I believe I know what you mean. It's not safe and civilized like the countryside at Home, but somehow inimical. Even though there are no large dangerous animals as in Africa.'

'Though we do have *Thylacine*.'

'The Tasmanian tiger? But she's not really a tiger at all.'

'And becoming very rare, I imagine. No, it's something in the atmosphere – my wife felt it. I was delighted with my appointment to Circular Head because of the chances for botanizing, but if my wife had been with me I couldn't have accepted.'

'You are married, Mr Gunn?'

'I *was* married. Now my five children are motherless. My wife died at her parents' home in Ireland, more than a year ago.'

'I'm so sorry. She must have been quite young?'

'Only twenty-nine – a year older than I. We had been very happy! But she became depressed and – and took to the bottle. In many ways it has made an old man of me.'

'You poor man! Your face in repose has a look of strain: I had noticed it. But you are certainly young yet.'

'And then, as well, I lost my young friend Lawrence – another tragedy. His wife died after their child was born, and he followed her to the grave. Now botany is all I have left.' He sighed.

Jane pressed his hand and turned to look towards the coast of the Tasmanian mainland they were now approaching. The sun was setting above it in lurid splendour.

'Nature is very wonderful, Mr Gunn. She does not fail her devotees,' she said softly ... 'I must go and call Sir John. We shall have a beautiful sunset.'

Chapter Six

'Of course we don't expect you to share all your finds with us,' said Sir John, very dignified. 'But since this rare echidna was found in the grounds of Government House, and since you know my wife is making a collection for her proposed Tasmanian Museum –'

Mary Maconachie's black eyes shone balefully. It was she who had found the echidna, and her husband who had preserved it for her in spirits. She looked across the library at her husband, as if to say 'There! You see how he treats me!' but Captain Maconachie shrugged very slightly and said nothing. He was not going to buy into this quarrel. His wife's tongue was more than a match for Sir John, and relations were strained enough already.

'Lady F.'s collection is already much larger than ours,' said his wife. 'And after all, *she* is not a scientist, while *my* husband is a former secretary of the Royal Geographical Society of London. And while I'm on the subject, let me add that it was never intended, never dreamed when he took this appointment, the Captain Maconachie was to remain permanently as a household drudge to Your Excellency. The Private Secretary's post was looked upon purely as a stop-gap, as you well know.'

'Madam, I offered the post to your husband in the name of friendship; he accepted it. If he is not contented the remedy lies in his own hands.'

'Exactly. I can always resign, Mary. But as Sir John points oot, it's better to avoid an open breach. That would only help his enemies and make it harder for me to gain anither poseetion.'

'Fiddlesticks! Of course he knows you are not free to resign. Where would we go? How would we pay fares for the children, and the cost of transporting our things? If this false friend will not lift a finger to find you another post here in the Antipodes –'

'Madam! I resent –'

'So you are a false friend! Sucking in every species of tale against him; listening to the barking and yelping of those curs, those half-bred hyenas of the Arthur faction. Can't you see that they want to separate you from the only man who can see through them? If only you had the wit to perceive it, but no –'

'Captain Maconachie! I must ask you to restrain your wife while she is living under my roof. I have never sought to quarrel; quite the contrary, but you know what the Bible says about "a broad house and a brawling woman".'

'Oh! Alexander! Take me away at once, at once –' and sobbing with fury, Mary Maconachie was half-supported out of the room and up the stairs by her husband.

Sir John strode irritably up and down the library a few times, then opened the corner cabinet of polished rosewood and poured himself a tot of brandy.

Really, that woman! It was very hard to have an uncooperative Secretary, a shrewd, conceited, meddling Scotsman who pursued his own ideas right or wrong, burning with missionary zeal to reform everything and regardless of how he embarrassed his employer; but hardest of all was to put up with Mrs M's spite and superciliousness. She was a clever woman, but with a two-edged tongue. How Jane could still like her and be friendly with her! It passed his comprehension.

Dashing her tears angrily away, forcing down her sobs, Mary Maconachie overcame her emotion and turned to her husband when they were in their own room. She was never one to fling herself on the bed and weep, as Lady Franklin might have done. It was sheer rage that had made her give way.

'Alexander, I'm sorry! It would be more dignified to ignore him, I know. But he *makes* me so angry! Blind, pompous, self-satisfied, obstinate old fool! He puts on such

47

a show of courtesy at dinner, serving me first like an honoured guest, and all the time I know he can't abide me. How much longer must we stay here?'

'My dear, I don't know. You said yourself, we have the children's future to think of. If only I could have the Governorship of this new Port Phillip settlement! I'm sure he recommended me for it; you must admit that he's fair-minded and above pettiness. He also strives to reign justly –'

'The imbecile reign of the Polar hero! He is only fit to govern the Arctic bears. I can just imagine them sitting round in a solemn circle, nodding their heads and clapping their paws in approval at his ponderous pronouncements.'

Maconachie had to smile; but he wished his wife would be more temperate, at least until his paper, *Thoughts on Convict Management*, and his letter to Lord Russell in the Colonial Office were received in England. Social science was his first love. The secretaryship had only been a way of getting to Van Diemen's land, where he felt his life's work lay; he fretted to begin it.

He was confident that his paper would be hailed as an enlightened plan for reforming the penal system. Perhaps he would be given charge of all the convicts in the island. That would be an appointment after his own heart.

He knew he was capable of great things. He longed to raise up the unfortunate wretches who shuffled out each morning from the penitentiary in the chain-gangs, their irons looped up to their waists, and clad in the degrading half-yellow dress of the felon. He felt convinced that all this unnecessary degredation and humiliation was the worst part of prison life; it crushed the weak, and irritated the strong into an implacable hatred of authority. The chain, the lash, the rule of silence, the solitary cell, tried to bring that noblest of earth's creatures, man, to the level of a beast.

And that was not all; the whole system, by degrading one class, operated on every other up to the Government hierarchy : the state of society at every level made this fact painfully obvious.

Particularly the assignment system was evil, a legalized slavery which corrupted the masters with too much power. The hardening effects of imperiousness, the ability to have punishment ordered at will, the fear of appearing weak, all combined to produce the slave-owner mentality. And there was no training of the convicts for their return to society. He felt he had to condemn the system root and branch.

Before sending off his paper to London, he had incorporated some of the ideas in an official letter to Sir John, which had been placed before the chief police magistrate; but Forster, of course, treated it with contempt.

As his Minute in reply remarked, his own ideas were not 'merely theoretical' like Captain Maconachie's; he could not agree that the system so well worked out by Colonel Arthur was at fault.

He had expected this, thought Maconachie. Forster was one of the old military martinet school, and to such as he the book of human nature was permanently sealed. And Montagu, his brother-in-law, had – naturally – backed him up with another Minute declaring 'he would feel grave fears of the Safety of the Property and lives of the Settlers if such impractical proposals as Captain Maconachie's were adopted.'

Well, they would see. When they read of his Mark system, his plan for gradual rehabilitation of the criminal, he felt confident that London would support him. If it only led to an enquiry at the top level into present conditions, he would not have worked in vain.

A man had died on the treadmill. He had complained of feeling ill, asked to see the medical officer, and been told that he was malingering. He was ordered fifty lashes for this offence, and sent back to the treadmill with his back still raw from the lash.

After half a day he became violently ill, with dysentery and vomiting. No doctor was sent for; he was returned to his cell in the penitentiary that night, and taken back to the treadmill in the morning. Within an hour he was dead.

Alexander Maconachie read of it in *Murray's Review*, and felt his blood boil in his veins at the injustice and horror of it. An 'official enquiry' would be instituted, he was assured by Captain Forster; but that would not bring life back to James Lovett, the unfortunate wretch who had died. He was a man, born of woman; some mother had loved him once, no doubt, and wept over his transportation – for 'skating on private ice'. A petty lord of an English manor had objected to a village lad disporting himself on his private pond. So James Lovett was sent in chains to Van Diemen's Land, where he had quite enough of ice when his pick had to break the frozen ruts while he worked in the road-parties in winter. In his misery and desperation he had attacked another prisoner who taunted him, and was sentenced to the secondary punishment of the treadmill. Now he was dead – murdered by officialdom.

This was just another example of the injustices of the system. Maconachie wrote a scathing letter to the editor of the *Hobart Town Courier*, under a *nom de plume*, to relieve his feelings a little.

He was still seething over this occurrence when another case of apparent injustice came before his notice. Without stopping to enquire into the details of the case, he intervened on the prisoner's behalf and personally rescued him from the clutches of the police.

The first Sir John heard of his Secretary's action was when Forster arrived at his office, red-faced and spluttering with rage. How, he asked angrily, could discipline be maintained among the prisoners when police regulations were mocked, and prisoners received the overt support of Government House officials? Who, he would like to know, was Captain Maconachie to –

Sir John placated him as well as he could, and sent for Maconachie, whose Scottish pride kept his neck as stiff, his back as straight as ever; though when confronted with the prisoner's record and the details of the case – a plot to kill an overseer – he admitted he might have been 'ower hasty'.

The upshot was a piece of humble pie eaten publicly by Maconachie in the columns of the *Hobart Town Courier*.

'I have been accused of favouring a prisoner against the police,' he wrote. 'I admit that my conduct was hasty, injudicious, inconsiderate, accidentally disrespectful to the chief police magistrate, and in many ways I regret it. But its purpose was merely benevolent ...'

'Really, it's beyond everything!' said Sir John to his wife that night in the privacy of bed.

Chapter Seven

Eleanor liked to slip out of the house in the early dusk, when Miss Williamson was busy getting dressed for dinner – for she ate downstairs with the family – the convicts working in the grounds had been marched back to the penitentiary, and the mounted police had gone back to their barracks.

The mountain was dark against the sky, lights were beginning to appear on mastheads and in portholes of ships in the harbour, and all was quiet but for the quick chatter of an acclimatized blackbird going to roost, reminding her of England.

She liked the grove of English elms sloping down to the New Wharf, the garden of English flowers, the green lawns underfoot. When she looked across the water to the tawny grass of the low bare hills, the colour of lions and deserts, or up at the sombre wooded slopes below Mount Wellington, she had a feeling of strangeness, almost of fear. She did not expect ever to feel at home here. There had been too many changes in her young life, passed from aunt to aunt while her father served in the Navy and her step-mother travelled round the world. She clung to the known, the familiar.

She was becoming used to the hard-faced men in dark grey suits of coarse and shapeless wool, shuffling along with their eyes down, or glancing up with a look of veiled hatred at the fair young English girl to whom their misery was only a spectacle.

When she visited Port Arthur, the place of doubly-convicted felons, their vicious and depraved looks had made her shudder. Her jaunting-car had been pulled by two of them running between the shafts like animals; and she had ridden in a trolley which they pushed along the tramline to Eaglehawk Neck, where the row of dogs was chained that kept them doubly prisoner. They wore the hated yellow dress.

She had become used; and here there were so many police and soldiers about that the streets of Hobart Town were really safer than those of London. All the same, she was not supposed to be wandering in the grounds alone at this hour. Miss Williamson thought she was watching her Mamma's toilette in the boudoir, and Mamma thought she was with Miss W. or the Maconachies – though she and Mary Ann, sensing the antagonism in the air between the adults, had become much less friendly.

If Hepburn, the Government House constable, should see her, she had only to say she was slipping out to pick some extra flowers for her Mamma's corsage, or to call her kitten, and he let her pass.

They had become firm friends on the voyage out, this old shipmate of her father's and herself. He had been with Papa on his last voyage to the Arctic. That was a link between them; they both worshipped Sir John. And he had taught Eleanor to make eye-splices and end-splices with a bit of rope's end, how to unlay the strands and weave them back together again.

Milly, her little black-and-white kitten, was stalking a late blackbird in the lower garden. Eleanor followed, calling 'Puss-sy, pussy pussy pussy pussy ...' as she jumped from terrace to terrace. The half-grown kitten was frisky. Pretending to be startled as she came close, it leapt off the ground as if it had springs in its feet, ears back and tail fluffed, and bounded off with an absurd sideways motion, stiff-legged, into the shade of the trees.

Entering into the game, Eleanor followed quietly, stalking the cat from trunk to trunk. It was already growing dark beneath the trees.

While the kitten was patting a fallen leaf she crept up on it, and was crouching quietly to put a hand out to catch it when, with a shock of horror, she saw a man's arm come stealthily from behind a thick bush of laurestinus, and his

53

large hand grasp her pet.

She felt her heart, her whole chest, turn to a solid lump of ice. She couldn't breathe, couldn't call out, couldn't move. Her knees ached with terror.

A head came after the arm, peering stealthily. The shock with which the man saw her was visibly as great as her own. His eyes became wide, his lips parted in a snarl like that of an animal at bay. So they crouched, almost touching, staring into each other's eyes for an interminable second above the struggling cat.

Eleanor, terrified as she was, was still her father's daughter, and he had been a young hero of Trafalgar. She raised her chin and regained her voice, though it came out in a squeak:

'What are you doing with my cat?'

'Ah, I'm fond of cats, h'I am.' He had recovered from his surprise and his grin of fear had become a more natural one, though still horrible for its mirthlessness. 'I like hanimals. H'i wuas rat-catcher and sow-gelder of the late Duke of Norfolk. H'i bleeds 'orses, cures colick, and treats other dumb animals. Cats includin'.'

'You're an escaped convict, aren't you?'

'Not escaped, me fine young lady; not escaped. E-mancipated. But I've 'ad me taste of the "cat", the Cat with nine tails, all on 'em knotted so cunnin'-like to draw blood. But this is a pretty little cat. I thought I'd like ter prig 'im and take 'im 'ome.'

'You had better go. If you're seen here you'll be sent to Port Arthur. Now give me my pussy-cat at once.'

'Ah, I've been to Port Arthur. They won't never get me there again, not alive they won't.' The kitten, which had become quiet in his grasp, now gave a convulsive leap and broke free. A claw raked across the back of one hand, drawing a red line. He gave an oath that made Eleanor blench; his eyes were full of blind fury.

He grabbed her arm and stared at her menacingly. 'I'm goin'! But if yer splits on me, look hout! I'll come back and bloody choke yer.'

In a moment he had disappeared behind the bush, but his hoarse voice lingered on the air, full of menace. Eleanor's paralysed limbs were stung into action. In a moment she was skimming up through the flower-beds, forgetful of the kitten. Once she tripped and skinned her knee, tearing a hole in her black stocking; but she was up in a second, panting and crying.

Near the house, feeling safer, she paused and tried to stop herself from trembling. Slowly she skirted the long veranda, entered the front door, passed through the anteroom where the orderly on duty scarcely looked at her, through the octagon-shaped hall where the great Maltese jardinière stood. She limped up the winding staircase.

In her room she rang for hot water. The nursery maid was helping her bathe a nasty graze when Miss Williamson came in. Her long face grew even longer as her jaw dropped in consternation. 'Whad have you done, child? Whad *is* it? You look veddy, veddy pale – shaking too, is id a fever? Give me that basin, Jessie, and ask Lady Franklin to step in here before she goes downstairs. . . . Now, Miss, whad have you been up to?'

'I was – I was walking on the balustrade of the veranda, and I overbalanced on to the gravel, I – think – m – my knee-cap is broken.'

'Tom-boy tricks! Not even Kiddy Maconachie gets up to such things, young as she is. Well, we shall have to call Dr Bedford id, I suppose.'

'Oh no! He looks so stern; he will be angry with me. It's not broken really, only very painful. I expect Jessie put too much muriate of soda in the water and made it sting. It'll be all right, truly it will.'

'Of course it will! I was always making holes in my knees at her age,' said Lady Franklin, coming in dressed for dinner. 'Miss Williamson will put some salve and a bandage on it, and you can lie on the couch and rest.'

'She cad have a tray by the coudge.'

'But what were you doing outside at this hour. Eleanor? You shouldn't have been downstairs at all. You've not even done your hair for dinner.'

Eleanor looked down and bit her lip. She didn't want to be forced into another lie. Already she was worrying about how God would punish the story she had told Miss Williamson. Yet nothing would make her tell about the man in the grounds. Somehow he would get her if she did. He would climb up a pillar and into her window, and choke her while she slept. She could see his strong, broken-nailed fingers caressing the cat.

'Very well, if you won't tell me! Miss Williamson, tell Jessie, no dessert for Miss Franklin tonight. She can have bread and butter instead.'

This was usually a dire punishment for Eleanor, who doted on sweet things; but tonight she felt too unwell to eat.

When everyone had gone down to dinner, and her own tray was removed, and even Marie had finished clearing up in Mamma's rooms and gone away, Eleanor began to be afraid. The Maconachie children were just round the corner of the corridor, but a wind had sprung up outside, a tree was creaking and scraping on the wall like finger-nails, and there was a throaty rumbling voice in the chimney.

This great rambling house of forty or more rooms – anyone could be prowling about in it. At last she fell into a sleep of nervous exhaustion, and dreamed of the kitten in the grasp of that hateful man. He was slowly squeezing the soft white throat, while the kitten's struggles got weaker ...

She woke screaming.

Miss Williamson came in with a candle and read to her for a while in her rather neutral voice. Before going to sleep again Eleanor commended her soul to God:

> And if I should die before I wake,
> I pray Thee my soul to take.

But she didn't want to die before she woke; she didn't want to die at all, or at least not before she was old. Yet death was so sudden, life so uncertain. Her own mother had died young. She had written in her diary yesterday, but without really meaning it: O God, make me ready whenever Thou shalt be pleased to call me!

She became so nervous at night that Miss Williamson moved her bed into the same room, and kept a nightlight burning. Later Mathinna came, the wild girl who was afraid of nothing but the thunder and lightning. But Mathinna waited in the future. So did Mr Gell, and the babies who were to cure Eleanor's morbid fancies forever.

Chapter Eight

For the evening's reception, Lady Franklin was wearing a gown of white satin with panels of silver lace. It was fortunate for the ladies that triangular woollen shawls were fashionable this season, for the Hobart Town evenings, however warm and sunny the day might have been, quickly developed a chill as a cold breath flowed down from the mountain or a southerly blew in from the sea.

Stewart wrapped a shawl of finest white Kerseymere with a deep silver fringe about her ladyship's shoulders. Jane went downstairs to see personally that the two great fires were burning brightly in the long drawing-room.

One advantage of this appointment was cheap firewood, far cheaper than coal at home. Plenty of timber was lying everywhere in the bush near at hand, with free convict labour to cut it. Besides, Tasmanian wood burnt with a brilliant flame as though releasing the stored sunlight of a hundred Antipodean summers.

She found Sophy already down, directing the footman whose job it was to see to the fires. The sparks were inclined to fly at first, so it was better to get a good blaze going before the guests arrived, and let it die down to a pile of glowing logs. Mrs Montagu's expensive dress had been burned at one ball by a flying spark.

Sophy leaned on the carved marble mantelpiece and looked at her aunt critically. The light colour of dress and shawl made her look younger. The dress fitted perfectly her slim waist, and her heavy necklace of sapphires set in antique silver matched her deep blue eyes. Her dark hair was dressed in Grecian style.

'Really, Aunt!' said Sophy half-complainingly. 'It is not fair to us young ladies to look as you do at your age. Especially those of us who prefer the company of older men. You will cut us all out.'

58

Jane laughed. 'Fiddle-de-dee! Why, you have poor Captain Ainsworth sighing for your hand, as we all can see with half an eye –'

'Captain Ainsworth!' Sophy drew up her neat figure in a stiff military pose, puffed out her chest and her cheeks, and mumbled, '*Your servant, ma'am ... Delighted, I'm sure ... The pleasure is mine* ... The pleasure is *all* his,' she said, relaxing. 'Oh dear! He reminds me of a great mechanical toy soldier. He eats, drinks, sleeps, walks, and can do everything but read – or think.'

She kicked impatiently at a tottering log with her small satin-shod foot.

'Sophy! You naughty girl, you'll ruin your shoes. And don't forget they take four months to get here from England ... And how is Mary's affair going?'

'Oh, Mr Price will be asking Uncle for her hand before the week is out, I shouldn't wonder. Have you not seen them mooning at each other? It's quite revolting. He's like a sick calf, and she's not much better. "Oh, Sophy, don't you think he has the most wonderful leg? Oh, Sophy, Mr Price gave me such a thrilling look at dinner, I declare I couldn't eat a mouthful!" Really, if that is love, give me indigestion.'

Jane laughed again, feeling her usual nervousness before a big evening evaporating and flying up the chimney with the aromatic smoke. Sir John was busy in his office with his interminable dispatches, his quill scraping across and across the paper, and would be until the first guests arrived. She often helped with copying them out, yet she hated the mere drudgery of writing, much as she enjoyed original composition. If only some sort of writing and copying machine could be invented, what a boon it would be!

When she had letters to send to more than one member of her family, Sophy would copy them for her. Whatever would she do without Sophy? She was like the daughter she had never been able to have in the body; and she took after her real mother, the charming Isabella Franklin, quick-minded and full of vitality.

It was a pity, but she could never feel that same spontaneous affection for Eleanor. She had always seemed rather a stodgy child, and except for her hero-worship for Sir John she was undemonstrative and rather reserved, almost cold in her manner.

Yet she had shown real distress when, the day after the episode of the grazed knee, her kitten had been found dead in the grounds – poisoned by something, it was thought.

All human beings, of course, were a mass of contradictions. Maconachie, for instance: children and servants loved him, and he was a champion of the under-dog like the Australian Aborigine; a noble-minded creature in many ways, yet self-opinionated to a fault and full of the vanity of his own ideas.

And John Montagu, now. What was she to make of him? He let her see that he admired her – not only as a woman, but for her intellect, which of course flattered her the more. He had asked her recently to write down her own ideas on how the penal system might be improved; and he always listened with courteous and serious attention to anything she had to say. She hated men who brushed aside her ideas with phrases like 'pretty heads should not worry over such matters'.

Sir John consulted her in everything, and she liked to feel her advice was sound. But that unpleasant Captain Forster, the bouncing blustering Captain, when she tried to explain her ideas for the better discipline of women prisoners, had simply stared and said nothing; it was a calculated snub.

On the whole, she did not get on with military men. There was something far more gallant and gentlemanly about the Navy. Mr Montagu was an exception, a hero of Waterloo.

Mr Alfred Stephen was not a naval man either, but his gay, witty company helped to make up for the boredom she often felt in Hobart Town society. He seemed inclined to single her out at official gatherings, and had asked her advice over his motherless brood.

Tonight, when all the guests had been greeted and were circulating, and before the musical programme began, he

60

asked her to step into the ante-room with him. He had a private problem, he said, peculiarly suited to the female intellect.

This was irresistible to Jane, who liked nothing better than being asked to solve other people's problems.

'My dear Mr Stephen, I shall do my best. Have you heard that I have a reputation here (and a woeful reputation it is in the minds of weak-minded people) of being *very clever*?'

'Indeed, Ma'am, I could distinguish that for myself; but why "woeful"?'

'Because if a governor's lady is *very clever*, and is known to sit a great deal in her room, and does not show her fancywork to other ladies, and has travelled on three continents and above all is suspected of *writing a book* – why then, if she doesn't soon overturn the State it's not because she lacks the means. They actually regard me as a dangerous, designing female, out to get the reins of office into her own hands.'

'I don't see how they could once they have seen you. A more warm and womanly nature they could not find, nor a less pompous and domineering manner. You haven't the aspect of a *manager*, my dear Lady Franklin.'

'Thank you, sir! Yet whenever I meet anyone for the first time, anyone who has heard of me that is, they exclaim, "But you're not a bit as we expected!" Apparently they expect a large, commanding-looking person, perhaps with a loud voice, too! I'm not at all enamoured of this visionary me.'

'I must confess to having been pleasantly surprised, myself.'

'So long as it was pleasantly! But I must return to the drawing-room; I am neglecting my guests.'

'Pray wait. I've not told you my problem. You know I have seven small children without a mother. My work at Court prevents me from supervising the establishment as I should like, and I've increasingly entrusted the household affairs to one Clapperton, an assigned servant ... He's been

61

stealing my funds all the time. As soon as I found out I had him arraigned, he was found guilty and sentenced to secondary transportation for fourteen years. And what do I find? He is not in the chaingang, but acting as chef to Mr Montagu.'

'To Mr Montagu? But if he was sentenced –'

'He has in fact been promoted – *that* is his reward for robbing a citizen who had given him a position of trust.'

'But how can this be?'

'How, indeed? It makes a travesty of justice in this colony. Not because I've been personally injured – I ask you to believe this – but on principle, and the strongest principle, I mean to have this wrong righted. Captain Forster interfered in the course of justice. So that Montagu should not want a cook.'

'Yes, of course, he's Mr Montagu's brother-in-law.'

'Brother-in-infamy! I found out by the merest chance. Well, what do you advise, ma'am?'

'You must write a letter to Sir John at once setting out the facts. Sir John has the strongest sense of fair play; he will never allow Mr Montagu to get away with it ... but ...' She faltered a little.

'Yes? I shall do so tonight. But –?'

'It will make the Colonial Secretary furious. He hates to be crossed. I remember Mrs M. was telling me she had acquired an excellent cook. Well, he will just have to *be* furious. Write to Sir John; I shall certainly lend what weight I have on the side of justice, Mr Stephen.'

'You know the golden figure of Justice above the Old Bailey in London – blindfolded, bearing the scales in one hand and the sword of retribution in the other? Justice, you see, is always depicted as a woman.'

'Why, so she is! I have some connection with the Law, you know – my sister Mary, my favourite sister, is married to a barrister.'

'Do I know him I wonder?'

'He is John Simpkinson, Q.C. London seems very far

away, does it not? Mary and Fanny were horrified at my coming all this way – such a distance! they said. Yet I had always wanted to see Australia.'

'For myself, I don't believe I shall ever return. My children were born here, they are little Van Diemonians; little savages I call them! I should like them to grow up in this brave new world. For I don't believe it will be always a convict settlement.'

'Nor do I! In spite of Colonel Arthur.'

'This new experiment of free settlers in South Australia is interesting.' They were walking back through the hall as they spoke.

'Yes, I long to go and see it for myself. I must travel on the mainland, and see the wild Aborigines and Port Jackson in New South Wales.'

'The mother Colony interests me .... I wonder, in a hundred years' time, how large it will have grown, and if people will have forgotten their convict origins? Transportation can be a blessing in disguise sometimes, when you consider the position of the poor in England. Not that all felons are reclaimable, of course.'

'Some emancipists here are already making good citizens.'

'Yes, indeed. Though I feel we must beware the dewy-eyed sentimentality of the excellent Captain Maconachie. These men, on the whole, are not the careless, good-hearted, reckless, generous fellows he's led himself to believe; but dogged, dark-tempered, and evil-disposed. It may not be their *fault*; the social system may be at fault; but so they are. Good treatment is thrown away on all such.'

Jane was inclined to agree; she felt that Mrs Fry, in spite of her wonderful work in women's prisons, was self-deceived, and that many of the women only pretended humility and gratitude. She had promised Mrs Fry to do something about the lot of women at the Cascades, and the whole system of assigning women servants which was inherently vicious.

'I tried to tell Captain Forster of my intense interest in

the women prisoners,' she said. 'He wouldn't even discuss it with me. But I should feel I had failed my sex if I did not do all in my power. I can't speak to you of the abuses of the assignment system for women, but you must know them well enough. After a sojourn at the factory, which many of the women regard as a sort of holiday, they're allowed to keep their illegitimate children, and the employer responsible can ask to have them reassigned. There is no real punishment for folly and wickedness.... You must think this is a very indelicate subject for a lady, Mr Stephen, but my feelings in this matter are very strong.'

'Not at all, madam. It's refreshing to talk with someone who doesn't pretend. I always admired a forthright mind rather than a simpering assumption of innocence before the seamier side of life.'

'Mr Forster will be even less co-operative, I fancy, when this man – Clapperton – is given his deserts. But no matter, Sir John will never be intimidated by "the Arthurites".'

'They are a powerful faction. They help control the Press.'

'It's scandalous that the papers can print such things as they do against respectable citizens. I'm glad to see you are suing the proprietor of the *Colonial Times*. I hope you win.'

The opening chords of the piano sounded from the drawing room; the lady singer of the evening was about to launch into the 'Casket' song from *Faust*. Mr Stephen and Lady Franklin returned to the general assembly.

Montagu, whose keen grey eyes missed nothing, had seen their departure and their return. The fact was recorded in his dossier-like memory.

He was about to make some little remark to Judge Pedder to make sure that someone else observed it too, when there came a brief scream from his wife. She had been standing in the centre of the room, a tea-cup and saucer in her hand, to show off her new blond-lace gown to its best advantage. Someone passing behind had jogged her elbow, and tea was

64

spilt on her skirt, making a brown stain on the beautiful material.

Montagu hurried forward to her aid with his best white linen handkerchief, but that sprightly ladies' man, Stephen, was there before him, solicitously offering his help. No wonder his unfortunate wife had been jealous!

Chapter Nine

The sun had set beyond Mount Wellington. The moon was not yet risen, but a pearly light lingered in the cloudless sky. Among the dry boulders in the bed of the Hobart Town Rivulet the rats were beginning to creep out, slipping from pile to pile of refuse. The convict-rats in the dismal 'Tench' had all sunk back to their holes.

At sunset, in the lumber-yard of the prison, three of them had suffered from the claws of the dreaded 'cat': a mere 'tester' each of twenty-five lashes. Face-down on their pallets, they let the evening air cool the crimson stripes on their backs.

The summer had been a dry one, and autumn had brought no changes but for the shorter days and crisper nights. Day after day the sun shone from a sky of uninterrupted blue, the hills across the harbour were still grassed with dull gold; and the wooded slopes with their sombre foliage never changed from season to season.

Now that the January sea-breezes had fallen, a mellow, waiting calm enveloped the warm-coloured stone of Customs House and Treasury, Commissariat stores and barracks, and the tombs of the earliest Europeans to sow this land with bones.

Down by New Wharf the English elms kept their green leaves. The new warehouses of convict-quarried stone held grain and wool waiting to be exported to New South Wales, and the exotic goods brought by ship after ship from overseas: spices and sultanas, Jamaica rum and tobacco, camphor-wood trunks and hogsheads of sugar casks of vinegar and chests of Indian tea, shawls from Kashmir, China silks and Genoa velvets.

Walking down Macquarie Street on her way to the Annual General Meeting of the Mechanics' Institute, Lady

Franklin, attended only by her French maid, met Mr Montagu coming in the opposite direction on his way to Government House.

His tall and gentlemanly figure, impeccably clad, was unmistakable. His olive-green surtout with a velvet collar was open in front to let show a green silk waistcoat figured in purple. He removed his tall hat with a flourish.

'Really, this road is becoming a disgrace, is it not?' he said after greeting her. Carriages and phaetons and a few late wagons from the country jostled each other on the one fairly smooth strip between the ruts and potholes.

'Yes, it's quicker to walk than take the carriage, I find ... and besides it's such a lovely evening.'

'Are you going to the phantasmagoria-lecture on astronomy?'

'No, to the Mechanics' Institute meeting; I'm on the committee, you know. Mr Alfred Stephen is to give the address.'

'Hmf! What can Stephen possibly have to say on such an occasion? I should think you will be bored.'

'I'm sure I shall not be bored, Mr Montagu. The limitations of the subject will only serve to show Mr Stephen's powers the better.'

He bowed ironically. 'Perhaps you are right, Lady Franklin. I admit he's eloquent – on his own behalf, at any rate.'

Jane bowed and passed on without replying.

Mr Montagu had no right to jeer, for Mr Stephen had won his libel case, though he'd been awarded only a tenth of the £1,000 he had claimed.

She had followed the case, (in which he challenged the proprietor of the *Colonial Times* for insinuating that he used to take bribes in his public office), and had sent him a note of congratulation on the outcome. In reply he had sent her a droll set of verses, a neat parody of Thomas Hood: it referred to the 'Drawing-room' at which Mrs Montagu had spilt the tea on her lace gown.

When lovely woman tilts her saucer
And finds too late that tea will stain,
Whate'er could make a lady crosser!
Whate'er can set all right again?'

and went on to conclude that the only thing to restore a
dress to 'proper colour is – to dye!'

He was already on the platform when she arrived. There
was a stir among the gratified officials as they welcomed
her and seated her in the front row. She made her apologies
for Sir John who was busy completing dispatches for tomorrow's mail packet for London.

Mr Stephen, studying some notes, seemed unaware of her
presence, but when he got up to speak he bowed to her and
began:

'We all know that His Excellency Sir John Franklin has
by his patronage conferred the greatest benefits on this Institute; by his frequent presence, and that of his lady – whom
we welcome tonight – at the lectures, he has given a stimulus
and attraction to them which accounts for much of the successful progress this season. ...'

When the small official supper which concluded the proceedings was over, she found him at her side.

'It was good of you to come,' he said. 'Have you your
carriage with you? May I see you back to Government
House, as it is on my way?'

'I told my coachman to call for me at nine, but I had
much rather walk. If he's here already I shall dismiss
him.'

Stephen gave her his arm down the steps, and with Marie
walking a few paces behind they set off for Macquarie Street.
He said, 'Do you remember when you came to see the
children? "That pretty lady" they still remember you as.'
The footpath became rougher and narrower, and once more
she took his arm, feeling beneath her mittened hand a faint
tremor as of a high-strung horse which frets at the curb. Mr
Stephen was talking jerkily, almost at random, quite unlike

68

his usual manner.

At last, stammering a little, he said in a low voice as they came in sight of the gates: 'Lady Franklin, there is something I wish to tell you – a personal matter –'

'Then pray come in, Mr Stephen. Sir John will have finished his chores and be pleased to see you.'

'No, no! A few words with you alone.'

She looked her surprise; however, he seemed so much in earnest that she spoke to Marie as they entered the gateway: *'Promenez en avance, s'il vous plaît – lentement!'* and added rapidly in Italian to Stephen, *'Ella parla Franchese solamente: non capisce Inglese.'*

'Ah – *capito!*'

She spoke to one of the two soldiers on duty at the gate, asking him to go and tell the coachman not to put the horses in. Then, pacing up and down on the drive patterned with leaf-shadows from a rising moon, she said, 'Well, Mr Stephen?'

He said rapidly, in a low voice: 'I want you to be the first to know, I am about to be married again. Not immediately, but fairly soon. I suppose you, being a woman, think I should be faithful to my first wife's memory?'

'Mr Stephen, you forget! *I* am a second wife.'

'Oh dear! I'm sorry, I'm terribly sorry. I am in such a state, sometimes I believe my mind is going. My health has not been good; then there was the strain of this case, and the Clapperton affair, and my nerves have been worn down by the backbiting and bickering in this accursed place. Only one thing has kept me here lately – surely you can guess! It is the opportunity of meeting you.'

'But, Mr Stephen –!' The darkness hid a quick blush.

'Sir John is a fortunate fellow.'

'And I am devoted to Sir John.'

'A happy marriage is an essential to a successful career. At least it is to me.' He paced away from her restlessly and swung back again. 'My first marriage was not – not entirely successful. Virgie –. However, I am about to marry a sweet girl, a former close friend of my wife's. Virginia would have approved.'

Jane started slightly.

'It is Eleanor Bedford – you must know her, though she doesn't go out a great deal in society. My children, I feel, must have a mother. And since the Clapperton affair there is no one I can trust to run my home.'

Jane was silent. Eleanor! A former friend of his wife's! A mother for his family! It was exactly her own situation in reverse. Was that why Sir John had married her, as a substitute mother for the little Eleanor? Yet he knew that small children bored her, and Eleanor had plenty of aunts ...

Once again there was that fateful letter N; she had quite a superstitious feeling about it now. Franklin, Stephen; Griffin, Porden; Jane, Eleanor; and now Eleanor again.

'Lady Franklin, I must not keep you out in the night air any longer,' he was saying. 'I can understand your silence. It was presumptuous of me. But thank you for listening to me, and for coming to hear my address tonight. You've been a bright star in a clouded sky. I – I value your friendship! I wanted to make sure I should not forfeit it by marrying again.'

He peered at her questioningly in the moonlight. There was something so wild in his manner that she patted his arm reassuringly.

'My dear Mr Stephen! Pray be calm. I assure you, you have my best sympathy. There is no need –'

'I'm sorry! I am not myself. I'm over-excited, over-tired. Forgive me, dear lady. Good night.'

He left her, and Jane went on up the leaf-patterned drive in a daze, only half aware of the freshness of gum-leaves and dew, and of Marie, who had been bored stiff at the meeting and was inclined to be sulky. She wanted to get her mistress to bed and be done with it. *Madame* was crazy, to go on foot when she had a perfectly good carriage at her command!

Sir John was already in bed in his dressing-gown with the lamp burning. His book, Volume One of Flinders's *Voyage to Terra Australis*, had fallen from his hand, his chin had dropped down, he breathed through his open mouth.

Jane blew out the lamp and removed the book, dropping a light kiss on the smooth dome of his head. Poor dear! He was tired out with the worries of his office; he let trifles trouble him unduly.

She went to sleep alone, turning over in her mind the strange behaviour of Mr Stephen.

Her nerves over-stimulated by the outing and its unexpected conclusion, Jane slept little and woke with one of her diabolically painful headaches. She felt as if an auger were boring into the bone above her right eye, and soon, she knew, the pain would make her vomit. Dr Bedford had tried blooding her, using cups as she refused to have those loathsome leeches on her head. She hated them almost as much as snakes, which made her ill even to think about. He also put her on a light diet with limewater to drink. She stayed in bed, directing Stewart to leave the blinds drawn for the slightest glare made her headache worse. Sir John came to see her after breakfast.

'Why don't you get Dr Bedford to cup you again, my love? I'm sure it's your blood that disordered. And while he is here, get him to do something about those painful piles. I believe there is an operation – oh, I know how you hate mentioning such a condition to him –'

'I couldn't bear it!' She had suddenly remembered that Dr Bedford was soon to become Alfred Stephen's brother-in-law. Of course he would not discuss his patients even with members of his family, but still ... Anyone but Dr Bedford! It was so mortifying to have such an undignified complaint.

'My love, he has treated more unusual female complaints than a simple case of piles, I assure you.'

'Oh yes; but he can't treat my headaches successfully. I

know he puts it all down to my time of life. How very convenient it is for the doctors; every complaint for years is put down to it: they are saved the trouble of diagnosis, and how comforting for the patients! Their suffering is "only to be expected"!'

Chapter Ten

Eleanor wrote in her diary:

> *Tuesday.* Got up at six, worked at lessons, then walked
> in the garden with dear Papa until breakfast. Dear Mary
> is to be married to Mr Price. We went for a pic-nic to
> Lindisfarne to see the pretty site he has chosen for their
> new house ... We tasted a bread called 'damper' which
> is baked in the ashes. It is rather heavy but not bad.
> Mamma has been unwell again.

The hateful operation had been performed after all; Sir
John had spoken himself to Dr Bedford. Jane, with her
faithful maid Stewart – a large, middle-aged person as quiet
as Marie was pert – was convalescing at Mr Price's peaceful
cottage across the bay.

Several miles of sea lay between her and Government
House with all its worries and domestic duties. She felt her
nerves unwind, her whole body relax in well-being and content.

Eleanor and Miss Williamson went out for long rides in
the bush every day. Miss Williamson's horse bolted with
her, but she was a person entirely without nerves and went
out riding again the next day. Mr Price was busy supervising
the building of the new house.

Jane enjoyed the day-long solitude, the silence broken
only by the calls of birds. It was a relief not to hear Sir John
coughing in the next room or sitting up to take snuff and
sneezing with a reverberating sound; not to have to listen
to the housekeeper complaining of the cook, or discuss
dinner-party menus with the butler. It was these petty worries which wore down her health. Already in this peaceful
atmosphere her headaches were better.

Here the air was pure and fresh; at home, after a big ball

or reception, the dining-room smelt of stale cigar-smoke, snuff, and port wine, which no amount of airing seemed to get out of the heavy folds of the curtains.

The doctor had told her to keep her feet up as much as possible. Stewart bullied her into taking the insipid lime-water. At night she lay on the sofa in front of the fire of blue-gum logs until she was drowsy, then went to bed and slept soundly.

This placid existence had gone on for more than a week when one night, while Miss Williamson was seeing Eleanor to bed, Mr Price hurried in with a flushed, excited face.

'Lady Franklin, I have some rather alarming news. The escaped convicts who've been bushranging in the interior – they have made their way to this side of the Derwent, plundering homes... They murdered one family of settlers. Madam –'

'How far off are they?'

'Not more than six miles. We may expect them in an hour or two. I have firearms, but not enough men. And to think that I have four females under my care!'

'Mr Price, there is your boat. Why cannot we cross over instantly to Hobarton? I'm thinking of Eleanor, you understand. A young girl –'

'But are you fit for it? And will you cross in darkness, in a little boat, in your state of weakness? What if we should be upset – how should I face Sir John?'

'My dear man, I'm not afraid of the sea; I am afraid of the bushrangers, however. I believe they are desperate men. And you will come with us, of course.'

'They may not come here at all –'

'Mr Price! Will you kindly go and get the boat ready, while I call the others. Quickly. They are nearly in bed.'

'But –'

'No buts! Just hurry.' Mr Price realized that he would get nowhere by arguing. He hurried. He would have liked a shot at the convicts; and he was not really alarmed for his own skin.

Eleanor was in fact already undressed and just saying her prayers. Jane hurried her off her knees and into her clothes, while trying to convince the placid Miss Williamson of the danger and the need for haste.

'Oh! Don't bother with your hairpins *now*!' she cried, exasperated, as Miss Williamson began poking under the chest of drawers, 'What does it matter if your hair falls down in the dark? We must get away before they arrive, or we shall be at their mercy.'

By now she was beginning to enjoy the drama and her weakness vanished. She called Stewart, who had been sitting by the kitchen range, and said as calmly as possible: 'Stewart, just throw on a cloak, there's a good woman, and get ready to set off this instant. There is a reason why we must cross over to Hobarton immediately.'

'Tonight, my lady?'

'Yes, of course tonight!'

'But what is it, my lady? Be some of the folks ill to home?'

'No; I will tell you everything when we are safely embarked. Now just get ready, do.'

Mr Price came in buttoning a pistol into a holster, and Stewart's eyes grew round. She still made no move to get ready, however, but began pulling the bedding from the sofa.

'What are you fidgeting about now?'

'Only getting your ladyship's pillows – you can't go without your pillows.'

'Oh, never *mind* the pillows! Come on!'

Miss Williamson and Eleanor, well wrapped up, went out preceded by Mr Price with the hurricane-lantern. 'C-ome quickly, Mamma!' cried Eleanor, her teeth chattering with fear or excitement.

'What on earth are you doing now, Stewart? We are going this instant.'

'But Your Ladyship's limewater!' she moaned. 'I must take the limewater. Dr Bedford made me promise –'

75

'Oh, fiddle-de-*dee* the limewater!' cried Jane, beside herself. 'Don't you know the bushrangers will be here directly?'

But Stewart, muttering that she 'couldn't abear to be flurried', grasped the great bottle of limewater under one arm, and two pillows under the other; and thus impeded followed her mistress down the steep bank to the water. It was not more than five minutes since the alarm.

A strong following breeze pushed the little boat out into the dark estuary of the Derwent; the sail was run up and soon they were making good headway. Cold water washed about in the bottom, and Stewart grumbled a little at the wildness of 'A-setting off for a voyage at an hour when Christian folks was all in bed.'

After landing at the private wharf and coming up quietly through the grounds, they caused quite a sensation at Government House. Jane was put to bed with a hot brick at her feet, and a dose of limewater triumphantly administered by Stewart.

Though she had been confined to a couch the day before, Jane was up and about again in the morning. As usual, strong excitement had acted as a tonic for her nerves, and she felt extraordinarily well.

Among her mail was an invitation from the Colonial Chaplain, the Rev. William Bedford, and Mrs Bedford to the wedding of their daughter Eleanor with Mr Alfred Stephen. She ordered the carriage and went out to buy a wedding-present suitable for a second wife.

A delicate bridal veil of snow lay incongruously on Mount Wellington's forbidding brow when Eleanor Bedford became step-mamma to seven little Stephens. The ceremony was performed at St David's Church of England, just across the way from Government House.

The wedding took place without Lady Franklin's presence, as she and Eleanor were sailing on board the *Eliza* for the south coast and the Huon. They saw all the new settlements along that lovely river, where the wild duck and black swans congregated in thousands.

There were already some permanent settlers growing apples and berry fruits in the clearings. Jane promised that when the new Government vessel, the *Huon Pine*, was built, they would get cheaper provisions. She had bought a piece of this land for Sir John out of some money her father had sent her; she loved buying land, and liked to give him presents. She promised her tenants she would later build them a church.

When they returned to Hobart they found Sir John in a 'state'. The Maconachies were not down to dinner, Jane noticed, in fact she had seen nothing of Mary Maconachie since her return that afternoon. They still usually met in the afternoons, as when the men were not there it was so much more comfortable.

In her upstairs sitting-room Jane found the English newspapers waiting for her after dinner. On top, folded back, was a London *Times* from the last mail.

'Just have a look at that, my dear,' said Sir John. 'Look what your precious Maconachie has been up to now.'

She took the paper gingerly. She had just come back, and some unpleasantness was waiting for her already.

'I've been longing for your return,' said Sir John, his sensitive lips trembling with feeling. 'After the papers came, Maconachie sent me a letter of explanation; he was upset by them himself; but I felt I must discuss it with you *at once*. I thought I'd just let you have your meal in peace. Of course it means dismissing him, in fact it gives me the excuse and I'm glad of it. But I need your help with the letter. It's a very delicate –'

'Just let me read this first, my love, so I'll know what you are talking about. Of course I do know: Maconachie has –'

'Yes; while under my roof, and employed by me –! Go on, read it.'

Her eyes flew over the single-column print. 'Incredible!' she breathed once, and 'Is it possible?'

For Captain Maconachie, as a private individual, had sent

his long-prepared report to the Society of Penal Reform in London; at the same time, in the private bag with the Governor's official seal, he had sent a summary to the Secretary of State, Lord John Russell, with a covering letter dated September 1837. This document had now been tabled in Parliament.

There in *The Times* was a complete copy of the report and of the letter. Maconachie had condemned, root and branch, the whole system administered by his superior, and particularly the assignment system, as degrading to human beings. He advocated rewards for good behaviour in a complicated system of marks, as in a boys' school; and he wanted the chain-gangs swept away.

He had never kept his views a secret, but this was unpardonable, a public statement which Sir John must seem to endorse if he kept him on as Private Secretary.

'And I am not prepared to be put in such a false position!' He strode up and down in his agitation, trying to control his emotion. It was such a relief to have her back, he told her; the strain and unpleasantness of dismissing Maconachie would be halved by having her with him, to help him and advise him with her clear mind. She was always the mediator; she would soften any unnecessary harshness; but she must see, as he did, that it was necessary to make the break.

He knew he was not brilliant; he was no theorist, he confessed – quite the contrary in fact; but he felt – he knew – he could be prompt and firm in action when action was called for. There was only one action possible now, much as she might deplore it. All he wanted was her help in compiling the letter.

Jane saw that he was right. Yet she could not help feeling a pang for her friendship with Mary Maconachie, and even for the Captain, misguided as he was. Friends of such mental calibre were rare enough among the small-bore minds of Hobarton. 'Need they leave our house?' she asked. 'I had hoped –'

'By no means. His enemies and mine would welcome such an open breach. And besides, where would he go? But he stays as a guest merely.' Sir John took out his pen-knife and sharpened several quills in readiness for her. She sat down at her escritoire and wrote to his dictation, suggesting a sentence now and then. But they could not agree; she kept objecting to a phrase here as ambiguous, a word there as too strong. At last Sir John, tired and overwrought, lost his temper and flung off to bed.

Jane stayed at her table, writing, the only sound the scratching of her pen across the paper : tearing up attempts and rewriting them, starting over again. At last some subtle change in the air, or in the tired yellow of the sinking candles, made her aware of dawn coming up beyond the windows.

She stretched her cramped limbs, put some more wood on the dying fire, and went to the window. No birds were stirring yet. All was hushed, breathless, indefinably expectant of the coming dawn. Jupiter, rising in the east like a herald of the great sun, shone with a steady yellow light, larger and yet less brilliant than a star.

Jane was light-headed with weariness. Her body felt hollow as an empty crab's shell. She needed food, but was too tired and sick to want to eat. Strange fancies slid in and out of her brain, forgotten almost as soon as they passed. She leant carelessly on the cold, dew-wet sill, and gazed into the clear lake of the slowly brightening sky.

Here she was in Tasmania, Australia, the 'land of simplicity and peace'. Dear God! There had been little simplicity and no peace for them since they had arrived in this beautiful island.

What indeed could be less simple than the tortuous intrigues of Van Diemenian politics? Perhaps it was a characteristic of small islanders to be pretty provincial? On the mainland, the real Australia, it must be different. There she would find the largeness, the space, the freedom of thought that should go with this exhilarating atmosphere, these pure and limitless skies.

She must get away. Her nerves shrank from the embarrassment of meeting Mary Maconachie every day, after the official letter of dismissal, for she worshipped her husband and could see no fault in him. Jane resolved on a trip to Port Phillip and Port Jackson, as soon as her duties would let her leave.

The final break with the Maconachies came opportunely, for as they moved out the whole Montagu family moved in. Mr Montagu had applied for two years' leave, sold his house, and was going to London.

Meanwhile the anti-Government papers had continued their bitter attacks on the Governor, and their support of Maconachie; and the last straw was when the Captain, whom Sir John suspected of writing these scurrilous articles himself, left a copy of the most offending paper, the *Advocate*, on the library table. There was nothing premeditated about it. It was merely typical of Maconachie's carelessness, his inability to see things from other people's point of view. But Sir John flew into a passion such as he rarely indulged in.

'This greasy, foul, lying journal under my roof – under my roof!' he spluttered. 'You continue to subscribe, sir, to this yellow rag, while sitting at my table and consuming my –! No, this is too much; this is the end. I must ask you to find other quarters for yourself and your family, from today week. Good evening.'

Jane came in at the end of this distressing scene, and as soon as she could saw Mary Maconachie privately. They embraced somewhat emotionally, shed a few tears, and promised to keep in touch. The Captain for once was ill at ease; he stood by impatiently, and at last said: 'Sir John might have been more friendly in his manner of turning me oot. But he could not have acted otherwise, being as he is, any more than he could fly. No; I don't blame him; the fault was on both sides. I admit it.'

And this, for Alexander Maconachie, was quite a hand-some admission.

Later, Jane went to call on them in their new home, and Mary Maconachie came to call on her, bringing the em-broidered footstool. It was the last time they were ever to meet. By the end of the year, the break was final. Eleanor had quarrelled with Mary Anne, and Mrs Maconachie had made her dislike of Sir John all too apparent. It was really much more comfortable all round when they had gone. Yet Jane felt sad. She could never quite cease to love anyone she had once been fond of, and she missed her friend; while there was something open, generous and fair-minded about the Captain, however, impractically he tried to carry out his ideas. She was so upset by all the enmity and strife and the unpleasant newspaper publicity that she scarcely went out.

Chapter Eleven

Dinner at Government House was rarely a family affair. Besides the Montagus, tonight there were the officers of the French frigate *Artemise*, now in the harbour; Mr and Mrs John Gould, for whom there was unfortunately no bedroom available though Jane would have liked them for house guests; Captain Parker, the new aide-de-camp, flirting with Sophy; and of course Miss Williamson, keeping 'her place' as usual; Mary, scarcely eating, with her soul in her eyes; and next to her the large, handsome Mr Price, her new husband; while on her other side sat young Henry Elliott, now acting as Private Secretary.

Sir John presided genially at the head of the table. Jane watched anxiously the number of glasses of wine he took, while keeping up a conversation in French at her end of the table. Mrs Gould was 'expecting' again, but continuing to paint for her young, dark-eyed, enthusiastic husband the exquisite bird-pictures which were to decorate his books on Australian ornithology. Jane thought she looked delicate, and was planning how she could make room for her in the house before her accouchement; she would be safer here with friends than travelling about New Holland with her peripatetic spouse.

The candle-light glowed softly on silver and on white napery, and on the brass-inlaid backs of the chairs Jane had been able to procure at last.

The footmen moved discreetly, serving from the left, taking away from the right, Tasmanian scallops from the coast, Tasmanian roast lamb, Huon valley raspberries with cream; for Jane had decided to give the Frenchman a completely local meal, except, alas! for the wine. Captain La Place had brought some bottles of Beaujolais with him as a gift from the ship; but one day, perhaps on the warmer mainland, Australian wine could be made.

Suddenly there was an excited babble in the hall. John Hepburn's strong voice, used to howling down a gale of wind, could be heard arguing: 'And I tell ye Sir John will wish to receive her at onst! How d'ye know she's not a princess of her tribe – she could be a little black princess for ought we know. He always liked to talk himself to the Eskimos when they came in, and the Red Indians and all them heathens ... I don't care if he is at dinner, send the under-footman to say I want to see him urgent-like.'

Sir John murmured an excuse to his guests and threw down his napkin. He was never deaf to the tones of the quarterdeck, though a polite murmur in company often eluded him, ever since the great guns went off at Trafalgar. He beckoned the butler to keep his meal warm on a chafing-dish and hurried out, shouting before he was fairly through the door: 'Well, Hepburn! What is it man?'

He stepped into the hall and stared at Hepburn, who stood there holding a small girl firmly by the wrist; she was pulled away from him to the length of her arm and seemed inclined to bolt. Her wide black eyes rolled wildly, the whites gleaming in her dusky face.

'By George – what have we here?' cried Sir John, but he saw at once what they had: a diminutive member of the Tasmanian race, one of the few remaining bush-dwellers of Van Diemen's Land. They were supposed to be all rounded up and safely exiled to Flinders Island, and here was one turned up at Government House!

She wore nothing but a kangaroo-skin cloak (not to hide any of her undeveloped figure, but rather as a decoration thrown over one shoulder, like a cape) and a pretty neck-lace of small blue shells. In one hand she grasped an empty food-dish of curved bark.

The Governor saw the wildness of her glance, the dawning interest at the golden braid and shining brass buttons of his blue naval coat, for in deference to the Frenchmen he was in full dress uniform. He squatted on his heels in front of her, his white breeches straining at the knees, his dress-sword touching the floor.

'Well, little girl!' There was no mistaking the kindness of his tone. 'May I see what you have there?' Gently he disentangled the convulsive grasp. 'Ah, a food-carrier, eh? I expect you're hungry. Want-it tucker?' Her free hand flew to her face, one finger entered her mouth. She rolled her eyes up at Hepburn and back to the brown, weathered, kindly face of Sir John.

'And where are your Papa and Mamma, I wonder?'

'If you please, sir, the little tyke was found by a camp-fire in the ranges up north. The family must have legged it when they heard the survey party comin', and she couldn't run fast enough and got left. P'raps they just lorst their heads and forgot 'er. The men brought her in.'

Sir John continued to gaze at her reassuringly from her own level. 'Let go, Hepburn; she won't bolt now. Will you, little one?' He took her other hand and removing it from her mouth, chafed it softly between his own. 'What name you? Me' – he pointed to himself – 'Mitta Guberna; you' – he pointed at her enquiringly – 'what name?'

She looked down at the string of shells decorating her breast. He seemed to be pointing at them, asking her to name them. Her wide, curving mouth opened at last and a faint breath of sound came out: 'Mathinna ...'

'Mathinna, eh? That's a pretty name. Now, John, take young Mathinna to Stewart, and ask her to put a dress of Miss Franklin's on her – never mind if it's a mile too big! – and Lady Franklin will come up and see her very soon. Tell Stewart to send for a glass of milk and some fruit: better give her something simple. And mind she doesn't bolt. She's as wild as a little possum.'

So Mathinna was led through a second big cave, and up a strange, hard hill with straight ledges one above the other and all the same size, and into another cave where there was a big pale person of peculiar shape, with no legs.

Then a pretty-coloured garment of soft, woven bark was put over her head, frightening and almost suffocating her for a moment, and with the strange smell which all these people had.

She was given a round juicy berry to eat, bigger and nicer than anything she had ever tasted before; she smelt it all over before putting it to her mouth. She refused the queer-looking white stuff, with its animal smell. Her eyes were stretched quite round with wonder, they felt as if they would never grow big enough to take in all the wonder of this strange place.

She squatted down to feel the ground. It was covered with a beautiful moss in many colours; more woven bark in pretty colours hung from the roof. There was a fire in a corner, the only thing familiar to her from the world she had just left, and another fire which gave a white light but no heat. She went over to the fireplace and crouched before it, staring unwinkingly at the flames.

She had been asleep in front of just such a fire, curled in her kangaroo-skin cloak, when confused shouts and the sound of running feet awakened her. She was alone by the fire; and above her towered two of the soldier-men she had seen only in the distance, with frightening red skins and three-cornered heads. All round her were members of the pale-faced tribe who were the enemies of the dark people. One of them held her while the other talked in loud unintelligible sounds.

Once she had heard from the silent bush beyond the fire-light a despairing cry. That was her mother calling her; but her mouth was too dry with fear to reply. The tall man had taken her away, with her food-gathering dish and her mathinna, her necklace of shells, and the fur cloak which were all she had left of the old life.

Tomorrow she would try to run away as soon as it was light, back to where her own people sat down.

Young Mr Gunn had forwarded a letter of glowing recommendation from Sir William Hooker, who described him as one 'devoted to science and one of Nature's true ministers'. Lady Franklin felt sure that all he needed to take him out of himself and restore his spirits after his unhappy experiences was some congenial company in a less isolated situation than Circular Head.

She made a suggestion, and Sir John proposed to Executive Council's next meeting that Ronald Campbell Gunn should be appointed temporary Assistant Police Magistrate in Hobart Town.

Gunn had not been in the south long before he established a horticultural society, of which he was the energetic secretary, and he had searched diligently in the hills about the town for a suitable area for her native garden. Already, she thought, he was looking better than when he arrived.

'Eureka! I have found it!' he cried as he came stepping energetically over the sill of the dining-room window one evening – for he often walked up through the grounds to take dessert and coffee with them on nights when there was no official dinner-party at Government House. 'Just what we've been looking for – but you'll have to travel by bullock-cart, Lady Franklin – there's not even a track for a horse and cart.'

'And *that* would never stop my wife, Mr Gunn, as you should know – quite the contrary, in fact.'

Gunn laughed. 'I know it.' He described how he had found at Lenah Valley, in the foothills below Mount Wellington, 200 acres of undisturbed bushland – huge gum trees, myrtle and sassafras, and large trees of *Acacia melanoxylon*, the Black Wattle, which would be covered with fluffy golden balls in spring; while the ground would be a mass of wild flowers.

He had found several varieties of orchidia, and the common though beautiful Epacris; *Bursaria spinosa* and the yellow buttercup, which had been called *Ranunculus gunnii* after himself.

Besides all this there was a tiny crystal stream dropping

down the hillside to join a larger creek in the gully at the bottom, and this was lined with green tree-ferns.

'It's the most beautiful place ever seen,' Jane agreed enthusiastically after her first visit, and ordered him to buy the land for her immediately. She wrote to Mary that, search for a Greek name to suit, she had come on Ancanthe, the 'Vale of Flowers'.

Later she meant to add a little summer-house or temple for nature's devotees at its foot. Or even, perhaps, a real museum of the arts and sciences. For this island with its dry summer hills, the rocky headlands and glass-clear water of its south coast, reminded her of Sounion and the peninsula of Attica. Why not the Athens of the south? So, she dreamed, Hobarton might one day be known, just as the ugly name of Van Diemen's Land, with all its associations of crime and penal stations, should be replaced by the euphonius name of Tasmania.

Already she had quite a collection of stuffed birds and animals and native weapons. Later she would commission portraits and import some copies of classical sculpture, to form the nucleus of an art gallery. . . .

Her nimble mind leapt on, envisaging the future, seeing a race of native-born Tasmanian painters and poets, who would be exported to the mainland just as now wheat and fruit were exported. They would not be exiled Englishmen, but Tasmanians; a new southern race, fostered by that genial climate which had made the Mediterranean the home of the arts in Europe.

Jane took up with her usual vigour and enthusiasm the project of civilizing Mathinna. She wanted to prove the intelligence of the native Tasmanians, and to show, by bringing up the girl in a Christian home among gentle-mannered companions, that they could learn good manners as well as how to write and cypher.

It was to be, in fact, an experiment in the influence of environment over heredity, which appealed to her scientific and enquiring mind.

No one knew for sure if a group of natives still survived in the depth of the bush, or whether Mathinna was actually the last of her race on the island. If banished to Flinders Island she would have less chance of survival, for the 'epidemic catarrh' was raging there, and the natives were dying like flies; whereas at Government House she would be surrounded by loving care.

At first there had been difficulties: the problem of keeping her clad, and discouraging her hunting and wandering propensities, for though so young she seemed to have sucked in with her mother's milk the ways of her people.

Mathinna was fascinated with the soldiers' red coats. It was the only colour she seemed to respond to; but as there were no red dresses in Eleanor's wardrobe, Jane had a tunic brought from the military stores and cut down for the child. It was more than enough for a full-length covering for the little thing.

The first garment they put on her, a white one, she had discarded casually as soon as she went out in the garden and found it impeding her progress. She simply pulled it off and let it fall in the dust.

'But Mathinna! You must wear your dress. All nice girls wear a covering – Eleanor, and Sophy, and everyone.'

'What por?'

For everything that engaged her infant curiosity she had this useful question: what por the piece of soap that went in the wash-stand dish, what por these queer, sharp 'porks' for eating with, when fingers were so much easier; what por these loose, removable skins which got in the way and seemed to stop her from breathing properly?

'Soapy', whose name she had changed because the hard 'f' sound was beyond her, was endlessly patient with Mathinna; Eleanor was rather scandalized at her uncivilized ways.

It had proved impossible at first to get her to sleep in a bed. In the morning she was always found curled up on the floor, near the fireplace. When they had washed the matted grease and clay out of her hair, it was found to be shiny and curly. Lady Franklin put a red paroquet's feather in the dark curls, and showed Mathinna her image in the boudoir mirror. She drummed both feet on the floor with delight.

A little later Eleanor found her crouched in the hearth, crushing charcoal between her hands and gravely rubbing the black into her already dark cheeks and forehead.

'No, Mathinna! That's dirty!' cried Eleanor, but Jane said to let her be. She had noticed the air of satisfaction, even of coquetry, which anointing herself in this fashion had given to the little face; Péron, she remembered, had described this custom among the wild Tasmanians, and it was no more reprehensible than for a white lady to dust her face with rice-powder.

The housekeeper came to complain that Mathinna kept strewing handfuls of sand on the verandas and about the doors. When Jane remonstrated with her the child took her hand and led her downstairs, smiling gravely. She already spoke a kind of English with fair fluency.

At the side entrance to the veranda she squatted on her heels and examined the sand smoothly dusted over the red and black tiles. A narrow, curving track was visible, emerging from the thick creeper growing on one of the veranda posts.

'Sunnake!' cried Mathinna, pointing. 'Taggeerar longa creeper. Me catch-it him sunnake.'

'A snake!' Jane shuddered and drew back. She hated snakes with a sick loathing; even the name was horrible to her. She had arranged with Captain Moriarty to give a bonus of a shilling a head for every snake killed in the length and breadth of Van Diemen's Land. 'Good girl, Mathinna, you leave it now, another time, another fellow kill-it dead. Look, here's a shilling for you for find-it. Now, no-more sand, no-more snake; finish.'

'Pinish?' Mathinna looked downcast. She had wanted to show her skill as a hunter, and contribute something to the larder. 'No-more eat-it?' she asked hopefully. 'Sunnake, him narra coopa tucker –' and she rubbed her plump little belly and rolled her eyes.

'*Eat* – ! No, no child, nice girls never eat snakes. Garh! The very thought of it! Hepburn will have it removed.'

There were so many things that 'nais' girls never, never did; like rubbing grease and clay in their hair, or charcoal on their faces, or eating grubs and lizards, or sitting on the floor. Some of the permitted things, like horse-riding at New Norfolk, or riding in the carriage to the other side of Hobart Town, made up for all the sitting on chairs and scratching with pointed feathers dipped in ink, and reciting meaningless white-peller chants like:

Two times two is por,
Por times por is six-teen. ...

She could write her sign now. It went M, like two pointy knees sticking up, and F like a broken-backed snake with a stick lying across it. That sign stood for Mathinna Flinders, which was her name. The Sir-Guberna had given it to her. He said that 'Plinders' belonged to his uncle who was the first white-man to sail all round this island; and an island was a piece of land 'pletely sounded with water; all sorts of other mysterious things like that she knew.

Eleanora and Soapy and the others had their own marks too, and Eleanora's and the Lady-Mumma's and the Sir-Guberna's all began with F, the same mystic sign as her own. That meant they belonged, they were all of one group.

Sometimes she wondered why they called her 'Necklace'. She supposed it was because she always wore her string of shells, the only reminder of her old life.

Far off, away in the dim half-remembered, was a world of firelight and moonlight, of sun through flickering leaves, where dark figures moved silently among tall straight trees, and where she had answered to another name ... But what it was, or where that place might be, she had no idea.

Chapter Twelve

Sweating in their red coats and high collars, the members of the 51st Regimental Band launched into a *pot-pourri* of classical music in the Octagonal Room, while the guests circulated in the large drawing-room below.

Candles twinkled in the crystal chandeliers, and a cheerful light was thrown by the fires in the two great marble fireplaces and from the oil-lamps on their stands. But in spite of the gaiety of the scene, there were mutinous looks on many fresh young faces, and many red lips were pouted in discontent.

Apart from the Birthday Ball last May – nearly a year ago now – there seemed to be no balls held at Government House any more. There were plenty of 'improving' evenings of classical music, scientific lectures, and conversations, while Lady Franklin held a soirée every Tuesday for members of the Tasmanian Natural History Society. But what young woman wanted to get all dressed up to spend her time in such boring occupations?

Another cause of unhappiness among the fair daughters of Van Diemen's Land was that the males attached to the Vice-Regal entourage did not seem interested in matrimony.

There was Henry Elliott, now acting as Private Secretary, the elegant and charming son of Lord Minto and the most eligible man in the colony; but he was always laughing in a corner with that clever, affected Sophy Cracroft. Tom Cracroft, his assistant, was a sickly boy and seemed interested in no one but his sister; and the gorgeous Captain Bagot, ADC, was equally courteous and gallant to all (including Miss Cracroft) without showing a preference for any.

The pretty and vivacious Sophy would have been voted easily the most-disliked person in Hobarton society.

Yawning, fanning themselves with feather or painted-silk

fans, the young ladies looked resentfully at the large-bosomed singer who was to provide the main entertainment of the evening, preventing them from even the pleasure of gossiping among themselves.

Suddenly their ennui was dramatically relieved.

A messenger who looked as if he had come straight from the forest called one of the footmen aside, and the footman called Sir John. The man presented him with a large sheet of curving bark, covered with a strange design in black and yellow.

Sir John Franklin's face blanched; a look of settled gloom spread over his usually cheerful features. He and Mr Alfred Stephen studied the drawing and conferred with Mr Gould. A rumour spread round the room, and voices were heard:

'Wild blacks! We must catch them and kill them before they get up to their old tricks.' That was blunt Captain Forster, very grim and fierce. Sir John held up his hand for silence. The band finished its piece and sat waiting.

His far-seeing eyes seemed to be looking beyond the well-dressed crowd, the ladies in their satin and *peau-de-soie*, the men in gold-braided uniforms or cut-away coats – beyond to that motley group on Flinders Island with their eyes full of a lost darkness.

'No!' He shook his head sadly. 'They are perishing fast enough. This will be just a small group left behind when the others were rounded up by Mr Robinson in Governor Arthur's time. What possible harm can they do?'

But the murmur spread round the great drawing-room like a grass fire in a dry paddock. 'Savages! Not more than fifty miles from Hobart Town! We could be murdered in our beds!'

For everyone had thought there were no Aborigines left on the main island. Now this charcoal and yellow-ochre drawing of a kangaroo had been found, unmistakably of Aboriginal design and recent execution. Those who had lived in the country during the 'Black War', or who had relatives or servants murdered by natives in earlier times, felt their old fear and hostility aroused. 'Catch them! Send them away!' came another murmur.

Sir John turned to his wife, who had come over to study with interest this example of Aboriginal art. 'My dear: could you have Mathinna brought down?'

'Mathinna! She will be asleep – and besides –'

'I think not. I heard some whispering between her and Eleanor this morning, about waiting at the top of the stairs till supper-time. Sophy or Henry had promised a smuggled feast, I suspect.'

'Well, I shall go up myself. She must be properly dressed.'

While she went upstairs the guests gathered about the bark-painting, held up by the messenger and a footman. Soon there was a stir in the ante-room. The crowd swayed as if a wind had passed through it, a breath from the eucalyptus-scented forests, the dark, haunted scrub of the far west and the gloomy shores of Macquarie Harbour.

Holding Lady Franklin's hand, Mathinna descended the stairs: Lady Franklin in black with a fine silver check, with carved jet ornaments; Mathinna in a soft, pretty gown of red muslin, with a round neck and simple puffed sleeves, and her native necklace of shells.

Her wide mouth was curled upward in a smile of suppressed excitement. Her enormous dark eyes, seeming without pupils, shone in the lamplight like those of some wild creature of the northern hemisphere, gazelle or deer. She had the grace of the wild, yet she walkd modestly and gently beside her benefactress.

'Here she is,' said Lady Franklin, smiling at her encouragingly. 'You have all heard of Mathinna, or seen her riding with me in my carriage, or out walking with my daughter. She was taken in the bush, in the central highlands, as a tiny tot. From time to time we have heard rumours of what may be her family, living wild in the far north-west.

'Now she is one of our family, and goes to school with Miss Franklin. Mathinna dear: say "Good evening" and let us see you curtsey.'

Mathinna took the red muslin skirt in her slim brown fingers and curtseyed low, to left and then to right. 'Goot eb-ening,' she murmured.

There was a little ripple of amused approval.

'That's my good girl,' said Lady Franklin, squeezing her hand.

Mathinna beamed, white-toothed and engaging.

'May I present my compliments?'

She giggled delightedly as that funny Mr Stephen bent over her hand with a courtly bow. She had met him when out riding in the carriage, and one afternoon when he called when there were no other visitors. He had let her ride on his boot while he sang a song:

> See-saw, Marjorie Daw,
> Johnnie shall have a new mas-ter ...

She had no idea what the words meant, but they made her laugh. Now he and the Lady-Mamma smiled at each other over her head, and he murmured, 'A very effective entrance. My congratulations.'

'She did very well, did she not?'

'Indeed, yes. Her good manners, her charming appearance make her the best of ambassadors for her race ... ambassadresses I should say, I suppose, if one could imagine such a thing ... Hullo, little ambassadress-in-a-red-dress!' He twinkled down at her. 'The *Hobart Town Courier* will have in its news columns tomorrow: "The Ambassadress for the Macquarie River Tribes was becomingly gowned in red; she wore her hair *au naturel*".'

Mathinna pressed a brown hand nearly into her mouth to stifle her giggles. The guests were crowding round to gaze at the little black girl. Lady Franklin made a sign to Henry Elliott, who came to her side. She transferred the child's hand to his.

'Henry, take her through to the supper-balcony, and let her choose the biggest cream-cake there is. Oh, and one for Eleanor.' (Eleanor had squinted and scowled when she found Mathinna was to get dressed and go down, while she was not. She was preparing to pinch her hard when she came back.)

'You see how well she can behave?' said Lady Franklin to John Gould. She took credit on herself for Mathinna's manners. 'If you take the native young enough, there is nothing to stop him acquiring our civilization. Yet people used to think them of little more account than the kangaroos.'

Sir John held up his hand again, and began rather pompously to elaborate her idea for the general assembly.

'That, ladies and gentlemen, is my daughter's play-mate and school companion: a wild girl from the north. The group responsible for this painting consists probably of one or two children like her, a black woman or "gin" and perhaps a single male – hardly calculated to terrorize a population of 200,000 whites; quite the contrary!

'Mathinna is an example of what can be done by kindness and example with her race. She is not perfect – eh, my dear? She sometimes shows a rather hasty temper in the schoolroom – but you can see by her looks and manner that she's a good girl, amenable and affectionate.

'She's never been treated as a servant, and has a natural dignity. Let her example persuade you to be patient with the unhappy remnant of her race occupying some corner of this island. They must indeed be lonely, and will probably give themselves up before long.'

There were murmurs of dissent, but more cries of 'Hear, Hear'. Arguments broke out in groups around the room, and passing quietly among them, Jane Franklin noted sadly that gentlewomen like Mrs Meredith, wife of one of the early pioneers who was in town with her husband, were among the advocates of violence.

'– or it will be like the early days over again, when none of us was safe from being murdered in our homes. They might increase –'

Mr Gould, in his natty pearl-grey trousers and waistcoat

95

embroidered to his wife's design with birds and flowers in coloured silk, came up to Sir John, who offered him a pinch of snuff from his gold box.

'It is good to know that there are some of the poor creatures still alive in the bush,' he said, declining. 'How many are left now on Flinders Island?'

'Only eighty, or thereabouts. The natural increase cannot match the death-rate. It seems as if they are doomed to extinction; yet Robinson keeps assuring me they are quite happy, and "healthy as can be expected". I have called for an independent enquiry and report on their condition.'

'I was not greatly impressed with Mr Robinson,' remarked Ronald Gunn. 'He's not an educated man, I fancy.'

'Nor I either,' said Jane. 'Mr Robinson spouts noble sentiments while looking slyly sideways at you to see they are having an effect. Besides, his eyes are to small!'

Sir John laughed. 'The relative size of the organs of perception, my love, are not really an indication of the size of a man's soul. I have the utmost faith in Mr Robinson's goodness. I believe he is a noble, disinterested worker for the Aborigines, one of their truest friends. Look what he's done for them –'

'Yes, and look what he has been paid! It was he who recommended the Flinders Island situation as "healthful", yet now he affirms they are dying of the bad water and the exposed situation. He said they would not miss their homeland, yet Dr Barnes and others are convinced that they are really dying of homesickness. Robinson is a small man with a longing for power, and they help him to indulge it.'

'Certainly they seem clean and well-cared for enough,' said Ronald Gunn mildly. 'But it's true they have no real will to live.'

'If nothing else, they would die of boredom at Mr Robinson's sermons!'

'Tut, my dear Jane you are too hard on him. He seems an honest, well-meaning feller to me.'

'We should make another journey to Flinders Island, to make sure.'

'Any excuse for travelling, my dear Gould, is sufficient for my wife! She's never happy unless she's travelling about the world.'

'Yes, and I'm leaving for Port Phillip and Sydney in a month or two. Is not that exciting, Mr Gould? The mainland I have heard so much about!'

'You will find it strange and stirring even with your ladyship's known taste for the original. And the most beautiful birds of the parrot family! The scenery's not so grand nor impressive as in Van Diemen's Land – what I have seen of it – but there is an immensity ... a feeling of space, of freedom ... 'tis reflected even in the reckless way the larger birds fling themselves through the air, with a wild screaming.'

'There is a great river I much wish to see, discovered by Mr Hume.'

'Ah, the Murray as it is now called. Yes, one day I believe it will make a highway into the unopened interior, as soon as steamboats become general.'

'Steam, electricity, galvanism – what an exciting age we live in, Mr Gould, to be sure! Oh! I should like to live for a hundred years more – or at least come back in 1939 to see what we have made of the world! It will be a wonderful place, I feel assured. All will be discovered or invented –'

'All! My love, leave me out of your visionary world, I pray. Nothing left to discover! Eh, Gould? No new lands, with new flora and fauna, no North-west Passage to search for, no mysteries at the Poles, and a thriving town, perhaps, in the heart of Australia! No, no, leave me out, I beg you.'

'And by then, perhaps, there will be not one of the original Tasmanians left,' said Gunn soberly. 'As a race, they will have vanished from the face of the earth.'

Chapter Thirteen

John Gould went off to the mainland first. Jane immediately invited his wife to stay at Government House until after her baby was born. She might not be back for the event herself, but Miss Williamson and Eleanor would look after her and see she was comfortable.

Sophy was delighted that Lady Franklin had chosen her to go to Port Phillip and Port Jackson. She hoped the sea voyage and the change of air would be good for her aunt, who was depressed and out of spirits.

The newspapers had been attacking her indirectly through Sir John. Now they announced that she was the owner of the *Tasmanian Advocate* which was most forward in attacking him. As soon as the proposed journey was known the 'vile colonial press' said that the journey was to 'collect material for her book of travel'.

'I shall not write a book, nor care to do so,' she wrote to her best confidante, her sister Mary, in London. 'I should hate to be thought one of your bold, clever women. . . .'

For her it was an escape from all the complexities of domestic life and Hobarton society. She and Sophy were to find in each other the perfect travelling companion, and to set a pattern, on this trip, for a thousand future expeditions all over the world.

Jane was pleased that she would avoid having to entertain the Alfred Stephens to dinner before their departure. (She'd met Mrs Stephen, and thought her a pleasant, sensible person who would make a wonderful mother, but she was certainly no beauty.)

She'd had an uncomfortable interview with Mr Stephen. He had called on her one morning when she was writing in her boudoir upstairs. Mathinna and Eleanor were at school lessons with Miss Williamson; Sir John was receiving his daily petitioners and officials in his office on the ground floor.

Alfred Stephen strode up and down the room, picking up pieces of fossil rock, examining shells and birds' eggs with apparent concentration. Then he swung round on her abruptly as she sat watching him, and she saw the wild, baffled look in his eyes.

'I'm going away,' he said.

'You mean up the country?'

'I'm going right away from the colony, to Sydney, to live. I have, in fact, been offered a Judgeship there; and I cannot any longer stay here, madam.'

'But why, pray? You can't leave us, Mr Stephen!' cried Jane. 'Indeed you must not. How can we spare you from Van Diemen's Land?'

'We?' He smiled rather sadly. 'You personally will not miss me at all then?'

'I, Mr Stephen! Why yes, I shall, of course. We – we have much in common. I value your friendship, and so does Sir John. I hope it is nothing ... nothing –? You know the rumours went about that you were driven from office by his neglect.'

'Bah! The vile newspaper gossip. You know me better than that, ma'am, surely. I am leaving for – for personal reasons. I have a family to provide for, and soon will have a second family on the way. My wife is everything that is amiable and good. That is why I must go where I shall not see you at every turn.'

'Fie, sir! What could I –'

'Surely you realized, you who must have been plagued by unwanted admirers all your life, how it was with me? What a fascinating girl you must have been, when even now –'

'When I was a girl, Mr Stephen, I was so tongue-tied and gauche that you would not have looked twice in my direction.'

'Impossible!' Yet he was remembering his first appearance in court, how he'd been unable to utter a word of his prepared address. It was bottled up inside him, but he'd bungled at pulling the cork.... He had wanted to crawl away and die.

Jane's sense of humour, never far from the surface, was beginning to bubble up. 'This is really ridiculous, you know. But I cannot help feeling the great impropriety of your remarks, and of my listening to them, here in my husband's house.'

'Yes, I am utterly to be condemned. I thought that marriage would give me stability, but it has not altered the pure and high-minded sentiments –'

'Enough, enough, sir!'

'I am going. I meant only to tell you my plans for leaving; and to ask you, whenever you may visit the Sydney settlement, to call on me.... And so, farewell until then. For if I thought it were forever, I doubt if I should have the strength to utter the word.'

He took her unresisting hand, shook it once, and withdrew.

Jane went to the long windows and looked down to watch him leave on foot, his trim figure disappearing swiftly among the garden shrubs.

Really! The man was a little unbalanced, surely. Yet there had been a ring of sincerity in his voice, and no hysteria; it had been calm and reasoned as if he were arguing a case in court.

The whole thing had its amusing side. When Mr Stephen had resigned as Attorney-General through ill-health, the Press had immediately proclaimed that they had cold-shouldered him. Now that he was going to New South Wales they would say it was because they did not properly appreciate him; yet if all were known they would say she had encouraged him too much!

She examined her behaviour carefully in retrospect. She had enjoyed his company, but she could not accuse herself of having flirted with him. She was devoted to Sir John and to furthering his career.

Sometimes she thought she loved him better when they were apart, and she did not have to submit to his rather bear-like embraces (though she did so always with a good grace). She lavished on him all the warm, maternal affection, tender and protective and proud, which the rather self-sufficient Eleanor did not seem to need, and which she might have given to a son.

Even so, she would miss Alfred Stephen; his going would leave a blank. And before he left, she would be going away herself.

> Poor Sir John! Mr Stephen was the only one who had tact and talent about the Governor; but while suffering from bad health and mental distress he was forced to become an official drudge, and so resigned his office. Now he is to be lost to this Colony. ... Heaven send Sir John and the Colony a good deliverance! For the Government is in a most deplorable pickle.

Thus ran the leading article of the *Hobart Town Chronicle*; and such offensive sympathy was, as Sir John remarked to his wife, 'calculated to try a man's temper'.

She saw that he was passing it off lightly, but that in reality he was deeply wounded. 'Poor Sir John,' indeed! He who had been lionized in London, who had dined as an honoured guests with the Tsar of all the Russias and hob-nobbed with princes and millionaires, was being pitied by the guttersnipe Press!

'Of course these scribblers and their vulgar twaddle are beneath notice,' she said.

'If they keep at it too long in this tone, I shall begin to wonder if I really am fit to govern,' he said with a trembling lip.

'What nonsense! You are too sensitive, my love. This is a country where people must have hearts of stone and frames of iron.'

'Even a stone can be worn away by constant small frictions. And even iron will rust in time. God grant my health doesn't give way.'

'I feel sad and guilty at leaving you when you are so beset.'

'No, my love, I thoroughly approve of your going. I only wish I could come too. But the voyage is worth it if it can cure your headaches. The worst thing for me is to see you suffer.'

'You are the best of husbands.' She gave him her sweetest smile and sat upon his knee. He kissed her white neck, where the fine skin was beginning to grow loose and slack. His strong arms tightened about her possessively.

'This business of Gregory worries me,' he said with a sigh, stroking her hand. 'He's become positively abusive – I think the man must be a bit unbalanced by his fancied wrongs. Apparently he was expecting to be appointed Colonial Secretary when Montagu went, he was quite certain of it. But when Montagu himself recommended Forster to take over his duties, what could I do? I can't go back on the appointment now. He'll never forgive Montagu, who used to be his friend; what must he feel for me?'

'It's inevitable that you make some enemies. Don't worry about it, my love; it will work out. Gregory can't stay in a dudgeon for ever.'

'He says he'll never set foot in Government House again except on official business.'

'Good! That will save me having to entertain his dull wife.'

'But, Jane –'

'But me no buts,' she said, and kissed him on the nose. 'The Gregory-pot will simmer down in time. And he's an excellent Treasurer.'

The morning was sunny and somnolent. High in the blue sky Mount Wellington, usually know as Old Storm Mountain or The Cloudmaker, belied his name, spreading in misty smiling blue beneath his frown of rocks.

Mathinna, very bored, was supposed to be making pot-hooks in her writing-book, but was actually herding a harassed black ant with the point of her pencil, never letting him get away over the edge of the book. When the Lady-Mamma came in she looked up with a smile. The ant escaped.

'Mathinna, dear – may I take her away, Miss Williamson? Thank you, Mathinna. I want you to put on your best red muslin and brush your curls. Mr Bock is waiting to do your portrait; I want it finished before I go.'

'Mathinna come with you.'

'No, pet, you would be seasick and unhappy. I am going across the big water. You must stay at home and go on with your lessons like a good girl. And I'll bring you a present from the country over the water.'

Mathinna was interested in the portrait-painting; she stared at the dried-up little man with his paint-stained velvet coat. She pounced on his watercolour tubes and began squeezing out long snakes of colour. 'O! Red sunnake, blue sunnake, green sunnake –' until Mr Bock snatched them from her.

She sat down quite good-humouredly at last, and crossed her ankles and folded her hands as she had been taught. Little Mr Bock looked so funny, darting quick glances at her like a bird, then dabbing at the paper with the brush, that she could hardly keep herself from laughing; but she kept her mouth closed tightly, though a smile would curve the corners, and her eyes were alight with fun.

Mr Bock was feeling a little put out. Lady Franklin, by taking him up as a semi-official Government House portrait-ist, had helped him back to self-respect and a useful life, after the dreadful degradation of the hulks and the irons which he tried to forget. He would do anything for her. But it was hard to ask him to copy his own early portraits of the wild, outlandish Aborigines with their fur cloaks and clay-daubed hair.

He had done a whole series for her proposed museum.

103

This painting from the life appealed to him more. He added a highlight to the expressive eyes, added a curve to the wide, gentle mouth.

Perhaps, one day in the distant future, his paintings would have a great deal of scientific interest as she said; just at present he felt his brush might have had worthier subjects.

However, he was an artist, and soon the old excitement set in like a fever. He found himself putting all his care and skill into recording the youthful visage of one of Tasmania's savage inhabitants.

'Stupidly, stupidly old books,' said Mathinna, violently flinging the *First Child's Primer* on the schoolroom floor. 'Me knock-up longa lessons. What por all-a-time sit in tchair, look in book?'

Eleanor looked rather scandalized, but she giggled, ducking her head over the table so that her straggly fair hair fell across her eyes. Miss Williamson's long face set in an expression of disapproval. A bump of knotted muscle appeared in her forehead, which was her way of frowning, and her lips came down over her large, regular teeth.

She said primly, 'We read, Mathinna, id order to improve the mind. Now, pick up the book and bring id here to me.'

Mathinna did so, relieved to get down off her chair, which irked her; she hated having her legs suspended above the floor.

'Now, Mathinna: here is the picture of the pussy-cat: see? Where is he sitting? He is sitting od the *mat*. M-A-T, like your name. Now, whad does this say?'

'The-cat-sat-on-the-Mathinna.'

'Od the *mat*. And where is the mat? Say after me: "The mat is od the floor".'

'The-mat-is-on-the-p-ploor.' Oh, it was a stupidly, stupidly way to spend a sunny autumn morning. The mat is on the ploor, two-times-two-is-por, see-saw Marjorie Door, what did it all mean? And who cared, anyhow? She would rather sort rocks and shells in the Lady-Mamma's collection if she *must* stay inside. But she longed to be outside, stalking moths and butterflies with the kitchen cat, or waking up the possum she had tamed to go riding on her shoulder, or picking fruit for him in the orchard.

'Mathinna wants to go,' she stated definitely.

'Very well, but we will just finish this page first. Now: "See the cat. The cat is not big. He can eat a rat."'

Just then the kitchen cat, a sleek tabby, came strolling past the french windows, licking his chops as he went. He had been hunting little birds under the eaves. A feather, curved like a shell, clung to his chin.

Mathinna bounded away from Miss Williamson. 'Poosy! Poosy, Poosy-cat,' she cried, standing on tip-toe to reach the door catch.

'Mathinna! Oh, very well. There's do keeping you still this morning, I declare.'

Eleanor did not look at the cat. She had never had another pet since the parrot and the white kitten died. Sometimes she still woke from nightmares about that hateful man who had threatened her, though she no longer feared him when awake. Mathinna in her cot across the room was company then.

Sometimes Mathinna frightened herself with stories about the debbil-debbil, Rageoorappa, who walked by night and made the noise of the thunder and lightning. Eleanor was not frightened by such things, and smiled when Mathinna buried her head beneath the quilt to hide from the dreadful lightning-flash. Eleanor was frightened of only one thing: sudden death.

She had seen much of death on the ship coming out from England. Small babies had died, mothers had died in childbirth, a man had been lost at sea. Since they arrived that nice young man, Lieutenant Burnett, had died, drowned in the harbour while surveying, and Sir George Frankland died soon after the first Hobart Town Regatta.

She did not want to die yet; she was a sinner with worldly thoughts and not enough love in her heart for her fellow men. How could she be sure she would go to heaven? She must be very careful not to die, at least until she was better prepared for eternity.

When her birthday came in June she wrote in her diary:

9 June. Another year gone ... Shall I live to see another?

And a little later she had written:

Dear Mary this day gave birth to a son. She suffered much, I fear.

Life was full of mysteries, half-guessed and frightening. It was terrible to be at such an age, neither a child nor a woman; and darkening all her days was the awful uncertainty of human existence: for 'man is like the grass, which today is, and tomorrow is cast into the oven and utterly destroyed'.

Mortality hung heavy on her soul.

Chapter Fourteen

Long letters sailed back and forth from Hobart Town to Melbourne, from Sydney to Hobart Town. Sophy and Jane had had wonderful adventures in the bush, with Mr Bagot and Captain Moriarty to look after them, and Mr Hobson as guide.

They were the first ladies who had ever travelled overland from one settlement to the other, camping out as they went. They had seen a 'corroboree', with painted and feathered savages leaping and chanting while their women beat time on folded kangaroo-skins. They had crossed the Murray in a flimsy native canoe of bark, an elderly Aborigine inviting them to step into it, as Jane remarked, 'with the air of a king'.

He had later demonstrated his tree-climbing ability in the huge red-gums along the banks. In writing of this Jane did not mention that the demonstrator wore nothing but a very short shirt. Mr Hobson had been rather shocked, and she was sorry if it had upset Sophy; but she had been able to watch with scientific detachment.

One experience she did not mention in her letters – it had shaken her severely. She was always a little fey, and would respond to certain places with a chill felt in the timid flesh, without conscious reason. Their first camp across the Murray River was such a place.

She had sunk into an uneasy sleep under the great spread of branches, the high sparkling of stars, and woke about midnight.

She lay listening for what might have woken her. Then she heard a shot, echoing among the trees. It was followed by a wild 'coo-ee'! She rushed over to wake Mr Bagot, who woke Mr Hobson; but the others had heard nothing, and all was quiet.

By now she was trembling with an unexplainable dread. By the dying coals of the campfire the great tree-limbs writhed in almost human contortions against the sky. A night-bird called away in the forest, and the river slipped secretly past.

To pacify her Mr Bagot fired several shots into the air, but though he hallooed for some time, waking Sophy too, there was no reply: only the unsilent silence of the bush.

It was not until morning, when bacon was sizzling in a pan over the fire and the earliest sun was painting the tree-tops with red-gold light, that Mr Hobson told her the history of the place. It was here that Mr Faithful's servants were murdered by the natives not many years earlier. Eight men had been speared and clubbed to death, and they had managed to fire only one shot in defence.

He would not have camped there, he said, if they had not had to stop and make a fire to dry their wet things after having been washed out of their last camp by a rain-storm.

Never again did she feel that sense of dread when camping out, but she remembered Mr Ronald Gunn's words about haunted places in the deeps of the Tasmanian bush.

The Governor of New South Wales, Sir George Gipps, sent a wagonette and an escort out to meet them on the Paramatta road.

Once arrived, Jane was indefatigable in seeing everything. She won the Bishop's approval for going to see the church buildings and schools in spite of pouring rain. She had received Sir John's letters by the hands of Mr Stephen, who had left for Sydney after she left for Melbourne, and had heard of her dangerous overlanding, he said, 'with joy and apprehension'. The first letter she opened told her:

My dearest Love,

I was delighted to receive your letter telling of safe arrival in Melbourne. Mr Stephen has particularly requested to be the bearer of my letters to you, and I shall therefore write by him to Sydney and send the newspapers. He and the Bedfords dined with me yesterday, with the Archdeacon, Harding, and McArthur.

The conversation was general, unconnected with the Island, except as to a few of Harding's officers making an an excursion to Mt Kermode ... Mr Stephen appeared out of spirits at first. He expressed the most anxious desire to see you at Sydney and will no doubt call on you, and then having the charge of my packet will be an additional reason for calling ... I had occasion to ask Stephen something relative to the Judgeship in Sydney which the Chief Justice wanted to know, and therefore begged to speak with him in another room after dinner.

Our being alone gave him opportunity of alluding to his leaving the Colony which he said caused him much pain, but he was persuaded it was for the best.

I told him I agreed as, 'You are gaining a larger income here but it may be uncertain if your health is not equal to the constant application to the business of Advocate.' He then said, 'With respect to my delicate health I must tell Your Excellency that because of my ill-health I am often very excitable and unstable and in such state of body I have done several things for which in a more healthy state of mind I have been sorry; and I think the calm and uniform duties of a Judge will do me good, and prove better for my temperament than the constant bustle of a Barrister's practice. I must also assure you at this time that in whatever I may have done here I deeply regret if it has been supposed that I have shown the slightest disrespect either for yourself of for Lady Franklin. Such a feeling I never entertained, but the contrary for you both. I have a sincere respect for you and I can assure you that a similar feeling is entertained for you and Lady F. throughout the Country ... and I will further say that Lady Franklin is looked upon with *admiration* ...'

He said 2 or 3 times I much wish to see Lady Franklin and hope that I may have an opportunity at Sydney; and I request if you have parcels or letters to send that you will entrust them to me. Which I promised to do....

He added that Mr Gould was in 'high glee' over his latest bird collections, and Mrs G. was still active. Eleanor sent a message, but 'had not time to write'. Jane wondered a little about that. Certainly she had more time than her harassed father, who wrote at length and in detail.

She had noticed the look with which Eleanor had followed Sophy as they embarked; next time she must contrive to take Eleanor with her, and leave Sophy behind. There was some jealousy there.... But Sophy was a marvellous companion, gay and adventurous and never tired. She had not complained when they were washed out in the flood, or when she had been injured by her horse running beneath a branch which struck her head and knocked her to the ground.

She looked again at the letter, and smiled. How like Sir John to give every word of the conversation, not knowing how much he was revealing. So, Mr Stephen had seemed 'out of spirits'. And Mrs Stephen was not present, which suggested that she was already in 'an interesting condition'. There was no doubt that, for men, a marriage even of convenience had its compensations, and whatever its earliest motives love must surely follow.

Sir John sat writing in his downstairs office, with the red curtains drawn and a fire flapping lazily in the fancy cast-iron grate. The pile of fat, sealed letters, not yet franked, was growing by his left elbow. He had just completed a long missive to his dearest Jane. It was almost as good as talking to her.

Telling her of his problems helped to sort them out in his brain, his mind fell tranquil like a pool in which the mud stirred up by the day's events settled quietly to the bottom, and his ideas came clear.

He'd had a more than ordinarily trying day: dispatches from the Colonial Secretary forecast yet another change in policy over the management of convicts. The Molesworth Committee was enquiring into the assignment system condemned by Maconachie; farmers and orchardists in Van Diemen's Land were sending delegations to the Lieutenant-Governor in alarm at the idea of losing all their servants and labourers.

He believed himself that the assignment system, though open to abuses, was preferred even by the prisoners to working in chain-gangs and being locked up in penitentiaries, hundreds of men herded together in unnatural conditions which must lead to vice. Assignment provided the nearest to normal conditions for the period of the sentence, and prepared a man better for the return to a free life when it was over.

He had been making notes of new regulations according to his own ideas: 'Very formidable punishment at first, to be gradually relaxed, each mitigation depending on good behaviour. Those convicts proving amenable will be graduated from the road-parties, freed of their chains, and put to work around the lumber yard. Then they will be given less arduous duties; next they will become "trusties" or model prisoners. The door of hope is thus proved to be open; and regeneration depends on themselves.'

Yet, 17,000 convicts! How was it possible to see that justice was done to so many?

Besides the convict problem, there was the ever-present worry of the perishing Aborigines. Dr Officer had been to Flinders Island to see if he could find the cause of their falling-off; eight more had died already since his return.

His report seemed to make it necessary to remove both the surgeon, Dr Walsh, and the superintendent, Mr Robinson, at least until they could be cleared of the suspicion of wrongly appropriating stores. Dr Officer had found the natives malnourished, in spite of the large amount voted for their commissariat and the flock of sheep which were supposed to provide fresh meat.

'Certainly they are not consuming the amount of food

shown on the returns,' Dr Officer reported. 'My own feeling is that they are dying partly of homesickness.

'One poor "gin" asked me if I could see the snowy peak of Ben Lomond away across the water – it was a clear morning and the mountain quite visible. The tears rolled down her black cheeks. "That me-country," she said. "Well, mitter, all blackfellow soon gone! Little-feller, me run about that country. You take-it him country, blackfellow all die." '

Sir John got out Robinson's reports of 1837 and read: 'The settlement is in a very powerful, tranquil state. The only drawback to their complete happiness on the establishment is the great mortality amongst them.'

Death *was* rather a drawback, certainly. What did the fool mean?

And here, farther back, was one of Arthur's memoranda on the establishment of the Flinders Island settlement: 'Mr Robinson is of the opinion that if the natives were placed on an island in Bass's Strait they would not feel themselves imprisoned there, or pine away nor wish to return to the mainland or regret their inability to hunt and roam as before....'

Dr Officer said the winds were violent and cold. The native huts were exposed to rain and sleet on an open sandy plain. The water was brackish and not good for drinking. But what else was to be done? He began drafting a letter to Robinson.

Sir John signed and laid down his quill, flexing the fingers of his right hand which had grown stiff from writing too long. When Jane was home she often helped with Duplicate Dispatches which were such a chore. Henry Elliott too was a great help, dutiful and affectionate as a son. He must write and tell Lord Minto so. Not like that foolish Peter Barrow, Sir John Barrow's boy, whom he had been forced to rap over the knuckles for taking sides in the Maconachie affair. He had since gone off home in the sulks.

It seemed that the Captain might get an appointment at

last; Lord Russell mentioned in his last Dispatch a plan to appoint him to Norfolk Island.

Sir George Gipps had the appointment to bestow. As for himself, he would recommend Maconachie, or at least not say anything against him. No, he would recommend him. He might do quite well as commandant of a penal colony, and it would give him a chance to try out his rather strange ideas for reform.

Ah, if he could only discuss all this with Jane! He picked up his pen and added a few lines: 'I know you will bring a full account of the Colony over there. Bear in mind, my love, that Sydney people are jealous of Van Diemen's Land. Do not make a longer stay there than is desirable. You must not make any unnecessary delay, for I want you back.'

Eleanor could see that her father was fretting for Mamma, as he always did after urging her to go away. He wrote every night, giving her details of all that occurred. Eleanor hated writing letters, though she liked getting them; and Mamma's were always long and interesting. She'd had one written on the banks of the Murray, another from Wiseman's Ferry on the Hawkesbury.

She wished she had a letter from her own true mother; but she died long before Eleanor was old enough to read. Among her papers Eleanor had found a poem she had written, supposed to be addressed by an Eskimo girl to a traveller leaving her country:

Yes, yes, thou hast gone to the climes of the East,
Thou hast welcomed the Sun as he sprang from the sea;
And thou car'st not, though sorrow lie cold on my breast,
Though the night of the grave may be closing on me ...

Had her mother a premonition of her end? It almost seemed like it, though the poem was written long before her death. It read now like a reproach to the husband who had gone off on another Polar expedition when she had only a week to live.

Oh God, thought Eleanor, make her heart pure like that

other Eleanor's, so that she might join her one day in heaven! But not yet; she was not anxious to join her just yet. She would like to marry and have children one day.

Mary's son Jemmy-Buttons was a perfect little pet. She loved to be allowed to hold him and smell the sweet baby smell, like honey. But she feared to suffer as Mary had done, perhaps to die in childbed.

Mrs Gould had been brought to bed of a fine boy. He was called Franklin after Sir John. She was already regaining her strength; but Eleanor had heard her scream. She had seen John Gould, who doted on her, pacing up and down, white to the lips.

Life was wonderful and terrible, and over all was God. His watching eye in every place, His ear listening to every conversation.

Chapter Fifteen

Jane was worried about her husband. She had returned to find him nervous and unwell, full of fears and indecision, quite unlike the firm, sensible letters he had been sending her.

What had happened? It was Gregory again: he had now been further antagonized by being dropped from the Legislative Council. The order to reduce the Council to only four members had come as a Royal Instruction, and certainly could not be disobeyed by Sir John; but Gregory insisted on regarding it as a personal insult.

It was, he said, a slur on his character, and had damaged him in the eyes of the public. He had lost rank, consideration, and station in society after years of faithful and zealous service.

There was every chance that the whole thing was a storm in a tea-cup. A clerk in the Colonial Office could have made a mistake in copying the instructions, and Gregory might not have to lose his seat after all. But it would take months for the thing to be sorted out because mails were so slow and uncertain, and the damage was done. Gregory had become an implacable enemy of both Sir John and the Government.

Sir John was so upset by Gregory's bitter attacks that he seemed stupefied. He sat about, refused his meals, took too much spirits on an empty stomach, and sometimes came to Jane's room and knelt by her chair shedding tears and self-reproaches. 'She would no longer respect him – she would cease to love him – she could never bear it if he were recalled in disgrace! But he could not live without her, she was his life and strength....'

As he babbled on she became stiff with impatience, and filled with a kind of horror at these unmanly tears. Yet she

115

forced her voice to be gentle and calm, she reasoned with him and reassured him like a child. Often she had to sit up half the night writing Dispatches and dealing with his personal correspondence; for a while he was unable to settle to anything. Henry Elliott was her great standby, but even from him she strove to conceal the extent of Sir John's collapse.

He had taken to pacing up and down his room at night, compulsively. Standing in the doorway, she watched as he walked to the window, held the curtain aside for a moment, looked blankly out; paced back to the end of the bed, rested a hand on the bedpost, and crossing the right foot over the left, remained thus in a brown study for half a minute; then walked back to the window, held the curtain aside, looked out; paced back and rested a hand on the bedpost....

At last she would speak, move into the room, do anything to break the senseless rhythm of his pacing and staring. He would start and gaze at her blankly, 'My love – you startled me. I was thinking; thinking; let me see; what was I thinking about? Ah yes: Gregory, Gregory, Gregory. D'you think the Secretary of State would uphold me if I were to dismiss him? Perhaps Lord Glenelg would think ... Perhaps ... What shall I do?'

'Sir John, it is time for bed.' And while she rang for his valet she picked up the empty glass from the washstand and smelt it. Rum and water ... No wonder his voice was a little thick, his manner distracted. Oh, she should never have gone off to Melbourne and Sydney and left him! Yet it would be even worse if they both cracked up, and without that perfect break from the deadly round of Vice-Regal dinners and duties she could not have carried on.

Miss Williamson was a pillar of strength: she could manage the house alone, and Eleanor as well, but Sir John was the problem. Certainly his position was beset with difficulties. Gregory's latest act had been to take an active and vocal part in defeating the Feigned Issues Bill, a Government measure in which Sir John should have been able to count on his support.

116

Sir John, very worked up about it, had come to her to announce that he meant to suspend Gregory from office at once. His view was that the Treasurer had behaved like a mutinous member of the crew. He felt he had to discipline him; but then a doubt crept in. Coming so soon after his dismissal of Maconachie – though that was a private affair, surely – it might look as though he were hasty-tempered and hard to get on with. Whereas it was not so – quite the contrary, in fact! Gregory was the hot-tempered one, impossible to get on with these months past.

He insisted on believing that Lady Franklin was the cause of his misfortunes, that she was behind the appointment of Forster as Acting Colonial Secretary. Was it in fact, wondered Sir John, some diabolical plan of Montagu's to disrupt the Government while he was away in London? But for what reason?

At last he had reported Gregory to the Secretary of State, and asked for direction: was he, or not, justified in asking Mr Gregory for his resignation? This, though, meant waiting nearly a year for a reply!

He'd never considered that factor when coming out here. Everything had to be wearisomely committed to paper, and sent to London; answers came to questions which were eight months out of date; action had to be delayed while permission came slowly from the remote Colonial Office. No one from the London office ever came out here to see things for himself, and no one over there understood the problems of the man on the spot.

There was this Molesworth Report on Transportation, now; he'd read its findings in *The Times* long before he saw an official copy. Then he had received blunt instructions that he must be ready for the approaching discontinuance of the practice of Assignment. Yet the whole Colony, and particularly the landholders, depended on assigned servants for cheap labour, and the free settlers were clamouring for reassurance. And there was still no proper provision for female convicts. . . .

What a frightful burden to be on the shoulders of one

117

man! If he had known all this he would never have taken it on. He was not cut out for it, the details worried him, he became tired and confused.

His place, however, was on the quarterdeck of his command until he was relieved from duty. He had offered for a term of at least six years, and he had been here less than three! That great mountain hanging there in the sky weighted his mind like the burden of office. He got up, paced to the window, and held back the curtain, staring out at the frowning rocks with their burden of ice and snow.

With Sir John in this state of mind, Jane was alarmed when she heard that a letter on the way from London – its contents had been confided to a friend of Henry Simpkinson's, Mary's husband – was calculated to distress him even further. Sir John Barrow of the Admiralty had written abusively, complaining of Franklin's 'ungentlemanly' treatment of his son Peter.

Jane cautioned both Henry Elliott and Sophy Cracroft to keep watch for this epistle whenever a mail-packet came in. They would know it by the baronet's crest on the outside, and they were to bring it instantly to her. But by some mischance it was sorted and placed on the Government House breakfast table with other of Sir John's private letters, while Jane was still in bed one morning.

While Eleanor stared, wondering what was going on, the quick-witted Sophy snatched up the letter and darted upstairs to Lady Franklin's bedroom.

'Sophy! Come back here! That letter was addressed to me, not to my wife, you daft girl! *Sophy!* D'you hear me?'

He threw down his napkin and strode after her, half-angry. In her room Jane grasped the letter, tore it in two, and thrust it in the fire. She was helping its destruction with the poker when Sir John came in. His face was ominously red.

'What are you two up to? Where's my letter?'

'In the fire, my love.'

'In the fire!' He grabbed the poker from her and tried to

rescue the paper, but it fell apart in a few blackened wisps. He flung the poker down with a clatter. 'What – do – you – mean – by – this – unwarrantable – interference?' he shouted at Sophy, who kept nervously behind Jane.

But Jane stood up to him bravely. 'It was on my instructions that Sophy brought the letter to me. I destroyed it; I would do the same again to save you the pain of reading it. You see, I knew what it contained. It was a complaint from Sir John Barrow. He would thank me if he knew, I'm sure, and already regrets his impulsiveness. He said things he didn't mean.'

'I don't believe you. What was in that letter? How am I to trust you when you behave like this?'

'My love, you know how sensitive you are. I only wanted to protect –'

'I don't want that sort of protection! I'm not a child to be mollycoddled by women. Sophy, leave the room! Jane, I want a full explanation of your conduct. How often have you meddled with my correspondence in the past?'

Jane looked at him with wide eyes. Oh, it was wonderful to see him in such a temper! He was a man again, ordering her about, taking command. She said meekly: 'Never, Sir John, I swear! And this was not *official* correspondence. Barrow wrote privately, and vindictively from hurt pride in his son. We know that the boy was in the wrong, but his father is too proud to admit it.'

'How do you know all this?'

'Mary let it out in a letter – Mr Simpkinson heard about it. I've been waiting to intercept it when it came. It was for your sake, for your peace of mind.'

'Bah!'

'Please sit down! Let me pour you some tea. You make me nervous, pacing up and down like an enraged leopard.'

'I *am* enraged. Women are so devious. Why could you not have told me of this letter, Jane – forewarned me so that I was ready for what it contained? But to burn it unread!' He was dangerously flushed, the veins stood out in

119

his temples. Jane began to grow alarmed.

'I am sorry! There, it will never happen again, Sir John. I had thought to save you an upset, and instead have caused one. I didn't mean to make you angry. I – truly –' She wiped a tear from a blue eye and gave a pathetic sniff. She looked very small sitting on the side of the big canopied bed.

'So you should be.' He sat down beside her. The bed creaked beneath his weight. He was beginning to soften. In half an hour he was appeased, but he extracted a promise from her never, never to do such a thing again.

Jane lay and hugged herself when he had gone back to his interrupted breakfast. The shock of finding how much she was taking on herself, the burst of anger, had done him the world of good. He had come out of his apathetic state, and had made love to her so vigorously that she was quite amazed.

At Christmas he had a short holiday in the peace of the Governor's Retreat at New Norfolk, on the lovely and tranquil higher reaches of the Derwent. Since his outburst his spirits had steadily improved, and by the new year he was almost his old self. The expected arrival of such men of science as Count Strzelecki and his old Arctic friend James Ross helped him to get his present troubles into perspective. Whatever the Colonial Office might think, his reputation in the Navy and the world of scientific discovery stood as high as ever.

Chapter Sixteen

Eleanor wrote in her diary:

1 January 1840. Another year past.... Shall I live to see another?

9 January. Beware of levity or familiarity with young men. Modest reserve without affectation is the *safe path*. We are never more in the midst of temptations than when we are most pleased with ourselves. Remember the Ear of God is in every company.

February. Mary has had a letter from Mrs M. The Maconachies are due to sail for Norfolk Island in the *Nautilus*. Papa recommended him for the position.

March. Mr Gell, the new Principal of the Queen's School, is staying with us. He is going on 24, but very agreeable, lively and clever.

Henry Elliott had gone away back to England at his father's request, for Lord Minto was getting old and needed his son. Sir John mourned as if he had himself lost a son; but in his place came John Phillip Gell, the charming and cultured young man sent by Dr Arnold of Rugby to establish secondary education in Van Diemen's Land at the highest level. Lady Franklin took to him at once 'Dear Lady Franklin,' as he wrote home to his father, 'was kindness itself.'

Young Eleanor was inclined to idolize him. When he offered to hear her Latin verbs or help her with Greek history her rather plain, placid face glowed with animation. Together they had made up nonsense verses on Regatta Day in the new year.

The Poet's prize will be a sprig of wattle,
But who will win I'm sure that I can-not tell....

It had been a sunny, breezy day with whitecaps out on the blue-green waters of the Derwent estuary: coloured flags flapping, sailing boats heeling over and cutting through the water behind a feather of sparkling foam.

Eleanor kept the white satin programme, with the odd names of the competing whale-boats for the Tasman prize – *Platypus, Squint-Eyed Sal, Native Cherry* – as a memento of one of the happiest days of her life.

There had been all sorts of opposition to Sir John's proposal for establishing a college for boys at New Norfolk, where he had donated ten acres of land and the Government Farm for a site. It was this new college that Mr Gell had come to establish, but the foundation stone was not yet laid, though £2,500 had been voted by Executive Council.

That dour lot, the Presbyterians, had their jealousies and suspicions about Mr Gell. Because he wrote home to the Anglican Dr Arnold for a charter they felt they would be delivered into the hands of the Church of England. The Press referred to the college scheme contemptuously as a 'baby-bubble', and for a while it was shelved. Mr Gell went on teaching at Queen's School, a boarding and day school for boys.

Ronald Gunn was now Private Secretary. A comfortable two-storied cottage was made available for him in the grounds, with room for his young family.

One morning while Lady Franklin was writing, as usual, in her boudoir, Mr Gunn came upstairs with a letter from an acquaintance of his, a German botanist and naturalist; perhaps she would like to receive him at Government House?

'But of course, Mr Gunn! Any friend of yours is welcome, and you know how Sir John and I dote on science.'

'Indeed, everyone knows it. You have started a new era. You don't know how I value your encouragement! But Dr von Lottke – he's not exactly a friend, and I'm not sure I'd call him a scientist. He dabbles, rather. He went collectng with me out from Circular Head, but he never spent a single night in the bush. He never climbed a mountain that I know of; and he used to buy his rare shells from others, because he's too plump to bend and pick them up! Yet now he's talking about writing a book on Tasmanian conch-ology.'

'Well, at least his intentions are good.'

'Yes, and he's a most interesting fellow – entertaining, rather. Can mimic birds so that he fooled me, and he has this odd German way of speaking English. I call him Dr von Doosenmatter.'

'You call him what, Mr Gunn?'

'Dr von Doosenmatter! He's easy-going, everything that happens he just says airily: "Ach! Dot doosen' matter, my friendt!" And: "It vos better to be vise than to be vealthy."'

'I think perhaps I would like your German doctor – of medicine, or letters, do you know?'

'Just a courtesy title, I imagine, which he has bestowed on himself since coming out here. He's a bit of a charlatan, I'm afraid.'

'Well, I believe I shall ask him to afternoon tea, and if I like him he shall stay to dinner.'

When Dr von Lottke arrived, he proceeded to charm everyone with his mercurial ways, his quaint speech, and his high good humour. He was a huge man, at least eighteen stone, with a bright red beard and large spectacles with strongly magnifying lenses, so that his pale-blue eyes had a mesmeric quality.

He made friends with Eleanor and Mathinna at afternoon tea on the lawn by giving a demonstration of juggling with four rock-cakes and a saucer, which was no rounder than Mathinna's dark eyes as she watched him.

When he didn't drop the saucer, or drink his tea with loud noises, Lady Franklin decided to invite him to dinner.

'Dis a most indteresting island vos, Sir John,' Dr von Lottke expounded at dinner. The days were drawing in, but light still lingered outside the dining-room windows, beyond the veranda. A willy wagtail flirted his black fan on the wooden rail, scolding a passing cat with a quick rattle of harsh notes. 'Vere else,' cried the doctor, 'vere else in the vorld vould you a letel bird findt, who is so brafe a cat to chase? Black and vite, I haf noticed, are many birds of New Holland also, and brafe as if dey vos tigers. *Chik-up – chirck-up, chik-up chirck-up chirk-up.*' he cried suddenly, echoing the bird exactly.

Willy perched on his legs of black wire and wagged his tail applaudingly.

'Also, they vill der cuckoos chase, who in their nests der wrong eggs lay. Ja!'

'You mean there are cuckoos in Australia?' asked Lady Franklin. 'Sir John, we must look them up in the Goulds' new book when it appears. I've never heard the cuckoo here.'

'Ach, he iss not der Cu-coo! Cu-coo! sayingk; but Twee-twee-twee-twee-twee-twee-twee-twee!' cried the Herr Doctor, whistling a rising scale in a minor key.

'So you are a ventriloquist as well as a conjuror; and a naturalist too, Dr von Lottke!'

'Ja! Mein lady; I haf dot accomplishments,' admitted the doctor complacently.

'And a botanist and conchologist too, Mr Gunn tells me. Surely you must have studied geology as well?'

'I am geologist also.'

'Then afterwards you must come and look at some of the specimens I have gathered for the proposed museum. There is some uncommon interesting fossil fern-tree, and calcareous limestone from the Sassafras Valley –'

'Most indteresting; most indteresting,' murmured the doctor, while Gunn gave him a rather malicious look. He knew the doctor's geological knowledge to be flimsy indeed. And during his stay as Circular Head he'd grown a little tired of Dr von Doosenmatter's airy way of borrowing things and forgetting to return them.

Lady Franklin with womanly interest was now pursuing the question of her guest's domestic arrangements. 'It is uncommon difficult to get laundry done here except in private homes. Does your landlady see to your shirts and socks, Herr Doctor?'

'Ach, *nein*, mine shirts I myself vash; I haf iron in my room, und der fronts und cuffs only I bress. For vy? Der rest is not seen. Mine socks I t'row away ven dirty dey vos, und der new ones buy. Ven vashed dey vos shrinken und shrinken.'

'He is *un original*, your Dr von Doosenmatter,' said Lady Franklin afterwards, smiling at Mr Gunn. She collected odd characters like this German doctor.

'Well, at least his shirts are clean. That's quite true, he does only press the parts that show, but he washes the whole garment. But he's a firm believer in "what the eye doesn't see …"'

'One evening I called for him for some function or other, he'd been busy mounting some specimens and painting the stands, and there was yellow paint all over his boots.

'He got dressed while I waited, put on a clean stock and a smart clawhammer coat, and was ready. When I pointed at his feet he said : "Ach, dot doosenmatter, my friendt!" He just dipped the brush in some black paint and painted over the yellow patches on his boots!'

'Oh dear! Did you hear him thanking Sir John in the hall last night? "Pleasant efening, sir! Feast of reason – flow of soul! *Wunderbar*! und now, *auf wiedersehen*. Upon your so kind hosspitality I must cock-roach no longer." Oh, we must have him again, Mr Gunn. He is priceless!'

Mathinna and Eleanor thought so too. Dr von Lottke came on Saturday afternoons and took them round the grounds, imitating the birds so that they came up to him, and throwing pieces of cheese from the capacious pockets of his jacket as a reward for the melodious whistling of the native thrush.

Sometimes he sang for them, '*Stille Nacht*' or perhaps a lullaby in German that was soft and melodious. Mathinna would stare at him, fascinated. She thought his great red beard must contain a bird's nest and a little tame bird which sang and whistled for him.

He found a spiny ant-eater and showed them its long tubular snout for sucking up ants, and a little marsupial mole, creamy-white and blind, which he dug out of its tunnel and held up gently in his big freckled hands.

Mathinna's pet possum took to him at once. When he was invited up to Lady Franklin's boudoir to see the specimens, it ran up his trouser-leg and popped into the pocket where he kept crumbled cheese, biscuits, and lumps of sugar for enticing animals and birds.

Soon its pointy snout looked out, munching, while one paw held a sugar-lump and the other a piece of biscuit. Its big blind-looking eyes stared vacantly. There were crumbs on its whiskers. With its trophies it now retired to the top of the doctor's head, where it relieved itself with a patter of brown pellets which bounced off his shoulders to the old-rose carpet.

'*Donner und blitzen!*' exclaimed Dr von Lottke.

Mathinna shrieked with laughter, folding her hands between her knees as she stamped on the floor.

'Hush! Mathinna,' said Lady Franklin, frowning but finding it hard not to smile. Eleanor blushed. 'Possie will have to go outside if he forgets himself like this. I'm sorry, Dr von Doo – er, von Lottke, he is usually house-trained. Excitement –'

'Ach, dot doosen matter! A leedle animals such as he vos, nodings mooch he does. Nodings mooch!' But he prudently removed the possum to a curtain.

Trees in asylum garb of green strait-jackets marched across the island in a line as straight as the stockade walls. Mary Maconachie had never seen such trees. They were called Norfolk Island Pines, but instead of soft pine-fronds they

126

grew green prickles. Instead of hanging down, the leaves stabbed upwards at the sky. Arranged in perfect symmetry round the trunks, the branches tapered at the top as if each tree had been cut precisely out of cardboard.

Pine-shingles made the roof of the commodious, single-storied Government House where they lived. Outside the seawind sang with a mournful sound, keening through the armoured boughs.

From the veranda there was a view of the sea and the two smaller islands with their fringe of foam. The Pacific's brilliant blue and green encompassed this green island where two thousand men were confined, completely cut off from society and the company of women.

Above the house the high land began, rippling away in a series of hills and valleys, each valley watered by a stream of sweet clear water and filled with a rich growth of tree-fern, wild lemon, guavas and wild cotton. Long-established orange groves scented the air with blossom. Grass grew everywhere, and sweet potatoes flourished in the rich dark soil. The place should be an earthy paradise; yet among the prisoners its name was synonymous with hell.

At night after the children were in bed Alexander would tell her dreadful stories of the condition of the 'old hands' – the doubly-convicted felons who had been sent here as the worst place of punishment in the Antipodes.

Indeed she had seen their wild, dark, sullen faces, more bestial than human. A Norfolk-Islander could be recognized among other men by his face, said Alexander, it was the index of his soul, and was largely the result of inhuman treatment.

He meant to alter the harsh and oppressive system, had already begun to introduce his humane ideas. The island alone was sufficient prison, he said, and transportation a severe punishment in itself, Irons and the lash were not needed in addition. When a prisoner had completed his day's labour for the Government, he should be free to culti-vate his own garden or his own mind, whichever he preferred. Alexander had brought musical instruments and books for a library with him, both unheard of before in the settlement prison.

On the Queen's birthday last month there had even been a party, with play-acting and an issue of rum. The prisoners had seemed dazed and half incredulous of their good fortune. There had been no stealing, no violence.

Only the bars on the veranda windows – put there to protect unpopular commandants from rioting prisoners – made Mary Maconachie a little uneasy. Otherwise the house was her delight, after so many cramped and shared abodes.

Marriage was her vocation, as penal reform was Alexander's. Sometimes he talked over with her his problems, his attempts to break the 'Ring', the secret society of the most hardened men, and their appalling jargon by which a 'good man' was a hater of society, a 'bad man' one who tried to obey its rules.

Sometimes he shut himself away from her for days, working late into the night and sleeping in his study. Then he would come back to her with renewed passion, letting all his worries and tensions unwind and unravel, flow out in the stream of their love like strands of silk.

Now, with the thought of 'more mouths to feed' no longer haunting her – for she had reached the menopause early and was free of that constant worry – she received him with an utter abandon of self, her mind filled with images of smooth-flowing waters and sea-polished shells invaded by the waves. The welling of the seed within her was no longer a menace to security but a deep, unmixed joy.

She thought of childless Jane Franklin, who was being so cruelly hounded by the newspapers of Van Diemen's Land. Jane was charming and intelligent, but limited in her understanding, almost as limited as a royal princess brought up in a palace must be. She had never known want. If she wished to travel, she had travelled; if she needed a new dress, she bought one; to read an expensive journal, she subscribed. She'd always been indulged by her weathly

128

father. Now, with John's salary and her own income, and no sons to educate, she could have anything she wanted . . . except a son, thought Mary, feeling suddenly sorry for Jane.

She remembered the first time they had met, in that dreadful little villa by the Thames.

Jane had called in the afternoon with her wealthy Guillemard aunt. Mary had all six children in the living-room with her, for she couldn't afford a nanny. She'd had a pile of old clothes on the table, piecing them to cut down for the children.

The little maid, knowing no better, had shown the visitors straight in. She had swept up the bundle of garments into a cupboard, but not before Lady Franklin had caught her first glimpse of genteel poverty.

It had been a constrained meeting all round. Only later when she got to know Lady Franklin better had she realized that her stiffness was due to shyness and an excessive sensibility at having caused embarrassment. She was really the kindest-hearted creature, but by her upbringing incapable of understanding much.

She'd warrant the lady had never stood over a hot stove making a family stew from cheap cuts of meat. The nearest she'd ever been to a kitchen was the Confectionary Room at Government House, Hobarton, when she put on a frilled apron and begged the chef to show her how to make tartlets and puffs.

A lady might make tartlets and puffs, even small cakes – but a common stew, never!

'Mamma, Mamma, this is the beautifullest place!' Kitty danced in, bright-eyed with excitement, followed more slowly by Mary Anne. 'Mr Reid drove us right across the island, and we have seen the view from the summit for the first time –'

'Are you tired, Minnie?' asked her mother, giving a warm smile and half an ear to her younger daughter's chatter, while she took Mary Anne's hand and drew her down to a chair. She was worried by the girl's slight but chronic cough. Her dark auburn hair was clustered damply on her brow, and her cheeks were brightly flushed.

'Only a little, Mamma.'

Inarticulately her mother chafed her hand. She found it hard to express her love for her children. She rarely indulged in demonstrations of affection, endearments and kisses, but she loved them all equally – or nearly so. For the eldest, Minnie, and the youngest boy she had a special affection.

She looked anxiously at Minnie, sitting with her head drooping over a slender, blue-veined hand. What future was there for a girl at the ends of the earth like this? She would hardly find a husband, unless among the military staff, and there could be little gaiety in her life. Alexander was so tactless in pursuing his ideas that most of the island's officials had quarrelled with him already. . . . The best hope perhaps, was for a visiting chaplain.

BOOK TWO

Recall

Let them proceed in their envy and malice, and blacken thy name after the most spiteful manner ... yet what art thou the worse?

The brave generous mind, whose all is in God, and who refers himself entirely to His judgement, is above the terror and discouragements of men, and lays no stress on their notions of things.

Thomas à Kempis,
The Imitation of Christ

Chapter Seventeen

With the first wattle bloom in August came Her Majesty's ships *Erebus* and *Terror*, which were to give their names to part of the empty white map of Antarctica. In command of the expedition was Sir John's old friend James Clark Ross, while Captain Francis Crozier commanded the *Terror*.

There had already been some French captains calling at Hobart Town: d'Urmont d'Urville in the *Astrolabe* back from charting the coast of Adelie Land, Captain la Place in the frigate *Artemise*. Lady Franklin with her fluent French and Sir John with his naval traditions were already popular with the French Navy, spoken of as ready to give visiting ships a kind reception. But this time the ships were British, and the atmosphere at Government House became charged with excitement.

In the perfect spring weather Sir John strode about with new vigour, a broad smile playing over his benign features, filled with pleasure in this congenial company. Jane set herself out to please with her not inconsiderable charm, tiring herself out with planning meals and excursions.

Eleanor basked in the new warmth, feeling the relaxing of tensions she had hardly understood. Sophy, who had been rather quiet since Henry Elliott left, lit up and sparkled like a Christmas tree.

James Ross fascinated her, with his long nose and brilliant black eyes set rather close together, his wildly curling hair beginning to recede from an intellectual forehead, his slim, trim naval figure in its smart blue and white uniform with brass buttons and gold epaulettes.

Poor Captain Crozier, larger and quieter, seemed dull by comparison; and he was no scholar. She arranged with her aunt to have Ross seated next to her at dinner, for the officers dined nearly every evening at Government House, walking across from the cove in a few minutes.

Sophy asked intelligent questions about the expedition, wore her most becoming gowns, and believed she was making some impression. But while she laughed and coquetted with Ross, Frank Crozier was watching her quietly from across the table. He thought he had never seen such a girl. She was so pretty and clever, yet so feminine, almost fragile-looking with her thin face and big dark eyes.

(When she had left London she'd been pale and sickly, but the wonderfully healthy climate of Hobart Town, with its bracingly cool summer evenings and clear sunny days, and its sea-breezes and fresh mountain winds, had brought a delicate colour to her cheeks and a gloss to her dark hair.)

When she came down to dinner in a third different gown in one week, her brother Tom pretended to fall back, dazzled, against the newel-post at the bottom of the stairs. And indeed she was a dazzling sight in stiffened net with diamanté over white taffetas – not that Tom knew what it was called, but his sister seemed to move in a filmy cloud sprinkled with sparkling dew.

To Crozier she was the Snow Queen, that legendary figure of the Arctic regions: coldly beautiful and unapproachable. Ross noticed only that she was in a scintillating mood at dinner, and let himself respond to the glances of her dark eyes.

Her laughter was silvery, like a tinkle of ice crystals, her neck was like a bank of snow. She called gaily to Jane down the table 'I was just telling Captain Ross, Aunt, that he should take some ladies on his expedition to the South Polar regions. This would make it unique, and add a certain grace to meals of seal blubber and penguin steak.'

'A wonderful idea, I declare!' said Jane. 'I would choose to go in Captain Crozier's ship, as he looks better fed.'

There was a laugh at this, Crozier looking down rather ruefully at his solid figure.

'I would choose *Erebus*,' said Sophy instantly. 'I declare I should feel enough "terror" at the icebergs, the terrible wastes of snow and the Antarctic storms, without being re-minded of it by the name of my ship.'

'I think Miss Sophy is teasing you, Frank,' said Ross with a smile. (She noticed with a thrill that he had dropped the more formal 'Miss Cracroft'.) 'I think she would be an asset to any expedition with her sense of humour. If only ladies could be persuaded to wear more sensible clothes –' and he indicated the filmy gown whose full skirt brushed, as they sat, the well-fitting white trousers of his uniform.

'Oh, but they can – look at riding habits.'

'But even they are only designed for *sitting* gracefully.'

'Pray don't discuss such a thing, James,' said Sir John, tossing off a glass of sherry wine after holding it up to Jane, 'or my wife will begin packing instantly. You don't know what difficulty I have in keeping her at home. And I warn you, she would take so much stuff with her that your ship would be overloaded to a dangerous point. Nothing will stop her –'

'Fie, Sir John! You should have seen me in the Australian bush, with only one carry-all in the spring-cart: I was Spartan, was I not, Sophy? And everything we had got soaked in a flood, and I wore the same clothes for a fortnight.'

'But you are a very remarkable person,' said James Ross with a bow. 'Most ladies would be impossible at the Pole. If I had to take females on an expedition (which Heaven forbid!) I should choose you and Miss Cracroft to go.'

'What a Jesuitical rogue he is!' cried Sophy. 'He pays compliments in the most charmingly insulting way, does he not? Ah, Captain Ross, I had thought the Navy was more gallant.'

'All naval commanders are gallant when on land, but at sea their ship is their only mistress. That is why ships are called "she": they're as capricious and demanding as a beautiful woman, and won't tolerate a rival. Isn't that so, John?'

'Well, most ships are so, that's true. *Dorothea* was like that, and no wonder, with her name. But *Trent* was a good,

135

no-nonsense sort of ship; and *Rainbow* – she was perfection.'

'The "Celestial Rainbow", eh? Yes, a remarkably happy ship, I always heard. And easier to steer than the Ship of State, eh, John? From what you tell me –'

'Don't let us speak of it,' cried Sir John, a shadow darkening his round, bland, beaming face. 'Instead, I give you a toast: Ladies and gentlemen, to *Erebus* and *Terror*, and their gallant commanders: may they return safely, and visit us once more at Hobart Town.'

Young Lieutenant Hooker, ship's surgeon and unofficial botanist to the expedition, trailed rather unhappily behind Lady Franklin as she led him up the hill above 'Ancanthe', talking all the time.

He was rather disappointed in her 'Vale of Flowers' so far. Part of it appeared to be a bare hillside, with what looked like the remains of a turnip garden. Certainly the creek itself was interesting, with its tall acacias with their leopard-spotted trunks, its fern-trees and myrtles; but he had expected to find the ground carpeted with flowers.

Lady Franklin was more interested in showing him the view from the top, though he kept his eyes obstinately cast down so as not to miss any rare plants.

He was almost intoxicated with the wealth of native flora in Tasmania: the snowy, twining *Clematis blanda*, the bells of pink boronia, the yellow banksias, the pink epacris and mauve tetratheca, and above all the dainty orchids.

His hostess was just above him on the slope when he let out a cry, almost a scream of excitement, and pounced. She leapt about two feet in the air and stood clasping her bosom, staring down at him.

'What is it, Mr Hooker? Did I nearly tread on it?'

'Yes, you could have ruined it – a beautiful specimen.'

'*What*! I thought you'd seen a snake!'

'No, it was a new orchid – the one I needed to complete the family. This is really marvellous!' and he held up a small flower for her inspection.

'Well, I'm glad of course ... but really, you did give me a turn! I have a horror of snakes, an absolute phobia. Even the picture of one makes me go cold with horror.'

Then why don't you stay safely in your drawing-room, thought Hooker rather irritably. He hated dancing attendance at Government House, dressing up for dinner-parties and receptions. All the daylight hours he wanted for collecting, and all the evenings for writing up and correlating his finds.

He wrapped the small orchid tenderly in his silk handkerchief to take down to the collecting jars he had left at the bottom of the hill, filled with creek water.

Botany was a passion with Joseph Hooker. He didn't expect to find plant life in Antarctica, except perhaps as lichen on rocks, and beneath the sea; but Van Diemen's Land was a happy hunting-ground, abounding in unknown species and unspoilt since the days of creation.

Afterwards there was a picnic on the lower slopes, the place Lady Franklin had chosen for the museum she proposed building. Young Eleanor took a serious interest in botanizing, gravely examined his finds, and kept bringing him useless specimens of common flowers he had already.

Ross, he noticed, was sitting at the feet of that flirtatious young Miss Cracroft, a sprig of yellow wattle-blossom in his buttonhole, while Crozier was plying her with food. Fools for a pretty face ... He would be more interested in love and so on if the human race had evolved a more dignified form of reproduction, more like that of the bisexual plants, or even by budding. The animal antics imposed on man by nature constituted a rather tasteless joke, he considered.

More than all the social life of Hobart Town, he was looking forward to an excursion with Ronald Gunn, his father's correspondent and collector. Here was a man after his own heart, unattached (though with several children) and with an ardent interest in botany. He was not more than thirty-two or -three, though to young Joseph this was 'getting on'; he was only twenty-three himself. Gunn had

137

sent one of his convict servants to act as guide when he was too occupied with Government business to go himself; but afterwards they'd had the pleasure of studying and classifying in his library the plants found in the field.

To both of them this was the supreme happiness, better even than discovering a new genus. With a newly-collected pile of specimens waiting to be sorted, the *Prodromus Flora Nova Hollandiae* of Robert Brown open on the table, they worked far into the night, comparing, annotating, and arguing in happy companionship.

To Gunn it was as if his dead friend Robert Lawrence had come back; to Joseph Hooker, fresh from months of sailing the barren blue fields of ocean, the richness and strangeness of the Tasmanian flora were almost miraculous. Both were to remember for the rest of their lives those enchanted weeks when they wandered together over mountain and through forest, camping under the brilliant southern stars, or poring over their plants by candlelight.

Generally, Joseph Hooker preferred plants to people. When Lady Franklin had taken him to Port Arthur she had expected him to be interested in the scenery and the convicts – but what really interested him was the chance of gathering *Anopterus glandulosus*.

At the picnic, Frank Crozier had managed to slip a folded paper in to Sophy's hand. He was inarticulate, and appeared more so beside such a vigorous speaker as James Ross, but he had a bulldog perseverance in the face of Sophy's evident lack of response. She had glanced at the paper and coloured a little, however, before slipping it into the roomy pocket of her morning-dress.

When she got home she spread it out to read, and found a verse:

To S –

> Beleeve not what the Landsmen say,
> Who tempt with doubts thy constant Mind;
> They'll tell thee, Sailors when away

In every Port a Mistress find.
    Yes, yes, beleeve them when they tell thee so!
    For thou art Present whereso'er they go.

La! Who would have thought Captain Crozier a poet! But she suspected that the piece was not original, though the spelling certainly was. All the same, he had more in him than met the eye. She wished she could feel more interested, but she had eyes only for James Ross, and today he had been very attentive to her. ...

Like Hooker, he was fascinated with the flowers of the Antipodean spring. 'Your golden wattle!' he had said, turning the little spray he always wore in his coat. 'An amazing tree! It's like an explosion, like a great yellow firework bursting against the blue. I hope we come back again when it's in bloom.'

'Wattle!' said Hooker. *'What'*ll they think of next in nomenclature, I wonder? There's that lovely and unique tree, the eucalyptus – now what could be more euphonious and descriptive? And what is the popular name? Gum! The beautiful little *Bossiaea cordigera* – that's Eggs-and-Bacon! and *Acacia melanoxylon* becomes Black Wattle. An ugly name for a beautiful tree.'

'It seems to be an Australian characteristic,' said Lady Franklin. 'I noticed it on the mainland : fields and meadows become "paddocks", streams are always "creeks", and a small level is usually a "flat" or even a "bottom"; a shallow lake is a "claypan". The harsher word seems to suit the character, or climate, or something.'

'I think,' said John Phillip Gell in his mild, cultured voice, 'that it is more the habit of understatement. A river is just a creek, a plain is only a flat, and a gum is a gum, not any high-sounding botanical specimen, however magnificent a tree in fact. It's all part of the Australian's dislike of "putting on side".'

He enclosed the slang phrase in elaborate verbal quotation marks.

Said Eleanor, greatly daring: 'Yet "billabong" is given, Mamma says, to a small lake, and is quite a euphonious word.'

'Yes, my dear. That is the exception which proves the rule.' Gell smiled indulgently; Eleanor's face became radiant. Jane noticed it, but the unworldly Gell, she was sure, did not. As for Sophy, she had eyes for no one but Ross. The merest child could see which way the wind blew there. She should really have a word with Sophy about it.

Terrestrial magnetism was Ross's special subject. An observatory was being built for him on Mount Nelson, where observations would be made on the astronomical term-day next month. The convict masons detailed for this work seemed almost to be enjoying it. The Governor had talked to them, man to man, telling them how important it was to get the building up quickly. The explorers must check their instruments before they left, and they could not delay once the ice began to break up in the frozen seas to the south.

The building went up at a great rate. Two of the men were marched down to *Erebus* to help bring up the telescope and other equipment; and they had been struck by the portrait of Sir John Franklin in Captain Ross's stateroom.

'La, Jim, 'ere's our Guv'nor!' cried one.

'So 'tis. The spittin' image!' And they both laughed at the strangeness of it.

Before the ships left there was a gay farewell party on board *Erebus*. Sophy was trembling with emotion as she got ready. How did she know that these brave men would ever return from the dangers of being frozen-in in the pack, which they described so light-heartedly?

Jane knew the state she was in, and gave her hand a reassuring squeeze as they mounted the gangplank to the brightly lit deck. The ships were to sail tomorrow, and Ross had made no declaration of his feelings – while Captain Crozier, Sophy feared, was screwing himself up to do so.

140

It was such a cold night that the party was held in the wardroom. Later in the evening they all went along to Ross's stateroom to admire the portrait of Sir John by Negelin. As everyone was crowding out again, remarking on the likeness, James Ross caught Sophy by the hand and drew her back into the room while the others were filing along the narrow alleyway.

'I should like to say goodbye to you here,' he said in a low voice. His brilliant eyes searched hers, and saw the flare of hope in them. 'I shall often think of you here, during the long Polar days,' he said slowly. 'You and all the good friends who have made our stay so happy in Hobart Town. A sailor becomes sentimental about his last port of call before a dangerous voyage, you know. I hope – I hope I have not given you a wrong impression, my dear.'

'I declare I don't know what you can mean, Captain Ross.'

Pride had come to her rescue as her heart sank; her voice was steady, her face cold and still. She looked down, refusing to meet his eyes, afraid he would read the disappointment in her own.

'Then I am mistaken, and I'm thankful to know it. You see ... I have someone waiting for me at home, back in England. I write to her every week, whether the letters can be posted or not. And she has promised to wait for me.'

'She is a fortunate young lady.' Sophy forced herself to look up and smile. She met his gaze steadily. He took her hand and bent over it, feeling its faint tremor.

'This is not goodbye – we shall be back in a year or two at most. Meanwhile, this will remind me of you, and the happy days here, even when it has withered.' He touched the buttonhole of wattle-blossom he always wore.

'Then *au revoir*, and *bon voyage*, Captain Ross.'

'*Au revoir*, Miss Sophy.'

The tears she would rather die than shed in front of him were gathered in a hard, painful knot at the back of her eyes. She went blindly along the alleyway and caught up with the others. In the wardroom Captain Crozier was waiting for her.

'Jupiter is just now rising over the water,' he said. 'You remember we looked at it through the telescope? I thought you might like to see it. I have your wrap.'

He placed her shawl tenderly round her shoulders and led the way up on deck. The great shape of the mountain towered over the ship, blotting out that quarter of the sky.

'You see?' He stood close beside her and pointed to the glowing yellow orb low in the east. She could see his face as a white blur above his dark blue coat and gold epaulettes. Ah, if only this were the other! but *he* had a girl at home, he wrote to her every week. . . .

'Captain Crozier,' she said clearly, 'you are leaving tomorrow on a voyage of some danger; perhaps you may not all return –'

'Oh, come now!' he began to protest.

'You know it is dangerous, that's part of the attraction, isn't it? Well, I am feeling dangerous tonight. Would you like to kiss me, Captain Crozier?'

She heard his just audible gasp, felt him stiffening with shock, recoiling a little, wondering if she had perhaps had too much wine.

But he was not one to miss an opportunity, this bold explorer. In a moment she felt herself grasped in arms like hoops of iron. For a sailor and a man past forty it was not a very expert kiss, but it was fervent.

'Oh, Miss Sophy!' His voice was faint and husky. 'Dearest girl, does this mean you will wait for me? I shall be the happiest of men if – if I can make you mine some day.'

'But it means nothing of the sort. I was just saying goodbye, that is absolutely all.'

'But – but –' He sounded comically bewildered. 'D'you mean you let all the fellows –?'

'Of course not. I'm very *fond* of you, dear Captain Crozier, and I thought perhaps you liked me a little.'

142

'Liked you a little! Oh my stars! I would do anything; you're the most marvellous girl I have ever known.' He tried to take her in his arms again, but she stepped adroitly away.

'Goodbye, and come back to us safely! Now I must go, before my aunt sends after me.' She was calm and unmoved. Her feelings seemed locked in ice.

'No, wait! Please wait!' But she retreated firmly to the companionway and he had to see her down. He went first, then lifted her down the last three steps. His heart beat furiously as he felt her warmth and lightness.

Through three long voyages, two to the Antarctic and one to the opposite end of the earth, he was to have a special affection for that companionway. Years later he was to touch its rail in farewell, before abandoning his ship for ever to the cold embrace of the Arctic pack.

Chapter Eighteen

Mr Gunn's 'friend', Dr von Lottke, had begun to make himself rather unpopular in Hobart Town. He had borrowed from anyone who would lend him money, including Ronald Gunn. Then he set up a so-called museum in the Mechanics' Institute with admission at half a crown each.

Those who paid this large sum to go in were disgusted to find not much more than a trunkful of rubbish: unlabelled bones, the skull of an albatross, some pieces of basalt such as they could pick up any day on Mount Wellington, and a small black snake in a jar of spirits.

His next advertisement in the local Press was for a public lecture on 'Scientific, Geological, Entomological and Ornithological Subjects, with a glance at the Flora and Conchology of Van Diemen's Land.'

By now his reputation as an imposter and literary pirate had spread; his 'audience' rushed the door and got inside without paying. As soon as he began to speak his voice was drowned by a roar of laughter and stamping: boos, catcalls, hisses, and loud cries of 'Dr von Hot-Air! Go home to Germany!'

With the utmost coolness, the big man folded his arms beneath his formidable red beard, and waited for the noise to die down. Then he spread his arms and said blandly, 'Wery vell; I see you an ignorant peoples vos. You do not onderstand dese t'ings. So – I shall valk.' And out he walked, leaving the audience rather stunned.

Ronald Gunn had warned Lady Franklin not to invite him again. He now seemed a person utterly devoid of good moral principles, though such an entertaining fellow. He had been pestering Gunn, to whom he already owed a large sum, for more money to pay his passage home, or to find a buyer for his trashy 'museum'.

His last exploit in Hobart Town had been to supply a tea-chest packed with seeds for a learned German botanist, who had ordered them through a respectable merchant, Mr Orr. Not knowing von Lottke's reputation, Mr Orr had advanced him thirty pounds for expenses. He soon turned up with a carefully packaged chest, secured with ropes and wire. He cautioned against opening it as air would get in and ruin the seeds.

Later Mr Orr received an indignant letter from the recipient in Germany. On unpacking the chest he had found it full of plain sawdust.

Von Lottke was quite unabashed; he even came up to the merchant in the street and offered to shake hands.

'I wonder, sir,' said Mr Orr with dignity, 'that you have the effrontery to speak to me after the deception you practised.'

'Vot deception?'

'Filling that chest with sawdust instead of seeds.'

'But, sir, you haf the money back vich you haf to me gifen?'

'Yes, but my client –!'

'Ach, so! Dot doosenmatter; you haf nodings lost. Goot morning!'

No one lamented his going when the 'doctor' finally set off for London. Gunn wrote to Sir William Hooker, fearing that von Lottke might use his name as an introduction: 'Be careful of him, and his writings. He is, I fear, nothing but a Black Sheep in a red Beard.'

Lady Franklin's famous iron bedstead, which could be easily dismantled and set up again by loosening or tightening a few nuts, was cleated down to the floor of the *Abeona's* hold. It could not move, in spite of the movement of the ship – though this was lively enough – in the violent cross-seas of Bass Strait.

Both Eleanor, in the lower bunk opposite, and Stewart, in the upper, were very seasick. Mr Bagot and Mr Gell were more comfortably accommodated in the Captain's cabin.

The schooner, of only a hundred tons' burden, had been chartered by Jane for the voyage to South Australia, where Mr Gell's brother was private secretary to Governor Gawler. He had written to say that Lady Franklin proposed accompanying him, and Jane had written personally to Gawler, though so far she'd had no reply.

Though the hatch-cover was left off for ventilation, the hold – the only space available for the ladies – had a musty, fusty, cockroach smell. On the first night, bugs came out of every crevice after dark. Between their attentions and the moans and groans and retchings of Eleanor and Stewart, Jane slept not a wink.

On the second night she decided to let the bugs have the bed, which was fixed against the cracked and infested wall. She made up a bed on the cleaner-looking floor, and got to sleep. Some time in the night she woke with a scream, feeling an animal as big as a dog walking over her; but on making light found it was a huge rat, one of the many scuttling everywhere away from the light.

The deck was too wet with spray for sleeping on. With a shudder, Jane went back to the bed, and the next night it rained in torrents. Water cascaded into the hold and soaked the bedding. She sat all night on the dry end of the bed, and as a final misery developed toothache.

'Oh, why do I do these things?' she moaned. 'Why don't I stay home in comfort, like other women?'

Yet next day the sun shone; and reclining on a kangaroo-skin rug on deck, eating cold roast goose and watching King Island and the low coast of the Port Phillip colony go slowly past, she felt her spirits lift and sing with the wind in the rigging.

She was so looking forward to meeting Colonel and Mrs Gawler, who were described as a pious and upright couple; though she wished he had been a naval rather than a military officer.

146

The voyage was taking longer than expected, for Captain Blackbourne's was a scratch crew and seemed to know very little about working the ship. It looked as if they might not arrive until just before Christmas (which might be awkward) though they had sailed on the thirteenth. The load of gooseberries from the Huon Valley was beginning to rot in the after-hatch. It was as well she had made Eleanor bring her lesson-books; it gave them both something to do. Life would never be long enough for her to see and learn and know half the exciting things in the world ... She entered up her diary with seamanlike precision:

Sunday 20 Dec. King Island bore W. $\frac{1}{2}$N. Read Lesson at Evening Service, the Parable of the Sower. Sky clear, wind S.S.W.

Eleanor was not so pleased about the lesson books – after all, this was supposed to be a holiday. At least, though, she had stopped being seasick, and she was delighted that Mamma had chosen her to be her companion. She had Mamma all to herself, no Sophy, no Mathinna to divide her attention. And Mr Gell was such an amusing, good-tempered, easy-going person that all must go well.

Sophy had been very hard to get on with lately; snappish and irritable, and inclined to mope in her room. On the day that *Erebus* and *Terror* sailed they had walked together to the Signal Station at Battery Point to wave goodbye as the ships rounded Sandy Bay Point with all sails set, and disappeared perhaps for ever.

'I pray those brave men have not gone to their deaths,' she said piously, when Sophy rounded on her and called her morbid. She then walked off home at such a rate that Eleanor could scarcely keep up with her.

Captain Ross had been wearing his usual sprig of wattle, and was in high spirits at the start of this final leg of his expedition; but Captain Crozier seemed rather cast down. Papa had been down at the Cove landing to see them off, but poor Mamma was in bed sick, worn out with entertaining the officers. This voyage, Eleanor hoped, would do her good.

Sir John, left at home while his friends sailed off to the far south and his wife to the north, was filled with restlessness, a longing for the uncomplicated life on board ship, where everyone had his place and his fixed duty, and to disobey a commander's orders was mutiny.

He had watched Ross and Crozier make their final preparations for departure with envious eyes. Ah, how he would like to be going on another expedition to the lands of ice and snow! Yes, even if it means living on lichen again, what the French Canadians called *tripe de roche*, with boiled shoes and burnt reindeer bones for dessert. Frostbite and hunger were nothing to the cold malevolence of the political factions in Van Diemen's Land and the cowardly Press which supported them.

At sea he'd never had any trouble making decisions over things like shortening sail or gaining an offing from a lee shore, but in the affairs of Government he was tormented by doubts over whether some action was for the best. And Jane, bless her, was so definite in her views, and always urging him to do this or that before he had properly considered the matter! She had excellent judgement for a woman, but it was the nature of women to let emotion rule their intellect, however bright.

The continual criticism in the newspapers was beginning to worry her, and she was not well. If it were not so far he would send her home to London for a spell. He was glad she was going to South Australia, the land he had seen as a midshipman with Flinders, and which had first filled him with the urge to be an explorer.

Ross would be sure to discover some more territory for the Queen in the Antarctic, even if it should never prove of any practical use. Oh, for the empty uncomplicated wastes about the Pole!

Tired out with the emotions of the day, he went to bed

early and some time towards morning had a most vivid dream. He was back on the shore of the Arctic Ocean. Or perhaps it was the Antarctic? For the ship was not *Trent*, it seemed rather to be *Erebus*, one of the ships he had just farewelled. They were in company with another vessel, both held perfectly motionless among the pack; yet all the time the roaring of waves on the outer edge of the pack-ice showed that farther out a heavy sea was running.

He stood looking up at the sky with a feeling of awe. Overhead the vane at the masthead scarcely moved. The sky above it showed the unnatural clearness of a calm and silvery atmosphere, but towards the horizon it was bounded by a dark hard line of sullen cloud. There was not the faintest movement of the ship, no creak of timbers, only the silent tightening of that fearful icy grasp: a grasp which might crush the vessels' sides as he had often crushed a walnut in the nutcrackers when the port circulated after a formal dinner.

He walked to the side and looked down at the frozen sea: not smooth, but piled in broken jagged hunks all congealed together in confusion. Gradually he became conscious of a lightening of the air, a faint pink glow; and looking up was amazed to see the beautiful mackerel sky which often presaged the return of the sun.

Then, how it happened he did not know, he was in a small open boat with Frank Crozier, exploring along a great wall of ice.

They were making for a deep cavern, mysteriously blue and chill, in the foot of a berg as big as an island, when a terrible rumbling thunder began. Even as they looked an immense piece of ice broke off and slid down two hundred feet into the sea. Cracks and growls and grinding noises were followed by an enormous splash, as the new berg disappeared a moment beneath the sea, then came plunging and labouring to the surface, pouring water from every crevice.

He tried to row, but the boat seemed glued to the sea. He

could only wait helplessly for the tremendous wave which presently rose and dashed them away to oblivion. . . .

He woke sweating, still making futile rowing motions with his arms. The rending noise of the calving berg yet sounded in his ears. Then he heard the tail-end of the thunderclap which had woken him.

Yes, surely it was *Erebus* he had dreamed of in the freezing grip of the pack. He could still feel the uncanny sense of that silent, menacing sky, that distant roar of the waves in the midst of silence and stillness.

Odd that he should dream he was with Crozier! He remembered now an experience with Davy Buchan of the *Dorothea*, when the ship's boat had been swept on shore by just such a wave. But that was twenty years ago . . . Was it a bad omen for Crozier and Ross? He hoped all was well with the two ships in those dangerous high latitudes, those notoriously storm-tossed Antarctic seas.

The thunder sounded again, farther away; then a heavy shower descended, drumming on roof and windows. He lay awake listening in the dark until the whole world seemed to be drowning and dissolving in that pouring flood.

The *Abeona* tied up at Port Adelaide on Christmas Day, at six o'clock in the morning. Eleanor dragged Captain Bagot down to the wharf in her excitement, for the *Cygnet* had just come in with a monster shark, eleven feet long; she thought it must be what a whale would look like, the one that swallowed Jonah, but Mr Bagot said a whale would make the shark look small.

Jane sat on the shaded side of the deck, away from the wharf, feeling numb with distress. A letter from Colonel Gawler was in her hand.

Chapter Nineteen

Eleanor and Lady Franklin, attended by Mr Bagot, sat waiting in the Customs shed at Port Adelaide, the only shelter available. They had been waiting for nearly two hours, feeling the dry burning heat strike upward from the earthen floor. Sandflies and day-biting mosquitoes attacked them, while the imperturbable Stewart dozed on a bench in the corner. The Port River smelt of mud and tidal water.

Jane had been looking forward to dry land after the discomforts of the *Abeona*'s hold, but now, if it had been possible, she would have gone back on board and sailed away. She had been mortified to receive a note from Colonel Gawler to the effect that he had just this morning got her letter confirming that she was coming. He welcomed her to the Province, said he would of course provide what accommodation he could, but Government House was not yet finished and Mrs Gawler had just been confined.

It was embarrassing, to say the least. Mr Gell set off on horseback for the city seven miles away to find out what other arrangements could be made, and to send a carriage or a spring-cart to collect them. Before he could do so Colonel Gawler arrived in his own gig. He was small, dark, impeccably dressed in a hot military uniform, and formal in his manners.

He offered Lady Franklin a dignified welcome, an apology for his tardy arrival, and his arm to assist her into the gig.

She began to protest her distress at causing him inconvenience, her willingness to make other arrangements; but he insisted that *of course* she must stay at Government House. He began to grow agitated in his turn, while they both perspired in the heat.

His firm lips quivered as he assured her, 'It is quite all

151

right, Lady Franklin. Mrs Gawler has already removed from the spare room where she was lying; it is being prepared for Your Ladyship's reception at this moment –'

'Removed! She had to get up from her bed! And she was confined, *when*?'

There was complete silence for a few moments. Jane wondered if she had committed an impropriety in the eyes of this stern-looking Governor. At last he said, 'Two days ago, Lady Franklin.'

'Oh, the poor woman! If I had only known –! I cannot conceive how my letter was so delayed.' She turned away, hiding her face with her bonnet to conceal the tears in her eyes. Her voice trembled. Gawler's silence made her feel worse. She had not yet got used to his habit of thinking deeply before opening his mouth. At last he said impressively:

'My dear Lady Franklin, do not distress yourself, I beg you! We are delighted to have you visit our Province, both for your own sake and that of your distinguished husband. It's an honour, not an inconvenience, I assure you. My eldest daughter is quite able to take over her mother's duties as hostess.'

'I confess I had not realized ... In Hobarton, you see, we often have fifty or sixty callers in a day, and rarely less than three or four house guests staying at Government House, so that one more or less makes little difference.'

Colonel Gawler smiled a little grimly. It was certainly different in Adelaide; ships from Sydney and Van Diemen's Land by-passed them on the way to England, and the overland route was scarcely open yet. 'We don't get many visitors here,' he said. 'And until recently I and my family, my secretary and my servants, were living in a mud hut.'

'Good gracious! I nearly descended on you a year ago, but they wouldn't let me come overland from Victoria. I hope, Colonel Gawler, you're not going to stop me from exploring on the ground that it is *dangerous* or *difficult*. I find that when a man says something is "impossible" for me, he

152

usually means merely uncomfortable. And I can stand any amount of discomfort.'

'I am relieved indeed to hear it. I fear you will find plenty of that commodity in Adelaide.'

As they drove towards the blue hills that lay behind the town, Jane looked about her with lively curiosity. That slightly higher peak must be Flinders' Mount Lofty – she would climb that first of all. North Adelaide, on a slight rise, gave a view of the town.

Jane decided to withhold her first impression from Governor Gawler. Adelaide appeared to her no more than a straggling village lost in the bush.

There were not two houses opposite each other along the wide dusty streets, and the Torrens could scarcely be called a river. It was a mere chain of water-holes linked by a trickle, and crossed by a wooden bridge.

'Somehow it all seems so different from what I imagined,' she said, looking at the stumps of gum trees in the dry-looking 'parklands'. Adelaide had a very temporary look indeed, and was monotonously flat and square after Hobarton. And were these the grounds of Government House! – another open tract of bushland, with a winding path from a gateway marked by a red flag with a white coronet in the corner. The two-storied building was no more than half finished.

The eldest Miss Gawler welcomed them graciously, smoothing over the awkwardness of arrival. She was very little older than Eleanor, Jane noticed with surprise, but had been much more brought forward, in the manner of colonial-born girls.

Dinner consisted of a bit of left-over beef and hot bacon, Christmas notwithstanding. In the morning the Governor took her to the Survey Office to look at maps and meet Mr Frome, who was bidden to a dinner-party that night, with Captain and Mrs Sturt and Mr Jackson.

Frome was an odd-looking person with drooping eyes, but Jane always got on well with surveyors and explorers.

At the dinner she enjoyed talking with tired, blind-looking Captain Sturt, telling him about their Tasmanian Natural History Society. Then Mr Jackson engaged her in conversation.

'Are you not surprised at Adelaide, Lady Franklin?' he asked importantly.

'Surprised? Er – in what respect?' she asked carefully.

'Why, at its size!'

'Well, I am surprised,' she said, 'at its extent, that is the extent of its *surface*. But I had expected to see more of a town. Melbourne two years ago was more of a town than Adelaide.'

Colonel Gawler coughed, Captain Sturt and Mr Frome smiled ironically, and Mr Jackson made an irritable movement, spilling his wine. 'Really! Melbourne! I would not have thought so,' he muttered.

Oh dear! thought Jane, she had been warned by Sir J. that Sydney people were jealous of Hobart Town; and of course Adelaide people were jealous of Melbourne. They were all so touchy on the mainland!

Meanwhile the Governor's servants had brought an opened bottle of wine to the table, which had to be sent away; a footman had tipped the dinner platter so that gravy was spilled on the Governor's collar; another set down a jug of whipped cream with such a bang that the contents flew up in his face. But Colonel Gawler sat immovably correct, his heavy brows unlifted, his mouth straight and firm, appearing not to mind. Ever a student of human nature, Jane found him a fascinating subject.

To placate Mr Jackson she said, 'I like the idea of firing a gun at noon. Everyone can hear it, without needing to see the town clock.'

'It would be of little use if they could,' said Frome drily. 'The clock hasn't worked for six months because there's an argument over who should keep it going.'

Really, it was hard to find a safe subject for conversation! She turned to Captain Sturt and asked him about Norfolk

154

Island, where he had once helped to put down a convict rebellion. He seemed inclined to think that Maconachie would not last there for long.

Eleanor wrote in her diary:

Today we made an excursion to the top of Mt. Lofty ... The view is beautiful from the summit of the plains spread out below, smoky with fires. We had dinner at an Inn – clean and comfortable. Very stiff and sunburnt after the ride. Mamma had Miss G's pony ...

Jane had brought back some quartz rocks from the summit, milky-white and crystal-hard. She added them to her other acquisitions, some dried plants and a small water-colour of Holdfast Bay by Mary Hindmarsh, who had come out from England in the same ship with Alfred Stephen; he had encouraged her sketching.

And how, wondered Jane, was Mr Stephen settling down in Sydney? He had seemed much more composed when she saw him there, but she'd had little time for him; a new star had risen in her sky.

Count Paul Edward de Strzelecki, 'a Polish nobleman of high Family', as she wrote enthusiastically to Mary, was a frequent visitor at Government House where she was guest of honour. He had made himself entirely charming, kissing her hand with courteous grace, always respectful yet subtly conveying that he would, in other circumstances, have wished to kiss more than her hand.

His accent was fascinating, his manners were impeccable, and his face had that rugged strength, that air of decision of the outdoor man of action, which had always attracted her more than mere drawing-room good looks. He was already *persona grata* among the older colonial families, the new aristocracy of the settlement, the Macarthurs and the Kings. He had promised to visit Van Diemen's Land before long, and she had assured him of Sir John's welcome.

Colonel Gawler was a very different type of man: more reserved, even stiff in his manner, but with an innate dignity and transparent integrity about him. He had told her he'd never heard of South Australia until three weeks before setting out. Then, wanting work, he applied for the position of Governor of the advertised Province. Only then he looked up its position on the map.

He must often wish himself away again. The climate was very disagreeable; the nights too hot for sleeping, hot winds laden with dust scorching the plain by day.

Yet beyond the mountains, she had heard, the air was most pure and beautiful. Mr Frome had promised to take her down to see the mouth of the Murray beyond Encounter Bay where Matthew Flinders (and Sir John as midshipman) had met the Frenchmen. Then she was off to Port Lincoln in the *Abeona* to find a site for a monument to Flinders overlooking the harbour he had discovered. Nothing would please Sir John more than this honour to his old commander. He had been only about fourteen years old when the *Investigator* was there, in 1802. To the people of South Australia this seemed like ancient history. They'd looked almost incredulous when Eleanor remarked that her Papa was the first to unfurl the British flag in this part of the world.

She sat down to write the day's entry in her journal:

7 Jan. 1841. Gov. House is full of boys and the air is dusty, the day wretchedly hot. Freddy is ill with the heat, ditto Mrs Gawler, and an ill-starred child is going up and down the house with bad eyes and nothing to do – but what does all this signify to the Gov.? He reigns calmly over the puzzling affairs of this puffing Province, tho' is reduced to hunting bugs to secure himself a night's rest ... Adelaide is a most disagreeable place; all the so-called streets are mere imaginary spaces of trodden grass or mud or a tract of bare sand and dust scattered with trees. The flagstaff in front of Gov. House is a very useful landmark in this half-reclaimed bushland.

Meanwhile George Gawler was visiting his sick wife. The

new baby squalled in its cradle, until he called the nurse to come and carry it round. He was not particularly interested in the child – it was his sixth – but he was worried about his wife's health.

He had just received, too, a letter from the South Australian Company officials in London, reprimanding him for his expenditure on public works, and threatening to dishonour his bills. However, he was still outwardly calm as he kissed Maria's damp brow and asked how she did.

'It's the heat,' she said listlessly. 'Lying in bed makes me so hot, yet I am too weak to get up.'

'You must not get up. Everything is going on very well without you, my dear wife.'

'You are so good!' Tears of weakness stood in her eyes. 'And you have all the worry of Lady F.'s visit. I really must summon the strength to receive her before she goes, yet I dread it. She's so learned, so famous –'

'My dear, you don't need to dread it. She is one of the most amiable, unassuming persons I ever met, and if her stockings are rather blue, her petticoats hide them. She's very little trouble, out exploring and investigating most of the time, and leaving on another expedition tomorrow. I've never seen anyone so eager in gathering information. Mr Frome says she asks very intelligent questions for a female.'

This was such a long speech for Colonel Gawler that his wife looked at him in surprise. He must indeed be impressed with the lady! She felt some curiosity herself, and wished she might soon feel stronger.

Chapter Twenty

There was consternation at Government House, Hobart Town. Mathinna had run away, back to the bush. 'Soapy' had been preoccupied and cross; Miss Williamson with Eleanor away was having a well-earned holiday, lying in bed and reading novels; and Marie, the French maid, had been unkind to her, and had chased her possum away because he wet the carpet.

Mathinna felt that all her friends had deserted her. The Sir-Guberna, though always kind, was busy all day and night in his 'oppiss' where she was not allowed to go. The white people were all very fond of this business of writing.

'What por?' she had once asked, puzzled, as she stood beside Lady-Mumma's desk and watched the little black words climb off the end of the writing-feather and spread themselves evenly along the white stuff called paper.

'What for what, little one?'

'What por all-a-time ri-ut, ri-ut, ri-ut? Like-it this!' And she bent over and scrabbled furiously with her hand across the desk.

The Lady-Mumma had laughed, and said she was writing up her journal, so that when she wanted to remember what happened on any day, it might be ten years ago, she could look in her journal and there it was. 'You know how to read, Mathinna. Well, if there was no writing, there would be nothing to read.'

Mathinna had since learned to write, but didn't like it much. Now there was no one with time or patience to answer her questions. She wandered, disconsolate and bored, about the great house with its forty rooms which to her were forty prisons.

So she had made up her mind to 'go walkabout' in the bush. None of her people ever showed any foresight in the

158

matter of tomorrow's provisions. Mathinna set off with an apple in one hand and a few biscuits in the other. The blanket from her bed was draped round her shoulders, as once she had worn her skin cloak. She had become used to blankets. Though it was now the middle of summer the nights could be bitterly cold.

She made her way first to the fern-tree glade in Lenah Valley, scene of many picnics with the Government House party. There she spent a happy day in the open air, tracking lizards, chasing moths, chewing young fern-tree shoots and digging the soft pith from a fallen stem with a sharp stone, and spitting out the fibres after she had extracted the sweet juice.

Later, when the heat of the day had passed, she climbed from the cool green valley with its arching roof of feathery boughs, and on the sun-scorched rocky hill looked for the little berries of the pig-face which grew there, and so made her dessert.

A clear stream tinkled through the valley with its dwindled summer voice, as it fell in crystal threads from pool to pool. She climbed down again to get a drink where plaques of sunlight were spread by rays falling through the green roof, or were reflected back from the water in a shimmer of gold.

Mathinna stayed in the valley, curled in her blanket, till morning. She had forgotten to bring a tinder-box and did not know how to make fire, so she was both cold and frightened of Ragearoppa, that bad debbil who walked by night and carried off little girls to his cave of thunder. She curled up in a tight ball and pulled the blanket over her head.

In the morning it was wonderful to wake up in the fresh air, with birds beginning their dawn chorus, the magpies carolling in notes as clear as the frail blue of the sky. When she went up the hill a flock of black cockatoos with yellow-banded tails were quarrelling there, like old men of the tribe painted for a corroboree.

Except for the birds and beasts the bush was empty. No dark figures among the trees, no happy laughter sounded from lubras' throats, no boys played with their throwing-sticks, with tree-trunks for targets, at hunt-the-wallaby.

She had almost forgotten her people, the singing round the fires at night, the feasts of baked shellfish when they went down to the coast. But young as she was, she felt the ghosts of the vanished dark people all about her. As she skipped from stone to stone (happy to have left behind those red stockings and black shoes which made her feet sore) her quick dark eyes noticed everything the surface of the ground had to tell her of the passage of animals small and large.

There, in the moist sand beside the stream as she followed it upwards, was the neat track of a spotted cat. Mathinna wished she still had her pet possum for company, but Marie had driven it away. She was beginning to feel lonely, to think of Gub'mint House as a happy place where there had been someone to talk to. Perhaps by tomorrow the Lady-Mumma would have come back. She had promised to come back.

Mathinna had long since shed her encumbering dress. She had hung it somewhere on a twig and forgotten it. Her restricting pantettes of white madapalam, kept up by buttons on a white bodice, followed the dress; then the petticoat went, with its rows and rows of small tucks round the hem. Now she wore only her shift, for she had grown used to some covering over her chest and felt cold without it. The blanket from her bed she rolled up and hung round her neck like a collar.

She ate some of the frilled, honeycombed cyttaria growing on a little stem on the trunks of the myrtles. She dug round the roots of the gum-trees for another fungus which she remembered – or had someone shown her since? – that her people used to eat, and that the white-men called 'native bread'. It was the wrong time of the year; the ground was bone dry, and the few pieces she found were tough and withered. She washed them down with a draught of cool

160

creek water. The water tasted of rocks, of grass and leaves, of the sky from which it fell. It was 'open air' water, quite unlike the dead stuff she drank at home, long stored in tanks and cisterns.

Lady Franklin made a note in her journal about the first bull-roarer she had ever heard – 'a thing kept secret from the boys and women, a piece of bark attached to a string, and whirled round and round to make a humming sound'.

She had given sugar-plums to the natives who came round every day for their rations, noting their different physique from the Tasmanians', their straighter hair and taller build. She had seen more natives on the way to the mouth of the Murray, where Gell and Bagot swam in the fresh water but did not attempt to cross, for the post commemorating the spearing of Captain Barker could be seen quite clearly on the far side. They had also seen on the way the grave of Captain Blenkinsopp, who had been drowned in those tremendous breakers beyond the mouth.

Leaving Adelaide without regret, she felt that it was most unsuited (with its lack of good harbours and its dreadful climate) to be the scene of the experiment the South Australian Commissioners were trying there : that of transferring a civilized, free community to these wild Antipodean shores. It was likely, she felt, to remain a bush settlement for ever. Certainly it would never be a great city.

At Holdfast Bay the *Abeona* danced high out of the water, for she had taken on no cargo to replace the Huon gooseberries. It was not an easy climb up the tall ship's side, but rope-ladders held no terrors for Jane – forty-nine this year, but still as active as a girl.

'I'm sorry it's such a climb,' she told Mr Frome, who escorted her on deck. 'But you see, having got rid of our cargo of rotten gooseberries, we couldn't find anything to take away in their place.'

Frome gave her a droll look of reproach; they were good friends since the expedition to the south. 'That's the severest thing I've yet heard you say about our province, ma'am,' he drawled.

'O dear!' Jane began to laugh. 'I have been saying the wrong thing ever since I arrived. What I *meant* was, after all the gooseberries were *rotten*, and we couldn't find anything bad enough to equal them. And just look at all the purchases I've made in your shops.'

Smiling, the long-faced, long-legged surveyor climbed down the ladder. The representatives of South Australia sailed away in their little sloop, waving their hats, and the *Abeona* weighed anchor for Port Lincoln.

As the Mount Lofty ranges, indigo-blue in the heat, faded farther back into the distance, Jane sat writing up her journal on a sheltered part of the deck. The sun shone brilliantly, the sky was flawless, the land beckoning and mysterious. She could imagine Flinders charting this coast with his usual thoroughness – though he had missed the entrance to Port Adelaide – and the young midshipman Franklin, already deciding to be an explorer.

She looked tranquilly at the distant summit of Mount Lofty. That was one more mountain she had collected. And over there lay Kangaroo Island, spread along the southern horizon; she must go there too on the way back. They would not be returning to Adelaide.

She was rather relieved at this. Her departure had been a nervous affair. Colonel Gawler she found singular and interesting, but she could never feel at ease with him. It was surprising to find such a man in charge of the South Australian experiment. There was something about his set, energetic, mournful face that moved her; she hoped he would find a solution to all the difficulties he had hinted at, including an insolent, carping Press.

She had been saddened to find that even on the mainland of Australia, that 'land of simplicity and peace', there were the same feuds and petty discords as in Van Diemen's Land.

At Hobart a search-party had been organized by the Con-

162

stable of the Yard, John Hepburn. He knew how fond Lady Franklin was of Mathinna, and Sir John had urged him to take all the men he needed. They were all 'trusties': ticket-of-leave gardeners or assigned servants. They intended to beat the bush all the way from the Derwent to the upper crown of Mount Wellington.

The commandant of the military forces also sent out a party, accoutred in full uniform. The unfortunate soldiers in their red tunics and white bandoliers were extremely uncomfortable in the heat. They were soon, all of them, in a thoroughly bad temper. Sent out to look for a runaway black, an 'abo' kid who was probably more at home in the bush than she was at Government House! It was a lot of fuss, they thought, about nothing, and they were the ones to suffer.

Eleanor sat on the deck of the *Abeona* watching her mamma sketch the rugged outlines of the Althorpes as they passed those islands for the second time. She wished that she had a talent for sketching. With a sigh she took out her journal and began bringing her South Australian impressions up to date. 'Col. Gawler is a little dark man but with gentlemanly manners. He weighs every word he utters. Miss G. plays the harp and piano. She is tall and nice looking,' wrote Eleanor (who would have liked to be tall and nicer-looking).

'I wonder how Miss Williamson is getting on with only Mathinna to teach,' she said aloud.

'I don't know, dear, I'm sure.' Jane's voice was abstracted. She was relaxed in complete enjoyment of the hour: the sunny afternoon, the dark blue sea, the fabled coast of the South Land off to starboard: that coast which had been the last to reveal itself to the discoverers of *Terra Australis*. She was following in her husband's wake. Away to the south-east the stony ramparts of Kangaroo Island loomed up, like the flat-topped walls of an enormous gaol. She had asked Captain Blackbourne to call at Kingscote. He was a most obliging man, a Lincolnshire lad like Sir John, and had himself carried the heavy box with the azimuth compass to the top of Stamford Hill at Port Lincoln, for fixing the position for the monument. She had paid in advance for an inscribed obelisk in the local stone. Then she paid out five golden guineas and made Sir John possessor of half an acre of South Australia, the land of his earliest exploits (for nearby, at Memory Cove, he had taken the chance of unfurling the Union Jack while searching for survivors). Providence moved, indeed, in a mysterious way. A young friend of his, another midshipman, had been chosen to go in the boat that was swamped; and so John Franklin survived to become a famous explorer in his turn, preserved for what different death, in what colder seas? Somehow she felt sure he was destined not to die tamely in his bed like lesser men.

Mathinna had moved each day farther up the mountain. The soldiers had beaten the scrub from the Organ Pipes downward, on the first day of their search. Her white bodice was dingy from sleeping on the ground by then, and she had easily slipped between their ranks. The terrain was too rough, with its gullies and ridges and great grey fallen trunks of peppermint and blue-gum, for an orderly search.

She liked the feeling of freedom which the height and the view over town and harbour gave her from the top of one of the great square boulders of basalt fallen from the rocky bastion.

The party under Hepburn were more likely to have found her, as there were several bushmen among them; but they had confined themselves to the upper reaches of the Sassafras Valley and the Cascades, knowing she would keep near water. They had found her clothes, and signs of a night's camp, but that was all.

Looking out of the upstairs windows of his dressing-room towards the mountain, where the foothills were beginning to be dotted here and there with the homes of settlers and orchardists, Sir John saw a brilliant gush of flame. The smoke billowing above it was ruddy with the fire's reflection. Could it be a house on fire?

He'd had a tiring day. As his valet helped him off with his uniform jacket he rubbed his broad shoulders and thanked God there was no one coming to dinner tonight, and no one staying in the house for once. If Jane had been here to share a tête-à-tête meal with him upstairs, he would have been quite content.

Jane ... But he had not told her yet about Mathinna. She had disappeared in the bush as completely as an opossum or a kangaroo. If there were only some of her own people available, they could probably have tracked her. But for a white to find an Aboriginal in the bush when he didn't wish to be seen was almost impossible – hadn't Arthur wasted thousands of pounds proving it in the abortive 'Black War'?

He shrugged on his velvet jacket with an irritable movement, and took a pinch of snuff. Things always went wrong when Jane was away. Still, he was delighted with her idea of setting up a monument in his name to Matthew Flinders. That she would carry it through with her usual style he had no doubt. Just let the South Australian authorities try to stop her!

He smiled to himself, beginning to feel better. He could just imagine her, listening to their objections with the greatest good humour, and then with one of her sweetest smiles and sharp remarks demolishing them utterly.

'A bush fire, Your Excellency – and a big one!'

What? What was the man talking about? 'Oh, ah! A bush fire on the mountain, eh?' He strolled back to the window and saw that the fire had topped a small rise that hid it before; it now glowed and flickered in a great arc of flame. The front was moving diagonally along the mountain, seeming to crawl at that distance; but in fact it was leaping through the thick undergrowth and up to the tree-tops filled with volatile oil, roaring and devouring like a savage lion which drove the timid bush creatures ahead of it, confused with its smoky breath.

Gentle wallabies, kangaroos and opossums – and of course, Mathinna! Sir John was not given to a belief in intuition or psychic intimations, but he suddenly felt certain that Mathinna was on the mountain, and that she was in danger, somewhere in the path of the fire. She was such a *little* girl – not more than five or six, unless she was very small for her age.

He rang the bell for his orderly. 'Send for Colonel Elliott. I want the military turned out at once to fight that fire in the hills.'

He was justified, surely, if there was a chance of saving a human life. And there was the magnetic station at the Rossbank Observatory on Mount Nelson that might be endangered – his nephew Henry Kay and several naval men had been left behind to man it.

The mere fact of the Navy being here gave him new strength to fight his enemies. It was partly being a naval officer on a military station that had led to all the trouble.

Mathinna amused herself counting berries as she ate them: 'Wu-un, two, t'ree, por, pagunta ...' Miss Williamson had despaired of getting her to count correctly. After four she said 'pagunta', which meant not five, but many, or plenty. It seemed to her unnecessarily fussy to go on counting in ones when you got past four.

She had made a wreath for her dark curls of the white clematis which festooned the bushes and smaller trees with starry flowers. Her hair, glossy and attractive now that it was kept washed and brushed by the nursery-maid, grew in short curls close to her head.

(Eleanor's long, fair, straight locks fascinated her; she would creep up and stroke them until Eleanor, who hated anyone to touch her hair, became aware of what she was doing and jerked her head away.)

Mathinna had trimmed her own hair with Lady Franklin's gold-plated scissors. Having read the work of Péron on Tasmanian Aboriginal customs, she did not reprove Math-

166

inna, but marvelled rather at this evidence of racial instinct, for the Tasmanian women had always kept their hair short with sharp shells or stones.

Mathinna had spent her second night in a hollow, burned-out tree, curled in her blanket and tolerably warm.

The last night, spent at the two-thousand foot level, had been bitterly cold towards morning, even though the sun was hot long before midday. As evening came on Mathinna began to think again about going back, though she had watched each day for the small ship in which the Lady-Mumma and Eleanora sailed away, and it had not returned.

She was happy and contented all day long, but each day as the sun sank down and the long shadow of the mountain stretched out across the harbour, she felt her spirits sink too; the darkness was sad and lonely, full of strange terrors, spirit-people and debbils. Also she was becoming hungry for white-feller tucker, for sweet 'biscotty' and tea with sugar. The ants' eggs she had dug up with a broken stick (some faint memory of going with her mother on an expedition to find ant eggs had come back to her) were tasty, but roots of the elephant-grass, though sweet and refreshing to chew, left her feeling unsatisfied and rather sick.

The ground, the scrub, was intensely dry up here; in the clear January weather with its strong drying breezes there was no dew even in the early morning. Searching with her long-sighted eyes, she had seen a spring coming out at the base of the great cliff of basalt which formed the top section of the mountain, and she decided to camp under that cliff tonight, in one of the natural clefts now filling with evening shadows. There would be cress and fern-roots to eat there, too.

She had never taken to shoes except for short periods. Her hard-soled little feet stepped lightly over the rocks and pebbles, fallen boughs and grisp curling bark, prickly shrubs and paper-dry grasses. She stopped suddenly with her nose lifted like an animal's, her eyes searching for some-

167

thing ... Smoke. It was rising from the next gully round the shoulder of the mountain. A camp-fire lit by some wanderer like herself? Suddenly she stepped into the open, her small figure rigid with dismay.

This was no camp-fire! Hidden in the hollow of the gully, a raging bush-fire had begun, and was rapidly driving towards her in front of the steady breeze from the harbour.

Mathinna paused undecided for a moment. Should she run down towards the fire and try to skirt it before it became too big? Or move ahead of it, traversing upward towards the spring where there must be moisture and greenery to arrest its progress? She decided to move upward, following her original plan, and trust that the breeze would drop with darkness and the fire die down or circle round her harmlessly.

By the time she had reached the stone bastion she was tired and thirsty. She dropped full-length to drink at the small stream of limp, ice-cold water issuing from the rocks. Beyond it was a hollow cave, but it was shallow and dry scrub grew right in its entrance, which was filled with an inflammable heap of leaves and debris. No place to sleep if the fire should come this far.

Below her the lights of Hobart Town were beginning to twinkle out through the twilight; the wind-ruffled, white-crested harbour was fading from sight. A lighted ferry moved across the water.

The breeze, instead of dropping with evening, usually increased in Hobart Town at this time of the year. Tonight was no exception. She wrapped herself in the blanket as a gust of cool air from the water came rushing up the side of the mountain to take the place of the hot air rising above the bush-fire.

With it came an acrid smell of smoke and the sound of crackling, increasing to a muted roar as a ridge of sun-dried brush burst into flame.

Mathinna began to be afraid. She sniffed the smoke and

168

trembled like a terrified horse. It was too late to run downwards, to try to skirt the edge of the fire, now coming up the ridge in a great semi-circle. Behind her the unclimbable wall of the mountain, in front an advancing wall of flame.... Soon she would be dead, 'pinished'.

She must get away from the rocky wall before she was baked there like a lizard in the ashes. The stream from the spring dropped over a little waterfall, then formed a small pool, then another tiny fall. She hurried down along it, her eyes rolling fearfully, looking for a larger pool which might be fringed with green rushes and moss, where perhaps she could lie up and let the fire pass overhead. It was just as well she had the blanket. She trailed it in the water, soaking the wool until it was heavy and wet. Already she could feel the hot up-draught in front of the flames. Their roar filled her ears like the angry voice of Ragearoppa; their heat burned her face like his scorching breath.

Chapter Twenty-one

The soldiers of the 51st Regiment of Foot were drawn up at the bottom of the gully. Above them the fire raced away towards the top of the mountain. To fight it was obviously impossible; there was no hope of stopping it now the wind had got up, and it was foolish to have sent them to try. They scowled and muttered; they wanted their tea. The little black girl would have perished before this anyway, five days in the bush already with nothing to eat. They waited for their officer to march them home to the barracks.

Meanwhile Sir John paced up and down his room upstairs, going over to the windows every now and then to look at the brightening line of fire creeping up the mountainside.

At last it had burned its way round a rock shoulder out of sight; only the glow thrown up on the cloud of smoke above showed that it still raged, while a trail of glowing stumps marked its course. Two of these, slanted towards each other, looked like the ruby eyes of some ancient image, savage and Mongolian; and in front of them rose a drift of smoke like incense.

A huge malignant god, revengeful and unappeased, seemed to lie along the edge of the night. Was Mathinna to be a sacrifice?

Sir John was not unduly fanciful, but tonight he felt in his bones, as he had felt sometimes on the frozen coast of the Arctic Sea, that nature was not so much indifferent as positively inimical. If man was born with original sin, then nature was created with original cruelty; and it would be a long, long time before the lion lay down with the lamb as the Bible said would come to pass.

On the mountain the law of survival was being worked out among the smaller bush creatures. The kangaroos and wallabies had already fled to safety, bounding ahead of the smoke and flames; but the slow-moving stumpy-tailed lizards, the grubs and beetles which lived beneath bark, the birds which became dazed with smoke and fumes before they could escape, the snakes asleep under warm stones, the ring-tailed possums and bandicoots sleeping through the last daylight hours in hollow logs, were trapped and roasted alive, or fled screaming with burning fur to ignite new patches of scrub.

Mathinna, like the other wild creatures, felt the urge to run; but an instinct of self-preservation made her take shelter in the first fairly big pool of the creek, where a rocky shelf held back the water above a small cascade. As she submerged all but her head she heard a sudden snarling cough. A fierce, black, whiskered face with wicked little dark eyes glared at her from a few feet away. A Tasmanian devil was sharing the haven of the little pool with her.

Mathinna backed away a little, but there was no room to move far.

'You cheeky-pfeller, you,' she scolded the little animal. 'You keep-it 'way, longa you-side.'

Then the overhanging bushes caught at their tops, and the fire was upon her. A baby possum with singed fur came blundering into the water and crouched beside her; they trembled with the same fear. The green fern fronds withered and curled, but did not ignite; the green bulrushes made a living shield. Mathinna covered her whole face and head with the blanket and breathed through its wet folds for an eternity. She felt the water growing hot.

At last the furnace-heat was past. Coughing and with eyes streaming from the smoke, she sat up and looked about her. The 'debbil' was gone, but the little possum was pressed against her, trembling violently.

'You too-much scared,' she said softly, forgetting her fear in soothing the little creature. She put it on her shoulder where it crouched in a limp wet bundle, its soft nose buried in her neck, its claws pricking through her bodice.

171

When she stood up it clambered to the top of her head and sat there, holding on to her curls with its tiny hands while its curving tail kept a firm grip round her shoulder. The possum felt safe only in a tree; and this human tree with its dark shiny limbs was the only one which was not glowing with red-hot coals.

While she waited for the ash-strewn ground to be cool enough to walk on, Mathinna pulled some of the bulrush-like 'cats'-tails' from the edge of the stream, and put their roots to cook. She was hungry. Her stomach rumbled with emptiness.... Her eyes rolled round and fixed themselves on the plump, trembling possum, who had climbed down again to her shoulder, and feeling better, was licking its singed fur.

Here was a meal of meat, just asking to be cooked and eaten! As if it felt her gaze, the possum stopped licking itself and sat quite still, its hands clasped in an almost human attitude. Its great eyes stared back at her solemnly.

Suddenly Mathinna began to giggle. 'Silly-pfeller you!' she said. 'What por you washem? Wash-em you hand and pface por dinner, that it?'

And very gently she stroked the possum's soft fur. It reached out its pointed snout and sniffed doubtfully at her cheek. She held up a piece of raw bulrush-stem. The possum gripped it in one little grey hand while she still held the other end. It began to gnaw energetically, still watching her warily from its large, soft eyes. In the daylight it was almost blind. With a sudden tug it pulled the stem away from her and retreated to the top of her head to finish off its meal in what seemed greater safety. Mathinna could only just stop herself rolling on the ground laughing. 'Silly-pfeller you!' she gasped.

That night the possum, though usually active at night, was still suffering from scorched paws. It slept curled up in a furry ball on a rocky mound free of red-hot stumps and ash. Mathinna curled around it, happy to have found a companion. She would go back tomorrow, and take the possum for a pet. It would be better company than that old stuck-up kitchen cat.

She was pleasantly full, for she had cooked some fern-roots over the coals of a smouldering tree, and had hooked out of a hole in a half-burnt banksia some tasty white grubs, already roasted by the bush-fire.

Gazing up at the friendly stars, looking small and yellow through the lingering smoke-haze, she knew that it was true what someone had told her long ago; that they were the camp-fires of the dead tribes who had gone to live in the sky country, on the banks of that mysterious river of light which the white people called the Milky Way. She was no longer lonely. Still, she would go back.

Eleanor had thought of an excellent joke: the *Abeona* seemed likely to arrive fairly late at night, and her idea was that they should creep up through the grounds from the private landing, taking with them the gong used to announce meals on board. They would then beat on the gong louder and louder, to the stupendous amazement and bewilderment of the occupants of Government House.

She could imagine the sleepy guard being turned out, John Hepburn struggling into his uniform, and Papa standing on the stairs in his nightshirt demanding to know 'what was that frightful din'. Then imagine his surprise and amusement when it turned out to be only Mr Gell, Mr Bagot, Mamma and Eleanor!

'Oh, please, Captain Blackbourne! Couldn't we manage to get in just at midnight?' she begged. 'It is such a thrilling hour.'

The Captain, who had never seen anything very thrilling about the cold, dark 'graveyard' watch, looked sceptical. He said he would try his best, but a head-wind could delay them until morning. Jane privately hoped for a head-wind. She always hated the end of a voyage, the return to the deadening domestic duties of her position after a holiday, whatever the discomforts of shipboard life; and the

173

Abeona's hold was certainly uncomfortable enough. She would like to arrive in daylight, and see once more the fluted stone capes, the romantic wooded shores, and the great brooding mountain which made this one of the loveliest harbours in the world.

Eleanor was to be disappointed; it was full morning before they dropped anchor in Sullivan's Cove. She seemed to blame poor Captain Blackbourne for the weather, and said goodbye to him rather sulkily. As Mrs Blackbourne dropped a curtsey in farewell, Lady Franklin took her hand and promised her a new handkerchief of the finest lawn to replace the one she had requisitioned on Stamford Hill at Port Lincoln, to give a mark for sighting the theodolite.

'Isn't she a lovely lady?' sighed the young bride to her husband that evening. 'I liked her ever so.'

'I'd rather have *you* than all the Lady Franklins that ever was,' replied her spouse. 'At least I can have you with me again tonight, without a lot of gentlemen sleeping in my cabin. Eh, love?' and he gave her a wicked wink, so that young Mrs Blackbourne coloured prettily.

In her boudoir the same evening, Jane sat relaxed in a comfortable peignoir, sipping the mocha coffee for which she had acquired a taste in Greece, and telling Sir John of her adventures while he turned over the pages of her journal.

'That's good! Very well expressed: "The houses were like empty shells, still beautiful but the life departed from them",' he read from her description of Kingscote. 'There's no doubt, Jane, that you could have written a book on your travels – and a jolly fine one, too.'

'Fie, Sir John! I have no ambitions to be an author.'

He was delighted at receiving the title-deed to the small piece of South Australian land, and blessed her thoughtfulness in arranging for the monument to Flinders.

'You are the best of wives, my dearest Jane! You knew there was nothing that would please me more than to honour my old commander. I feel distressed that I didn't look after your little charge better.' He glanced at Mathinna, curled up asleep on the hearth-rug with the possum, wide awake, staring out from the shelter of her arms.

The child had rushed at Jane when she arrived that morning, and hugged her so tightly round the knees that she couldn't move, burying her little dark face in the skirts of her travelling dress.

'There – there! Did you think I was never coming back?' had said Jane, surprised and a little moved at this display of affection. Eleanor had never greeted her so. Where had she failed with Eleanor? Other people's children always liked her; she had made friends with a young sailor-lad at Kingscote and given him a book, and young Freddie Gawler had been her slave.

Sir John told her afterwards of Mathinna's 'walkabout', how they feared they had lost her for good. She had turned up at the Government House gates early the day before, with the baby possum on her shoulder and not a stitch of clothing but a filthy, blackened bodice with holes burnt in it by the bush-fire, half-covering her down to her little pot belly.

John Hepburn had picked her up and brought her in – wrapped in one of the red coats from the soldiers of the guard.

Jane imagined it all as Sir John described it, the child sitting on the Constable of the Yard's shoulder, her little black face and dark eyes showing out of the bundle of scarlet, and beside it the pointed snout and wistful round eyes of the possum.

When Sir John had questioned her she would only say, 'Me bin go walkabout longa bush, longa mountin.'

Then she had smiled her wide curly smile and held out the possum to be admired. He stroked it, and it promptly nipped his finger. He had scolded her for worrying them all, but was too relieved to be very angry.

'I didn't know how to face you, my love, and say I had lost your pet,' he said now, as he sat on the arm of the couch where she rested.

She frowned slightly, 'Don't call her my pet, as though she were just another animal, Sir John. You know she has a soul as much as a white child, and is a Christian now.'

'Yet she's apparently been happy and quite at home wandering in the bush. A white child would have died of hunger and fright in six days. I pray God we have done the right thing in bringing her to a civilized home.'

'She's happy now, at any rate.' For Mathinna was smiling contentedly in her sleep. She had been wild with joy all day. She had drummed with both feet on the floor, scampered up and down the stairs, and laughed immoderately. Finally, she had fallen into an exhausted sleep in front of the small fire which burned in Jane's room, more for ventilation than for warmth. The possum, which had already been in trouble with Miss Williamson for leaving droppings on the nursery floor, had a grass-lined box on the hearth.

They talked until late, for he could not hear enough of the growth of the young province of South Australia; the financial difficulties of Colonel Gawler with the officials of the South Australian Company had their parallel in his own troubles with the Colonial Secretary. Affairs had gone more smoothly while Montagu was away; but he would soon be back.

A servant came in to build up the fire, and was dismissed for the night. Mathinna still slept. Jane, who had been wound up and full of talk, suddenly yawned. Oh, she was weary. . . .

'Time for bed, my love,' said Sir John. 'I – thought I would come and sleep in your room tonight. That is, if you are not too tired?' His round face was anxious; he looked like a small boy who fears to be denied a treat. Jane hesitated only a moment.

'No, of course I am not too tired. You know that travelling agrees with me excessively. Let's not disturb Mathinna and Master Possum; they look so comfortable.'

In Lady Franklin's bedroom, Stewart was sleepily passing the copper warming-pan between the sheets of the big bed, 'just to hair it like, because it wasn't what you'd call cold'.

'Well, Stewart, and how did you enjoy the voyage? Lady Franklin will be making a sailor of you yet.'

'Not I, Sir John! No, not I! That's something you won't never see in your wildest dreams, me being a sailor! I 'ates the sea.'

'You may leave it now, Stewart,' said Jane. 'You must be tired out; I can get myself to bed. Good night.'

'Very well, my lady. And that there possum?'

'Is asleep in the next room, with Mathinna. Don't disturb them for now.'

'No, my lady. Good night, my lady. Good night, Sir John.' Stewart went out and closed the door.

Sir John Franklin, short and stout, a little deaf, more than a little bald, turned his gentle, far-seeing eyes to his true north, the magnetic pole of his being. As he folded his dearest Jane in his arms, his lips sought the soft breast that had never been denied him. He sank down and down into the warm, dark safety of the womb.

Chapter Twenty-two

Eleanor's lips moved as she read the advertisement in the *Hobart Town Courier*: 'The Monster, after pursuing his unfortunate creator, leaps into the burning crater of Mount Aetna, which will be represented vomiting flames and lava!'

'Oh Mamma!' she begged. 'Pray let us go and see it at the Theatre Royal next week! I should so love to see it!'

'What, my pet? You know Papa doesn't approve of the theatre, and it's certainly no place for a young girl.'

'But Mamma! It says here, "THE MONSTER" in big type, "founded on Mrs Shelley's beautiful novel". It must be *Frankenstein* – Miss Williamson and I read it together at New Norfolk, and we were afraid to go to bed afterward. It's excessively exciting! Oh, I should dearly love to go.'

'Now, Eleanor! All that strong excitement is very bad for you; remember the nightmares you used to have. We might go to a concert, perhaps, but not a play of that type. I want you to keep your mind on serious things while Miss Williamson and I are away, and work by yourself at the tasks she will set you.'

'Yes, Mamma.' Eleanor looked sulky. She never pouted as a sign of inward mutiny, but the whole expression of her face changed: she squinted and her mouth set in an ugly line.

Jane chose to ignore it, and went on: 'I hope you will look after Papa for me, be company for him when he hasn't official business, and unless there are special guests I think you might start having dinner downstairs. I'll probably still be away for your birthday, but I'll bring you back a nice present from New Zealand.'

'You mean *always* come down to dinner from now on?'

'Yes, as I said, except for State dinner-parties.'

'Oh, Mamma!' Eleanor's face relaxed again.

'And be kind to Mathinna so that she doesn't run off. I think she realizes now that I will always come back.'

'But what about when we return to England?'

A shadow fell on Jane's brow. She said firmly: 'We'll just have to take her with us. She is so attached. Anyway, that's not for years yet.' She hoped. Or did she fear?

'Perhaps I could have a pet rabbit?' Eleanor was still reading the advertisements: 'TAME RABBITS, Sale of 100 rabbits and 20 hutches.'

'Yes, perhaps you could have a rabbit. They seem to keep quite healthy here, in spite of the hotter summers....'

But Eleanor was not listening. With wide eyes she was reading:

It is time Captain Booth should exercise a different system of discipline at Port Arthur than that which has caused so many instances of desperation. The most recent murder was when two lads, Maxfield and Sheffield, agreed to abscond. In getting off their irons, Sheffield struck Maxfield by accident in the face, whereupon M. took a branch and beat him to death. It is horrible to contemplate! Again, one Henry Belfold, only 22 years old, for no reason battered a fellow-prisoner to death while he was drinking at a water-hole. This lad, an orphan, was deported at 15 for burglary; flogged repeatedly; given 6 months 'solitary' for insubordination; and spent 22 months in chains for disobedience. He tried four times to abscond. He has now found the only means of escape, by way of the gallows.

Only fifteen when he was transported, Eleanor told herself, trying to feel something for this unknown lad; her own age last birthday! But she could feel nothing, nothing; her heart remained cold as stone.

These horrors were exaggerated by the newspapers, of course. How could they be true, when her own dear kind Papa was the head and chief of the whole system: the gentlest and most sensitive of men, who spoke so movingly to the new convicts when they came off the ships? Mr Gell had told her that sometimes the less hardened of them were moved to tears.

More and more were being unloaded all the time – she saw so often when she looked out the window the Mulgrave Battery signalling with the flag of 'a ship in sight', plain red for male prisoners or red-and-white for females.

Lying awake at night, listening to the soft chirring of crickets in the summer dusk, sometimes she would find herself thinking of all the suffering that was going on, the boys, some of them only eleven years old, being flogged at Point Puer, the hanged men swinging on the gibbets. . . . 'Oh God!' she often prayed. 'Take away this stony heart, and give me a heart of flesh, warmed with love of my fellow creatures.' Because she should love them, even if they were bad . . .

And all of them, perhaps, were not as bad as the evil-faced men in yellow and grey who had pushed the car on the tramway at Port Arthur, whose hatred she had felt like a miasma in the air. Beaumont Smith, for instance, sent out for defrauding the Exchequer, and the man who threw a stone at King William: they had not the depraved look of the others.

She had heard Mamma and Mr Gell discussing Captain Maconachie's ideas for reform, and Papa arguing with them. . . . She wished she were clever and knew several languages like Mamma, whose company Mr Gell obviously enjoyed.

Once again she felt the dark gnawing of envy and jealousy. Papa had a new friend too, in Count Paul de Strzelecki, a name she could never spell in her diary. He had arrived straight from the bush, in walking-jacket with buttoned-flap pockets and strong corduroy trousers, a knapsack full of geological specimens on his back and wide-brimmed felt hat on his head. It was just when they were having a big dinner for the officers of *Erebus* and *Terror*, but Papa had welcomed him like an old friend: 'Come in, come in!' he cried heartily. 'Never mind your bush dress; we are all travellers here.'

Well, at least she would have Papa to herself at breakfast, and no Miss Williamson to drag her off to lessons. And when Mr Gell came to dinner she would be there at table as his hostess, just like a grown-up young lady. Surely he would notice her more? She must have her hair put up in curlers every night, a thing she usually refused to do because the curl-rags were uncomfortable.

Il faut souffrir pour la beauté, as Mamma always said when she wriggled as the curl-rags were pulled tight. Eleanor Gell ... Mrs John Phillip Gell ... How elegant it sounded!

Jane was off again on a voyage to New Zealand. The senior officer of the sloop of war *Favourite*, Captain Stanley, an old friend of Sir John's, had offered her a passage. Sir John urged her not to miss the opportunity with his usual unselfishness, and Jane did not need much urging. This time she was taking Miss Williamson, who needed a holiday.

'Montagu will be back by the time you return,' said Sir John. 'You know, I feel I can cope with him much better with Strzelecki to advise me. He's impartial, he's not involved in any way, and he sees these local disputes with a clear eye and mind.'

'He has an excellent mind. I'm so happy you have his friendship to sustain you among all your worries. He's one of the most cultivated and delightful men I have ever met.'

'Well, he will be back from the north-west next week, so I shall not be lonely at dinner.'

'And then you can always invite Mr Montagu.'

'I wonder, now, why he scarcely wrote a word to me from London, except the most trivial notes. D'you think he's up to something?'

'I don't know ... I'm uneasy about him. Perhaps I shouldn't go.'

181

'Nonsense, Jane! I must fight my own battles. I'll have 'im on deck and demand to know why he didn't communicate. I'll let him know who's in command here.'

'That's the stuff! Aye, aye, Captain Franklin, sir.'

Visiting Korarareka in the beautiful Bay of Islands, Jane had a glimpse of what a Pacific island must be like, and resolved that her next travels would take her across that enormous ocean, perhaps all the way to South America.

The back of the house opened directly on to a fern-tree hill, where cicadas shrilled in the steamy heat. From the balcony she saw the ship lying between arches of bougainvillaea and hibiscus that flamed in blazing colour against the blue water.

The Maoris she found very different from the Tasmanian and Australian natives. They were bolder, more on an equality with the whites, though they seemed happy enough to carry her in a litter part of the way to Hokianga, adjuring each other not to drop 'the great lady, the sister of King William', as they seemed to think she might be.

At Akaroa she had the great pleasure of meeting Captain Lavand, that frank honest-hearted Frenchman, in command of the frigate *Aube*. She took to him instantly, as she had to Count Strzelecki: indeed she got on better on the whole with Europeans than with Englishmen; hadn't she nearly married a Swiss?

He entertained her and Miss Williamson royally, with *pâtés de Périgord* and wines from Beaujolais. She sent him across a piece of Tasmanian roast lamb.

He begged her to give him the pleasure of delivering her back to Hobart in the *Aube* and surprised her with a punning reference to the work of a modern English poet: 'Bliss was it in that "Dawn" to be alive –'

And what, said Jane, if France should declare war on England again while she was on board? – He would do as he promised, and deliver her safely back to her husband!

'Oui, mon capitaine?' said Jane impishly. *'Mais – mais sans saccager la ville?'*

'Ah, madame!' said the Captain, shocked. Never – never would he sack the town. *Jamais de la vie!*

They parted excellent friends. Later he told Captain Bérard of *Le Rhin* of kindness and affability, her fluent French, her charm: 'What an ambassador she would have made for her country, if women were appointed to such posts!'

It had been an auspicious meeting. As for Sir John, when she told him of it, he said he could never quite like the French as much as she did, because of the way they imprisoned poor Flinders all those years.

Sir John had found a change, hard to define, in his relations with the Colonial Secretary. Since his return, Montagu was studiously polite, but not affable; and he showed in numbers of indirect ways that he was implacably opposed to the idea of founding a secondary college at New Norfolk, the *raison d'être* of Mr Gell's presence in Van Diemen's Land. The newspaper opposition to it increased at once; the *Tasmanian* speaking in a leader of 'this visionary twaddle'.

But it was something in Montagu himself which was subtly disturbing to Sir John, always sensitive to atmosphere. Could it be that Jane and Maconachie had been right: that Montagu was devious, untrustworthy, and finally interested in nothing but his own aggrandizement?

He had come back with an irritatingly superior air, as if he knew something which the Governor did not know. His handsome face had always worn a rather self-satisfied expression, but now he irresistibly suggested the cat that has eaten the cream. And he was, to say the least of it, uncooperative.

Eleanor was a great comfort in these days. With her mother away she suddenly seemed to grow up into a responsible young lady; and she did not frown at the brandy and hot water he took before dinner to 'stimulate his digestion', or the wine he took with his meal and the port after it.

He never drank during the day, keeping his head clear for business. Surely a man could be permitted a little indulgence in the evening, when resting from his never-ending labours? It was all very well for Jane. As soon as she felt off-colour or depressed she went off on a new trip, and came back refreshed, but it was rarely that he could get away even for a few days to New Norfolk.

He had offered the Government cottage there, besides ten acres of land, for the college project, and the foundation stone had even been laid, but that was as far as it seemed likely to go at present. He couldn't spend more than £200 in any direction without specific permission from the Secretary of State for the Colonies; but he was willing to put up £500 of his own money; Jane intended giving her valuable properties in trust for the project.

At breakfast he always tried to be cheerful. He and Eleanor played little practical jokes on each other and were very merry after their early-morning walk in the grounds, which they took every day that the weather was fine.

In that early-morning hour in the dew-sparkling garden, with the grey shrike-thrushes calling from the shrubs in notes as clear as dew, he felt washed clean, renewed by the pure island air. He missed the sea, he would have liked to give up his troublesome colony for a simple naval command, and envied Ross and Crozier down in the clean white world of the Far South; but at least in Hobart Town you were never without a glimpse of the sea, or a breath of its briny tang.

He did not let Jane know how worried he felt. She must have peace of mind on her holiday, or it would do her no good. He wrote: 'Montagu has resumed his office and Forster his, everything is going on very quietly.... I really feel happy now. Come back as soon as you can and increase the happiness of our family circle.'

Eleanor had had a letter from Colonel Gawler in Adelaide to tell her that the baby had died of croup, but that Freddy was very well. He did not tell her what was already

184

rumoured over there – that his own recall was imminent.

Eleanor wrote in her diary:

9 June 1841. It is our duty to prepare for Eternity. Another year is past.... It may be my last on earth.

She had been shaken by the sudden death of Archdeacon Hutchins while Mamma was away. He had come to Eleanor's birthday party. They had all been very merry; then he went home and dropped dead without a cry.

When she and Papa went to comfort Mrs Hutchins, she wondered why the widow was not happier at the thought of her husband safely and comfortably in heaven – for who could doubt that such a good man would go straight there? As for Eleanor, she often had sinful thoughts, sometimes about young men, and if a good man like the Archdeacon could be hustled off without warning, it might happen to her even right in the middle of a bad thought, and then what would become of her?

It almost seemed as if the safest thing was to die young, before you could learn to be wicked ... or to live for ever, but of course that was impossible.

She became even more conscientious about saying her prayers, kneeling on the floor by her bed for some ten minutes of urgent communication with the Almighty before getting into it. She had got into the habit of kneeling up in bed with the covers hunched round her shoulders in the chilly Tasmanian nights.

She opened her diary again and added: 'God grant that when I am called I shall be found watching....'

Chapter Twenty-three

'Papa,' said Eleanor as they walked one morning in the garden, 'I have been thinking, will Hepburn accompany us when we go back?'

'Go back! Who is talking of going back, pray? My term of office is not completed yet.'

He spoke sharply, for he was still upset by the news, just received from South Australia, of Colonel Gawler's ignominious recall: the relieving Governor, Grey, had actually arrived in the same ship as the notice of his dismissal.

This was so unlike her gentle Papa that Eleanor was confused. 'I only meant ... I meant *one* day we'll be returning, and Hepburn seems to like it here. You know how good he is with young people? Would he not be an excellent man to take charge of the boys at Point Puer?'

'And what do you know about Point Puer, my dear child?'

'Nothing, except *"puer, pueris"* is Latin for boy; and I was surprised on my visit to Port Arthur to find how *young* some of them are. And I have read things in the papers ... of punishments ... floggings ...'

'When I was a midshipman we were flogged just as hard with a rope's end if we misbehaved. But still, I shall consider the matter. You have a brain in that little head, Nell. I believe Hepburn *would* be the man for the post; I was looking for some outside appointment for him.'

Eleanor smiled happily. He called her 'Nell' only when he was feeling pleased with her.

'– I shall talk it over with your Mamma when she returns.'

Eleanor's face fell. Of course he would do nothing without Mamma. It was ridiculous the way he would tell people to 'wait until he had discussed it with Lady Franklin'. They

186

would get the notion that Mamma ran the colony, whereas it went on very well without her, and so did Government House, Eleanor thought.

However, when Mamma came back at the end of the month she was limping badly, her face drawn with pain, and Eleanor felt contrite. Mamma had fallen when she stepped out of a Maori hut in the dark, forgetting it was several feet above the ground. They'd had to call at Sydney for a doctor to see her.

She had brought Eleanor a beautiful Maori feather cloak, a piece of greenstone for Sophy, a wooden doll for Mathinna, and a carved figure with paua shell eyes for Papa.

'I don't like the look of the creature much,' said Sir John, turning over the piece of carved totara wood with its grimacing features and protruding tongue. 'Are you sure it's not unlucky, with those greeny eyes?'

'Sailors are always superstitious,' laughed Jane.

He stared at her soberly. 'Gawler has been peremptorily recalled from South Australia.'

'No! I can't believe it!' She sank into a chair and stared back at him, shocked and disturbed.

He put the thing on the desk in his office, but after a while its baleful face began to worry him. He hid it away in a drawer.

Ross and Crozier had come back in April. He went out in the Government barge to meet them; so brown and fit they looked, though their faces were scored with new lines and weather-beaten by freezing winds. He'd of course invited them to stay at Government House for a change from shipboard life, though Mary Price was there again waiting for a new baby, and Count Strzelecki was a guest whenever he was in town.

On 6 July, the day before they were to sail for the Far South again, they gave a ball on board *Erebus* for the officers to say farewell to their many friends in Hobart Town.

The invitations were printed on pieces of pale-blue satin

ribbon, with a picture of the two ships. The night before the ball Sophy lay tossing on her bed, strung up to such a pitch of excitement that she could not sleep. First she was too hot, and threw off all the bedclothes; then she began to shiver with cold; but as soon as she covered herself she felt as if she were stifling, and threw back the covers again.

In despair she got up and stared out of the window at the frosty stars in the winter sky. Oh God, she must sleep! She would look like nothing on earth tomorrow, great dark circles under her eyes, or worse, they would be red and puffy.

Captain Ross had come back a hero of unimaginable dangers, and she was more in love than ever. She had listened enthralled while he spoke of the great Ice Barrier, like a solid wall through which one would no more think of sailing than through the cliffs of Dover; and how, when they reached a lower part of the Barrier and could see from the masthead the surface that lay above that endless wall, it had appeared quite smooth, like an immense plain of frosted silver.

He had brought back a piece of rock from his farthest south, which he had called Franklin Island; and he had such things to tell in his energetic, incisive manner, of waves that froze as they fell on board, of a fish frozen in the rigging; of the aurora coruscating in the heavens in flashes of red and green, or softly undulating in a filmy curtain; and the great snow-clad volcano which he had named Mount Erebus, from which the red flame and the black smoke burst forth incredibly in a land of cold unchanging white.

She sat like Desdemona before Othello, drinking in his words, and seeing him larger than life against that heroic background. Poor Francis Crozier had braved the same dangers, but he was not so eloquent in recounting them. Besides, he was busy all the time at the Rossbank observatory, supervising a series of comparisons between the magnetic instruments carried on the voyage and those in the fixed observatory.

On the term-days, when magnetic observations were taken all over the world, every officer and all the gentlemen from Government House had spent the whole day and night there – Uncle John and Lieutenant Bagot, Mr Gell and Mr Henslowe, the Private Secretary who had taken over from Ronald Gunn.

She had managed to avoid Captain Crozier except at the dinner table, but it was obvious from the way he gazed at her that he had not got over his feelings in the cold southern latitudes.

When she'd had to meet Captain Ross again she became quite ill with nerves and had to go to bed for a few days. By the time she got up she had command of herself, and by a tremendous effort of will managed to greet him coolly. Her aunt had scolded her a little for showing her feelings too openly before, and her own pride had come to her aid.

Tomorrow – tomorrow night was the last time she would ever see or speak with him. The next day the ships sailed for New Zealand via Sydney, and then turned to the deep south again. They would not come back by way of Tasmania.

'James Ross, James Ross,' she whispered into her pillow, over and over. 'James Clark Ross.' Three short unbeautiful syllables ... Would he dance with her? Of course he would, he must! He was, after all, one of the hosts.

The clock downstairs chimed three. She felt each stroke like a blow on her trembling heart. Dear God, would to-morrow never come?

'It is like a fairyland!' exclaimed the guests, with more enthusiasm than originality.

The two ships lay in Ross Cove in a glassy calm. Strings of lanterns outlining hulls and masts were reflected like stars in the dark water. Overhead the real stars sparkled frostily.

On board *Erebus*, all the flags from the two signal-lockers gaily decorated the enclosed decks, in red, white and blue rosettes. On the dais for the official guests pale blue candles burned among white and blue flowers.

As Sophy twisted her programme, with its silver print and pale blue tassel and pencil, in her faintly trembling fingers, she felt a woman's greatest strength fortifying her; the consciousness that her gown was right for the occasion, and that it suited her. She had chosen a cool blue silk surah and had it made in sweeping lines and gleaming folds. It was like a fall of ice, like the colour of the ice-caverns in a glacier. It blended perfectly with the decorations.

Pale and feverish with excitement, with glowing dark eyes and shining hair, she felt herself burning like a blue flame. The intensity of that flame must be felt by James Ross; he must be melted a little by the clear burning of her mind and will.

'Miss Sophy. May I look at your programme? If the supper-dance is not taken –'

'You may, Captain Ainsworth, you may. But pray give it back to me when you have written your name *once*.'

'Ah, Miss Sophy! You are too cruel. Only one more, that's all I ask.'

'Oh, very well.' She took it back from him, giving him a playful tap with her folded blue-satin fan. She turned at a voice by her shoulder:

'The Ice-Maiden! Am I too late to ask for the first dance?'

'Why, no, Captain Crozier.' She flicked open her fan and hid behind it her bitter disappointment that it was not the other.

'And the last, and the supper-dance, and –'

'Fie, sir! What impetuosity! The supper-dance is taken, and as for the last –'

But Frank Crozier, made bold by desperation – for did they not sail tomorrow, not to return again to this home of his Snow-Queen, his Ice-Maiden? He might never see her

190

more! – was writing his name all down the card, holding the dainty pencil clumsily in his big fingers.

She snatched the programme from his hand. The silk cord holding the pencil tore out from the corner.

'There now, I declare! You are *provoking*, Captain Crozier!' Anger had brought some colour to her pale cheeks, her eyes flashed like the Aurora Australis. He thought she had never looked so enchanting. Lieutenant Bagot, handsome in military red and gold, came up to claim a dance, and Sophy began to despair. Her card would be full before James Ross asked her.

Lady Franklin was sitting on the dais among a bower of fern-tree boughs and blue flowers, with her injured leg resting on a footstool. She would not be able to dance for many weeks yet; not that this was much loss to her, she did not care for dancing these days, but she hated to be confined in any way.

Once she used to dance until four in the morning.... The music, the women's gowns, the glowing candles, made her mind drift back to those youthful days. That wonderful evening at Mary's when she'd worn a pink gown, with white ostrich plumes in her hair. Waltzing romantically with Peter Mark Roget ... Her heart had thrilled with emotion, and she had felt his emotion answering hers. Now each of them was happily married to someone else. If only youth could understand, she thought sadly, that its heartbreaks are not eternal.

Her eyes sought Sophy in her gleaming ice-blue, and her heart went out in sympathy as she saw the girl, her face upturned to Captain Ross, who had taken her programme in a masterful fashion and seemed to be filling every blank space left in it. Sophy had two bright, feverish spots of colour in her cheeks; her eyes were alight with a perilous joy.

Ah, how well she knew that lift of joy, and the terrible pangs of hope deferred! She had let her feelings show that night, but Roget had made no declaration, then or ever.

And so here she was in the Antipodes, leading a life of immense interest and variety, and with the position of first lady in the land. It would have suited her admirably if it were not for the wretched newspapers, and her own morbid fear of publicity.

She was keeping an anxious eye on Eleanor. This was her first ball, and she did hope the child would enjoy it. There seemed, however, to be a satisfactory cluster of young officers about her. They'd had rather an argument over her gown. She had taken it into her head to want to wear emerald green – a young girl coming out, who of course should wear nothing but white! (She did not know that a half-forgotten picture of herself in brilliant emerald and peacock shimmering silks had stayed with Eleanor since the first days they had been in the colony.)

They had compromised in the end with a pretty pink-and-white striped *gauze de Chambéry*, but really, Eleanor's colouring was so mousy that pink was not very becoming. She was treating her would-be partners with admirable composure; she was not anxious to fill up her programme, for Mr Gell did not dance, and when she sat out it would be on the platform near him.

Sir John was gay and frisky as a young midshipman: gallant to the ladies, exchanging jokes with the men, laughing heartily, and full of bright quips; almost witty, thought young Henslowe in surprise. He looked well in his naval dress uniform, in fact he had never shown to better advantage. Henslowe had seen the transformation in him these last months so that he scarcely recognized the dull, prosy, stammering old 'Guv' he had become used to and felt rather sorry for.

In fact, with the arrival of his friends – they had lost young Mr Gunn at the beginning of the year, and it had left a blank when he returned to Launceston to manage a friend's estate – Sir John had felt once more a sense of belonging, of being appreciated and at home among his peers, which was necessary to his nature. With Jane's poor health and frequent absences he had been thrown on his own resources, and since Montagu's return and unco-operative attitude had felt less and less sure of himself. When Count Strzelecki was in town he rallied, but the Count preferred to make his headquarters in Launceston, where there were less distractions from his work.

Franklin had tried to bolster his well-being with brandy and rum, but though the spirits had an immediately cheer-ing effect, they let him down afterwards. The doctors in England had warned him that if he had much mental work to do, he should avoid spirits altogether, because the day after indulging, however mildly, his head felt thick and woolly and the smallest decision was difficult.

Now, stimulated by congenial company and conversa-tion, he had found it easy to stay up all night taking read-ings in the observatory on term-day, and his head remained as clear as when he was a young man. Not that he was old ... a mere fifty-five, he probably had twenty effective years ahead of him!

'You remind me of the white Antarctic petrel,' said James Ross as he whirled Sophy to a standstill at the end of the waltz. She kept her white-gloved hand on his arm. He walked for'ard with her to where the awnings ended and they could see the starry sky and the towering mountain above Hobart Town.

'Is it a bird of good omen?' she asked lightly.

'Not exactly.' He laughed at her quick frown. 'But it's a very beautiful, elegant bird. It's found in the thickest pack-ice; it means dangerous water. When it is left behind we know there's clear sailing ahead.'

She gazed at the clear sky where the Southern Cross, swinging in a great arc, now began to rise away from the horizon below which it never set.

'If there is a parable in this, sir, I interpret it badly.'

'It means ... that there is danger for me in your proxi-mity. Perhaps it's as well we are returning by way of Cape

Horn and shall not be calling here again. You see, I expect to be married as soon as I return.'

'Is – is she beautiful?' asked Sophy pitifully.

'She is as kind as she is fair. I have known her family many years.'

'What is her name?'

'Anne. Anne Coulman.'

'*Oh!*' Sophy grasped the ship's rail and held it as if to prevent herself from falling.

'My dear, are you all right? Can I get you something? An ice – a glass of punch? You're trembling.'

'Oh, I cannot bear it!' You will sail away for ever when you leave the Cove tomorrow.'

'My dear girl, I had no idea – forgive my facetiousness. I had thought – you seemed so composed when we met again – and I thought you indifferent.'

'Indifferent!' Strong shudders went through her frame from head to foot; she was quite unable to control them. 'Indifferent!'

'Sophy, I'm sorry. It's something quite outside my experience; I'm not a ladies' man, you know.' He raised her gloved hand and kissed it.

Sophy looked up at the brilliant Cross.

'I think of you always when I look at that constellation, Captain Ross. And the two Pointers, like a pair of steady, glowing eyes. I shall look at it every night and pray for your safety.' Two teardrops glittered but did not fall.

He touched her shoulder gently.

'We will take a walk round the deck until you are more composed. Let me look at your programme. The next dance is with Frank Crozier; he won't mind if you're a bit late.'

She put her icy hand on his dark-blue sleeve and went with him without another word. There was a strange timelessness, a sense of unreality, as if the solid deck might melt beneath her feet, thaw and resolve itself into a dew.

The last guest had departed. The decks were quiet and deserted.

'She is made of ice!' cried Frank Crozier despairingly to his brother officer, as they had a nightcap in Ross's stateroom before he went back to his own ship. 'I call her the Snow-Queen.'

'Miss Cracroft? I call her the White Petrel. The bird of the ice-pack.'

'Her heart is made of stone. But oh! Isn't she a stunner, old fellow? Coral lips and teeth like pearls! And her hair has just a sheen of copper in it –'

'Come come, she's not as hard-faced as all that.'

'My dear James! She's adorable. Hard-faced! Why –'

'No offence, Frank old man. I was pulling your leg. All those stony and metallic comparisons! She's fresh and charming, I agree. Intelligent, too.'

'Oh, it's all very well for you! Your heart is safe in England. But I've been a lost man ever since I first set eyes on her. D'you think she'll ever have me, James? I intend to keep asking, if I get the chance.'

'Good man. Never give in.'

Ross accompanied him up on deck. They walked to the rail and looked towards the sleeping town, the dark loom of Mount Wellington. It was like a second home in the southern hemisphere, this English-seeming city on the far side of the world. Both felt regret at leaving it, but the lure of fame and danger, the possibility of sailing right to the South Pole, was stronger than love or comfort, than the call of sweetheart or home.

High in the southern sky, the Cross glittered, beckoning and pointing the way they would follow: to failure or success, to glory or to death in the frozen south.

Chapter Twenty-four

To 'take Sophy out of herself', Jane proposed that she should become secretary of the Ladies' Committee she had just formed for attempting some sort of reform at the Female Factory, the notorious women's prison at the Cascades. But Sophy would have none of it; she hated ladies' committees and all such organizations for doing good among her own sex.

A Miss Kezia Hayter, strongly recommended by Mrs Elizabeth Fry, had arrived from England to give Jane support. She was as full of crusading fervour as Captain Maconachie, and was sure she could appeal to the better nature of the women and bring about a change of heart among the most depraved of them.

Jane had her doubts. Most of their hearts, she felt, were like adamant for hardness: they regarded a sentence to the Female Factory as a kind of loafing holiday, and many of them came back regularly to have their illegitimate children there.

Miss Hayter became secretary of the committee, which was made up largely of unmarried ladies of uncertain age who found plenty of time on their hands for good works. They agreed to visit the prison once a week.

On the first visit they were accompanied by the Rev. William Bedford, and this Jane felt to be a mistake. The women probably had quite enough of his sermons at compulsory service on Sunday, without having to listen to him on a weekday as well; and since he enjoyed the sound of his own voice he was not likely to remain silent.

However, Mr Bagot A.D.C. was always a great success with the ladies, and Squint-Eyed Sal, Nosey Meg and their fellows at the Female Factory were no exception, when gathered in the hall before the visitors.

'Cor ... lumme! Lookatim, willyer?' they begged each ther. ''Arf is style! Enough gold braid ter trim a dozen ushions ... I alwus was partial to that shade o' red.... Cop he whiskers!' Then a loud, cheeky voice from the back of he room: 'Wotyer doin' ternight, luv?'

The prison superintendent was now almost as red as Mr Bagot's tunic. 'Silence!' he thundered, but the women merely laughed. Then the visiting ladies' bonnets were xamined and commented on aloud and mockingly.

Jane wished she had Mrs Fry's majestic figure and commanding presence. She felt her temper and her colour rising, while Miss Hayter in her precise English explained their mission, how they hoped to teach the inmates fine sewing and other handicrafts, and help them to help themselves.

'We knows 'ow to 'elp ourselves!' yelled a witch-like creature with an incipient beard. 'That's why we'se 'ere, ee?' Titters went round the room, and Mr Bedford felt moved to read a reproving lecture.

'My unfortunate sisters, sinful as you are –' he boomed, but the women began to cough him down. When he raised his voice they started clapping in unison. It was remarkable the rhythm they kept, as though the whole thing had been rehearsed. The visitors had to withdraw, defeated, to have afternoon tea with the superintendent and his gloomy wife, who was matron, and whose face, framed in a cap with a pleated frill, had the shape and likeness of a pickle bottle. Jane glanced at Miss Hayter. She saw that in the shelter of her bonnet her face was stiff with shock. She refused anything to eat, but sipped her tea in silence.

Next day the newspapers were full of critical comment. *Murray's Review* even accused the Ladies' Committee of indelicacy, suggesting that it was 'not fitting' for unmarried ladies to enter upon such a task, and printing a list of the committee members.

Some of the ladies, shocked at this publicity and at their reception in the prison, withdrew one by one, and Miss Hayter declared she would never set foot there again.

197

Jane talked her round, rallyingly, but when the next visiting day came, Miss Hayter sent a message that she was 'unwell'. It turned out that Mr Price (Mary's husband, now the Assistant Police Magistrate) had warned her the women were hostile, believing that she meant to introduce the cutting of their hair as a punishment. She was told not to go unattended to the wards, or the women would tear her to pieces.

'What stuff!' said Jane, and set off in the carriage alone. She got through the visit without incident, but when she returned Miss Hayter's resignation awaited her. She was returning by the next ship to England.

The rest of the Ladies' Committee soon followed suit. After less than a fortnight Jane's cherished project collapsed.

'I should like,' she said to Sir John that night, as she paced up and down her boudoir in a rage, 'to see the gossiping ladies, and the men gossips who are just as bad, and the vile newspaper editors, and the colonial chaplain and Mr Price, all shaken up in a – in a – I won't say *what*! But they make me so *furious* I could scream! And Miss Hayter with her sickly schoolgirl sensibility is going back to England without accomplishing anything! I don't know when I've been so disappointed.'

'Well, my love, you have done your best, and I thoroughly approve of what you have tried to do; but public opinion is against it, as it is against the college at New Norfolk and every project which has no immediate advantage in pounds, shillings and pence! I fear there is little room for higher things in a colony made up of merchants and emancipists and military cliques.'

'Oh! I had expected so much of Tasmania, and our stay here.'

'Well, Jane, I suggest you turn your energies to something else. You have decided to let the snakes rest in peace; the ladies have decided you must leave the convict women alone.'

'Well, I shall bring something "useless" and cultural into their lives against their will! This very night I'll write to Mary for a design for the Tasmanian Museum. I don't care what it costs! We will leave a little corner of Greek learning in this barbarous place when we go.'

'You mean to pay for it entirely yourself?'

'Yes, just as I did for the Ancanthe garden. And what better setting for a "glyptothek"? We will have art treasures as well, copies of Greek sculptures, portraits of explorers like Ross and Strzelecki – oh, it is a wonderful idea!'

'I believe you'll do it, too,' said Sir John admiringly. 'You're a remarkable determined woman when your mind is set on anything, my love.'

'And it shall be called the Sir John Franklin Museum in your honour. Whatever happens to us, it will remain as your memorial.'

'And yours, my dear Jane.'

Perhaps she had been too hard on Kezia Hayter, a girl fresh out from England. She wrote bravely to Mary that she treated the scandal-mongering papers with the contempt they deserved, but her sensitive nature shrivelled in the hot blast of invective. Even worse were the blatant attacks on Sir John and his administration, for it was now known that he and his Colonial Secretary did not get on, and that Government business was held up as a result.

There had been a drought for two years, so that the Hobart Town and New Town rivulets almost ceased to run. The papers seemed inclined to blame Sir John even for this.

The Town rivulet is now little more than a common sewer, emitting, after the heat of the day, exhalations of the most noxious odour.... At the same time there is a 'deadlock' in Government works, because of the rumoured quarrel between His Excellency and the Colonial Secretary, Mr Montagu....

Count Strzelecki, who had been staying at the Government cottage at Launceston, came down to Hobart for a few weeks. He listened with sympathy to Jane's woes over the Ladies' Committee and Sir John's troubles with his Colonial Secretary. Jane brought out all the designs she had so far collected for her museum, including her own sketch of the Grecian front elevation, and the design by Captain Swanston, creator of the Model Prison at Port Arthur.

The Count approved her drawing but dismissed Swanston's plan. 'Zis is too large, too expensif,' he opined. 'Somesing elegant and imposing wizout being pretentious is what you require, Ma'am.' As usual Jane found him full of good sense and good advice.

Afterwards, as he was demonstrating his coal-testing instruments for analysing the gas content of a piece of Tasmanian coal, setting them out on the library table, Jane noticed with some surprise that Sophy was full of interest. Not only that, but the Count was quite aware of this interest, and laughingly held her hand to steady it while she tried to operate the equipment for herself.

Really, Sophy had been very odd lately, ever since the South Polar expedition left; one day pale and moping, and the next full of a febrile gaiety. Count Strzelecki (unattached, though he had hinted that his affections were bound up with a sweetheart of his youth who still waited for him in Poland) had noted the challenge in her eyes, her arch laughter, and probably thought it only good manners to respond. One could not blame the poor man for flirting a little; he led a Spartan life much of the time, camping in the field or working at his *Physical Description*, which looked like becoming a big book. He could hardly be persuaded to attend any Hobarton festivities.

Why then this strange pang as she looked at him and Sophy, a little flushed and merry, bending over the blue flame?

When she met him in Sydney, she remembered, he had talked to her almost exclusively; but she was older than he by almost five years, and Sophy was young. Examining her heart critically, Jane saw what it was that disturbed her. It was the realization of a woman past fifty, who once used to charm men almost unconsciously, that she is growing old.

When later she mentioned the incident in a letter to Mary, she carefully refrained from the slightly bitter phrase, *'young enough to be his daughter'* .... Mary was an expert at reading between the lines.

Ronald Gunn, once more living in the north of the island, had found Strzelecki a congenial companion on many bush rambles, but a fall from his horse had resulted in a comminuted fracture of the leg, which was to keep him home for months. He had a letter from that odd character, Dr von Lottke, from London; he had heard from some Van Diemen's Land correspondent that 'you did promenade from your Horse to fall and your Leg to break', and offered his condolence. Gunn did not reply; he still resented the large sums of money Dr von Doosenmatter had abstracted from him under various pretexts.

He read with indignation the latest diatribe against the Governor in the *Launceston Advertiser*: 'Poor Sir John! He should be left to the quiet and undisturbed enjoyment of a peaceable unpopularity....'

In Hobart Town meanwhile three young lads cheered themselves hoarse for Sir John Franklin as their ship moved out into the waters of Storm Bay. Bill Bridges, Tommy Martin, and Jem Garaghan had each been given a free pardon for good conduct so that they could join the ship as able seamen. A contrite bushranger, reprieved from the gallows, was heard to say: 'May God bless the Governor!' Another act of clemency brought Montagu's suppressed animosity suddenly boiling to the surface.

It was known afterwards as 'the Coverdale case'. The Police Commissioner of the Richmond district had reported to the Colonial Secretary that Dr Coverdale, the district medical officer, was guilty of culpable negligence causing the death of a patient. On the evidence Montagu asked for his immediate dismissal, to which Sir John agreed.

Dr Coverdale appealed against his dismissal. Nearly the whole population of the Richmond district signed a petition asking for his reinstatement. Lady Franklin, who had recently been there on a visit, heard from friends that they thought the doctor's punishment too severe; she mentioned what she had heard to Captain Forster, whom she happened to meet shortly afterwards.

Sir John hated dereliction of duty as he hated the Devil, but after considering the petition (which showed that Coverdale had not known where to find the patient he was supposed to have neglected, but had stayed in all day waiting to be called to him), he decided to reinstate the doctor.

The immediate result was a visit from Montagu, white in the face with rage. He disliked the people of Richmond, free colonists who were against 'the faction', and he was furious that his recommendation had been revoked on their account.

'Of course,' he said, mouthing his words with cold venom, 'Lady Franklin has stirred up this agitation in the Richmond district, because she has developed an unaccountable dislike to me since my return. Just because the college –'

'Sir! You are speaking of a lady, sir – I would remind you –'

'I cannot help it, Sir John. I must take leave to protest against the lady's interference in affairs of State, and her unwarrantable remarks about me.'

'I am sure, Mr Montagu, that Lady Franklin would not so far forget herself as to criticize your actions publicly.'

'She has spoken in derogatory terms, sir, to Captain Forster, who has reported it to me.'

'Is this true?' For a moment Sir John was shaken. Jane was impulsive and not always discreet; had she made some unguarded remark? It was certain that she had never stirred up the Richmond protest. At last he got rid of Montagu, and went in some agitation in search of Jane.

She was writing, as usual, in her boudoir. At the look on

his face she laid down her quill and rose in apprehension.

'Jane; I have come direct from a most unpleasant interview with Montagu. Tell me the simple truth, my dear: what did you say of him to Forster?'

'Why, nothing; I have never discussed him with Captain Forster.'

'Never? Not over the Coverdale case?'

'Never.'

His shoulders slumped in relief. He sat down on the box-couch and put his head in his hands. She was as shocked as he at the depths of Montagu's hostility – more so, for they had kept up a friendly intercourse on the surface, whatever her suspicions of him might be.

That night she wrote him a long letter of wounded sensibility, and received a stiff and unbending note in reply. He would not set foot in Government House again except officially, nor would Mrs Montagu be permitted to do so. All pretences of friendship were gone.

After this attempt to shake his faith in his wife, his one remaining ally, Sir John could not meet Montagu with the old openness. He could not dissimulate. At their next official meeting he was cold and formal. Montagu saw that he had failed to drive a wedge between husband and wife. He had failed to become the hidden ruler of Van Diemen's Land. His cold anger lay coiled in his breast like a serpent, waiting its opportunity to strike.

Attended by Mr Gell, whose school was on its summer vacation, and with Eleanor and Miss Williamson, Jane retired to New Norfolk for the hot month of December, but she wrote to Sir John and heard from him every day. He told her that public business was held up because Montagu now refused to co-operate with the Governor alone, and everything had to go through Executive Council.

'My Dearest Love,' he wrote, 'I fear Montagu means to continue in his obstructive ways, but I shall tire him out by summoning him continually to the Council.... I cannot dismiss him for merely *negative* misdemeanours, and he knows just how far he can go....'

Jane, however, knew her husband's peace-loving nature, his inability to bear a grudge, and she feared that all would be smoothed over again. She would not have left his side, but while her head ached continually she was of no use to herself or anyone else.

She was pleased to see that *l'affaire Eleanor* was progressing. She went riding with Mr Gell before breakfast every morning, with Miss Williamson or an orderly in attendance, and came back glowing, her face animated and even pretty. Jane never asked to see her diary, but it was full of revealing references:

Copied out the sermon given me by Mr Gell, in full.
Mr Gell read me Thomson's 'Spring'.
Rode this morning 12 miles before breakfast....
This morning had a delightful ride to the forest falls with Mr Gell and an orderly. The views both up and down the river were exceedingly beautiful.
Mr Gell drove Mamma in the cabriole....
Mr Gell took me to church.
Mr Gell ... Mr Gell ... Mr Gell ...

She was not yet eighteen.

Sophy had stopped at home with Mathinna, promising to bring her one day on the excursion steamer up the river to the Governor's Retreat at New Norfolk.

They were all pleased with her development. Lady Franklin had written home glowing accounts of her protégée to her sister; she thought of sending too the charming portrait by Mr Bock.

The little wild-eyed savage who had been brought in from the bush seemed now almost civilized. Everyone was struck by the softness of her looks, their affectionate and sparkling expressiveness, her lively contented air and perfect innocence.

Sophy was fond of her, but had misgivings: what would happen to Mathinna when she grew up? Into what niche in society could she possibly be fitted?

For herself, she felt apathetic and dull since Count Strzelecki returned to Launceston. Ever adaptable to his company, he had seemed to sense the recklessness, the readiness to be diverted, the longing for reassurance in her since the too-transparent offer of her heart had been rejected by Ross.

That heart was still entirely his even if he did not want it. Young as she was, she felt, she knew such intensity of feeling would not come again in a lifetime. Anything else must be a shadow.

The Count had diverted her, and given her back her self-confidence and poise. Behind his vivacity and fire, his amusing anecdotes, his wide, laughing, mobile, bitter mouth, she had sensed some hidden tragedy which drew her to him – not knowing that he too was faithful to the image of one lost love, lost for more than twenty years. Mary was no longer her confidante. Since her cousin had married Mr Price, they had grown apart, for Sophy could not like him: there was something animal about him, about his cold eyes and his big hands covered with reddish hair. It was rumoured that he was a tyrant in his office, as he certainly was at home; and that as Police Magistrate in charge of all the convicts in the south, was known to hand out savage punishments. He was feared by his subordinates, and hated by the prisoners.

She had been reading *The Rime of the Ancient Mariner*, by Samuel Taylor Coleridge. The description of the ship bursting through the ice 'into that silent sea' might have been prophetic of James Ross' last voyage.

Now *Erebus* and *Terror* were again in the far south, making the most of the midsummer days when the sun wheeled round the horizon for twenty-four hours without setting.

Sitting up long after midnight, heavy-eyed yet strangely restless and disinclined for sleep, she turned the day's page in her diary, revealing the date: 18 December, 1841.

205

She was still copying out some verses when the summer dawn began. The room began to grow steadily brighter as the candle guttered lower in its holder. She snuffed it and went downstairs and opened the drawing-room shutters, stepping out on to the veranda to breathe the fresh, damp, aromatic air of early morning. Some soft-edged clouds drifted in the zenith, or wreathed the noble brow of Mount Wellington.

While she watched, the dawn showed briefly its traditional colours, pink, white and blue: but it was a cool and subtle pink, with much mauve in it; the blue showing between the clouds was the faintest, coldest blue imaginable; and the moon over which they slowly dragged was neither white nor gold, but a dull silver-gilt like a tarnished trophy.

Cold, cold! She shivered in the dawn wind, and thought of the austere white world beyond the Antarctic Circle, and those frozen seas where the giant petrel and the Mariner's albatross wandered...

Far to the south, James Ross was writing up his Expedition Journal. For 18 December he wrote:

Last night a strong iceblink appeared in the sky to the S.E.; the temperature of the sea also falling to 29° at midnight, gave notice of our aproach to a large body of ice; and at 3 o'clock in the morning the main pack was seen stretching across our course, from east to west. At this time there were forty large bergs in sight.

All the circumstances appearing favourable, we at once ran into the pack, and at first made good way through it, the ice being remarkably light and very open; but as we proceeded south it became heavier, and more strongly pressed together. Immediately upon entering the ice we found the temp. of the seat at 28 deg., that of the air being 32 deg.; and *for the first time the beautiful snow-white petrel was seen.*

Chapter Twenty-five

'Want of talent in the ruler of a province is more mis-
chievous than want of principle ... but this is what has
been revealed by the administration of this Colony by Sir
John Franklin.

'To his too-evident incapacity – to his demonstrated
feebleness – can be traced all the errors of his administration. He has long outlived respect! His policy has been
distinguished by time-serving expediency.... The
Queen's School is at this moment, through the vicious
ambition of Sir John, an *incubus* upon the land.'

The *Van Diemen's Land Chronicle* was crumpled, flung
to the floor.

'By heaven! They go too far, Henslowe,' cried Sir John.

'They are certainly shameless, Your Excellency. In fact
their insolence is almost incredible.'

'And yet Montagu – Montagu solicited my patronage for
this – this off-scouring from the gutter! It was to be a semi-
official publication. He was to give them Government news
in advance, they were to borrow the latest scientific and
literary journals from Lady Franklin – they have borrowed
them! No, it's too much. I must ask Montagu formally to
withdraw his support from this rag.'

The season of peace, goodwill towards men, was over;
an open season of backbiting and slander seemed to have
been declared. Young Henslowe said to the A.D.C. in his
office: 'Quick, where's some paper without the Government House letterhead? I'm going to write off my own bat
to that slippery Montagu, and ask him to deny that he's connected in any way with the *Chronicle*. The last article's
really too much. His Ex. is in a wax about it, and he can't
very well write himself without causing a crisis.'

'What have they said this time?'

'See for yourself.' He tossed over the paper, which had been printed on Christmas Eve.

' "Deplorable indolence ... immense sums of money have been wantonly and disgracefully lavished upon ridiculous journeys and fantastical deviations from the paths of men...." Phew! That's pretty hot, eh? A dig at Lady Franklin and me for going to Adelaide I suppose – and she chartered the *Abeona* from her own purse – and to New Zealand, when a British warship offered a free passage there and back. Fantastical imagination they've got!'

Young Henslowe wrote his letter, marked it 'Personal', and sent an official memo to Sir John on his action. A characteristically devious reply having come from Montagu, he pressed him to be more explicit, and received the snub direct: 'Sir, you have taken a liberty with me which our short acquaintance has not warranted.'

Henslowe gave up with a sigh and handed the file of correspondence over to Sir John with a note to the effect that he thought the articles highly disrespectful to the King's representative.

On 11 January Sir John wrote himself, reminding Montagu how he had solicited Government patronage for the *Chronicle*, and referring to the scurrilous articles. Montagu coolly denied it.

'Damnation!' said Sir John, which was strong language for him.

'I fear, Sir,' he wrote with chill formality, 'that in this case the Lieutenant-Governor can only conclude that the Colonial Secretary's memory is at fault.'

Back came a letter which for studied insolence made the Governor gasp. He showed it to Jane, just back from New Norfolk and inclined to be rather horrified at his high-handed calling of Montagu's bluff. She went pink with anger and surprise. There was nothing for it, she agreed, but to suspend the Colonial Secretary from office.

Yet she felt a pang; that handsome, proud, clever man to be brought so low! She had been hurt by his sudden display of enmity for herself, his announcement that neither he nor Mrs Montagu would set foot in Government House again as guests or friends, but now he was to be sent home to England in disgrace she felt sorry for him.

She appealed to Sir John to reconsider. Sir John was affected by her nervous eloquence; but, as on a few other occasions, she found him immovable. He set his jaw firmly and to all her pleas replied, 'What's done cannot be undone. He has gone too far this time, and must take his medicine.'

'But what if – if Lord Stanley should not back you up? If –'

'I cannot help that, my dear. In this case I feel absolutely certain of having done right, and nothing will shake that conviction, not the censure of the whole of Her Majesty's Home Government. It's not just this last letter, that's only the culmination of a hundred pinpricking insolencies. He was determined to wear me down, ever since he returned, and I feel morally sure he's behind the attacks on you in the Press.'

Jane was silent. She felt in her heart that he was right, yet she was uneasy at the outcome. Might not the Secretary of State for the Colonies begin adding up the number of dismissals under the present administration, and wonder if all was well? Captain Maconachie; Captain Sheyne, the Director of Roads and Bridges; Mr Gregory, the Colonial Treasurer; and now the highest officer of the Government, the Colonial Secretary himself!

They had been so long in the colony, she found it hard now to see its affairs in perspective. This was only a portion of her life, and Sir John's. Yet she felt they would be judged by their success or failure here.

How little she had known, when she went aboard the *Fairlie* full of joyful expectation! *Uneasy lies the head that wears a crown* – even when it is only a tinsel, proxy crown that can be snatched away at a moment's notice by an edict from fourteen thousand miles away.

In a few weeks Mr Montagu had packed up his family and his goods and left for England. The oppressive heat of an unusually severe summer had given way to cooling breezes from the sea; the thunderclouds rolled away, the hot winds ceased, the air cleared.

High above the spreading town the summit of Mount Wellington shone clear in rocky grandeur against a sky swept and polished by the winds. The harbour sparkled like a bowl of saphires. The inhabitants of Government House felt their spirits rise in spite of themselves.

Mr Gell's boys from the Queen's School often came round in the afternoon. They found the Governor a new man, genial as always but without the haunted worried look they'd come to associate with his blue and bloodshot eyes. He had not looked so well since Ross and Crozier sailed away. As Lady Franklin wrote to Ross, the dismissal of Montagu had done him good in every possible way: it had roused him to new vigour, sharpened his perceptions and calmed his mind.

All the good would of course be swept away if the Secretary of State failed to uphold Sir John's act in suspending his Colonial Secretary. Yet he was fortifying himself for just such a reversal. They both knew by now the extent of Montagu's power and malice – or so they thought. For the present there was nothing to do but wait for Lord Stanley's dispatches.

Invitations were sent out in March for the ceremony of laying the foundation stone of the Ancanthe Museum. Mr Gell helped Lady Franklin to compose an inscription in six languages, which was lettered on parchment in Mr Ewing's beautiful script ready to be placed beneath the stone. It read, in Greek, English, Latin, French, German and Italian:

Laid 16 March 1842 by Sir John Franklin
in the presence of the Masters and Scholars
of the Queen's School and others his friends
as the Corner Stone of an Edifice
to be given in Trust from Lady Franklin to the College
for the purpose of preserving
the productions of Nature
and as a Retreat
for her Ministers and Interpreters
Thomas John Ewing, Clerk
Curator of the Museum

Jane had acquired another ten acres of almost level ground
below the Vale of Flowers (which the unpleasant newspapers insisted on referring to as 'Lady Franklin's folly at
Kangaroo Bottom', though she called it Lower Ancanthe,
and its correct name was Lenah Valley – 'Lenah' being the
local native name for kangaroo).

Here in a bush setting, with a background of folded hills
rising to Mount Wellington and within sound of the Newtown and Brushy Creeks, the stone was laid. She refused
to have her own name upon it; the building was to be
shown on the title deed as 'The Franklin Museum'.

After the ceremony the party climbed farther up the hill
'Nsika' for a cold picnic lunch spread on cloths on the
grass, with jellied turkey and sliced ham and cold roast
chicken. 'Success to the Museum' was drunk in cold champagne, Mr Gell made a speech in Greek. and a libation of
wine was poured upon the ground – the hard dry ground
with its burnt grass and aromatic shrubs which might well
have been part of the ancient land of Greece.

Then tea was brewed over an open fire – watched carefully in case it started a bushfire in the dry scrub – and
stirred with gum-twigs to give it flavour.

Lying back against a shaded rock, listening to the monotonous soothing chirr of crickets in the heated ground. the
whirr and click of grasshoppers' wings, Jane felt content.

At least she had achieved *something*. Long after she and Sir John were gone from Tasmania and from the world, this building would remain as a monument to their interest in art and science. She felt sure the convict builder would make a thing of beauty from the architect's plan – a severely classical building based on the lines of the temple of Athene at Athens. It would be small, but perfectly proportioned, with a row of four fluted columns in front. She meant to inspect and supervise every step herself. It was a pleasant though bumpy drive to Lenah Valley, practicable in all but very wet weather.

Behind her the great trees rose in grey columns, unbroken by any branch for a hundred feet, like the portico of some greater Greek temple. Their shadows fell in long dark stripes down the side of the hill. Mount Wellington towered above, and below, the land fell away in gentle undulations to the winding Derwent. The air was redolent of eucalyptus and dry grass. A column of blue smoke rose straight into the sky from beyond the next rise.

She breathed deeply, inhaling the pure and stimulating atmosphere, enjoying the simple fact of being alive.

Chapter Twenty-six

On the far west coast lay the abandoned penal settlement of Macquarie Harbour, a place more dreaded even than Port Arthur. Only one man had ever escaped from it overland, and he, after eating his companions on the way, gave himself up in a starved and half-crazed state to be hung.

The bolters usually perished of cold and hunger in the dank unwholesome swamps of that terrible region, lashed by tempests howling in from the sea, sodden with rain that fell continuously from the low grey sky. In its chill and humid climate spirits sank to their lowest, and bird and animal life was almost non-existent.

Those who managed to make their way through the swamps and ravines and the nearly impenetrable 'horizontal' scrub, through the dripping forests bearded with moss and lichen, came to yet another barrier: enormous mountains covered with snow, which rose to the clouds like walls of adamant, with an air of rigour, ferocity, and doom.

Its inaccessibility made Macquarie Harbour an excellent place of confinement; but its known horrors drove men to desperate deeds to escape it, like the pirates of the brig *Cyprus* who overpowered their gaolers on board and sailed away to the South Seas. It had been abandoned in 1834 and was now deserted.

Sir John knew its character and history, and longed to explore the overland route himself. James Calder, the Surveyor-General, had already blazed a trail for him as far as the Gordon River which flowed into the harbour; but he was horrified when he heard that Lady Franklin intended going too. It was no place for a woman, however sturdy, let alone a lady used to the most refined comforts –

'Lady Franklin is one of the most intrepid travellers of her sex I have ever known,' said Sir John, cutting him short. 'She has managed to get to places no lady ever set foot in before. But quite apart from that, *she has made up her mind to go*; and I can assure you, my dear Calder, that when she makes up her mind to anything it will save time in the long run to agree at once.'

'Yes, well –' grumbled Calder. 'If Your Excellency is sure ... Perhaps we can arrange to have her carried over some of the worst of the track. It's not even as if she were a *young* lady.'

'Her spirit is young, that's the main thing. What does the Bard say?

> Your merry heart goes all the way,
> Your sad tires in a mile–a.

There's one thing I can guarantee: she won't complain.'

Indeed, Jane was game for anything, but she knew the journey would be arduous and perhaps dangerous. A medical man, Dr Milligan, who was also something of a naturalist, was going with them, but they would be quite cut off from any help if it should be needed, once they left the edge of the settled country and crossed the upper Derwent where it issued from Lake St Clair. Sir John insisted that she should be carried some of the way, as she had not been well lately (wounded, he suspected, by the slings and arrows of outrageous journalism, for the Press attacks on her had increased in number and bitterness of late). A light wooden armchair was fitted with rings for carrying-poles, so that four of the twenty picked convicts who were to go with them could take it in turns to carry it. She was glad for their sakes that she had kept her slight figure.

All the same, she was resolved to go as far as possible on her own feet. She disliked asking anyone to do what she was not prepared to do herself. Stewart had agreed to go, her stolid, stalwart, dependable Stewart. Even for a married lady it would be an embarrassment, Lady Franklin felt, to be the only one of her sex among a company of males. Sophy had been pale and peaky lately, quite lacking her usual energy, so she did not ask her. She spent most of her time at the piano in the great empty drawing-room, playing dreamily or fiercely according to her mood. Eleanor, of course, had no taste for discomfort; she was a born city-dweller. Marie had married a French settler on the Huon, one of Lady Franklin's own tenant farmers, and was busy raising a race of French-Tasmanians.

That left Stewart.

'Of course I'll come, my lady,' said Stewart when warned of the hardships ahead. 'I wouldn't rest easy if you was travellin' in them furrin parts without me to bring your posset at bedtime.'

'There'll be no beds, Stewart. Sleeping-bags on the ground, and a tent over our heads if we're lucky. Damper and black tea, salt pork and biscuits: we'll be on bush rations most of the time, till we join the schooner at the Gordon. Remember, *everything* we take has to be carried.'

'Remember, everything you take has to be carried on the shoulders of my men, Lady Franklin,' said Calder mildly.

'I can't help that, Mr Calder. I must take my books; I couldn't live without any books. And *this* bag contains a plum cake and a bottle or two of wine and some rum for the men, to celebrate Sir John's birthday or our arrival at Macquarie Harbour, whichever is earlier. And *this* one –'

With dismay Calder looked at the growing pile on the ground. 'Perhaps,' he suggested delicately, 'if I were to go through a list of necessities with your ladyship, we could work out which things are absolutely indispensable, and then ...'

Lady Franklin heard him to the end of his sentence, her head a little on one side, a winsome, co-operative smile on her face. Then she said firmly:

'These things are *all* indispensable, Mr Calder. I have already been through the list, checking and double-checking. Now, here is the last one. Please see that none of the bags is left behind "by accident". I shall not forgive you

215

if even one is missing.'

'Yes, Lady Franklin.' The big, bearded surveyor was vanquished with scarcely a shot fired. He had tried arguing with her before, and had found that one might as well argue with the wind about its direction. For such a small, feminine-looking lady she was excessively obstinate. Yet he couldn't help liking her. She could laugh at herself, as over that mad whim of getting rid of all the snakes in Van Diemen's Land; and she had such a droll way of looking at someone who was being a little pompous or didactic: humour sparkled in her eye, and even her silence was eloquent.

Eleanor had shown more emotion than usual when they set out. 'Everything seems to go wrong when you're away,' she said, near to tears.

Mathinna said nothing, but she strained her thin little arms round Jane's knees and looked up questioningly into her face.

'Yes, I will come back, little one,' said Jane.

Before they left they had been much grieved to hear of Mrs Gould's death only five days after the birth of her little girl. The beautiful book on Australian birds that she had illustrated for her husband with her paintings remained as her memorial.

Sir John wrote to his friend Strzelecki in Launceston about the coming trip, and how sorry he was that Ronald Gunn, who had broken his leg badly months before, was unable to come and botanize.

Knowing the Count's interest in the Aborigines, Sir John told him of the small group of men and boys caught recently in the north-west, in the act of spearing sheep for food. They had been sent off to join their fellows. 'So our little Native girl is the last of her race still remaining in the main Island,' he wrote.

Strzelecki was planning a visit to Flinders Island, for he wished to test a theory of his own for the dwindling of the race. He felt there was little hope of their survival, but while they survived he deplored the efforts of missionaries and others, however well-meaning, to graft a European set of customs and observances on to a primitive people. 'At least leave them alone to follow their own customs, and let their last remaining years be happy,' he said.

He'd had many an argument with Jane over the wisdom of keeping Mathinna and teaching her along with Eleanor. The result could only be disastrous for the child, because of the deep dichotomy between the Aboriginal and the white man's way of life and thought.

He was pleased that Sir John had resisted Robinson's grandiose scheme of taking all the Tasmanians from Flinders Island to the mainland: 'Where they would have a civilizing effect upon their wild brothers.'

'Zis man is mad,' Strzelecki had said with vigour. 'He has illusions of grandeur, of being the Conciliator for all ze mainland natives. Obviously he has no idea of ze size of Australia, ze immensity, ze distance involved. Zis was a scheme ze most foolish and ill-considered.'

It had certainly been unfortunate for Bob and Jacky, who were among the small group he was allowed to take with him when he was appointed Chief Protector of Aborigines at Port Phillip. They had wandered off, become involved with some whalers, and ended up being hanged for murder.

Mr Malcolm Smith had been put in charge at Flinders Island, with Mr Dove the Presbyterian minister and Mr Clark the catechist to help. A medical man, Dr Jeanneret, was to take over shortly. For the time being the swift decline seemed to have been arrested.

News of Ross and Crozier arrived just before the Macquarie Harbour expedition set out. Sir John wrote to tell Strzelecki they had reached Tierra del Fuego in South America after a fearful passage.

'What a narrow escape *Erebus* and *Terror* have had! They reached 78.94' S. Found the ice as before like a wall.

Erebus's bow was stove in by contact with *Terror* in a gale of wind; they collided while trying to clear an iceberg, in immense seas. . . . Almighty Providence has saved them for some further work.'

How closely connected with his own life and death that 'further work' was to be he had then no idea; or did some intimations of mortality reach him from a future yet hidden over the horizon towards which his course was set?

This was the first time Jane had ever been on an exploring expedition with her husband. She felt as excited as a child when they left the last homestead behind and set off on horseback into the New Country: past a gang of probation convicts working on a drainage project, through a forest of weird, dead trees of ghostly grey, still standing, but without a living twig or leaf, past Lake Echo and into the unexplored wilds of Transylvania.

They halted in the early evening on the banks of the upper Derwent, and went to see Lake St Clair. They stood in awed silence on the banks of one of the loveliest expanses of water in the world. The sunset-rosy peak of snowy Mount Olympus was reflected there, and the lesser mountains ringing it round. Dark myrtle-beech and pine grew downward in what seemed a purer atmosphere.

At last Lady Franklin broke the silence. 'I am excessively fond of mountains, Mr Calder, are not you?' she said.

'I can't truthfully say so, Lady Franklin.' Calder was a little dry with her. 'They strike me as objects of unprofitable sublimity and useless grandeur, simply impeding progress and making it difficult to open up new districts.'

'Oh, fie! What a Philistine!' laughed Jane. 'Is he not, Sir John? "Objects of useless grandeur" indeed. Think how boring if all the earth were flat!'

'Nevertheless, to a road-building engineer a bit more flatness in the Van Diemen's Land countryside would not come amiss, your Ladyship.'

'Poor Mr Calder! You've had a terrible time making this

218

track for us, haven't you?'

'It's the most harassing duty I have ever gone through, and it's not over yet,' said big Calder bluntly. 'I shall be immensely relieved when you and Sir John are safely aboard the *Breeze* in Macquarie Harbour.'

'Well, well, never fear our spirit, Calder. I'm an old campaigner,' said Sir John, 'and so is my wife. She can put up with an extraordinary amount of discomfort and even danger if she makes her mind up to it. You've no idea what a strong will she has.'

Oh yes, I have! though Calder to himself. She was the best and kindest person, yet she could never conceive that any arrangement she had made could be improved upon; you might as well tell her that night was day, or try to persuade Mount Olympus to move from its base.

If she couldn't talk you round to her way of thinking – or 'into reason', as she called it – she was sure to defeat you by some other ingenious means. It had amused him sometimes to see a stranger, a new Government officer perhaps, deceived by her great good humour into thinking he had persuaded her into another course than the one she had set her mind on. While her kindly if slightly satirical smile gave the idea that she would comply, he suddenly found himself floored by some witty sally or exquisite rebuke. And one was usually enough.

In the morning Jane's leg was stiff from the cold, so 'the palanquin' was hoisted on the men's shoulders, cheerfully enough for her weight was nothing among four of them; the carts and horses turned back; the expedition had begun in earnest.

There had been an iron frost in the night. Half an inch of ice formed on the water left in the washbasin. But the sun rose in glory, and by the time they were on the move the spicules of hoar-frost had melted from the glittering trees, and the spiked wheels of ice from roadside pools. Patches of mist wreathed about the trees like teased cottonwool, and

219

birds sang clear and free. Even the hardened convicts in the party seemed to sense the beauty and peacefulness striking deep into their souls.

Under a sky of intense Australian blue, in brilliant sunshine which lit up even the dark, dense foliage of King William pine and beech (so different from the light-filtering gum trees of the east coast), they went on to King William's Plains and camped among the timber. By the next day they had climbed on to the central Tasmanian plateau, and wherever they looked they saw mountains.

Nowhere in the world, said Sir John, and his lady agreed, was there a view to equal the prospect from Fatigue Hill. The monotonous dark forest clothed the endless rolling ranges; the landscape lay folded into immense mountain ridges like a frozen sea. Beyond was the great range of the Frenchman, with Frenchman's Cap disappearing into mist, and far below lay a distant sunlit plain, green and verdant and quite untouched by man – save for the wandering lost tribes of Aborigines – since the first days of creation.

Next day they were deep in jungle. Myrtle and fern trees, pandanus palms and sassafras, jumbled in an inextricable mass of fallen trunks and sprouting creeper. They began to realize what Calder had meant. The track had been cut foot by foot, with axe and tomahawk, through the horizontal scrub.

They crossed a river on a bridge formed by a huge fallen beech tree, and followed down its banks in deep forest. At last they emerged on the plain directly below Frenchman's Cap. The great triangular peak, glittering white with quartz, unveiled its head from the mist.

Now the vegetation was parklike, the streams were placid and winding, and little Burn, the Englishman who had asked to come on the expedition because he wanted to write, began to feel more at home. He had found the jungle terrifying, the dead trees oppressive. But the weather closed down on them; it rained and blew, the streams rose, and they were kept in camp for a week. On the first night lightning lit the buttongrass of the plain and the wind had blown the flames towards them so that he had feared being burnt to death; now it looked as if he would be drowned.

Calder was uneasy. He knew the *Breeze* would not wait at Macquarie Harbour after the eighteenth, and they still had the worst part of the journey to cover.

He knew better than to speak in front of Lady Franklin. He took her husband aside and said seriously, 'I think, sir, it would be wiser to return. The season has broken. The Franklin may be to high to cross when we get there, and our provisions by then will be so low that we won't be able to retreat. It's now or never.'

'We'll put it to the vote,' said Sir John.

Chapter Twenty-seven

Everyone agreed to go on; they felt, erroneously, that the worst was over now. Certainly they were geographically much nearer to Macquarie Harbour than they were to Hobart Town.

So Calder, huge and untiring, took half the convicts and trudged back to the Derwent for fresh supplies. Returning, he found the party isolated on a little triangle of ground between the mountain and a flooded creek. Their tents were sodden, they were sleeping on beds of damp fern, and it was so cold that snow was falling. Sir John was in his element. This was the sort of physical trial which called out all his resources of good-humoured resistance.

'Come, my boys,' he cheered the cold and sullen convicts. 'This is nothing, you should laugh at this.' And when Milligan wanted to curtail the men's ration and give more to Lady Franklin and 'the gentry' he wouldn't hear of it. 'No, no, let us go short if necessary; and the men who do all the work have the extra.' And his gallant wife agreed.

When at last the party reached the Franklin, it was in turbulent flood. There could be no going back now. They had come through the worst part of the journey, the valley of the Acheron, a stream as dark and sinister as its counterpart in Hades. It was enclosed by dark-foliaged trees through which no light penetrated from above. Underneath, among the slimy mosses and dank, bearded trunks, glowed points of strange blue luminosity, a weird and heatless light from a multitude of phosphorescent fungi.

Sir John had had a bad fall on the steep track, but with characteristic thoughtfulness called out before he even landed: 'I'm not hurt at all; quite the contrary!'

Jane laughed at him in her relief. 'What did you mean, *quite the contrary*? That in fact the fall had done you good? Oh, you are the most – Oh! Help! Sir Jo –' And she too slid out of sight over the slimy bank, and winded herself against a tree. Calder and one of the convicts had bounded down to her almost before she stopped, and lifted her bodily up to the track. Sir John brushed solicitously at the mud on her divided skirt: she would have preferred trousers to her riding-habit if the very thought were not unwomanly.

Poor Stewart slogged along in the rear, her head down, an expression on her face like that of a suffering cow. She had been on some wild trips with her ladyship, but this was absolutely the dead finish. Never, never again would she be let in for 'explorin''. Might she be shut up in the loony-house if ever she agreed to such a thing; It 'ud be a miracle if they got out of it alive, or at least with all their limbs left to them. Starving on salt junk and biscuits when they could be dining at Guv'mint 'Ouse on squabs and spatchcock! Lord, what fools these mortals be ...

Lieutenant Bagot, A.D.C., had thoughts much like those of Stewart. The Governor's orderly and the once-gorgeous aide-de-camp were indistinguishable now. No crimson cloth and gold braid decorated the Queen's soldier. He had several days' growth of beard beyond the side-whiskers he wore, and his face and hands were grimed with stinking mud. He would *never* want to be an explorer!

Dr Milligan, calm and philosophical, botanized among the fascinatingly different flora and made notes for Ronald Gunn. He could make himself at home anywhere. He watched with amusement the discomfort of young Bagot, and with admiration the wonderful good humour of Lady Franklin. 'She's the life and soul of the expedition,' he wrote to Gunn when they reached the banks of the Franklin.

Jane had been kept up by excitement, the unfailing stimulus of new surroundings. Only in this dank valley of the Acheron did she begin to feel the oppression which Mr Gunn had mentioned – Van Demons' Land! The coldly-glowing points of light in the gloomy undergrowth looked

223

like the eyes of trolls or gnomes. There was a continual hollow patterning of large drops from the trees shutting out the sky, on to the broad-leaved growths below. Strangling creepers wound upward like coiling serpents, and green moss and white-bearded lichen coated every tree, living or dead.

And all this with cold; a dank penetrating cold, clammy and depressing. The growth was tropical in its luxuriance, yet the island was far from tropic latitudes. It was a strange land indeed, a distant land, only half-tamed by man and perhaps never to be fully inhabited.

Down in the deeper gullies, shrouded in tree-fern and creeper, was always the sound of rushing water, which underlined the silence, the stillness where no wind ever penetrated from above. Down there lurked *Thylacine*, the Tasmanian Tiger, striped and savage; and in the murky swamps rotted the white bones of the few convicts who had tried to make their way overland from Macquarie Harbour through this soulless, hostile environment where they had come across no living thing, and no birds sang.

'God exists everywhere,' said Jane to herself, but felt thankful for the company of her fellow men.

At last they emerged and saw once more the stars, and the rushing waters of the Franklin. Poor Calder now had another headache. The *Breeze* would wait only another two days, having heard nothing of them. And the river was impracticable for the raft he had left there for the crossing.

Two of the convicts had been bargees on the Thames. They feared no river, they said. They launched themselves on the raft in an attempt to get word across to the schooner.

They were instantly carried out of sight on the raging waters. Soon, however, the anxious watchers heard a faint 'Coo-ee!' from downstream; the two men appeared on the opposite bank, and darted into the forest.

They could not have known that a free pardon would be theirs when they got back to civilization, though they hoped for some indulgence from the Governor. That night they returned with news that the schooner would wait, but her stores were very low. Poor Calder and nine weary men set out again on the dreadful journey to St Clair for a new load of provisions.

Before they went they celebrated Sir John's birthday. The plum cake was brought out of its bag, a little damp and mildewy but edible; with the addition of wine and rum, the salt pork became a banquet.

Still the river rose. Burn, who had once been a naval architect, and an old convict who was a ship's carpenter, began to work on a double canoe of Huon pine, a wood not hard to work. Sir John was quite unable to keep away or refrain from giving advice when any sort of craft was involved.

He kept hovering about, making suggestions and getting in the way, until the surly old convict turned on him in a fury.

'You be off directly,' he said with a menacing look, 'and don't come meddling with what you know nothin' about.'

Sir John retired quietly to his tent, while the others tried to suppress their titters. It had been so unconsciously done that not even the Governor of Van Diemen's Land, a Captain of the Royal Navy and a Knight Commander of the Bath could take offence.

When Calder's men returned the party crossed on the canoe, named the *Eleanor Isabella*. Ten miles up the glorious, green-sombre River Gordon the little *Breeze* was awaiting them, a schooner of twenty-eight tons. Calder's men, stocking up with what extras the schooner could spare, turned back to make the journey overland to Hobart Town. The others settled down in comparative comfort to write letters home, feeling they were almost there. A few days' voyage round the coast was nothing.

Anxiety was mounting in the capital. When Calder returned with news of the safe boarding of the *Breeze*, the travellers were expected daily. A week went by and there was no word.

It began to seem certain that they had been wrecked, and

that the survivors must be starving on that inhospitable shore. The Government cutter *Vansittart* set out to search the west coast for wreckage, the *Beagle* was diverted from her survey work, and the schooner *Eliza* sailed with provisions to make a search of Macquarie Harbour.

When the *Eliza* did not return, a land party of six convicts was sent along the now almost beaten trail across country, to search the harbour shore for wreckage or survivors.

Meanwhile the *Eliza* beat up and down outside the harbour. The weather was too rough for her to enter, and continuous westerly gales caused her to stand well out to sea from the dangerous lee shore. Long ago the doomed convicts who entered this hell-on-earth had named the rocky bar across the entrance 'Hell's Gates'.

Eighteen days out from Hobart Town, the weather began to moderate at last. The blinding rain squalls ceased, the wind tended easterly. Next day, which was a Sunday, as they turned north again after a long southerly tack, the *Eliza* sighted a small schooner's sail on the horizon. It was the *Breeze*, with seventeen famished sailors and passengers aboard.

They had many stories to tell of their three weeks' imprisonment. In that very place the half-starved convicts, lashed by cruel overseers and by furious storms of rain, cold and cramped in their cells, cold and miserable when out at work, had dreamed hopelessly of escape. The Vice-Regal party had had quite enough of it.

The acute shortage of food – for fish had been shy – the cramped quarters, with everyone living in one room, and above all the appalling weather had made it seem a lifetime. They had been in real danger of starvation if the sea had not unlocked those sullen gates and let them out. They transferred thankfully to the *Eliza*.

It had made a profound impression on Jane, always susceptible to the spirit of place. She had been able to think quite placidly about the men convicts before.

She had heard rumours that both Captain Booth and Mr Price were martinets, that Port Arthur was a place of suffering, but after all the men were felons, doubly-convicted most of them, and receiving their just punishment.

Now she had lived and shared discomforts in the bush with twenty convicts, and found that they were people, with human failings and human dignity. She had felt a bitter pang when poor Mumford put out his eye; and she had been impressed by the fact that these men had only to band together to murder them all with the tomahawks in their possession, then take over the *Breeze* and sail away to the South Seas; yet they had walked and worked with a will, carried her for thirty miles without grumbling, and had gone back quietly with Mr Calder over that dreadful trail, with winter already setting in. She – why, she *admired* them!

When the *Eliza* finally got back to Hobart – the *Breeze* having sailed ahead with news of their safety, for they were determined to explore Port Davey on the way home – Jane was distressed to hear of the new overland party of convicts, now overdue in its search for them.

Another party was sent on their trail, but little hope was held; they must have run out of provisions long since. Jane sent for Mr Calder and begged him to do all he could: she would most gladly bear the expense, whatever it might be.

She told Mr Boyes of her horror at the thought of leaving those poor gallant fellows to perish; she would never forgive herself if it were found afterwards that some means had been left untried that might have rescued them, or at least ascertained their fate.

She could imagine all too well the condition of the lost party, she told him; indeed, their image haunted her day and night. At last she burst into tears, with such unaffected emotion that even the stolid Boyes was moved, and promised to do everything in his power. She was glad that it was he and not the cold Montagu who was now the Colonial Secretary.

She knew at first hand the miseries of cold and hunger

and of hope deferred. They had almost given themselves up
for lost until that last Sunday when the day dawned clear
with promise, and the thunder of the reef at last was stilled.

They had gathered on the deck for morning service, and
there was not a sound – it almost seemed that the men held
their breaths – while Sir John read with impressive earnest-
ness from Psalm 107:

> They that go down to the sea in ships, that do business in
> great waters; these see the works of the Lord, and His
> wonders in the deep.
> For He commandeth, and raiseth the stormy wind, which
> lifteth up the waves thereof.
> They mount up to the heaven, they go down again to the
> depths: their soul is melted because of trouble ...
> Then they cry unto the Lord in their trouble, and He
> bringeth them out of their distresses.
> He maketh the storm a calm, so that the waves thereof
> are still.
> Then are they glad because they be quiet; so He bringeth
> them unto their desired haven.

She had prayed every night since her return for the lost
men. Surely the Lord would hear her cry? Sir John had
offered a free pardon to the two men who dared the flooded
Franklin in the raft, and there were tickets-of-leave for the
others. But if these six were uselessly lost she would never
be able to sleep with an easy conscience again.

However, a second party had now been sent off after the
first, well equipped with provisions. Eventually they met the
exhausted men returning, having eaten the boiled remains
of their leather knapsacks, in which they had nothing more
to carry.... They could not, they said, have held out
another day: unshaven, red-eyed, their boots in tatters.

They had left a pathetic note at Macquarie Harbour,
found by a search vessel, *'to let anyone no we have don our
duty what we was sen to dou ... May God give us power to
go trou our journey ...'*

228

Jane wrote to tell her sister they had been found, and added: 'You would not believe how all this has changed and aged me.' Perhaps it was partly the rigours of the expedition, the short rations and the exposure to weather, which had lined her face and sprinkled some threads of grey in her dark hair, so that she began to look her real age. She was in her fiftieth year.

The newspapers continued their attacks. They enquired the cost of 'Lady Franklin's palanquin', and suggested that she had procured free pardons for the 'palanquin bearers'. They chided Sir John for leaving his public business – the first real holiday he'd had in five gruelling years – for 'a wild and senseless freak'.

Murray's Review was the most vociferous. After speculating on the cost of sending the *Breeze*, it remarked that Sir John's unfitness for office had been manifest from the start; that 'miserably inactive as his Government had even been' it had now been left for almost two months without a leader; that the Macquarie Harbour excursion had been 'a book-making' expedition and that part of the lady's travel-book was already in a London publisher's hands.

'No doubt,' it added blandly, 'Lady Franklin's "history" will boast of much extensive exploring: when the interesting volume appears, in the concoction of which so much of the Public Funds have been employed, nothing will be found to have escaped the vigilant eye of the lady....'

All these insults had to be endured in silence. Sir John took his consolation from the *Imitation of Christ* of Thomas à Kempis, 'Trusting in God when men speak ill of us: *These scandals vanish and fly away like motes in the sun...*'

Jane could not be so philosophical. She burned with resentment; it made her go hot all over, in a great flash of impotent rage, when she read in the *Colonial Times*: 'Sir John's ineptness as a governor was never in doubt.... He has brought the colony to a condition bordering on ruin.' (They were blaming him now for the financial depression, which had been steadily worsening from various causes, not least the closing of mainland markets for Tasmanian wheat and wool, while steady labour was scarce and land values had slumped.)

She composed long, scathing letters in which she utterly routed the editors of the worst journals; but these compositions had all to be consigned to the fire.

The attacks on Sir John were harder to bear than those on herself. What, after all, did she care for colonial opinion? This was only a distant outpost, and no one at home would hear about these scandals in a tea-cup; she would get used to it, she would, she must. But it was Sir John's whole life – his ability as a leader, his integrity as a public official, his worth as a man – which was in question.

He was bearing up remarkably well. The holiday had done him good, but ever since Montagu left his spirits had risen noticeably. Anxiety left him, he no longer had recourse to brandy-and-water to make him sleep, so that his brain was clear in the mornings. The calm knowledge that he'd done the right thing upheld him. He felt confident that Lord Stanley would back him up. All was for the best, he kept assuring her.

Jane held her peace, but something, a foreboding or a feminine intuition, told her that the wily Montagu would win in the end. He was on the spot, he could get his story in first. She saw the word 'recall' hanging over their future. Montagu would do all in his power to make it a recall in disgrace.

Chapter Twenty-eight

Sophy could no longer see to read the notes. She closed the piano and stepped out on to the veranda, shivering in the clear cold air.

Where the sun had gone down a warm amber glow lingered, shading upward into clearest green and peacock blue. The pure and luminous arch of sky was unmarked by a feather of cloud, or even the white point of a star.

Against it every leaf of the thin-clad gum trees showed in separate silhouette: each tree's anatomy of bare trunks and shapely boughs was etched in black. For a moment she longed for her sketchbook and pencil, but she had given them up since her eyes were so bad. They were smarting now from peering at the music.

She rested them by gazing at the empty sky until the zenith deepened to a more intense and brilliant hue, the green and yellow were absorbed, and the first stars came out.... Yes, there were the Pointers, scintillating in the clear atmosphere like gems in water. Above them, in the arc of its great swing round the Pole, hung the Southern Cross to which they pointed. The fainter stars were missing still, but she knew its shape by heart. *James Ross, James Ross, where are you now?*

She knew that his two ships had been preserved by some miracle in that terrible collision among the bergs. He was still alive, and somewhere in the southern hemisphere. Perhaps his eyes rested on the same constellation at this moment. She sent up a passionate prayer. Not that he should be hers: she had given up that dream forever. But that he should be preserved to find happiness with that other.

Count Strzelecki, who had been gallant to Sophy, charming

to Lady Franklin, and a sympathetic friend to Sir John, had finally left them for the mainland, from where he would go to England to see his book through the press. He had added something of tone to Government House gatherings in Hobart Town.

He had enchanted the ladies with his graceful manners, his European ease of address, his vivacity and fire. How was it such a charming man was not married, they wondered?

Before leaving, the Count had confided to Sir John, who had told Jane with the strictest injunctions to secrecy, that he had found what was probably a rich gold discovery west of Sydney, during his explorations in New South Wales; but he had promised Sir George Gipps not to reveal it, for fear of its effect on the young colony.

'Ah, Mr Gell, I want *humility*.' Eleanor turned up her eyes and drooped her head to one side. 'How can I attain it? I have prayed –'

'Prayer must come from the heart to do any good, Miss Eleanor. The great attainment is love of God; after that the rest will follow.'

'But I do not even love my fellow men. At least not *enough*. My heart is cold and lethargic. I want energy to do good. If God would only warm my heart towards –'

'Truly, as Jesus said, "Inasmuch as ye have done it unto the least of these my brethren, ye have done it unto me. . . ." Would you care for me to read with you in the New Testament?'

'I should like that above *anything*. Oh, you have helped me so much! Papa is a good man, I know that, but there is a want of spirituality in our household. He reads the morning prayers, and then takes a great pinch of snuff! And the talk is all of practical things, science or geology or botany. Even Mr Bedford is a little worldly: I long for spiritual conversation.'

'You have a beautiful mind, Miss Eleanor. I did not quite

realize it before, you seemed still a schoolgirl. But I shall be happy to become your spiritual adviser.'

'Oh, Mr Gell!' Eleanor turned her eyes down so that he should not see the exultant light in them. Spiritual guidance she was willing to use as a hauling-post for his personal love. She wanted him for a husband, she knew now. She wanted to live with him in the delicious intimacy of marriage which Mary had only hinted at, though her smiles and blushes told much more.

She wanted to give him sons, like Bobbadil and Jemmy-Buttons, Mary's delightful eldest boys, who were joined regularly each year by a little sister or brother. How interesting to think what must occur *at least* once a year between Mary and Mr Price! Some ladies pretended that it was boring and distasteful, but Eleanor had her doubts. Even the Queen and the Prince Consort added to their family all the time, though they had surely done their duty by now in producing heirs to the throne. It was odd to think that the *Queen* ... All at once Eleanor's thoughts ran away from her.

When Mr Gell spoke again in his mild, cultured Oxford voice, she started and blushed becomingly. Mentally she scolded herself and called her thoughts back from the steep.

The newspapers were openly referring to an occurrence at Norfolk Island, where Captain Maconachie's experiment in humane government was very unpopular with the Colonial Office. Jane at first refused to believe it, until a letter from a friend in Sydney confirmed it.

Mary Anne Maconachie, Eleanor's former playmate, the little girl who had once shared a garden with her, had been trusted alone with her tutor – a convict on parole – and the result was 'the most terrible of domestic calamities which a mother could fear for her daughter'.

Jane wished she could write to Mrs Maconachie, even a line of sympathy, but how could she reopen their correspondence (after years of silence) on such a subject? Perhaps she might venture a few words to the Captain, whose trust in human nature had been so cruelly repaid. He must know she knew; she would have to make some gesture of sympathy, however clumsy, and however much she shrank from it.

Thank God there was nothing of the sort to fear with Eleanor! If anything, Eleanor was a little too prim and pious. Almost, in fact, a prig.

'I wish Mamma,' she had said recently, 'that we might have more instructive and *spiritual* conversation at our dinner table. But I fear it would be received by *many* with coldness.'

Whatever the child meant by that!

There was a monthly dinner at Government House for members of the Tasmanian Natural History Society, who had successfully brought out their first publication. The *Journal* had been received with acclamation in Melbourne and Sydney.

The dinner put everyone in convivial mood for the monthly meeting, and was looked forward to by all the members; but mammas with eligible daughters complained of the lack of Vice-Regal balls.

Jane had never cared for public opinion, but it came as a wounding shock to find how unpopular she had become. Everything she did or did not do was criticized freely in the Press. She spent too much time among 'savages' in New Zealand, and did not patronize local concerts; she visited Australian Aborigines but not the Tasmanians on Flinders Island; she went jaunting in Government ships, and followed her whims without regard for expense (it was her own money she spent, but no matter); she was a seeker after notoriety, a 'man in petticoats', a political intriguer....

As the attacks grew she began to dread going out in public. She could not reply to slander, and she could not pretend to be ignorant of it. Everywhere she went she seemed to hear sniggers of derision, and feel fingers pointing, eyes gloating. Her birthday was in December; Eleanor wrote in her diary:

> Dearest Mamma has been very ill lately, with a complaint that affects her left side entirely.... I tell her afflictions can be a blessing in disguise.

What had finally overwhelmed Jane was the discovery that the story of her interference in Government affairs had reached the London papers.

This was too much to bear. 'Is there *no* escape?' she groaned. She had become used, though not hardened, to the vicious attacks of the vulgar colonial press; but her friends in Van Diemen's Land all knew their falseness. Now she was shown up before all her London friends and acquaintances, as a wicked designing woman determined to get the reins of office into her own hands – a pushing, unwomanly person of the very kind she most abhorred.

She longed to leave Hobarton, the scene of her humiliation, and flee home to obscurity, yet now she shrank from appearing in London society. She longed to get away, yet felt she must not desert Sir John, who still had the threat of possible censure or even recall hanging over him.

This unresolvable conflict issued in an illness that struck her quite suddenly one morning. She had felt a strange tingling sensation in her left arm, from the wrist to the elbow, as though the nerves had 'gone to sleep'. At the same time there was a severe pain over her right eye.

As she tried to get up and put her feet to the floor, one leg crumpled under her.

'I'm paralysed!' she thought in a moment of panic. She lay there with her heart thudding wildly. She could not reach the bell, but she called weakly for Stewart. Sir John, Eleanor and Miss Williamson were all downstairs at breakfast.

Stewart heard her and came in clicking her tongue in consternation. She began fussing like a hen over a single chick.

235

'There now, did ye fall, my lady? I'll help ye back to bed, and ye'd best stay there. Now – up we come. No feelin' in the foot? Ah, I'll rub it with some camphorated oil. Just you bide there now while I fetch a hot brick in flannel. Me old aunt had rheumaticks in the foot somethin' cruel, and she was alwus callin' for a hot brick....'

While Stewart went to get the camphorated oil, Jane lay anxiously feeling her arm with her other hand. The tingling sensation had spread up to her shoulder now, and she couldn't lift her hand.

She reached out for a book from her bedside table with her right hand, and transferred it to her left. The book fell out of the nerveless fingers. She couldn't hold it at all. Her palms, she noticed, were clammy with sweat. The pain bored into her head like a twisting knife.

Gradually the headache receded, but the weakness in her left side, the strange tingling sensation increased.

'I think I've had a sort of stroke,' she said when Sir John, alarmed, had been summoned from the dining-room. She was fighting to keep down hysteria. She had always dreaded some incapacitating illness, which would make her helpless long before her death.

No more mountain-climbing, no more treading the heaving deck of a ship in a storm; even the climb up to Ancanthe would be beyond her. She could become a useless invalid, pushed about in a Bath chair for the rest of her life.

The doctor was sent for, spoke vaguely of 'over-strain', and 'difficult time of life', and prescribed an iron tonic for the nerves.

So he thought she was imagining it all! Was her brain going, then? Had all this worry and persecution driven her mad? At the thought a black pit seemed to open at her feet. A deadly vertigo made her swoon.

With Eleanor and Miss Williamson, and Mr Gell to attend them, she was taken to New Norfolk to stay in the Government Cottage for Christmas. Sir John remained on duty in Hobart Town. As he had written to Ronald Gunn,

236

when that young man resigned to go back to Launceston, a public officer had to work 'rather after the manner of a Horse in a Mill'. On New Year's Day, however, he came up by river and took them for a drive, trying to rally Jane a little.

Eleanor tried to sympathize with her mamma, who was certainly in a bad state of nerves though not apparently suffering any pain – Dr Officer seemed to think the weakness of her limbs was a kind of nervous affliction – but her own happiness kept breaking out of check.

John Phillip Gell was more attentive to her than he had ever been. On this holiday they went for long rides once more among the beautiful riverside scenery – always attended, of course, by Miss Williamson or an orderly – and Mr Gell several times took her to church. He was very gentle with Mamma, lifted her into the cabriole and drove her himself to afternoon tea at some of the neighbouring great houses.

Eleanor wrote in her diary:

Jan. 1843. My heart is still very cold. O God, water it, warm it, let Thy Holy Spirit breathe upon the dry bones and infuse life into them for Our Saviour's sake!
6 Jan. The Anniversary of our landing six years ago. We know not what another year may bring forth: some of our bodies may be mouldering in the grave.... Mamma still very unwell. Bad headaches. Rode twelve miles before breakfast.
2 Feb. This evening had a delicious ride with Mr Gell and Miss Williamson. Sat on rocks and walked in moonlight.
8 Feb. Returned from New Norfolk. *Mr M. reinstated publicly.* Mamma much overcome. I wish she would get idea of paralysis out of her head and keep earlier hours.

By the second week of January there had still been no word from Lord Stanley on Montagu's dismissal. Then Sir John had written to them at New Norfolk to report a rumour: Forster was supposed to have received a copy from Montagu, of Lord Stanley's decision, dated the September before.

Mr Montagu, it seemed, had been appointed to Cape Colony, to a better and higher-salaried position as Colonial Secretary there. Lord Stanley had set the seal of his approval on Montagu, and had publicly rebuked Sir John Franklin.

Sir John toned down this news in his letters to spare Jane as long as possible, but on her return he had to tell her that Lord Stanley's dilatory dispatch had at last arrived at Government House. It contained unqualified support of Montagu and the announcement of his new appointment, with the statement that 'his hold on the respect and confidence of Her Majesty's Government is undiminished'.

Lord Stanley added coldly that the Lieutenant-Governor's proceedings did not appear to have been well judged, and that his suspension of Mr Montagu from office was not sufficiently vindicated.

This meant that Stanley had endorsed Montagu's opinion of Lady Franklin; but he had merely hinted at her name in his dispatch, so that in future times the record would show simply that she was supposed to be guilty of some mysterious delinquency.

Jane read this clause and fell into hysterics, such as she had not given way to for many years. She cried and sobbed for two hours, until Dr Officer came, gave her a sedative, and enjoined quiet and rest. By now her left side had become quite rigid, but he felt sure it was not an apoplectic seizure, for her facial muscles were unaffected, and her speech was clear as ever. She could not rest, but sat up writing to Mary or in her journal long into the night.

His wife's collapse seemed to call out Sir John's reserves of strength. Sophy and Eleanor both remarked how calm he was in the face of Lord Stanley's intolerable harshness and discourtesy: for it had been the height of discourtesy to let Montagu have a copy of the dispatch before it had

238

even been posted to the Governor. Then the stern rebuke at the end of his communication was tempered by no expressions of esteem or goodwill. Sir John felt he had been publicly though unjustly humiliated. He wrote off at once to demand satisfaction: Stanley would either give him an assurance of his continued confidence, or allow him to resign his office. Meanwhile his duty clearly lay in not deserting his post until relieved. However cold and squally the wind of circumstance, the officer of the watch must stay on deck.

On Norfolk Island, Alexander Maconachie knew that his days in command were numbered. He'd not had a fair chance to try out his mark system of prison discipline because of hamstringing regulations and the hostility of Governor Gipps.

Yet if he had saved even one soul from degradation and misery it would have been worth while, and he knew he had done more than this.

Now that they were not cowed by the chain and the lash, the gag and the spreadeagle, and all the other humiliating punishments used under the old system, there was a different spirit among the men. He would not even listen to a man who whined and cringed. They had learned to stand up and speak out. He had not broken the Ring, but he believed its power was less.

'If only I were Governor, if only I had the power!' he exclaimed, clutching his greying curls in despair. 'Mary, I was right, I am right, but they willna admit it in Sydney.'

Mary Maconachie was silent. She had lost some of her faith in Alexander's wisdom since the affair of Minnie. The girl had been packed off to her aunt in England, travelling under a married name. Please God the scandal would not follow her there!

The man had been a 'trusty', one of Alexander's pet examples of reformation. He was still young, only twenty-three, but sullen and set in his hatred of authority.

Alexander had found that he once had ambitions to be a concert pianist. He set him copying music and playing for church services on Sundays. The young man had changed and softened, had been invited to their home, and Minnie had become his pupil at the pianoforte.

Oh, she would have watched her more carefully! But who would have dreamed –? And Minnie herself, when her condition became obvious, was unrepentant.

'I don't care! I love him! ' she sobbed. 'I love him, I won't be sent away. Papa, you said all men were equal in the sight of God. You said we must always remember the prisoners were men, and treat them with – kindness and – courtesy. It would not have been kind to spurn him just because –'

'You deceived us, Mary Anne,' said her father gravely.

'I know, I'm sorry for that, but not that I let him love me. You don't understand, you don't understand!'

And so it had gone on, exhausting scenes and recriminations, and every convict aware of their shame. The story had even reached Sydney; some of the viler rags had printed references to it.

There was nothing for it but to send Minnie away, back to the cold winters which were so bad for her delicate chest.

Chapter Twenty-nine

Convicts were arriving in the Colony in a great flood, since transportation to Sydney had ceased in 1840 and Norfolk Island was the only other substantial penal settlement. Soon there would be 30,000 of them; the balance of the population was changing, for free emigration was not keeping pace. Van Diemen's Land was turning into an enormous prison.

The probation system, which had followed assignment, concentrated the men who had just arrived into big labour gangs, in theory for their gradual rehabilitation. Actually the gangs were hotbeds of vice and training-grounds for the less corrupt to learn from hardened criminals.

'Sodom and Gomorrah over again!' cried *Murray's Review* in a leader.

Sir John, while aware of what was going on, had to obey the edicts from Home. He was given no extra funds for running the enormously increased prison system. There were not enough chaplains and no trained men to take charge of the gangs or watch over their morals. He had to see his cherished infant nation of Tasmania become a dumping-ground for the Empire's wrongdoers. Norfolk Island was to become a dependency of Van Diemen's Land, which would mean that Maconachie would be answerable to him; the Captain would not like this, but anyway his recall was imminent.

Captain Forster, Chief Police Magistrate, was at first appointed Director of the Probation System as well. When it became evident that he could not do both jobs efficiently, Sir John offered the Probation Officer's position to his friend Dr Milligan. Forster took offence at once. Sir John was forced to realize that Forster had always been an implacable enemy, just like Montagu; but he, the bluff no-

nonsense Captain, had seemed more open than the cold and wily Montagu.

Within the year came Lord Stanley's ultimatum: Forster was to be reinstated, and even promoted to a new office of Comptroller of Convicts as well, at a higher salary. This order arrived with the new Colonial Secretary, elderly, inoffensive Mr Bicheno, who had also brought a mysterious parcel from Montagu for the manager of the Derwent Bank.

In March a strange visitor had come to the Australian skies. The Great Comet of 1843 was first noticed by John Phillip Gell as he was walking up to Government House to call on the family after dinner.

He saw a gauzy veil of light stretching across the sky, quivering in the haze at the horizon. At first he thought it an aurora, but its shape was too stable and not far enough to the south. The skies had been overcast for more than a week, so that its approach had not been noticed, but now he realized that it was a vast comet with its head already set below the horizon.

Rushing inside, he insisted that everyone should come out to view the phenomenon, Lady Franklin being carried in a light armchair.

The Government House party stared in silence, awed by the sheer sweep and beauty of this heavenly visitor. Eleanor felt a nervous dread: was this a portent of death, the white spectre which haunted her waking hours and her dreams at night? But death for whom? Mr Gell said that it must be visible over all the southern hemisphere, though hidden by daylight in the north.

The shimmering tail spread over a quarter of the heavens, from Archernar to Orion, and through it the stars twinkled faintly like the eyes in the tail of an enormous white peacock.

Sir John, too, felt a twinge of sailor superstition. He saw the comet as omen of his own recall in disgrace; and he set himself to meet his final humiliation firmly and courageously, secure in the knowledge that he had done nothing to be ashamed of: to the very last he had done his duty.

Deciding that it was better to know the worst, Jane sought out Mr Bicheno, and asked him point-blank if Sir John's office was to be terminated very shortly, as the papers openly avowed?

Poor old Bicheno looked profoundly embarrassed, but admitted in a low voice that this was so. He had been told to 'learn the ropes' before the new Governor arrived; but had found (and here he had difficulty in keeping the surprise out of his voice) that Sir John had such a good grasp of affairs and that Government papers were in such good order that a week or two had sufficed him to become acquainted with everything.

Yes, thought Jane grimly, you had been well primed by the Montagu–Stanley line in London to expect a doddering, incompetent old fool whose wife has to write all his dispatches for him! While the realization of Montagu's success pained her, she was soothed by the evident respect which Bicheno now held for Sir John's powers.

It now looked as if, in a final insult, Lord Stanley meant to send out the new Lieutenant-Governor in the same ship as the notice of recall. She could scarcely believe this possible, if the same thing had not happened to that excellent Colonel Gawler, one of the most upright and intelligent public men she had ever met.

She said nothing to Sir John, but on his own initiative he decided to grasp the nettle firmly, and in a public speech made open reference to the scarcely-veiled hints of recall now appearing in the local Press. He announced with simple dignity that until he was relieved of office, or a new Governor arrived, he thought his place was still on the deck of his command. Though half his audience greeted this with contemptuous silence, the other half applauded his courage.

Jane felt so much better now that the uncertainty was at

an end that she was able to pay a visit to the Ancanthe Museum site. She was cheered by this visible result of her will and imagination: the columns, yet without their pediment, soared into the autumnal blue.

Here was an achievement no words could take away, though the Colonial Office might censure her obliquely, and the *Colonial Times* openly condemn:

Is this a time to employ up to a hundred men, and outlay the tools, in building a road to Lady Franklin's plaything, the mock museum, erected upon an almost inaccessible mountain? The road to which leading nowhere, can have only one object, that of improving the value of Lady Franklin's property....

It was an outward and physical sign of her inward and spiritual faith in the future of *Tasmania* – not Van Diemen's Land, though Sir George Beaufort declared the name could not be altered without an Act of Parliament. The demons of convictism and colonialism would be exorcised, and art and learning would flourish like the blue-gum and the wattle.

Free men owning their land, like the settlers she had helped and encouraged on the Huon, would export not only fruit and wool and wheat to the mainland, but poets and artists and professors, and Prime Ministers for an independent Parliament. This would be the cradle of culture in the new south land, this 'isle of Grecian beauty and Grecian climate' as Mr Gell had called it.

Jane began to walk without a limp. Once again she held her head high and her back straight. No, she would not die even of the Colonial Office or the London papers; her spirit would rise like the sea with its hidden tides against every obstacle.

Then a new blow came. At first there were only whisperings and rumours, conscious looks and conversations broken off suddenly among her friends. At last it came out that Montagu had smuggled into Hobart Town a book

244

of manuscripts containing not only the text of Lord Stanley's harsh rebuke to Sir John, but of all the arguments he, Montagu, had put forward to influence the Chief Secretary's mind.

Henslowe heard that Lady Franklin was described as an *intriguante*, and Sir John as 'no better than an imbecile'. It was clearly a libellous collection; and it was kept at the Derwent Bank by Swanston, the manager, who refused to give it up although he showed it privately to customers. This was the parcel that Bicheno had innocently brought.

Sir John protested about it in a passionate dispatch to Stanley, but the Secretary of State maintained his lordly silence. There had been no reply to Sir John's demand for an affirmation of faith in his administration, or leave to resign.

The waiting was like a war of nerves. He became more and more gloomy and anxious, yet had to conceal his true feelings from Jane for fear of making her ill again. His only confidants were Boyes, who had returned to private practice as an auditor, and Bishop Nixon, whose sympathy was enlisted too in the fight for the secondary college at New Norfolk.

The Bishop was a huge handsome man with black curls and black eyes and a big curling beard – most impressive in his gown and gaiters. He was also artistic, producing charming pencil sketches of the local scenery. He and his wife became their firm friends, writing home to London a true account of what the Franklins had to contend with in Hobart Town.

Poor Jane was shattered by this new blow. She kept to her room, refusing to see visitors, and though Sir John offered to carry her to the carriage she would not venture out for a drive.

As she lay on the *chaise longue* in her boudoir, drugged with sedatives, often weeping or falling into a fitful doze, Mathinna sat at her feet like a faithful dog. She did not understand what had made the Lady-Mumma so unhappy,

245

but she would like to kill the person responsible, or at least tear out all his hair.

She encouraged Possie to do his tricks when he woke in the evenings. She brought the cat in the hope that it would cheer the invalid, but Jane would only smile wanly and go back to her brooding.

One day Mathinna came in shielding something between her cupped hands as a great treasure. *This* would make the Lady-Mumma smile at last! Right under Lady Franklin's nose she opened her hands and a great long-legged grasshopper whirred up into her face.

Jane threw herself back with a cry: it had startled her terribly. Her heart was pounding.

'Mathinna, you naughty girl! That was not a nice trick to play.'

Mathinna was absorbed in recapturing her treasure, her face was turned away. When she looked up, however, her large dark eyes were shining with tears.

'Me catch-it present por Lady-Mumma,' she murmured. 'You no laik?'

'I'm sorry, pet. Did you bring it for me? For a present? Let me see him – a grasshopper, is it?'

'Yiss. Grarse-opper this one. Him pretty longa wings.' Holding the grasshopper firmly but gently, she stretched out one of the dry papery wings, which was striped in clear yellow and black.

'Yes, he *is* pretty! It was just that I got a big fright when he flew up like that. Put him on the bowl of pampas-grass in the corner there. He will decorate it beautifully.'

Mathinna did as she was told, but the grasshopper was still alarmed and took a whirring flight to the other corner of the room. He landed low down on the curtains; and the cat which had followed Mathinna in made short work of him. A leap, a tiny crunch, and the cat was swallowing the 'hopper while delicately spitting out the pretty yellow membranes of its wings.

'Naughty pfella you!' cried Mathinna, chasing the cat

away. 'You ole cat! Go 'way, go 'long. You no eat-it Lady-Mumma's grarse-opper. You go catch-it your own grarse-opper's s'pose you want eat-it. Sss! Out-you-go!'

When she came back from ejecting the cat, Mathinna found Lady Franklin laughing exhaustedly.

'Oh, Mathinna! You're as good as a tonic! That cat looked so guilty with a piece of grasshopper sticking to its whiskers and you chasing it round the room!'

'Yiss; but him all pinish now,' said Mathinna, picking up the pieces.

'Never mind, I'll put the wings between the leaves of a book – see, that's better than having the whole grasshopper, the wings make a lovely bookmark. Thank you for my present, dear. You are a thoughtful little girl.'

Mathinna beamed, a wide delighted grin. Lady Franklin smiled at her fondly. But a new worry was gnawing at the back of her mind: if they were suddenly recalled, what would happen to Mathinna? It would not be a kindness to drag her off to England with them.

At least, thought Jane, looking at Mathinna making her peace with the cat, they had taught her a few useful accomplishments like plain sewing, writing, and ciphering.

'Mathinna, let me see how you're getting on with your needlework. How much of that tablecloth have you done?'

The child fetched it and displayed it indifferently. She had liked the pretty pink linen when it was new, but now it was grubby and creased, bordered on two sides with dog-leg stitches in varying shades from white to greyish-brown, depending on the state of her hands at the time of picking it up.

'Dear, dear! You haven't done much, have you? Why don't you finish it, and then Miss Williamson will get it washed and ironed so it will be pretty again?' Her tone was indulgent, for she remembered how clumsy her own fingers had been at things like tatting.

'Mathinna knock-up longa sewing. Neenel all-a-time bite-it my pingers.'

'It pricks your fingers, you mean. Say: all the time pricks my fingers.'

'Alla-time p'ick my pinger.'

'Pick-my-pinger! Oh well, that's near enough I suppose. You'd better run along and have your lunch now. And ask Sophy if she will come and read to me for a while. My head ...'

'Lady-Mumma sick longa head?'

'Yes, my pet. She is very sick longa head.'

Chapter Thirty

A short sea voyage to the southern coast of New Holland, change of scene and excitement of travel, as usual did wonders for Jane's health and spirits. Then Mr Gunn was such an amiable and congenial travelling companion. She was delighted to see him so happy in his new life, managing the Lawrence estates and married to the bonny Margaret Jamison, who accompanied them. He no longer spoke bitterly of 'Van Demons' Land' but said he hoped his sons would all grow up good Tasmanians.

When she returned from Portland Bay the snow was already lying on Mount Wellington, softening the massive summit but leaving bare the vertical basaltic cliffs below. She felt sure she would not see the mountain under snow another year.

It was bitterly, piercingly cold. The cheeks of children in the streets glowed like autumn apples. The wind swept down Davey Street, cutting like a knife. The family at Government House drew closer about the roaring fires, trying to ignore both the cold and the sharp hostility beyond.

Sir John wished he could send Jane home to her sister but it would mean arriving at the beginning of the damp English winter. Instead he had persuaded her to go across to the mainland with Mr Gunn to escort her.

The settlement at Portland Bay had been established by the enterprising Henty brothers, one of whom had come out with them in the *Fairlie*. They entertained Jane while Mr and Mrs Gunn botanized among the sandhills.

It seemed obvious to Jane that the new settlement of Port Phillip across the Strait, and successful grazing properties like the Hentys', were taking capital away from Tasmania. The mainland market for wheat and wool was evaporating; prices had fallen steadily, and the land boom was turning into a slump. Skilled labour was almost unobtainable to work the land; free immigration had fallen off to almost nothing. The golden glow of prosperity was fading into the grey of depression. The land she had invested thousands of pounds in acquiring had fallen to a tenth of its nominal value.

The banks were alarmed about the increasing number of bankruptcies, and were restricting credit; this in turn prevented development and recovery. The Press, of course, blamed Sir John for it all. 'In a matter of a few years,' they complained, 'he has brought this Colony to a state bordering on ruin.'

Yet he was only the instrument of the Colonial Office at home, which from 14,000 miles away sent out its arbitrary orders, promulgated its vacillating convict policy, and expected local revenue to support a huge police system to control the convicts. Under the probation system they were herded in the Peninsula and not allowed to be assigned to useful labour, though the wheat dried up and blew away unharvested, and apples rotted on the ground.

Jane suspected that their marching orders would come from Lord Stanley without any warning. She must try to get Mathinna adopted, settled in a new home before they left.

She went to inspect one of her hobbies, the Queen's Orphan School, where there was accommodation for both girls and boys in clean dormitories. The children were many of them offspring of convict women who, unmarried, had become mothers; some of them half-caste children brought over from Flinders Island (regrettably, some of the soldiers stationed there had forgotten their duty and had to be removed). They seemed bright and well-fed enough. Jane tried to convince herself that Mathinna would be happy here; happier, in fact, among children of her own age.

She had still said nothing to Mathinna herself when one winter evening young Henslowe came into the smaller drawing-room where the family was sitting, and with a white face announced that the *Tyne* had just arrived from England with papers in which the appointment of Sir John Eardley-Wilmot as Governor-General of Van Diemen's Land was gazetted.

'Is this true?' asked Sir John quietly, while the others sat, dreading some outburst.

'I fear it is, sir.'

'Very well; so much the better.' He fumbled in his waist-coat pocket, brought out his gold snuffbox and took a large pinch in each nostril. 'So much the better ... I wish him joy of what he has in store for him.'

Jane thought he was putting a brave face on it; but she found as the weeks went by that he remained calm and even cheerful. The waiting in ignorance was over. He knew the worst Lord Stanley could do to him, and it was a relief to know. The date of the Government Gazette was early in March. His successor must soon arrive.

'Did you ever hear such confounded cheek?'

Sir John strode up and down the library on his short legs, blowing out his clean-shaven cheeks with indignation. A letter had just been delivered by young Henslowe. Written in an educated hand on cheap and dirty paper, it started without preamble:

Martin Cash & Co. beg to notify His Excellency Sir John Franklin and his satellites that a very respectable person named Mrs Cash is now falsely imprisoned at Hobart Town, and if the said Mrs Cash is not released forthwith and properly remunerated, we will, in the first instance, visit Government House, and beginning with Sir John administer a wholesome lesson in the shape of a sound flogging; after which we will pay the same currency to his followers.

Given under our hands this day at the residence of Mr Charles Kerr at Dunrobin.

CASH
KAVANAGH
JONES

'Dunrobin! That's not far from Hamilton,' said Jane. 'But what arrogance and bombast! They're not to be taken seriously, of course. This Mrs Cash is in the women's factory at the Cascades, I presume. No doubt she well deserved her sentence.'

'Dunrobin!' said Sophy. 'It seems a propitious name, at all events. If they have *done robbin*', they have given it up and must have mended their ways.'

Sir John's usually mild features relaxed again in a smile.

'All the same, it's nothing to joke about, Sophy,' he said with an attempt at severity. 'These fellows have no respect for property or person. They've bailed up I don't know how many householders in the north.'

Major Ainsworth, promoted from Captain since the days when he had begged for Sophy's hand, set off with a company of the 51st Regiment of Foot, to search the countryside round Hamilton.

By this time the bushrangers had, of course, left Mr Kerr's, and there was a curious reluctance among many of the local people to give information. The shepherds and farm-workers were openly on the side of the bushrangers, who frequently treated them to free grog while holding the master and his family in one room under their guns.

Cash & Co. had evidently 'holed-up' in some of the dense scrub hills. Ainsworth's company returned without any more success than the parties of foot police which had been scouring the area.

The soldiers' scarlet coats had made them perfectly conspicuous as they moved about the countryside, while the bushrangers' mufti helped them to melt into the background of drab and grey olive. Then they'd tried dressing their men in prison garb as decoys, but the bushrangers proved too wily for them.

'By gad, they're elusive, sir,' said the Major, reporting back to his Excellency. 'But we'll catch them yet.... They'll overreach themselves sooner or later.'

Major Ainsworth, his broken heart mended, had recently

married a pretty widow. He was glad to get back to head-quarters after this unprofitable duty. When called away he had been pursuing with enthusiasm the project of begetting a colonial child, and was anxious to resume it.

'Mathinna dear; come here to me.' Jane sat in the low quilted satin chair in her boudoir, and held out her arms to the dusky mite who was the most precious of all the trophies and specimens she had collected in the southern hemisphere.

Since Bicheno had confirmed her own fears for an early recall, Jane had been quietly packing up: Maori feather cloaks and Australian boomerangs, Tasmanian waddies and the quartzite from the top of Mount Lofty, were all packed in a trunk, not yet labelled but ready to be shipped home.

Mathinna remained, a living, human problem. What to do with her? Dr Milligan said she should go to Flinders Island with the rest of her race, and that she would never survive a winter in England.

The people caught in the north had not been her family; she was an orphan now, and still only seven years old. It would be better, surely, to send her to the Queen's Orphan School. The climate of Flinders Island seemed likely to be as fatal as London's; there were scarcely fifty Aborigines left alive.

Mathinna leant against Jane's knee confidingly, and gazed into her face.

'Little one, you know that Sir Guberna and the Lady-Mumma have to go back to England soon, away across the sea? You won't be able to live here with us much longer.'

Mathinna's great dark eyes were fixed upon her mouth as she spoke, as if she would read some other meaning behind the words. She gave no sign of understanding. Her wide lips curved in their habitual happy smile; she only leaned a little harder.

'We have to go back to our home in London, Mathinna.

'... You see, we have to do what the Queen says. And Eleanora too, and Soapy, and Miss Williamson and everybody. There will be a new Sir Guberna at Gub'mint House, and he will not have room for a little girl.'

'Mathinna come with you.' She stated it calmly. Her eyes shone with faith.

'But my pet, England is a cold, wet country. You wouldn't like it at all, you would get ill.'

'Mathinna stay with you always. Me belong.'

Jane sighed, and sent Mathinna out of the room to make a drawing. 'How can I leave the little thing behind when we go? I can't do it.'

Sir John gazed down at her, where she still sat in the low chair. He rubbed his forehead and shaded his eyes with his hand as he did when thinking deeply.

'I don't see what else you can do, my love. You know what Milligan said – and I'm sure Dr Bedford would agree – the first winter would be fatal.'

'She'll die anyway, if I leave her behind. She will be homesick for her friends, and for all the comforts we have given her.'

'At least you have given her the comforts of Christian religion.'

'Ye-es.' Jane wondered about the comforts of Christianity for primitive peoples. The most pious of the Flinders Island natives drooped towards death, sunk into a kind of apathy; whereas in the bush they had been happy, healthy pagans. Perhaps Count Strzelecki was right.

Was there perhaps some virtue which the nature-worshippers absorbed, and to which people like Mr Robinson (now returned to England with a comfortable nest-egg) and Mr Clarke the Catechist were blind? There was that strange poem of the new Poet Laureate Mr Wordsworth ...

She shook off such confusing thoughts and said, 'Well, Mathinna has been christened, and she knows her Creed and her catechism. I pray that she may be happier in the next life, anyway, than if she had been left a wild creature in the forest.'

'May Mathinna come back now? Me has drawed a wallaby, Lady-Mumma.' The soft, plaintive voice matched the large soft eyes.

'Let me see, pet. Yes, that is very like. Now what about sitting down and drawing me ... let me see ... drawing a – a bird. A *big* bird.'

Mathinna turned the paper over, sat down on the floor and began at once with her piece of crayon.

'The chair, dear. Use my desk. We don't sit on the floor. Remember you are a young lady; always remember what you've been taught.'

But even as Mathinna climbed obediently on to the chair, from which her little legs hung down without reaching the floor, Jane thought bitterly, *Cui bono?* She would end up in the blacks' settlement on Flinders Island when she was too old for the school: sitting round in the dirt, gossiping apathetically with the other women.

When she grew up she'd be a handsome girl. Jane thought of the depraved convict women, some barely eighteen, whom she had tried to rescue from a life of sin. Was that to be Mathinna's fate? She closed her eyes on a terrible vision, almost like a flash of foresight, of a drunken and diseased Mathinna sunk in the mire of depravity.

No, God would not allow it. Her Christian upbringing, the gentle nurturing of the last four years when her character was being formed, would strengthen her against temptation.

She must be taken to the Orphan School this very month. There would be time, then, to visit her in her new surroundings and help her to settle in while they waited for a ship.

The portrait by Bock she would give away. She needed no reminder of Mathinna's gentle, merry features and curly head; and those large, faithful dark eyes would haunt her for the rest of her life.

At Norfolk Island the Maconachie family was preparing for departure also. They were going to Van Diemen's Land on their way to London, but they would not catch up with

255

their former friends the Franklins.

'You can't all go with me, men,' said Captain Maconachie, smiling in spite of himself at the anxiety of the 'old hands' (who were being sent to the Tasmanian colony) to travel in the same ship with him.

This was the justification of his humane system. Men who had seemed brutalized by long and vicious punishment; men who had been cringing creatures unable to look him in the eye, had recovered their human status and were capable of loyalty, and, yes, affection for their superintendent.

Of course they hoped he would put in a good word for them on arrival, but also there was real sorrow at seeing him leave. They would be known favourably as 'Maconachie's men' for years to come.

Fresh maize-meal added to their bread, the fruit and vegetables grown in their own gardens, the indulgence of being allowed to bathe in the sea, all had improved their health and with it their morale. It was only the new arrivals from England who came down with dysentery and were corrupted by the homosexual practices he had been unable to stamp out.

As for his mark system – well, it had failed to work, but he was convinced that it could work given a proper trial. Governor Gipps had been amazed to find order and tranquillity reigning when he came on his tour of inspection at last. But it was too late for his report to do any good, for the edict for his recall had gone out long ago. The Colonial Office had only been waiting for a suitable successor.

Mary Maconachie could think of nothing but seeing her eldest daughter again.

'I wonder how Minnie is? Will she have got over it? Surely it's a blessing that the baby didn't live! It must have aged her.... How will she look, I wonder?'

It was all very well for Alexander, wrapped up in his prisoners – they were like a huge second family to him. But she wanted her daughter, whatever she had done. And she had never quite forgiven Alexander for introducing that man to their house.

She was glad, glad, to leave this green prison, to be going home at last.

BOOK THREE

Last Voyage

Let me assure you, my dearest Jane, that I am now amply provided with every requisite for my passage, and that I am entering on my voyage comforted with every hope of God's merciful guidance and protection....

– From Sir John Franklin's last letter to his wife

Chapter Thirty-one

Sir John Eardley Eardley-Wilmot arrived in mid-August, when the spring wildflowers were preparing their colours and the wattle already hung out its cloth-of-gold on the hillsides.

He came prepared to step straight into office and into Government House, yet it was three days before Sir John Franklin received the official dispatch from Stanley informing him of his recall. Its cold official language was not warmed by one word of praise or thanks for his six years of service; it merely 'presumed' that since he had completed the normal term of office, he would be 'expecting to be relieved of his duties'.

The Franklins made what hasty temporary arrangements they could. So did the Nixons, who were staying with them.

Major Ainsworth took them in while they arranged a sale of their effects: the grand piano and the brass-inlaid chairs, the box-couch and the drawing-room sofa upholstered in yellow silk. Then they went to the cottage at New Norfolk so as not to embarrass the new Governor by their presence in town.

The freedom from official drudgery gave Sir John a new lease of life. He put from him all thought of the foul wrong done to him by the Colonial Office: that could wait until he saw Stanley face to face. He sat out to enjoy his last few months during the lovely spring and early summer of one of the most beautiful islands in the world.

Jane sent out invitations to the opening of the museum. Her natural history specimens had been installed there when they made the move. Now they were unpacked from their crates and put in glass cases with labels hand lettered by Mr Ewing, the curator.

The painting by Bock, of Ross, Crozier and Franklin outside the Observatory, was hung, and the shelves of the small library were filled with books: John Gould's *Birds of Australia,* Flinders' *Voyage to Terra Australis,* a copy of Mr Burn's play and a file of the *Tasmanian Journal of Natural Science.* Only books about Tasmania or neighbouring colonies were to be. included, or those written by residents or former residents of Tasmania.

Jane hoped that the rent from the extra four hundred acres of hillside she had acquired would pay the cost of upkeep. She had small hope that anyone would keep up the native arboretum now that Mr Gunn was away in the north; but at least the building would remain.

It was not quite completed on the day of the opening ceremony, but she wanted to hold this before the weather became too hot. It was a perfect afternoon, still and sunny, in late October.

The mountain rose against the sky, its organ-pipe rocks sharply etched with cobalt shadows. Scent of late apple-blossom from orchards in the next valley floated on the air, mingling with the breath of wild sweet-briar and the aromatic eucalyptus exhaled by the leaves of the tall gum-colonnades.

A pang went through her heart as she breathed – soon for the last time – that enchanted, balmy air, and listened to the tinkling of the rivulet over its stony bed.

Now they were only waiting for the ship to take them to Melbourne, where they would board the *Rajah* for London. This was her last Tasmanian spring.

Eleanor walked up the hill with Mr Gell holding her parasol over her head, tenderly, to keep the hot Antipodean sun from her fair complexion. She did not know whether she was happy or sad. In a month's time they would be gone, and she would not see her beloved John Phillip Gell for what might be years. Yet if they had not been going, would he ever have brought himself to the point of making a declaration?

In the last weeks she had almost despaired. Then suddenly one evening, in the more intimate atmosphere of New Norfolk (where he was spending the weekend with them and where they had many happy memories of shared excursions) he had grasped her hand as he was lighting her candle from his own, regardless of hot wax dripping on the floor. He opened his heart. He could not bear to see her go, she meant all of England to him, the green fields and sheltered lanes, the spires of Oxford and the playing-fields of Rugby. Before she left would she promise to be his? The knowledge that she was waiting for him would make his remaining years of exile in this distant Colony possible to bear.

Eleanor's reply was almost inaudible from an excess of happiness; at first he thought she was refusing him. After all he was many years older, he would soon be thirty while she was not yet twenty.

At last he understood. He kissed her hand, and went to find Lady Franklin to tell her of his success: for he had already asked Sir John for permission to speak, and he had given it heartily.

In Jane's room he broke down and wept a little from the relief and confusion of his feelings. He told her that he felt at peace for the first time since coming to Van Diemen's Land. His life had direction now. He would stay long enough to see his college established for which Sir John left £500 of his own money, and Lady Franklin the Ancanthe estate and the museum.

As soon as he had saved a little and had the promise of a good living at home, preferably in a London parish, he would return and claim Eleanor as his bride. He would not expect them to give up their only daughter, and indeed he could never become a Tasmanian himself. At heart he had remained an exile.

Mathinna was established at the Orphan School. Weeping and rebellious, she had been handed over to the superin-

tendent who told Lady Franklin privately that he thought
it best to keep her locked in her room for the time being,
as she seemed likely to run away.

Jane had been confident of making her understand that
she must stay, that the home she had known for four years
was being broken up. She had not forgotten her own bewilderment when her mother died; she was only three years
old, but her nanny had remained, the solid walls of 21
Bedford Place had remained, and her father who had
always been a rather aloof and mysterious figure. And
then she had her sisters. She had adjusted herself fairly
quickly to the fact that her pretty blue-eyed mother had
'gone away to heaven'. To Mathinna 'going away to London' was just as final and mysterious a parting; from
now on the Lady-Mumma would be as if dead. But Mr
Gell had promised to keep a kindly eye on her, and Mrs
Nixon, the Bishop's wife. Mathinna would not lack
friends.

She was nearly eight, quite capable of understanding that
the parting was for her own good. But, oh dear –! Those
great, shadowy dark eyes overflowing with endless
tears; the desperate clinging of those thin, brown arms
to her skirts, the cry: 'Don't leabe me! Don't leabe
me! No! Mathinna stay with you! Don't go, Lady-
Mumma!'

It had been like killing an affectionate and trusting pet.
She had unwound the wiry clinging arms, dropped a blind
kiss on the curly dark hair, and stumbled out to her carriage too overcome to give the coachman directions.

She meant to go again and visit her often; she had been
steeling herself to it for weeks; but she dreaded the same
scene and its effect upon her nerves. At last she let her
doctor persuade her that it was best not to upset the child,
and that for the sake of her own nerves, she should
make a clean break. She went at once to say goodbye,
and found Mathinna sullen and apathetic, dull-eyed and
drooping.

She would get over it; she had been like a little sulky bear, refusing to eat or speak, said the superintendent. Jane, seeing her sunken eyes and the unsmiling, strained expression of her mouth, went away feeling the guilt of a murderer. She had killed something innocent and freedom-loving, bright and sparkling as the clear mountain brooks that bounded down the slopes of Mount Wellington. She would get over it, she told herself firmly. In time she would forget.

The excitement of final departure buoyed them all up in the last weeks. There were Loyal Addresses and farewell dinners; Sir John received testimonials and good wishes far beyond what they had expected, and Jane's wounded pride was appeased. Her own image had been damaged irrevocably by the dastardly attacks of the newspapers and the damaging assertions of R. L. Murray of *Murray's Review*, who referred openly to 'the all-grasping occupations of the Lady Governor of Van Diemen's Land', and said 'That the whole Colony knew that Lady F. takes part in the administration of the Government ...' Then there were the vile innuendoes of Montagu's 'book'; but Sir John, whatever the Colonial Office liked to think, was obviously liked and respected by the free colonists.

After a triumphal departure from Hobart Town, with women curtseying and kissing his hand, the Regimental Band playing, flags flying, the rattle of guns in salute, and thousands lining the streets and wharves to wave goodbye, he was almost too moved, honest Sir John Franklin, to give his address in reply.

His enemies had got to him through Jane, he thought, and perhaps she had played into their hands by not being a quiet, retiring, ordinary housewifely body who could never have been accused of trying to take over the reins of government. But he regretted nothing, except the recorded slur of Lord Stanley's rebuke which had now been indelibly written in the annals of history. Whatever happened, he meant to get justice from Stanley. He would haunt the man's doorstep until he admitted that injustice had been done, and recorded that at least the Franklin government had been an honest one, whether or no it had been succesful.

He wrote to James Ross before they left:

Jane cannot help being clever, yet it was that the Faction could not bear. They think they could have got on with a simple unsuspicious obstinate old fool like myself, but that her discernment has unveiled them; and it is true she saw through them sooner than I did....

Yes, it was all clear enough now; it was easy to be wise after the event. In all his life before he had had only honourable men to deal with. Political scheming, word-twisting, slander were beyond his experience. He always preferred to think well of everybody, until or unless something bad was proved, and this trusting nature had been his undoing.

Mr Gunn, who had been left to administer in trust Lady Franklin's holdings in Tasmania – for she owned, besides the Ancanthe estate and Betsy Island, nearly eight thousand acres of Tasmanian land – came with Mr Henty to see them off when they called at George Town.

He came out in a small steamer to take a final farewell on board before the ship weighed anchor for Port Phillip.

He felt a return of his old melancholy at this further loss of sympathetic friends – though this time it was not by death, he felt the parting was just as irrevocable. With a family to bring up and educate he would never have enough money for the voyage to England. He would never see the great gardens at Kew for which he had provided so many exotic plants, but at least he could thank his stars that his poverty had prevented him from losing anything in the economic crisis.

Property had fallen in value to a ruinous extent. The colony had got into a fearful state, and heaven knew what would be the end of it.

'Well,' he said to Henty as they stood waving goodbye

from the small boat, 'Sir John may not have been a brilliant Governor, but he was certainly a good man. I shall miss them both more than I can say.'

Chapter Thirty-two

It almost seemed as if Australia were loth to let them go. The *Rajah* hung about inside the Heads, waiting for a favourable wind and tide to take then through the Rip. Meanwhile John Gell and Eleanor went through the emotional strain of a prolonged parting. After two days they had lost the sense of urgency, when suddenly Sophy came down the companionway in a rush, to say the ship was weighing anchor immediately.

She went away and left them to the last intimate moments together. John Gell ran into the cabin next door to take a hasty but emotional farewell of Lady Franklin and Sir John. Then he came up on deck to give Sophy a brotherly kiss before he went over the side.

Eleanor, in tears, stayed below. Jane tried to comfort her for a while; but as the increasing motion told her they were out in the long swell of the Southern Ocean, she went up on deck for her last glimpse of the Australian mainland.

Farewell, you distant land, she thought, I shall never see you more. Farewell blue skies and lonely fenceless plains, sombre trees burdened with birds, and empty, haunted bush. Land of simplicity and peace, farewell!

They had spent six weeks travelling and camping in the country, in the beautiful Gippsland, discovered by Count Strzelecki; had been entertained at sheep stations, and made their way over the ranges in the wake of a huge brushfire, among charred and smouldering trees.

Once again she was impressed by the absence of hedges or enclosures, producing a sense of unfettered freedom and space. Even the long flat leaves of the eucalyptus hung down edgeways so that the sun's rays were obstructed as little as possible.

And the effect of the pure and exhilarating atmosphere on the frame and spirits! She was convinced that it actually developed the mind and ability beyond their natural capacity. New arrivals became more irritable and energetic, while the colonial-born showed a quick-wittedness and resourcefulness that was remarkable.

She had responded to the country immediately, as she knew she would when she first read of it. John Gell did not seem to feel the same, longing for his return to England. Hepburn, on the other hand, was staying quite happily at Port Arthur. He had a responsible post in charge of the boys at Point Puer, with whom he had great influence because of his true kindness of heart, combined with firmness.

She stood beside Sir John in the stern to watch the low coast recede. He put his hand over hers where it rested on the rail. Far to southward, out of sight over the horizon, lay the mountains and forests of Tasmania, the lovely lakes and rivers and the beautifully situated town of Hobart which was the scene of their few triumphs and many humiliations.

A large tear dropped on their joined hands.

'Cheer up, Jane, my love,' said Sir John. 'We mustn't despair, but trust in the wisdom of God and the judgement of time. They stamped on the seeds we tried to sow – universal education, improvement of the women's lot, and all the rest of it; but our intentions were good, and perhaps in time they'll bear fruit.'

'I feel sure of it,' she said, rallying a little. 'But isn't it odd how things work out – there's Montagu advanced, and Arthur who made a fortune, and Alfred Stephen, Chief Justice of New South Wales, while we –'

'And Maconachie is recalled in disgrace from Norfolk Island, and Gawler just as summarily dismissed in South Australia, and Gipps tells me the Colonial Office has ruined his health. No, my love; anyone who takes on the post of Governor, whether of a penal settlement or a free province, has my sympathy. I am truly sorry for Sir Eardley

269

Wilmot, and wouldn't be in his shoes for all the tea in China. I'm sorry for the manner of my recall, but not for fact of it. No, no; quite the contrary, in fact!'

They were still pacing the deck when evening fell, both delighting in the long, slow swell, the swing of the deck and creak of spars and timbers. The water was remarkably smooth and calm. Jupiter threw a sword of yellow light across the waves, and in the west towards which they sailed were two dark ribbons of cloud, joined by a frail new moon that hung between like a silver clasp. That was a good simile; Jane tucked it away in her mind for future use in her journal.

Mathinna moved across the yard of Orphan School with a crowd of girls yelling behind her:

'Yah! Yah! Black skin, black soul!'

Even if she had not been able to understand the words, the tone of the voices was enough: jeering and hurtful, an ugly chorus which greeted her when she came out after school in the afternoon, or when she tried to join the others at lunchtime.

She had seen a white crow once in the country, trying to join the others in their cawing and playing about a dead tree. They would suffer it for a while, then suddenly all the black birds would turn upon it, harrying and pecking, till the conspicuous white bird slunk away and hid in a bush.

Here she was the only black one, she was the freak; yet there were half-white children not much lighter in skin than she was. It was her other difference they minded: her soft voice, her gentle manners, her way of eating delicately while they gobbled and snatched. It seemed to infuriate them.

Sometimes, at night, when they were all shut in the dormitory and supposedly asleep, they would pull her out of bed and subject her to all sorts of indignities. A pillow would be put over her face to prevent her crying out, and several big girls would sit on her arms and legs.

'Oo, yes, she has got one! Just the same, see! And with curly hair like on her head, too. Pull out one of the hairs – go on, don't be a softy. Pull hard! Here, let me –' and excited and giggling, the bigger girls pushed and squabbled over the privilege of hurting and humiliating her.

When, after she was let up, she flew at them in revenge and pulled a handful of one girl's hair right out of her scalp, she got into trouble from the matron for being 'a little savage'. It was no use telling tales. The authorities wouldn't believe some of the things that went on anyway, and it would only make her more unpopular than ever.

Those first months at the Orphan School, after the Lady-Mumma's last visit which finally convinced her that she really had to stay there, had been the worst of her young life. She would never forget them; she would never be the same again. The effect of bottling up her rage and swallowing her pride had made her taciturn and sulky. She tried running away, but they brought her back and whipped her. She sank into misery and apathy.

So Dr Milligan found her when he was leaving to take up his new post in Flinders Island. He arranged with the Matron – for he was now Protector of Aborigines and had the power – for her to be transferred to Flinders Island in the new year, to be among her own kind. That Christmas she knelt down and thanked the good Jesus for delivering her out of the hands of her enemies.

Jane had never been away from England for so long before. Indeed, it seemed a lifetime ago they had sailed in the *Fairlie*, with fair winds and fair hopes. Strong excitement had borne her up during the last weeks in Van Diemen's Land. The excitement of arrival covered the conflicting emotions she now felt at the thought of being reunited with her family after so long, and after they had read such terrible things about her in the newspapers. Mary, she felt sure, understood; but there were others, cousins who had always been a little jealous of her good marriage and what

271

fame she had collected on her travels. How they would rejoice!

The Franklin relatives with whom they spent their first night in England, at Portsmouth, were of this order. Jane's nerves were quivering as she smilingly crumbled cake and sipped Madeira wine in their drawing-room, waiting for some reference to her part in what she thought of to herself as 'our recall'.

At last it came; a poisonously-sweet enquiry from one of the Porden relatives of the family: 'How will you settle down, my dear Jane, to being just an ordinary citizen, after having been "the Lady Governor of Van Diemen's Land"? For so we have seen you described –'

Jane sat very still. Her face froze. She felt her smile become stiff and brittle as ice; at any moment it might crack and fall on the floor with a cold, accusing tinkle. Sir John interposed with a cough. He was about to say 'Quite the contrary!' she felt sure. She could not bear it, she could not.... A thick sob rose in her throat, and in a moment she was weeping uncontrollably. Sir John carried her upstairs, but her loud sobs continued to echo through the house.

'Pray calm yourself, my love!' he begged, patting her hand, while Eleanor fussed round with smelling-salts and damp cloths which Jane thrust away.

'If you would only keep earlier hours, Mamma –' she began.

'Sophy, I want Sophy!' sobbed Jane.

Eleanor and her father looked at each other across the bed. At last Sir John said formally: 'Will you go and call your cousin, my dear Eleanor? Apparently we can do nothing for Mamma.'

Chapter Thirty-three

Eleanor had gone to the country to stay with her Aunt Isabella, Sophy's mother, who as a widow was very grateful for having her daughter's upbringing taken off her hands for so many years, but disappointed that Sophy had not, like Eleanor Franklin, managed to find a husband in Van Diemen's Land.

'I have always heard there was such a preponderance of males, dear child,' she murmured vaguely when they were alone in her daughter's room. 'Indeed, it must surely be so, for even Eleanor (who is not so *very* attractive) has got herself engaged.'

'There were plenty of men, Mamma,' agreed Sophy, 'but not the right sort of men – or not right for me, at all events.'

'You mean you *had* proposals – and refused them! I thought your letters sometimes hinted as much. And indeed, Jane mentioned a Captain Ainsworth, I remember.'

'Major Ainsworth he is now – and married to a plump widow. Of the others – alas! The most interesting men are always married already, or at least bespoke.'

Her mother would have pursued this interesting topic, but Sophy showed her impatience. She was missing her Aunt Jane, who never gossiped of stupid subjects like young men and did not think marriage the be-all and end-all of a woman's existence.

As soon as they reached London she'd realized that Sir John – kind uncle that he had always been – expected her to go back to her own family. He showed in many little ways that now the public life in a distant land was over, he would like his wife to himself.

Since Jane had seemed to take it for granted that she

would come back with Eleanor, Sophy wrote to her aunt to explain why she felt it impossible.

'I can no longer make my home with you,' she wrote. 'I am afraid that Eleanor is, and has been for sometime, distinctly jealous of me; and even Sir John, though uniformly kind, indicates that he would rather I did not come back except for short visits to London.'

She knew that her aunt, with her good sense and clear-sightedness, would realize she wrote no more than the truth.

She had been made uncomfortable by Eleanor's increasing religiosity. She had become much more gay and likeable for a while after John Gell proposed; but now, separated from him by thousands of miles of ocean, she became gloomy and introverted, spending much time in her room in prayer.

In the last year she had been confirmed and went regularly to Communion, getting up early to attend the special service twice a week. A minor kind of mystical experience had occurred to her.

As she knelt in her white dress and felt the bishop's hands upon her veiled hair, her heart began to flutter strangely; and high up under the dome of the church she seemed to hear the flutter of angels' wings, as though the roof were filled with angels. She became convinced that she was one of the Chosen of the Lord.

She did not tell the Bishop of Tasmania of her experience, as he seemed to her rather worldly-looking, with his vigorous black curls and full lips. Her dear John was much more spiritual in appearance, in fact he looked much more like a bishop. . . .

(Mrs Nixon, the Bishop's wife, had been aware of Eleanor's critical attitude. She did not take to Eleanor at all, though she invited Sophy to stay with her for several weeks, and confided that she felt 'quite vexed' that dear Mr Gell was engaged to Eleanor. 'Oh, it's only her manner that is

274

irritating,' Sophy had said charitably. 'I'm afraid she's not a very happy person.')

Now Eleanor was even more annoying. She was inclined to over-eat and was becoming quite plump, with a sancti-monious expression on her smooth, round face.

Separated in the flesh from her dearest John, she was able to suppress all carnal thoughts, and helped by his pious though loving letters she thought of their future mar-riage as a spiritual union. They had been brought together by the Lord's design, so that they might further the work of the Church of England, which of course was the true Church.

She made a list of people to remember in her prayers, feeling it a serious duty in one to whom the Lord was bound to listen:

1. John – Health.
2. Papa – Irritability.
3. Mamma – Bible. Worldliness.
4. Aunt C – Contentiousness.

and so on right down the scale to 'servants' and 'visitors'.

She did not waste any prayers on Sophy, who was, she felt, too worldly to have any chance of entering heaven, even with her intercession. She still hoped to save her mamma. She could not talk to her on spiritual subjects, she seemed always busy, taken up with some project or other, and her reading was all scientific and practical. With Mathinna left behind, and Sophy returning to her own mother, she had expected at last to find that closeness to her admired step-mamma that somehow she had never found in Van Diemen's Land. But she seemed entirely wrapped up in Papa's troubles with the Colonial Office.

Sir John's irritability, which Eleanor deplored, was under-standable. He had come home refreshed from the holiday in the Victorian bush and the long sea voyage, ready to put his case before Lord Stanley with all the vigour at his command, and all the strength of one who knows his cause is right.

Stanley refused even to see him.

Before leaving his office in Tasmania, Sir John had sent indignant dispatches about Montagu's 'book', 'in which Lady Franklin is designated as a bad intriguing woman'. He had never had a satisfactory reply from Lord Stanley on this point; and all he would now concede was that the recall did not reflect on Sir John's personal integrity: 'I do not doubt that during your administration of Van Diemen's Land your best endeavours were applied to the honest and faithful discharge of your duties....'

This, however, left Lady Franklin's position where it was: Montagu's accusation of 'improper interference in matters of State' was upheld. Sir John haunted the corridors of the Colonial Office, and sent message after message; Lord Stanley would not budge an inch.

Sir John determined to produce a pamphlet setting out all the facts, and publish it. Not all Jane's 'influence', backed by the advice of their friend Count Strzelecki, could deflect him from his purpose.

Once she saw he was determined, Jane threw all her energies into helping him, asking only that he leave out the part about her intercession for Montagu, but to this he would not agree.

They retired to the country to work on the *Narrative of Some Passages in the History of Van Diemen's Land during the last three years of Sir John Franklin's Administration in the Colony*, as it was rather long-windedly to be titled.

'Now, Sir John, we must have Sophy; she is absolutely indispensable in a matter like this, with her acuteness and memory,' said Jane.

'Yes, well, I suppose so ...' he grumbled. 'Then I'll get Richardson to come and stay as well; we don't want the thing to sound too feminine in its composition.'

Sophy was happy to come back. She loved paper-work, did not mind copying out long screeds, and had a flair for annotating and collating undigested masses of material. Eleanor, feeling shut out and unwanted, went to another of her aunts. It was a repetition of her unhappy childhood, when she had been passed from aunt to aunt about the country. She wrote long letters to John Philip Gell, spent much time in prayer and brooded. One day, she vowed, Mamma and Papa would be sorry; they would beg her to come and live with them, but *she* would be in a position to repudiate *them*. It was not a very Christian sentiment, but her cheek was tingling from a series of slaps; she did not feel inclined to turn the other.

By the end of the year the *Narrative* was almost completed, and a new interest had taken hold of their minds: the coming North-west Passage Expedition. As Sir John was fond of pointing out, English explorers and English ships had made a chain of discoveries off the north coast of America. England should have the honour of forging the last link in the chain. An English ship must carry the Union Jack through the Passage. He volunteered at once to go.

Admiralty Captains and Arctic explorers became regular diners at the Franklins' table when they returned to London. Eleanor had come back, Sophy was still with them. She had the pain of meeting Captain Ross and his charming wife, the 'Anne' after whom an Antarctic cape had been named, and about whom she had felt such painful curiosity.

She told herself she was glad to see him happy, though that happiness was like a knife in her breast. He announced that he had no intention of abandoning the comforts of married life to go once again to the frozen North. They had offered him command of the proposed expedition, but he had refused it. His wife smiled secretly. She had no intention of losing him either; her father had made it a condition of giving her hand that he should stay home for at least five years.

Sir John laid down his soup-spoon with a trembling hand. 'James,' he said, 'if you will recommend me to the Admiralty, there's nothing in the world I'd like better than

277

to go. You know that there's no service nearer my heart than the accomplishment of the North-west Passage.'

'I know, old man. I've already suggested you as commander.'

He did not add that he had also exchanged letters with Lady Franklin on the subject, to test her feelings and ask how important she thought it was to Sir John. She had replied that it was the only thing which could make up for Lord Stanley's injustice and oppression. He needed some honourable employment, and that soon.

Yet she dreaded to let him go at his age. She left the outcome to fate. She did not, as she would have done before her Tasmanian experiences, ask for the guidance of God. *Van Demon's Land!* She had lost something of her old faith there.

The Admiralty tried again to get James Ross to change his mind. Then, in February, Lord Haddington summoned Sir John for an interview.

Naturally, said the noble lord, they looked for a man of Sir John's experience and judgement to command the expedition; but had he really thought seriously of the undertaking at his age? For they knew his age: it was fifty-nine.

'Not quite,' said Sir John, whose birthday was not for another two months or so. 'You'll examine me, my lord, to see that I'm fit! Exploring could never be as hard work as governing a colony, I assure you.'

'But you're not as young as you were, Sir John.'

'If I were not equal to it I wouldn't go, my lord. I'm too stout nowadays for a walking expedition. But by ship – that's different.'

Two days later a letter came from the Admiralty informing him of his appointment. Sir John was eager as a schoolboy for a promised treat. The dining-room table was covered with sheets of paper on which he made out lists of men and materials, dates and estimates of arrival, plans and diagrams and maps. He worked at them even during meals.

Jane was indulgent, trying to be happy for him, yet with

something cold and heavy at her heart ... was it premonition? She remembered the dread with which she had approached the shores of Van Diemen's Land, much as she had longed for the appointment.

Sir John seemed to have no fears, and of course would never admit that he was too old. He gave up snuff and spirits entirely on his doctor's advice, took more exercise and was healthier than he had been for years.

Only once she glimpsed the anxiety that he kept hidden even from her. She was sewing a silken Union Jack for him to take with the ship through the North-west Passage. The last strip of white was added to the blood-red, the royal-blue, and she threw it, folded loosely, across to him where he was dozing on the couch beside her.

By an unlucky chance it opened and draped itself over him. He woke at its touch, looked down; his eyes flew wide with alarm.

'O, Jane!' he said. 'What have you done to me?'

She looked startled, too, but tried to laugh it away.

It was superstitious nonsense of course, but he was a thorough-going sailor in this as in everything else. For a moment, half awake, he had thought himself a corpse draped with the flag for ceremonial burial.

Chapter Thirty-four

Captain Francis Rawdon Moira Crozier made a last attempt to melt his Ice-Maiden. In a brief interval of fine weather in March, he walked home along the Embankment from an Arctic lecture in the Guildhall, from Westminster Bridge to Waterloo, with Sir John and Lady Franklin and Sophy Cracroft. The Franklins had very kindly asked him back to tea.

Walking a little behind with Sophy, he intentionally dawdled to let the others go ahead. Looking after them he said with a heavy sigh: 'There's a happy man! A marriage like that must make up for many other things in life. Your aunt and uncle always seem to me an ideal couple.'

'Yes, and so they are. But a cynic might say that the reason is their frequent absences from each other. They never get time to grow bored before one of them is off – Sir John on a naval service or expedition, my aunt on her travels.'

'Ah, no! They are ideally suited, I should say.'

'And then, of course, they had a second chance. I doubt Sir John's *first* wife would have suited him so well. And I believe, from little things she has let fall, that my aunt was in love more than once before she met him.'

'Miss Sophy!' He stepped squarely in front of her and stopped in the middle of the pavement. 'If you would only give a fellow a chance! I'm forty-eight, and old enough to know my own mind; I'll never love another. I'll not trouble you again; but I must try my luck once more. Won't you have me?'

Sophy stepped aside and looked over the stone balustrade at the grey-brown muddy tidal Thames, surging upstream with filth and flotsam on its turbid surface.

'The Thames is certainly not as clean as the Derwent,' she said.

'Ah, Sophy, acushla! Don't put me off like that. Remember you kissed me once, in Hobart Town.'

She looked at him through her dark eyelashes, her remote features becoming softer and more warm.

'But that was in the Antipodes, Captain Crozier! Here all is opposite.'

She walked on, but when they came to the next bridge he took her hand and drew her down the steps to water-level. Mist was rising from the river; a red sun burned murkily in the west.

He stood on the lowest step with her above him, their faces close. 'Please call me Frank,' he said.

'Dear Frank. There! You *are* frank, and honest, and brave. And I cannot love you.'

'You know I've volunteered for the North-west Passage. I may not come back. I shan't want to come back.'

'Ah, no emotional blackmail; that isn't playing fair. I've heard that you are to command *Terror* once more.'

'At least you know where you are with a ship,' he said rather bitterly.

'I've never misled you, Frank Crozier. At least, I never meant to. And now we must catch up with my aunt and uncle. Farewell, Frank; and God bless you.'

For a moment those red lips in that cold white face touched his. Then she was gone up the steps. Frank Crozier felt a coldness creeping up from his feet. He looked down. The swiftly-rising tide had covered the bottom step, and he had been standing in water for several minutes without feeling it.

On Flinders Island in Bass Strait it was the end of summer. Cold winds were beginning to sweep in from the south-west, in the pattern charted by Count Strzelecki in the book he was just seeing through the press, dedicated to Sir John Franklin – and paid for in part by the Tasmanian subscription got up by Sir John and handsomely begun with his own donation of a hundred pounds.

Lady Franklin had given Betsy Island to the people of

281

Tasmania, and the Ancanthe estate had been made over in trust to the college foundation.

Ronald Gunn was acting as her agent for the Huon river properties, gradually being bought by her tenants at low prices as they made a success of their fruit-growing ventures; and for her property in the north and east. She had invested nearly all the £5,000 her father had sent her. Legally it was all Sir John's, though they never worried over money matters. She had income from her mother's estate; he had a life income from his first wife's, which went to Eleanor at his death.

One of Gunn's duties was to visit Mathinna occasionally to see if she wanted for anything. Provision had been made for her under the Land Fund to defray the cost of her education until she was fifteen.

On Flinders Island, among her own people, Mathinna was happy at first. But the change in values was confusing. The people seemed to her both dirty and lazy; brought up to fill her days with activity and schoolwork, she found the hours of daylight at first too long. And she had been conditioned to believe that it was wrong to wipe greasy fingers in one's hair, to blow one's nose without a handkerchief, to squat down in the open to perform natural functions.

Yet there were compensations. When a party crowded into one hut for a sing-song – even if the songs were mostly hymns – the animal warmth and nearness of her kind gave her a peace she had never known before, in all the comforts of Gub'mint House, Hobart Town. She reverted to more casual eating habits, and found pleasure in holding a juicy bone in both hands, tearing at it with her strong white teeth.

She still wore her necklace of shells, and her red muslin dress now a little worn and getting too tight under the arms, where it was beginning to split. She was maturing early: already her womanliness was in bud. There were boys, too, to tease and play chasey with, and the older boys who looked at her in a way that made her feel queer so that she giggled shyly and dropped her eyes. There had been boys at the Orphan School, but there the boys and girls were kept more rigidly apart. Here it was one big, sprawling family, not exactly happy, but given unity by a consciousness of one fate.

By the end of the year, when she was nearly ten, she could hardly remember Eleanora, and Soapy, and Miss Williamson with her clogged voice and big teeth. Only the Lady-Mumma she could not forget. Sometimes she stood on the sand-dunes in the stinging wind, and looked over the blue water towards the Tasmanian mainland: feeling sure that a ship would appear with the Lady-Mumma aboard, come back to Mathinna as she had always come back before.

Then as the red dress wore out and the red stockings were thrown away or lost, she ceased to hope, and almost ceased to believe that there had ever been another life over there, beyond the mountains washed palely on the horizon, faint as a half-remembered dream.

She liked Dr Milligan, but she was not sure that she liked Mitter Clarke, the Catechist. She went every Sunday morning before church to the scripture class at his quarters, where she learnt each week a new verse of the Psalms and repeated it the following week. She also knew her catechism and her Creed, which she could gabble off faster than any of the other children.

Clarke was a hollow-cheeked, strange-looking man, very pious but with a fanatical look in his sunken eyes. He believed in mortifying the flesh. He looked at the nubile girls among his classes with a glazed look almost of hatred; but there were few enough young people. Only fifty-three natives were left altogether.

The last to die had been an old man with one eye: the natives were intrigued to know whether he would have two in heaven, but were inclined to believe that, resurrected in the flesh, their departed brother would be a recognizably one-eyed angel. They made up a song about it, Truganini and Wanganippi who had gone back to their own native names; and the others took it up:

> Angel a one-eye our Brudder gone,
> Our Brudder gone, Brudder gone:
> Mitter Clarke say in Heppen he rise,
> Our Brudder gone, Brudder gone ...

It was not a cheerful song. The voices died away in a kind of long-drawn sob on the last syllable. Like a comment on all who had already passed, and on all who must inevitably follow until there was not one left to mourn, the word echoed over the low swampy grasses and stunted tea tree, floating on the cold wind: Gone ...

Chapter Thirty-five

Sir John's last thought as he left Disco Bay in Greenland, the final port of call before he sailed into the unknown, was to reassure his dearest Jane about the coming voyage.

He wrote that *Erebus* and *Terror* sailed well together, and that he was perfectly content with his officers, his crew, and his ship. It was, he told her, one of the best-equipped expeditions ever to set out. Besides which James Ross always said that the Arctic Sea was not nearly so dangerous for navigation as the Antarctic....

He sent her a pair of sealskin boots made by the Eskimoes, and was her most affectionate husband, John Franklin.

At the same time he sent a very different letter to his friend James Ross:

> What I most fear respecting my wife is that if we do not return at the time she has fixed on in her mind, she may become very anxious.... James, I wish you were here. I would then have no doubts about our pursuing the proper course. What I fear is that from our being so late we shall have no time to look round and judge for ourselves, but blunder into the ice and make another 1824 of it....

Fear, anxiety, doubt. Yet he had kept up the façade so well that Eleanor was able to tell her Aunt Isabella that her dear papa left in excellent spirits, looking much better since he had given up snuff. She and Mamma had gone as far as Rotherhithe with the ships, then waved their handkerchiefs until he was out of sight.

Jane settled down to the long anguish of waiting. Hadn't old Sir John Ross, James's uncle, once spent five years in the Arctic? They had been frozen solid in the ice for the last year, and in the end had to nail the colours to the mast and abandon *Victory* to her fate. Emaciated, scurvy-ridden, frost-bitten, they had been rescued at last. *Erebus* and *Terror* had plenty of supplies for three years, including a great stock of tinned meat.

She waited in suspense till the autumn and summer were over, the second year, and as soon as winter sealed the northern routes she set off for India. She and Sophy travelled in bullock-carts from rest-house to rest-house, carrying with them the famous iron bedstead. Then back to London to wait for news, or the return of the ships; then off the following winter, for North America. She was popular with the Americans. They loved her title, and her years in Australia had made her less formal in her manners. On the return voyage she stopped at Honolulu at the invitation of King Kamahameha of Hawaii. She found the Royal Family most congenial, and the climate delightful. The King presented her with a beautiful feather cape, a semi-circle of yellow feathers with a red border such as could only be worn by the Hawaiian nobility.

By 1847 already Jane was fearing the worst. She had written to James Ross that she did not hope for a successful outcome, only for the safety of the expedition: 'Would you go in search of them, I wonder?' ... She wrote and re-wrote a long letter to Sir John for a rescue ship to take to him.

By the beginning of 1848 Ross was free; his publishers had brought out his book, *A Voyage of Discovery in the Antarctic Seas.* He had stayed at home four years as a model married man; now his wife agreed for him to go in search of his old friends. After three years, if they were caught in the ice (as seemed likely) the expedition must be in serious straits.

Jane was in a restless, excited state of feeling. She wished she might go with the *Enterprise* and *Investigator,* but felt it would be unbecoming. Besides, she really should not leave Eleanor, and if Sir John were already on the way back she might miss him.

She wrote long letters almost daily, as had been her habit whenever they were apart. They gave her some illusion of contact, though they could never be posted.

One letter was copied out by Sophy many times, and sent with whalers going to the Arctic Seas, with a promise of £3,000 from Jane if they could deliver it or even bring back news of *Erebus* and *Terror* and the 135 men aboard them.

James Ross promised he would not come back without *some* news, whether good or bad.

Jane sent a letter by his hand, telling Sir John that the prayers of all who loved him would surely prevail with Almighty God to spare him – the Bishop of Tasmania had proclaimed a day of prayer throughout Van Diemen's Land for the expedition – God was merciful, 'But we know his ways are inscrutable.'

If she thought he was ill, she added, nothing would have stopped her coming after the expedition, but she felt it her duty to remain.

At this stage they all thought that it was only a matter of sending a search expedition to the rescue, or to learn the worst. No one imagined that dozens of ships, a great list of famous Polar explorers, and years of patient search would yield not the slightest clue. *Erebus* and *Terror* had disappeared, it seemed, for ever.

The disappearance and the search had brought Sophy and her aunt even closer together. Sophy admired Jane tremendously, and to Jane she was her right-hand man, her favourite travelling companion, and her uncomplaining amanuensis. They both had a personal and emotional interest in the search, for though Sophy had obstinately refused to marry Frank Crozier, she was touched by his devotion and persistence. He had taken with him to the Arctic a small booklet she had given him as a memento, just as she kept in a secret compartment of her portable *escritoire* a silver-printed, pale-blue programme with a broken silk cord, and a blue satin invitation in memory of Captain Ross and a ball years ago on board *Erebus*.

In the year before, while they still waited in dreadful suspense for news of the expedition, Ross's book of his voyages was delivered to Lady Franklin.

Sophy gave a small gasp as the two volumes were unwrapped.

'It's an elegant production, is it not?' said Jane, turning the dark-blue covers in her small hands.

'Very elegant,' said Sophy quietly. Beneath the gold lettering of the title was the Southern Cross, imprinted in gold on the midnight-blue cloth as it had been patterned on the midnight sky over Hobart Town, the night she had said farewell to Captain Ross.

When Ross had not returned by the late summer of 1849, a second ship was sent out with supplies for *Investigator* and *Enterprise*, so that they could stay out and continue the search. But it had scarcely sailed when Ross and his expedition turned up off the coast of Scotland, back already, and without having found anything.

Jane was stunned. 'An experienced Arctic voyager like him, to come home so soon! Marriage has a softening effect on some men, I believe,' she said bitterly. Sophy was silent. Even she was disappointed in her idol.

In deep despondency, Jane read the chronicles of an early Dutch expedition in which the commander, Barentz, died on an ice-floe in 1594, after abandoning his ice-bound vessel. He had died calmly and bravely, thinking less of himself than the safety of his crew, his last words directed to the course they were to steer. How like Sir John it sounded! When Barentz died his inconsolable men, who had loved and revered him, could not dig a grave on the nearest land for the ground was frozen like iron. They had scraped a sarcophagus in the ice and left him there, to float in that vast and wandering grave of the pack, until at last it drifted to warmer waters and let him sink to burial at sea.

Jane's vivid imagination saw every detail of the cold, the hunger, the increasing anxiety of the men whose stores were running out and who must decide whether to abandon ship or to stay, in the hope that the ice would break up and set them free.

What were they doing now, in the growing cold of the Arctic winter? Were they safe aboard the ships, or wandering somewhere in those terrible wastes? She longed to know, to see. 'If only I could see you in a magic mirror as in the fairy-tales,' she wrote. And yet perhaps it was better not to know.

Mrs Nixon wrote from Tasmania that the present Governor would have nothing to do with the idea of a college, and had even filled up the foundations which were dug for the building. John Phillip Gell, disgusted with Van Diemen's Land, was coming home to claim Eleanor. John Hepburn had given up his post at Point Puer and was on his way home to join in the Arctic search for his old Commander. He was no longer young, he wrote, but he knew the Arctic seas and felt he must go. Ronald Gunn sent his sympathy.

Jane had prayed for patience; she had tried to have faith, she had kept up her hopes, in vain. Now in desperation she turned to Spiritualism.

The clairvoyante, Ellen Dawson, was a little, wizened creature subject to fits and heart trouble, but she had a reputation for remarkable visions of the future and the past while in a trance.

She chose Sophy as an interlocutor. When she had 'gone away' Sophy was to ask her questions.

Sophy was more sceptical than her aunt, but in spite of her self she felt a tingling of her spine as she sat alone with the medium in a darkened room. Ellen Dawson fixed her eyes on a point of light coming through a crack in the heavy black curtains. Slowly her eyes grew glazed, then her lids fell shut and she appeared to sleep.

When her voice came, rather guttural and deeper than

her waking voice, Sophy jumped nervously.

I have been a long way on the sea and into the ice, and saw a ship in the ice, and several people on it, all men ... one of them rather old ... rather short and stout ... rather dark, with such a nice face....

'Is he quite well, does he look ill or unhappy?' asked Sophy breathlessly.

No, quite well, happy and comfortable ... rather anxious perhaps....

'Where are the ships, when will they come home, can you ask him?'

No.... There is a cloud before me.

'But can't you see anything else?'

The old gentleman's cabin is quite clear.... Two portraits of ladies in it –

'Of course! That's true; my aunt's and the Queen's!'

And ... and ... no, it's growing dark.... There seems to be plenty of salt beef and biscuits.... All is well, all is quite right....

'What else, what else? Is there an officer, a younger man, commanding a second ship? Can you see him in his cabin?'

No. I can see nothing. All is dark. I can see no more.

Jane was comforted a little by this 'vision' as reported by Sophy, but she did not dare mention it to John Gell when he arrived. He and Eleanor were married and went off on their honeymoon, while Jane wept a little that Eleanor's father was not there to give her away, though she wrote him a long letter to tell him about it. She was completely certain that he was alive. She felt sure she would have known, without the corroboration of the medium, if he were dead. She planned a new expedition, using her own money and half of the income from Eleanor's mother which was hers to use under a Power of Attorney.

Chapter Thirty-six

Her last Christmas at Flinders Island was spent by Mathinna in 1847. All the natives enjoyed this time of year, the carol-singing by candlelight and the crib which Mr Clarke encouraged them to build, with real straw in the manger and a tiny wax doll for a Christ-child.

Mathinna's doll given her by Lady Franklin had been broken by some of the bigger girls at the Orphan School before Dr Milligan had her brought to Flinders. Now, at twelve years old, she was in her own eyes a young woman; she was more interested in boys than in dolls.

She had noticed before the funny way Mr Clarke looked at her from his shadowed and sunken eyes, but it was nothing to the way he looked when he found a group of them, three boys and three girls, exploring the delightful differences of the opposite sex in a hollow of the sandhills. It was no more than healthy curiosity, but to the Catechist they seemed sunk in the depths of depravity.

The old tribal customs by which a girl was made a woman and taught the things that a woman should know by the old women of the tribe, had been lost in the 'civilizing' process. In the same way the boys, each of whom would have been made a 'proper man' at the appointed time, with a long period of fasting, initiation rites, and separation from the womenfolk, were allowed to grow up without guidance from the apathetic Old Men. So, fumblingly, they sought the age-old knowledge and wisdom which the Bible classes and the Sunday school failed to give.

Mr Clarke was angrier with the girls than with the boys. He had always seemed a kind man with a genuine love for his charges, but now he was beside himself. He drove the girls along before him to his quarters in a seething

rage. There, half-dressed as they were (for he'd hardly
given them time to huddle their clothes on) he shut them
in an inner room and called them out one by one for
punishment.

Mathinna was trembling when she came out. She had
heard the screams of the other girls, and the swish of the
leather strap. Mr Clarke was trembling, too. There was a
strange glitter in his eyes and foam upon his lips.

'Come here!' he said harshly. 'Mathinna, kneel down
and ask God's forgiveness for your wicked and carnal
ways.' He grasped her shoulder and forced her to her knees.
The blue serge blouse which had lost some of its fastenings
slipped sideways, leaving one shoulder bare. 'Say, "May
God forgive me and make me pure".'

'May G-God forgib me and m-m-make me pure.'

Mr Clarke began to lash her back and bare shoulder
in a frenzy. 'Take that! And that. And *that*! And may the
Lord have *mercy* on your *soul*! You are a wicked, wicked
shameless girl. You are all shameless. I've seen you rolling
your eyes, leading the boys astray.... If I ever catch you
again, I will flog the lot of you until you can't stand up.
Now go!'

Sobbing and wiping her nose with the back of her hand
Mathinna stumbled out and joined the other girls. Though
their backs were painful, so painful that after a restless
night they went to Dr Jeanneret to ask for wet compresses
and ointment, there was much giggling as the story of the
thrashing was told and the stripes were proudly displayed.
In some odd way they didn't rightly understand, they had
enjoyed their punishment. 'My word, Mitter Clarke prop'ly
wild,' they told each other gleefully.

Coming on a tour of inspection, the Bishop was shocked
at the Catechist's intemperate action. He was worried by
the continuing decline of the race, and had recommended
that they should be taken back to the main island, to some
country retreat not too near either Hobart or Launceston,
where the climate was more equable and their decline
might be arrested. Jeanneret, reinstated by Lord Stanley,

once more lost his job. Dr Milligan was to take over.

Governor Denison (who had already replaced Sir Eardley Wilmot, hounded to death, it was said, by the Colonial Office) signed the order for the forty-four remaining Tasmanians to be taken to Oyster Cove, south of Hobart, between the mouths of the Derwent and the Huon – all but the young ones. They stayed behind, and on nearly the last day of the year, Mathinna found herself back at the Queen's Orphan School in Newtown, the place she had hated, with six other children from seven to thirteen. There were no babies any more.

It was three years before she managed to get away. In that time she grew into a young beauty, with a glossy brown skin and soft curling hair, fully aware of her attractions. The superintendent of the school begged that she should be removed before she ruined all the others with her spoilt, coquettish ways.

She was nearly sixteen when she was delivered back to Dr Milligan, and to Mr Clarke who felt his vocation was to give spiritual guidance to the natives as long as the poor creatures needed him.

When Mathinna got out of the spring-cart at the Snug, with all her belongings in a cloth bag with a drawstring over her shoulder, she stood quite still, breathing deeply and peacefully. Here was that scent, green and aromatic, which she remembered, or seemed to remember, from long ago, when the mere fact of living and breathing was enjoyment.

The gum trees soared 300 feet above her head, their trunks as smooth as stone columns, and along the creeks grew myrtle and banksia and fern-tree; the Tasmanian lily lighted the slopes with its orange and scarlet bells, and the crimson flower of the waratah burned in the depths of the bush.

She dropped the bag and opened her arms to it all. This was her place. Here she had come home.

In Launceston, Ronald Gunn had a sad letter from Lady

293

Franklin, who had planned to fit out an Arctic search ship
herself in the year of Eleanor's marriage, but had to give
up the plan. Eleanor's opposition was so bitter that she
was forced to the painful thought that she did not *want*
her Papa to return; for once his death was presumed she
would have the whole income from her dead mother's
estate.

'Eleanor has grudged every penny spent by me in my
efforts to find her father,' wrote Lady Franklin. 'It is a
cruel consolation, but should my dear husband never return, at least he will never have to hear of Eleanor and
Gell's actions!

'I brought my husband about £16,000, and tho' Ancanthe
certainly is a failure and Betsy Island only a useless invest-
ment, yet could the money have been better spent? It is all
in Sir John's name, and all left to Eleanor.... Ever since
their marriage I have handed over half of E.'s Trust income; the other half has gone in organizing the search....'

It was a shame, Mr Gunn and his wife agreed. He had
never taken to the daughter, with her round, smooth face
and rather smug expression, but he was disappointed in Mr
Gell, who had always seemed so spiritual.

In London, where Gell now had a good living, Eleanor
wrote in her diary, the following year:

> *March 1850* I see my last entry was a few days before
> my marriage. Now I am looking forward very speedily
> to becoming a Mother. It is a solemn thought. I am going
> to the gates of the grave, and it may be God's will that I
> go through them. To be with Christ is far better than to
> be with the best earthly husband! But I dread the
> thought of the blank I shall leave behind me. Lord, into
> thy hands ...

She was kept too busy producing little Gells and bringing
them through infancy, after this, to have time for the
luxury of such speculations. In place of spiritual matters,
spirits of turps (as a remedy for worms) appeared. Prescrip-

ions for infant diarrhoea replaced her dialogues with God, and recipes for hardening bones, liniments for softening boils, preoccupied her more than the state of her soul.

Her step-Mamma (as she now thought of her) knew nothing about babies, so there was no point in taking them to see her. Anyway, she was quite unbalanced over this business of searching for Papa, who had obviously gone down with both the ships long ago, or why had nothing ever been seen of them? She suspected a gigantic plot to keep her, Eleanor, and her darling John and her precious babes out of their rightful inheritance. She would fight that scheming woman in the law-courts if necessary. Let the dead bury their dead. She was alive, and that was all that mattered.

Chapter Thirty-seven

A whaler in Melville Bay had the last glimpse of *Erebus* and *Terror*. That was on 26 July 1845, not long after they set out. Since then the world had buzzed with speculation about their fate. Everyone had theories of where they might be, yet no one could find them.

From the dignified London *Times* to the cartoons of *Punch* the papers were filled with the Franklin Expedition and the North-west Passage; Lord Tennyson wrote poems and Sir Edwin Landseer painted pictures on the same subject.

By 1850 there were fifteen ships in the Arctic: American whalers, British naval vessels, screw steamers, schooners and auxiliary steam vessels, including an expedition sent by Lady Franklin and the *Felix* under command of old Sir John Ross, financed by the Hudson Bay Company. They were all looking for Franklin. McClure and Collinson set off by way of Bering Strait for the north coast of America, to be out for five years.

Captain William Penny, that rough diamond; Admiral Sherard Osborne, Commander Forsyth, Captains McClintock, Ommanney and Austin; Ellis Kane and de Haven, in the American expedition financed by Henry Grinnell; the *Advance, Rescue, Intrepid, Assistance, Pioneer, Enterprise, Investigator*; what a gathering of great names and noble ships!

The little *Prince Albert* came back first with news. The *Lady Franklin & Sophia*, with a figurehead of Hope leaning up an anchor, came back with its loving, anguished letters undelivered.

But the *Assistance* had found traces of the expedition. Near Cape Riley they found rope and canvas of British Admiralty make, and cairns, containing no papers. This proved at least that the ships had got through Lancaster Sound and Barrow Strait. From there they could have gone north up Wellington Channel, or south towards the coast of North America. Everyone seemed agreed that they had gone north.

Only the little *Prince Albert*, under Captain William Kennedy, the Canadian, set out in 1851. He carried homing pigeons which were to be marked with a red cross on the breast for good news, or a black cross for bad, if anything were found.

Kennedy came back with his pigeons; Sir John Ross and Dr Richardson returned with nothing after two years. Now Jane knew he must be dead, but she would not admit it. She could not rest until she knew her husband's fate.

Each night as she closed her eyes she prayed that she might go out of the body and voyage, even in dreams, to those cold inhuman regions which held the secret. If there were flying machines which would take her there just for a glimpse, or if by some magic, even, she had been able to hear their words! But such things were impossible.

She fell asleep muttering her usual prayer: 'May God bless you and preserve you, my own dearest love.'

Her Majesty's Government seemed content with the scrap of information discovered, and resigned itself to the loss of the ships and all their men. Jane scraped and saved to fit out another search ship herself. The Fellows of Christ College, Tasmania – for Jane's dream college had been established, and the island bore the name she had always given it – sent thirty pounds as a donation as a token of their affectionate respect for Sir John's memory in the Colony.

It was very welcome, for Jane had nothing left but the income from her mother's estate. Eleanor, full of bitterness, had gone to law over her father's will and her mother's estate, and all that had been Jane's now belonged to her. She no longer spoke to her Mamma, and Mr Gell replied coolly to Jane's letter begging for some sign of affection,

297

that 'such things could not be forced'.

The Tasmanian gesture was balm to her wounded feelings. All their work in that distant land had not been in vain.

'Be assured,' she wrote, 'that he whom you so affectionately regard as a benefactor would be amply rewarded for the deep interest he took in the Tasmanian College, could he witness this proof of the noble and generous sentiments which ...' Her pen faltered. It was well he could not witness the ignoble and ungenerous actions of his own daughter.

Early in 1854 the Admiralty sent out a notice that 'If intelligence be not received before 31 March next of the officers and crews of H.M. ships *Erebus* and *Terror* being alive, their names will be removed from the Navy List, and they ... will be considered as having died in Her Majesty's service. . . .'

Jane instantly put away the black dresses she had been wearing for years as becoming to her age, and appeared in light colours of pink and green.

She wrote with deep feeling about 'fixing upon one moment for consigning 135 seamen simultaneously to the grave,' and added that under the circumstances she would refuse to accept any widow's pension. She pointed out that the little vessel she had bought, the *Isabel*, and offered to the Navy, was lying unused as a monument to blighted efforts; but since no evidence had been found of a catastrophe the men could not be considered dead. She would continue the search on her own.

Almost as if in answer, a letter came in October from Dr Rae, who had been sledging out from Hudson Bay. The Eskimoes there had told him of two ships crushed in the ice, of a large party of white men dying of hunger: 'they fell down and died as they walked' not far from the mouth of the Great Fish River in northern Canada.

The final proof was the collection of relics of the lost party, silver forks and spoons and a small order or star with Sir John's name engraved upon it.

The Times gave columns to a description of the report and the relics, and to the following discovery by Sir George Simpson and the Hudson Bay Company of a boat with planks missing, some snow-shoes made of oak, discarded utensils; but not a scrap of paper or journals.

'And this,' ended *The Times,* which had opposed spending money on the search, 'seems all that we can ever know of the fate of the Franklin Expedition.'

It was noon in midwinter. Frank Crozier, fighting against tiredness, climbed on to the white and frozen deck and closed the hatch beside him.

Down there it was still comparatively warm. They had enough coal left for cooking and keeping the steam-pipes hot till the end of winter, but that was all. As soon as the sun returned, unless the ice began to break up and set them free, they must take to the sleds and walk.

Unless the ice broke up! He looked about him and laughed, a harsh and mirthless sound.

All round stretched a vast plain of ice and snow heaped with tiers of broken ice blocks and snow wreaths, all glistening brilliantly in the moonlight. At the centre of this emptiness lay the two lone ships, atoms in the empty landscape. Landward, to the south-east, far over the rugged and frozen sea, all was deathlike and silent.

The high moon rode through a heaven of deepest ink, where the constellations wheeled round the Polar Star like armies in review. Fleecy clouds slowly crossed the moon, so that the distant capes and headlands now receded into shadow and gloom, now burst on the sight in startling distinctness, so that the landscape seemed to waver like a flag in the wind.

He climbed down to the rigid surface of the congealed sea. As well expect the solid land to break up, as this mass of impenetrable ice!

It was hard labour, their lethargic state, even to cut

enough ice for drinking water, to keep holes open for sewage. It had proved impossible to dig a grave.

He followed the line of posts that had been set up as markers to the ship in fog and snowstorm, then deviated to where a large square edifice of ice stood on the frozen sea. They had built it of sawn blocks something after the fashion of an Eskimo dwelling; and there lay Sir John Franklin, draped in his country's flag, undecaying, yet never to wake, enclosed by walls of Polar ice – a fitting memorial, thought Crozier. They might have taken him to King William Land over there, but still would not have been able to dig in the frozen ground; and they liked to have him close. If the ice had broken up, they had thought to preserve his body and take it with them.

A simple inscription was cut upon a board set in the ice:

Here Lies Sir John Franklin, K.C.B.,
Captain, Royal Navy,
Commander, H.M. Ship *Erebus*,
Discoverer of the North-West Passage

For they had found the Passage – or a passage – though it was solidly blocked with ice, and by then they were already being squeezed in the relentless grip of the pack. Lieutenant Gore had come back from a sledging party with the news of the channel tending away to the west. He had told the Old Man of it: had he understood? He was very low by then. If he understood, had he cared?

He'd kept muttering, 'Tell them – tell them I wasn't too old, Frank; and look after the papers ... must keep the records ... the papers ...'

He had been quite well when Gore and Fitzjames set out. Then a fall on the slippery deck, and one of his brittle, ageing bones snapped and protruded through the flesh of his leg. It was what he had dreaded. When the leg failed to heal and the surgeon said it had to come off, he knew he must die. It looked now as if they might have to walk for it; and a one-legged man of sixty-two could hardly keep up. He would only be a burden.

So he decided not to recover from the operation, but set out quietly to die. He didn't eat, and as his vitality was already low after the long winter and the shock of the injury and operation, he soon sank, his mind turning more and more to the people at home.

Jane – how she would worry! No chance of the ice breaking up this year, and even if by some miracle the ships were freed next summer, they'd already have been out three years.

He coughed weakly, gave a little groan as the cursed leg that wasn't there ached and ached. His eyes sought the portrait of Jane on his cabin wall: tenderly smiling at him, with just a hint of mischief about the lovely eyes. Jove, what low bodices they wore in those days! Wouldn't be approved of now by Queen Victoria over there....

'Frank! Frank, are you there, old man?' His voice had become not much more than a whisper.

'Yes, John. Don't try to talk.'

'Tell my wife, Frank ... I want you to tell Jane ... I had an easy end. Died in my bunk, tell her. No pain. Quite the – contrary, in fact....'

In the cold moonlight, beside the sarcophagus of ice, Crozier turned and looked back towards the ships. At that moment a cloud crossed the moon. All became formless, unreal: the ships, the distant headlands, were blotted out, he could no longer see the line of demarcation between sea and land. He stood alone at the frozen end of the world.

Chapter Thirty-eight

Coming up from the lighted 'tween-decks into the inhuman night was like stepping from life into death. Down there the oil-lamps still gave a murky light though the candles were all gone. The steam from the hot cups of cocoa on the mess tables, mingled with the breaths of fifty men, filled the space with mist and fog.

There, below, was human warmth and life. Up here the bite of the frosty air hurt the lungs. The space, the silence, the deathly stillness of the frozen sea made Frank Crozier shudder. Dear God, it was a fearful place! What were puny men doing here, pitting themselves against the enormous indifference of nature?

Yet there was a strange poetry in the evanescent colours of the sky as the sun came closer. The southern horizon would be shaded through the most delicate tints from pink to blue, all through the twenty-four hours, like a perpetual dawn: growing darker and darker in tint until in the north a cold bluish-black scowled above the frozen ocean.

And in the long winter night the Aurora Borealis had danced and wavered its filmy curtains, from palest straw-colour to brilliant pink and green. The moon like a silver wheel had rolled round and round the sky, just above the horizon. For whose eyes to see? For what reason these wonderfully beautiful displays in a desolate and forever-uninhabitable region? What for, he wondered.

There was little conversation sounding through the closed hatch. The old cheerful hum down there had subsided, as in a hive where the bees are overcome with cold. Depression had settled about the ships like a miasma, scurvy had attacked most of their crews, and they were pale and lethargic after the long Polar night.

If they left it much longer they would be too weak to pull

the heavy sledges loaded with food, should they have to abandon the ships. And it seemed obvious that they would have to do so.

It was his, Crozier's, job to lead them now. Which way were they to go? Some wanted to try to make a beeline for the Hudson Bay Company outpost, taking to the boats when open water intervened. Others wanted to go almost due south for Back's Great Fish River which would lead them down into Canada. But with their heavy sledges would they ever make it?

His own idea was that their best hope lay in marching away from home, up near Barrow Strait and Lancaster Sound where rescue ships were most likely to be looking for them. The men, of course, hated the idea of going north. They would put it to the vote. He wouldn't coerce them. He only wished Sir John were alive, with his personal knowledge of the inhospitable North American coast, and his great influence with the men.

Heavily laden sledges, waiting to be man-hauled across the rough sea-ice, with tarpaulin covers lashed down, stood ready for the men to slip into their harness. Two were loaded with whaleboats for use when they came to open water.

There was still plenty of chocolate, pemmican, and tinned meat, but there was no fuel left for making hot food or thawing out frozen boots.

All they could do was keep moving, doggedly, painfully, until they dropped: the weaker sheltered by the strong, mates giving a helping shoulder to each other, officers trying to cheer the men with words of hope when their own hearts were cold with foreboding.

For a while they could laugh, and joke. Even Crozier, with all his worry, had to smile when he heard an old grey-bearded marine adjuring a youngster: 'Be sure an' always stay a simple seaman: 'cos that way, d'you see, you have to think of nothink; there are petty off'cers, Captins, Commanders and h'Admirals all paid for looking after you, and a-taking care o' you.'

Minute spicules of frost formed on the men's clothing and beards as they waited. Behind them, twenty-four man-made mounds of ice, smaller than the one that marked Sir John's resting place, stood on the frozen sea. Those who still lived, more than a hundred men, were ready to set out on their last walk.

Frank Crozier dashed back to *Erebus*, nodded in farewell to the portrait of Jane still smiling serenely on the empty cabin, and went along the alleyway and up the companion, where he had lifted Sophy down at a ball years ago in Hobart Town. He took off his glove and fur mitten from his right hand, and touched for an instant the rail, white with hoar-frost. The cold seemed to burn his hand.

He walked for the last time across to the icy cairn with the flag which marked his old commander's grave. He stood before it and mentally vowed he would get the records and letters back somehow, if he lived.

The return of the sun had cheered them a little. One of the younger seamen, climbing to the masthead, had caught a glimpse of gold over the southern horizon, and hailed its return with a weak shout. They celebrated with the last of the rum, giving the sailors' toast, 'The Queen, God bless her', and 'Sweethearts and Wives'.

Crozier came back and drew a small book from his pocket. It had been given to him by Sophy just before their departure. He intended to take it with him, even if it meant extra weight.

Breath steaming in the icy air, he said, 'I want to read you something before we leave, men.'

He cleared his throat. His voice grew stronger as he read:

'Each must act as he thinks best; and if he is wrong, so much the worse for him. We stand on a mountain pass in the midst of whirling snow and blinding mist, through which we get glimpses now and then of paths which may be deceptive.

'We do not certainly know if there is any right one.

'What must we do?

' "Be strong and of good courage." Act for the best, hope for the best, and take what comes ... If death ends all, we cannot meet death better.'

There was silence for a moment, then a cheer, dying away in the vast emptiness around. The sky overhead was perfectly clear and serene. At the zenith a most intense indigo blue, it became paler and paler towards the horizon, where the sun was skimming along at an altitude of two degrees, large, golden with promise.

The march began.

Outside the grog-shop at the Snug, far away in Van Diemen's Land at the opposite end of the earth, Mathinna counted the money tied up in the corner of a dirty rag. The weather was hot, and she was thirsty. No, it was not quite enough yet. She twisted up the rag again, savagely.

'Carm on, Sweet'eart. Ow's about it? Come on down ter the beach.' The drunken sawyer put an arm round her shoulder to steady himself.

Impatiently Mathinna shrugged him off. 'What por?'

'Oh, ho, you knows what for. Eh? Carm on, luv, I got money. Ow much ter come down the beach?'

Mathinna's dark eyes stared over his head at the tall, clean trunks of the soaring trees. Her curving mouth was sullen. She shrugged again. 'Penny. I want penny more to get 'nuff for bottle o' giblee.'

' 'at's the girl. Carm on, carm on. We's wastin' time.'

She went with him indifferently.

It was ten years since Mathinna had been taught to mind her manners at Gub'mint House, to keep herself clean and value her person. For the last year she had lived at Oyster Cove among the hopeless dying remnant of her race, scraping with her fingers for food in the communal cooking pot which the dogs licked afterwards.

The sea broke in slow, clear waves on the firm sand of D'Entrecasteaux Channel, as it had through thousands of years when the women of her people came here to dive for oysters or bring up a live crayfish for the men, their lords and masters. Thousands of years of submission to the male was bred into Mathinna.

Why had 'they' taken her up and almost made a white girl of her, she had often wondered? For she could never be a white girl, she could never be one of 'them'; and she could never be quite contented as a black girl, for the ways of her own people disgusted her.

So did the dirty sawyers and splitters and whalemen with their white-man smell strong on them and their harsh ugly voices and red skins. But they had money, and money would buy drink – 'giblee', and a few hours' obilivion.

The man had gone, leaving her spent and used. She rolled over, resting her face on a shapely brown arm. A scalding tear ran down the side of her nose. It dripped on the sand, forming a tiny pockmark there.

Something pricked her breast – the pointed shells of her necklace, still strung on their worn strip of kangaroo sinew.

With a fierce tug she broke it through, scattering the shells which sank and were lost in the sand. There went Mathinna, 'Necklace' as they called her, the red muslin dress, school with Miss Williamson and Eleanora and the Lady-Mumma she had loved and trusted.

Soon they would all be gone like the shells: Mathinna and Truganini, Patty and Bong, Walter and Mary Anne – gone from the leaking, filthy huts where she shivered all night in one flea-ridden blanket because they'd sold the rest for drink; gone from the grog-shop and the beach, lost and forgotten, dead like poor old Mitter Clarke, who had been three days dying, calling on Jesus to come and take him, and who had told them all to 'be sure and meet me in heaven'.

There was only a handful of her people left, and nobody cared if they lived or died. Why had they been born, why ever had they been born. *What por, what por?*

Chapter Thirty-nine

'I wish you would take more rest, Aunt,' said Sophy anxiously. She was afraid Jane's nerves would give way as they had in Van Diemen's Land, though physically she was well and full of energy, and looked ten years younger than her real age. Her hair was still dark, though Sophy's was turning grey.

Sophy had worked untiringly with her, but from so much copying and working late at night her sight was going. She wore glasses all the time now, with tinted lenses by day to shield her eyes from the bright light. She knew that she would never marry. She was nearly forty, and looked her age; time was slowly closing the gap between her and Jane, who had once been twice her age, so that now they seemed more like sisters.

Jane was determined to discover something more, some written records of the expedition. Instead of relaxing her efforts now that definite evidence of the loss of ships and men had been found, she redoubled them. She would not give up, though everyone in authority seemed to have lost interest.

What! Give up now, when at last they had a clue? And one which pointed to the very area, off the coast of Boothia and near the mouth of the Fish River, which she had suggested to the Admiralty back in 1850 – when, according to the Eskimoes, forty men were still alive. Were her husband and all those brave men to have died in vain, with no record of their sufferings and discoveries?

She had once written to Mary that she would hate to be thought one of those bold, energetic, clever women, fit for anything. But the title had been thrust on her in Hobart Town; now she set out to make it a reality.

As Admiral Sherard Osborn had said in dedicating his

Arctic Journal to her and her noble efforts at rescue, or solving the fate of the missing men. "The name of Franklin, and the mystery hanging over his fate, the sufferings he and his followers must have undergone, are on every tongue in every civilized land.'

With tremendous and single-minded energy she had set out to urge or shame the Government into continuing the search. Her last, most strongly-worded appeal, written with all the practised eloquence of her pen, was rejected by Lord Palmerston and the Lords of the Admiralty in 1856.

Undaunted, she saved and scraped together all the money she could, about £7,000, and organized lectures and appeals to raise another £3,000. Mr Charles Dickens wrote a moving sketch. 'The Frozen Deep', the proceeds from which went to the Search Fund. Sir James Ross, William Thackeray, and her old flame Dr Paul Roget added their eloquence.

Naval men and scientists stood behind her to a man, including Captain Maconachie; she had always known he had a generous spirit. She had written to him when his daughter Mary Anne died of tuberculosis in the Isle of Wight. She had lived to be thirty-two.

Ronald Gunn raised what he could in Van Diemen's Land, though most of her land was now legally Eleanor's under Sir John's will; for married women had no legal rights to their own property. Sir John's niece, Mary Price, was now a widow on a Government pension. For after a tour of duty as Commandant at Norfolk Island (where he put down insubordination with a ferocious, cold inhumanity the very opposite of Alexander Maconachie's methods) John Price had been murdered by a group of maddened convicts on Williamstown Pier.

Eleanor now had several children. The eldest, Phillip, took after Sir John, but Jane had not seen him since he was a baby.

There had been some bitter exchanges over the will, and now the two families did not meet. 'I'm afraid Eleanor positively *hates* my aunt,' as Sophy wrote sadly to her mother. Jane was disappointed in Mr Gell, who had turned out to be less spiritual than he had seemed, but she put it down to Eleanor's influence.

She had been negotiating for the purchase of a private steam yacht of under 200 tons, the *Fox*. In April 1857 she wired triumphantly to Captain McClintock: YOUR LEAVE IS GRANTED THE FOX IS MINE REFIT WILL START IMMEDIATELY.

She and Sophy worked day and night helping with the refit, making lists of stores, for they must not lose another summer.

Jane felt confident that Leopold McClintock was the man for her work. He was an experienced Arctic navigator, with the short, wiry, slender but muscular frame of James Ross, well fitted for endurance. Quick and decisive in his movements, he was always perfectly calm, overseeing every detail of stores and equipment without fuss.

The second in command would be William Hobson, son of an old friend, the Governor of New Zealand during her visit in 1841. She had offered him a home at Government House, Hobart Town while he completed his education, if it had not been possible for him to go to England (for she had not doubted, then, that Christ College would be speedily completed).

The tension mounted until at last the little *Fox* was ready. She steamed away, with smoke trailing from her tall funnel set among the masts, and followed by prayers and good wishes. Then began the long anxious period of waiting.

At last, in the spring of 1859, Captain McClintock returned. After hope had been deferred for so long, Jane could not believe the news at first. Young Hobson had found a message left by the retreating party, ten years earlier.

A little to the north of Point Victory he had found a rusted tin containing a printed Admiralty form. The paper was stained, one corner had rotted away, but the writing was legible.

310

There were two records, a year apart. The first, using
the body of the form, gave the latitude and longitude of
the spot where the ships were caught in the ice, to the north-
west of King William Land, in an ice-bound channel which
led on (had they been able to move) to Bering Strait and
the North Pacific. It added simply, 'All well.' It was dated
April, 1847, and signed 'Lieut. Gore'.

The second message had been scrawled round the edge of
the form, evidently in haste and with partly thawed ink, a
year later.

Jane set off with Sophy for Scotland to meet the *Fox*,
and handle and read for herself the precarious scrap of
paper, the reward of all her years of struggle. She went
out in a small boat in a storm, and up the rolling side of the
yacht like a sailor.

The Scottish fishermen who rowed her out gaped after
her. 'Whut a mon the mon must be, when the wumman
is sic' a braw ane!' they said. 'Och, she moves like a lassie
o' sixteen.'

McClintock and Hobson placed the small, rusted can in
her reverent hands. They went away and left her alone
with the message, which she already knew by heart. Written round the edges of the form were the words which
said so little, yet gave the answer to her long musings and
imaginings over Sir John's end, most of them too terrible
to contemplate for long.

The message ran:

Terror and *Erebus* deserted on 22 April, having been
stuck since Sept. 1846 – nineteen months in ice. 105 souls
landed here.
Sir John Franklin died on 11 June 1847 and the total
loss by deaths in the Exped. has been to this date 9
officers and 15 men.
           Signed, James Fitzjames, Capt. H.M.S. *Erebus*
           Crozier, F.R.M., Capt. & Snr. Officer.

Below the signatures was scrawled:

311

And start on tomorrow 26th for Back's Fish River.

That was all. It was tantalizingly little, but it was enough for her to let the matter rest, and find some measure of peace: as Sir John Franklin had found peace at last.

Frank Crozier had been there with him to cheer his last moments. He could not have dreamt that not a single man would get through, and that all the records would be lost; or that the prolonged search for him would do more for Arctic discovery than all the expeditions up to date.

Jane sat for a long time with the paper in her hand. She believed that it was real now. In a way she had felt sure of success this time, and that young Hobson would be the instrument: the fatality of that letter N again! She must call Sophy and let her see the paper. It belonged to the nation, it was not hers to keep.

So Frank Crozier had led the men on their fatal march. He was an experienced sailor, but not used to sledging and footwork. How long before he dropped out? Sophy said he used to call her the Ice Maiden and the Snow Queen. Jane imagined him plodding on in the last extremity of exhaustion, his tired brain dreaming of mounds of food and steaming cocoa, seeing perhaps the wraith of his old commander walking beside him.

And then ahead, through the powdery drifts of snow, a white figure beckoning: clad in white fur, with snow-pale cheeks and glittering dark eyes, and red lips cold as the kiss of death. Stumbling forward, falling into that icy embrace, he had sunk into blessed oblivion.

The next year Eleanor died and went to join her Papa and her real Mamma in heaven, where all would be forgiven and understood. She was only thirty-six. She had been expecting and preparing for this event ever since she was fourteen; yet she was loth to go, and leave her dear John Phillip Gell and all her little ones.

He asked if she would like to see Jane, but she thought

not, though she didn't mind if he invited her to the funeral. Perhaps they would be reconciled over her grave. She had pictured the scene so often in past years, the flowery bier, the weeping relatives, and Jane had always been among them.

The children were ranged beside the bed. The youngest was lifted up to kiss her Mamma for the last time. Then Mr Gell prayed with her, and she gave up her breath with a regretful sigh.

In the same year Jane received the Gold Medal of the Royal Geographical Society for her work in promoting the Arctic search. She had already set up a fitting memorial for Sir John, just as she had for Matthew Flinders in South Australia.

McClintock had taken out a marble obelisk and set it up at Beechey Island, where the 1850 expedition had found traces of his first winter camp.

Jane composed the inscription herself. It was characteristic of her that she improved a little on the Bible in her quotation:

To the memory of
FRANKLIN
CROZIER, FITZJAMES
and all their
gallant brother officers & faithful
companions who have suffered & perished
in the cause of science
and the service of their country
'And so He bringeth them unto the Haven
where they would be.'

COOPER'S CREEK
by Alan Moorehead

The true story of one of the most amazing cross-Continent treks of all time. Of an expedition pitting courage and incredible bravery against the Australian outback — millions of miles of unbearable heat and sand.

It is the epic tale of the fateful attempt in 1860 of an extraordinary band of men to unlock the territory from Melbourne to the Gulf of Carpentaria and back to Cooper's Creek in the 'Red Centre'. It is also the tale of Burke, the dashing but inexperienced Irish leader of the expedition; of Wills, his heroic second-in-command; of Wright, but for whose delays all might have been saved; and Brahe, who deserted his post.

NEW ENGLISH LIBRARY

HOW GREEN WAS MY VALLEY

by Richard Llewellyn

In the beginning were the green mountains and the fertile
valleys and the people were happy.

Then below the meadows they discovered coal. And the
men of the fields were transformed into people who
laboured in darkness. People who fought, loved, drank and
sang in the shadows of the great collieries. People who
lived with danger and disaster – who had forgotten how
green their valley had been.

'Vivid, eloquent, poetical, glowing with an inner flame
of emotion . . . To write from the heart, to measure
experience in love and sorrow, to bear witness to nobility
or the idealism of men – this is not the sort of thing a
serious novelist tries to do nowadays. It is what Mr
Llewellyn does, however. His story makes a direct and
powerfully sustained appeal to our emotions . . . deeply
and continuously moving.' – *The Times Literary Supplement*

'A work of fiction which enlarges for us the whole
bounds of experience . . . I say with all my heart : read it. It is a
most royal and magnificent novel.' – *Yorkshire Post*

NEW ENGLISH LIBRARY

TIMES OF TRIUMPH
by Charlotte Vale Allen

Spanning more than three decades in the turbulent history of our
century, Charlotte Vale Allen's magnificent saga traces the life
and loves of a woman born to struggle against every adversity
with dauntless courage and unflinching love.

Leonie came to New York with all the world against her and
built her tiny eating-house into a mighty business empire.

Gray, the London journalist who followed her across the ocean,
was the father of her children and the love of her lifetime.

Through the First World War, the hard and hungry years that
followed, through love and pain and bitter sadness, through the
growing years of their son and daughter destined to retrace
their mother's footsteps into a Europe once again torn apart by
war — Leonie's life was a time of triumph.

NEW ENGLISH LIBRARY

MEET ME IN TIME
by Charlotte Vale Allen

Meet Me in Time is a story about love, its intensity and destructiveness, its needs and satisfactions. It is also the story of the Burgesses, a brilliant, tormented family.

Gaby: bitter and unstable, cheated by the failure of her marriage and resenting the child she never wanted . . .

Dana: a talented playwright who recoiled from the truth about himself . . .

Glenn: the artist, haunted by her mother's death, expecting more love than anyone could humanly give her . . .

All three had dreams of fame, and passions that demanded fulfilment. All three shared the bittersweet inheritance from their mother, whose need to love had been overwhelming, and whose need to be loved was an inescapable legacy to her children.

NEW ENGLISH LIBRARY

Book Tokens

**Give them
the pleasure of choosing**

Book Tokens can be bought
and exchanged at most
bookshops in Great Britain
and Ireland.

NEL BESTSELLERS

T045 528	THE STAND	*Stephen King*	£1.75
T046 133	HOW GREEN WAS MY VALLEY	*Richard Llewellyn*	£1.00
T039 560	I BOUGHT A MOUNTAIN	*Thomas Firbank*	95p
T033 988	IN THE TEETH OF THE EVIDENCE	*Dorothy L. Sayers*	90p
T038 149	THE CARPETBAGGERS	*Harold Robbins*	£1.50
T041 719	HOW TO LIVE WITH A NEUROTIC DOG	*Stephen Baker*	75p
T040 925	THE PRIZE	*Irving Wallace*	£1.65
T034 755	THE CITADEL	*A. J. Cronin*	£1.10
T042 189	STRANGER IN A STRANGE LAND	*Robert Heinlein*	£1.25
T037 053	79 PARK AVENUE	*Harold Robbins*	£1.25
T042 308	DUNE	*Frank Herbert*	£1.50
T045 137	THE MOON IS A HARSH MISTRESS	*Robert Heinlein*	£1.25
T040 933	THE SEVEN MINUTES	*Irving Wallace*	£1.50
T038 130	THE INHERITORS	*Harold Robbins*	£1.25
T035 689	RICH MAN, POOR MAN	*Irwin Shaw*	£1.50
T043 991	EDGE 34: A RIDE IN THE SUN	*George G. Gilman*	75p
T037 541	DEVIL'S GUARD	*Robert Elford*	£1.25
T042 774	THE RATS	*James Herbert*	80p
T042 340	CARRIE	*Stephen King*	80p
T042 782	THE FOG	*James Herbert*	90p
T033 740	THE MIXED BLESSING	*Helen Van Slyke*	£1.25
T038 629	THIN AIR	*Simpson & Burger*	95p
T038 602	THE APOCALYPSE	*Jeffrey Konvitz*	95p
T046 850	WEB OF EVERYWHERE	*John Brunner*	85p

NEL P.O. BOX 11, FALMOUTH TR10 9EN, CORNWALL

Postage charge:

U.K. Customers. Please allow 30p for the first book plus 15p per copy for each additional book ordered to a maximum charge of £1.29 to cover the cost of postage and packing, in addition to cover price.

B.F.P.O. & Eire. Please allow 30p for the first book plus 15p per copy for the next 8 books, thereafter 6p per book, in addition to cover price.

Overseas Customers. Please allow 50p for the first book plus 15p per copy for each additional book, in addition to cover price.

Please send cheque or postal order (no currency).

Name ....

Address ....

....

Title ....

While every effort is made to keep prices steady, it is sometimes necessary to increase prices at short notice. New English Library reserve the right to show on covers and charge new retail prices which may differ from those advertised in the text or elsewhere. (3)